Under the Spell of the Serenissima

Book III

in the French Orphan Series

by Michael Stolle

i

ISBN-13: 978-1494217594
ISBN-10: 1494217597

Dedication

To Nina, Sandra & Chris

Contents

The Story So Far...

Brought up in a monastery school in Reims, Pierre believes he is a penniless orphan until his best friend, Armand de Saint Paul, decides to root out the truth. When Pierre discovers that he is in fact the heir not only to the aristocratic de Beauvoir family on his father's side, but also to the Duchy of Hertford on his mother's side, life suddenly becomes very complicated...

Pierre also finds he has a cousin, Henri de Beauvoir, so like Pierre in looks, but with a heart of pure evil, who wants more than anything to be Marquis de Beauvoir. Then there is the cunning and extremely powerful Cardinal Richelieu, who one minute is aiding Henri (tempted by the thought of claiming some of the de Beauvoir inheritance for the Church) and the next apparently acting as Pierre's protector. In addition to this, Pierre, utterly inexperienced in matters of state, has to walk a tightrope of diplomacy in negotiations to secure his inheritance on both sides of the Channel and then learn how to manage his vast estates.

All of this would be too much for one young man, but Pierre is not alone. Amongst his allies he can count his best friend Armand, who is always at his side (unless he is at the side of a pretty girl, that is); his English cousin, Charles, a strong and powerful ally; his faithful and quick-witted valet, Jean; and then he also has the love of Marie to spur him on.

When we last saw Pierre, he and Armand had narrowly escaped death in a tavern brawl in Milan orchestrated by Henri whilst they were in the company of Edoardo, a young and genial member of the Piccolin family of bankers in Italy.

In this final stage, Pierre's aims are simple – avoid being killed by Henri; marry Marie; oh yes, and find a priceless treasure, allegedly in Venice, in order to fulfil a promise he made to his supporters in England. What could possibly go wrong?

On The Road Again

"Why the hell is Edo *still* talking to that stupid peasant?" Pierre was not only extremely irritated, but his stomach was rumbling and he was exceedingly tired. "I mean, how complicated can it be to ask for directions to Verona?"

"Seems that they have a lot to discuss... With them both being Italian, I guess they simply can't help talking. They'll probably take ages to get to the point, better be patient," answered Armand, scratching his head reflectively.

Pierre watched his friend suspiciously and moved a step further away from him. "You've got lice!" he accused his friend.

"Could be," Armand answered, unperturbed. "I'll ask Jean tonight to have a look. Don't look at me as if I'm a leper, it's almost impossible not to catch them when you're travelling. Come on, stop pulling faces at me!"

Pierre suddenly felt a strong urge to start scratching himself; he could almost feel an army of blood-thirsty lice crawling all over his own body. He shuddered but secretly he had to admit it. Armand was right, there was no realistic hope of escaping any of those beasts – from lice to fleas or bedbugs – as long as they were travelling and had no choice but to stay in all sorts of dubious post stations along their way.

At last Edo seemed to have finished his discussion as he was waving his hat towards his friends, gesturing them to come and join him.

"In the name of all the blessed saints, what took you so long with this peasant?" Pierre exclaimed, irritated. "Did he at least tell you the quickest way to Verona?"

Edo smiled. "Actually I didn't ask him *that* particular question," he answered calmly.

"You didn't ask?" repeated Armand, almost mechanically.

"So why did you keep us waiting so long?" Pierre cried in frustration.

"There *is* the possibility that I asked him to recommend a hospitable farm or post station close by – somehow I had the inkling that my travelling companions might otherwise turn into cannibals and have me for lunch," Edo answered with a glint of laughter in his eyes.

Pierre looked guilty. "I'm sorry, Edo, I guess I'm behaving like a spoilt child!"

"Since he's been named a duke and kissed by King Charles, he's become extremely difficult to deal with," Armand commented, ignoring Pierre's furious glances. "His lackeys usually serve a full picnic at this time of day – and he becomes really nasty if everything isn't served exactly as he likes it."

Edo saw Pierre kick Armand and laughed. "Sorry, I can't offer such a treat, but the peasant did tell me that there is a noble estate nearby, so let's spur on the horses and hope they'll offer us a late lunch. I'm so hungry that I could devour a whole pig!"

"That sounds fabulous, I'm really hungry too. But what about Verona, then?" interrogated Pierre. "Do you know how to get there, your discussion with this man seemed to go on forever!"

"Oh, we're not going to Verona," Edo said casually. "We're riding north instead."

"But you told the innkeeper in Bergamo that we were heading to Verona in order to meet some of your relatives there."

"Yeah, I was pretty convincing," Edo answered smugly. "Maybe it's about time to confess that I had a long discussion with my brother last night when you had already gone to bed."

His glance met two curious pairs of eyes. "I must admit that my brother may be stuffy and thrifty, but indisputably he's got the brains of the family. He made me recount our adventures in the tavern in Milan and looking calmly at the facts he came to the conclusion that Richelieu's involvement seemed rather unlikely – which leads…"

"…which leads us directly to my murderous cousin, Henri," Pierre groaned.

"Exactly." Edo beamed at Pierre like a teacher encouraging a dim pupil who had – finally – understood a difficult point. "Therefore my brother instructed me to be careful and cover our tracks and suggested we ride to a remote castle in the north close to Lake Garda and stay there over Christmas. The owner of the castle is not only a close friend of the family but he also has good connections with the Venetian aristocracy and could help you to find the ring you seem to be looking for."

"I don't feel very comfortable imposing myself on your friends," Pierre interjected. "Just imagine the reverse, four total strangers knocking at my door in Montrésor to spend a surprise Christmas with us!"

Edo waved nonchalantly. "Don't worry, the owner is not only a close friend, he owes us a favour. You'll see, he's really very nice. We'll have a great time – some peace and quiet will do us good after our last adventure."

"That's what I've been saying for the past two years," Armand commented gloomily, "but somehow peace and quiet never seem to happen."

"So tell me, what were you discussing at such length with this peasant?" Now Pierre was openly curious.

Edo laughed. "He was telling me a long, long story about all the misfortunes that have befallen members of his family lately. I think he had it all from miscarriage to the untimely death of his wife and of several of his numerous children. Oh yes, I forgot to mention the perfidious witch who put a spell on his goat."

Pierre was shocked. "But that's no laughing matter!"

Edo made a face. "It was so obvious, he saw our expensive clothes and thought he could cream some money off us. I don't believe a fraction of what he told me, he sounded far too cheerful, although he tried hard to shed some tears to make the story more credible!"

"Pierre always believes in the goodness of mankind," Armand commented drily. "It's become quite a bad habit. So what did you answer?"

"Oh, I retaliated and I told him about our own terrible misfortunes, that we're on our way to Verona but were robbed in Milano by gangsters who almost took our lives and haven't a penny left for our journey – he shouldn't even think about us being able to dispense any charity."

"Good!" Armand beamed at Edo. "You know how to deal with this kind of bloodsucker."

"Of course I do," Edo answered. "Lesson number one I learned from my brother: A banker never opens his purse unless it's to receive something!"

While they had been chatting animatedly the four riders approached at a leisurely pace a stately home, a solid old square estate built from local stone and bricks. Plaster and paint looked worn by age but strangely this only added to the dignified aspect of the building. A hysterical dog could be heard barking inside the courtyard, the only noise that seemed to disturb the peaceful winter day.

"This should be the estate the peasant described to me." Edo looked around, appraising the building. "It certainly looks wealthy enough to offer us a decent lunch!"

As they entered the courtyard several curious servants started to gather around them, gawking at them as if they had arrived from the moon. Apparently visitors, especially strangers, were a rare occurrence – not to be missed on any account.

Jean had dismounted first and was shouting at the grooms to stir themselves and wait on his masters when the scene was interrupted by the arrival of the lady of the house. Traces of long-gone beauty were still apparent in her face but deep lines of grumpiness were matched by blazing eyes and a shrill voice as she addressed the strangers. "We have nothing to give and the master of the house is busy, he cannot receive anybody today!"

"What a witch," Edo murmured to Armand. "I wonder how she managed to get here so fast. She must spend all her time supervising and whipping her servants into action."

Pierre looked at her in disbelief. He had imagined himself already seated at a table loaded with delicacies – never had he expected such a bold and impolite rejection. While he was still wrestling with his disappointment and this sudden turn of events, Armand dismounted from his horse and nonchalantly approached the lady of the house. He ignored her apparent displeasure and waved his hat while bowing low as if they were at the royal court. He greeted the lady and addressed her in his charming mix of French of Italian.

"My lady, please accept my most profound apologies for our untimely intrusion. My friend, the noble Comte de Reims, and I are come from France on our way to visit friends in Verona and all we wanted to ask was a cup of water and a piece of bread. Never had we intended to disturb the lady of the house – but please let me add that I'm pleased that we did so all the same. I'm enchanted to meet a lady of timeless beauty and elegance."

He finished his introduction with the famous smile that rarely failed to impress his female victims and – once again – Pierre could witness the immediate effect of the shameless charms of his friend. The lady of the house turned scarlet and instinctively she tried to arrange the curls of her hair while clearing her throat.

"Oh, you're from France!" she exclaimed in a slightly croaky voice. "I love France, I spent my youth at the court of Queen Maria de Medici. I will never forget the beauty and refinement of her courts. Do you know Her Majesty, by any chance?"

I'm too young by far, thought Armand, but quickly bit his tongue and answered, "I regret that I never had the chance to meet Her Majesty, as you probably know, His Majesty and his mother are not on the best of terms... but it's a pity that we won't have the opportunity to exchange some words about the royal court – by chance we happen to know the present King quite well – and his mother's sudden exile was such a scandal..."

The lady of the house suddenly seemed to realize that they were surrounded by her gawking servants. Regally she turned around and admonished them sharply. "Stop staring at us, you silly idiots, can't you see that we have noble guests here? Take care of their horses, get cook to prepare a decent lunch, and if I say decent, I mean decent!"

Smiling coquettishly at Pierre and Armand, a totally altered hostess ushered them inside while whipping her servants into a frenzy of action. Minutes later they found themselves sitting at a large table laden with all kinds of regional delicacies, the best wine of the house gleamed in expensive glasses from the famous Murano glass factory and toasts were raised to the King and the Queens of France.

The master of the house was dragged reluctantly from his study where he had been hiding and brooding as usual over the estate records – but if he was astonished to find three strange guests at his table his manners were polished enough to hide his true feelings behind a façade of faultless politeness. In the meantime their hostess had undergone a complete transformation; gone were the deep lines of misery and ennui. Sparkling with joy, laughing and joking like the young maid of honour she had once been, she sat in the middle of the merry party, listing enraptured to Armand's ever so slightly but delightfully indecent stories from the French court.

Only when the servants started to light the first candles did the party become aware that dusk was falling, and indeed quite early, as they were approaching Christmas.

"I must apologize," cried Armand. "I had completely forgotten the time. We must leave quickly now as night will be falling soon and we want to reach the next post station. It has been the most delightful afternoon – rarely have we encountered such a charming hostess – and host," he added dutifully.

He had not even managed to finish his sentence when the lady of the house intervened. "There can be no question of your leaving tonight!" she cried. "You must stay as our honoured guests! It's far too dangerous to ride in the darkness – and…" She paused.

"And?" repeated Armand.

"And you absolutely must finish the story about Queen Anne and this insidious Duke of Buckingham, I mean did they really….?" She giggled. "I'm *burning* with curiosity! Queen Marie never liked her, by the way, she always used to say, '*You can't trust the Spanish*'!"

Which didn't stop Queen Marie from taking their gold, mused Pierre, but preferred to refrain from echoing his thoughts aloud. Clearly the lady of the house still held a very sentimental opinion of Marie de Medici.

Armand made a good show of refusing their kind invitation to stay, on the grounds of not wanting to disturb their noble hosts any further – but relented soon enough as the lady of the house wouldn't hear any more talk of them leaving. Thus they spent an agreeable evening topped off with a sumptuous dinner and sank into their beds well nourished and slightly tipsy from too much wine.

Armand was soon to discover that there is no such thing as a free meal, as not even an hour later the mistress of the house visited his room, clad in an almost transparent nightgown and explaining that she needed to be reassured that his room was to his liking. Armand kept masterful control of his expression and it didn't really come as a surprise to him when all of a sudden she pretended to feel dizzy and sank down on his bed. As a true gentleman, Armand knew what was expected of him and fulfilled the duties that her bookish husband had apparently neglected for some considerable time.

The next morning a worn-out Armand mounted his horse along with the rest of the party and waved good-bye to the whole family. Pierre looked surprised at his friend's apparent fatigue but when he saw their hostess radiant with happiness he immediately drew his own conclusion.

"Busy night?" he asked his friend with a wink.

"Exhausting," Armand whispered back. "She wouldn't stop until I was almost dead, never had a woman craving it like that before!"

"Maybe she was afraid that it might be the last time," Pierre commented, looking at her aging, pallid husband.

The ensuing journey towards Lake Garda slowed down, as the weather had reserved a nasty surprise for them and was on the turn. The pale but bright sun that had made them almost forget that it was the height of the winter season disappeared timidly behind a thick veil of clouds. The more they rode north towards the steep slopes of the mountains, the more the clouds seemed to descend, piling thick and menacing above their heads. The next day the light drizzle was replaced progressively by a thick curtain of rain that poured down relentlessly upon the hapless voyagers. Dripping wet, they continued their journey, freezing and miserable, as even the thickest coats and blankets made of leather and woollen felt couldn't withstand this deluge.

"Didn't you promise us that this would be one of the most beautiful sights on earth?" Armand challenged Edo when they finally set eyes on Lake Garda for the first time.

"It usually is," Edo answered, prevented from going into a more lengthy comment by a vigorous sneeze.

The friends looked incredulously at the brooding lake that stretched out below them, a vast greyish mass of water reaching to the horizon that blended seamlessly into the clouds of darkest grey. The lake that had been described to

7

them as a blue gem in a lush setting of green certainly did not live up to their expectations – cold and grey, it held no invitation for them to stay and enjoy the scenery.

"We'll reach our friends' castle before sunset; it's about three to four hours' ride from here," said Edo, trying to inject a more optimistic note into their discussion.

"Let's hope that our welcome there will be warmer than the one Mother Nature has reserved for us," Pierre sighed. Secretly he still felt highly uncomfortable visiting strangers uninvited.

The path Edo had chosen continued steeply uphill and soon their conversation died down as they had to concentrate all of their attention on the slippery path that was the only access to the castle perched like an eagle's nest on top of the mountain.

After many hours of this difficult terrain Edo started to crane his neck and look hard into the distance. "We're close now!" he shouted excitedly, hoping to cheer up his fellow travellers.

"Close to what?" muttered Armand. "I can only see clouds, nothing but clouds!"

Edo was spared the effort of an answer as the dark veil was torn apart and the silhouette of a tower and high walls of quarried stone shimmered in the distance. Invigorated by the expectation of dry clothes and the lovely thought of hot mulled wine the friends spurred on their horses and tackled the last steep slope.

"The gate keeper is a bit special," Edo cried good-humouredly. "I've known him since I was a kid, so don't be surprised if he cracks a joke or two, he's got a weird sense of humour!"

"I don't mind," answered Pierre. "As long as he opens the gate quickly, I'm fine with all kinds of jokes!" Pierre shuddered; he felt miserable. It was not only wet and cold, but they must be approaching late afternoon as the daylight was already dimming quickly. The trees and shrubs along the path seemed to be dissolving into indistinguishable shadows of grey, and the whole world seemed misty and unreal.

As they approached the castle, the horses kept puffing along, leaving behind clouds of steamy breath. The heavy breathing of the horses and the noise of their hooves were the only sounds that could be heard, a monotonous rhythm accompanying their slow and tiring ascent to the castle. When the gate of the castle was finally towering above them, their mood brightened considerably. Even though Edo had put on a cheerful face, he had been

8

worried to death that the dense clouds might descend even more and make any further progress impossible.

With relief he rang the bell at the gate, happy to hear the clanging sound echoing through the castle walls. Seconds turned into endless minutes of waiting – but nothing happened. Angry and frustrated, Edo pulled at the bell rope several times, but this time the clanging noise wasn't cheerful any more, the bell faithfully conveying the message that an angry visitor was expecting immediate attention. It took some more minutes until the shuffle of dragging feet could be heard and a shutter in the solid oak door was slowly opened.

"What d'you want?" a voice growled through the iron grille. "We ain't giving nothing out."

These inviting words came with a hiccup and the penetrating smell of alcohol. Edo could only discern the lips and a red scarf – yet he didn't need to see anything else to understand that this could not possibly be the gate keeper he had been expecting. He frowned and whispered to Armand, "That's strange, there's something wrong here."

Armand was utterly exhausted and didn't fancy finding his way back down the slippery path in the darkness that was falling fast. Impatiently he shoved Edo aside and   without further ado he grabbed the ends of the red scarf that were dangling out of the grille with his left hand. Then he pressed the face of the totally surprised gate keeper against the grille with an iron grip, and waving his gleaming dagger in his right hand hissed, "Either you open the gate immediately for us, you son of a bitch, or this dagger goes straight into your throat!"

A gurgling sound from the other side could be interpreted as a sort of acceptance and indeed they heard the noise of a key grinding in the lock of the door. Armand maintained his iron grip until the party had safely entered the courtyard and could have a closer look at the strange gate keeper. He was an old man of medium height, his frightened and sweaty face gleaming in the light of the torches that had already been lit inside the castle compound. As soon as he realized that he was surrounded by four well-trained men with the unmistakable airs of gentlemen he fell on his knees whimpering, "Have mercy, most noble Signori, I was only following the butler's instructions, that no visitors were to be admitted!"

Pierre was not sure if he had understood the gate keeper correctly as his thick rural accent and some missing teeth made his speech hard to understand. But Edo had no problems understanding the plea. Unmoved he barked at the gate keeper, "You brainless idiot, shift your useless arse and show us to the butler immediately or we'll show you the quick way to paradise."

Keeping the frightened man safely in their middle they marched through the poorly lit courtyard and entered the great hall where flabbergasted servants were gawking curiously at the newcomers. The nervous gate keeper instructed a fellow servant to rush and fetch the butler as noble guests had arrived unexpectedly.

Thus announced they stood motionless in the great hall, but Pierre didn't mind, as a comfortable and inviting fire was burning in the large fireplace, an imposing work of art where an unknown master of his profession had not only carved the count's coat of arms into the now blackened sandstone but had also chiselled all kinds of artistic ornaments so that a closer look allowed the discovery of ever new and enchanting details such as acorns, sculptured leaves, and even birds that were interwoven into a delightful pattern. Pierre's feet and hands started to thaw and his spirits start to rise again. Maybe this strange welcome was nothing but a silly misunderstanding?

Pierre had just discovered a birds' nest complete with offspring hidden in this intricate pattern when he heard the noise of marching feet on the marble floor. He raised his head in time to be gratified with the sight of the butler, a man who easily made up for his lack of height by his personality. Holding himself erect he approached the guests majestically – but his arrogant attitude changed significantly as soon as he set eyes on Edo.

"Oh, Signore Edoardo!" he cried out. "I must apologize for this miserable reception, but this idiot must have completely misunderstood my instructions!" And as he spoke, his hand made a telling gesture classifying the gate keeper unmistakably among the ranks of the lower animal life, probably on a level with a cockroach.

Edo looked relieved. "I'm truly happy to see you again, Giuseppe. I was really wondering what was going on here. I have never seen this strange gate keeper before and I don't recognize any of the servants standing here gawping at us – have they nothing better to do?"

As if Edo's remark had been a cue for the servants that had been standing around idle and gawping, the butler clapped his hands and cried, "Don't you see that we have noble guests here, get moving and prepare the dining room, immediately!" He bowed towards his guests apologetically. "I must ask for your lordships' pardon and express my profound distress at receiving you in such inadequate circumstances but I have bad tidings. My master and his son had to leave unexpectedly because his lordship's beloved sister fell ill and he took most of the servants with him. I'm therefore left without any servants worthy of this name, in essence, my lords, I have to deal with a bunch of idiots."

Edo looked crestfallen. "Oh, dear Lord, what has happened? We were actually planning to spend Christmas here with your master's family! My brother Giovanni is also planning to come over and join us!"

A shadow of unpleasant surprise seemed to dart across the face of the butler, but it vanished so quickly that Pierre started to doubt he had ever seen it.

"I regret it profoundly, Signore, but this will be impossible. You must certainly grant us the honour of staying tonight as it's too late to head back for home, but I'm afraid that not only is my master absent, but the master's apartments have been shut down for renovation. I can only offer you accommodation in the north wing." The butler looked distressed now, but this was nothing compared to Edo, who looked positively scandalized.

"The north wing!" he cried. "But it's half ruined, I don't even remember ever having seen it in use!" Edo was furious. "What happened to your master? He would never have had his guests treated like this!"

"As I mentioned before, Signore, my master had to leave in a hurry to attend to her ladyship, his eldest sister. Knowing that he'd be absent for several weeks he gave orders to renovate the apartments of the family. I'll do my utmost to have the north wing prepared and made comfortable while I invite you, most noble Signori, to sit down for dinner here in the great hall."

There seemed nothing that could be done other than accept the situation in good faith. Pierre was exhausted from the trying ride and was relishing the warmth from the fire that he felt spreading slowly through his body. Several glasses of the excellent wine of the region added to a feeling of lightness so that even the prospect of having to sleep in the abandoned and draughty wing of a castle couldn't really unsettle him anymore.

The butler condescended to serve at table himself and dinner passed fairly quickly – but in a strange mood. Edo still appeared to be gloomy and taciturn and Armand's attempts to cheer up his companions with some risqué jokes quickly died down as he remarked soon enough that his friends were lost in their own thoughts and only reacted mechanically to his efforts to spice up their conversation.

Once dinner had been finished the butler politely but firmly insisted that they should move over to the north wing. Edo opened his mouth – apparently to protest for one last time – but shut it when the butler looked at him with a stern glance and opened the door of the great hall to cross the cobbled courtyard.

Outside the rain had turned to a light drizzle that made the cobbled stones shimmer dimly in the light of the torches but drained away all colour, so that walls, windows and even the remaining servants turned into indistinct shadows. Quickly they reached the north wing where the butler had given orders to have one of the old tower rooms prepared for the three friends and their valet.

Freezing and tired, they climbed uneven and worn-out steps until they reached a huge room that must have been abandoned for generations. Makeshift beds had been erected and a miserable fire with bluish flames was burning in the old fireplace. The room reeked of smoke, testimony to the servants' efforts to light a decent fire, but they must have given up as the chimney was clogged. Some furs had been heaped on two beds and in a corner; ravaged by moths, they too had seen better days.

Edo was speechless as he appraised their home for the night – at least he didn't protest when the butler addressed him formally.

"Signore Edoardo Salvatore, may I wish you and the noble gentlemen an agreeable night. I propose to come and fetch you tomorrow morning to partake of a hearty meal before you leave the castle. Good night!"

To their great surprise he quickly shook Edo's hand – as if he wanted to apologize for the miserable dwellings he had to offer to them.

"Good night," Edo retorted. "But I fear it won't be a very agreeable one!"

His words were spoken in vain as the butler had already left. "This is unbelievable, your *friends* have left us in a pigsty!" he cried accusingly at Edo.

Surprisingly Edo answered aloud, "It doesn't matter. Actually, I know the castle quite well, it's far too dangerous to leave this room, half of the building in this part is ruined. I guess simply wants to protect us! Let's go to bed now, I'm dead tired. I think the wine and the long ride have done for me. Look at Pierre, he's fallen asleep already!"

While Edo was talking loudly he made gestures to Armand and Pierre to keep quiet, then he tip-toed to the door. Pierre couldn't help himself – he thought it fitting to make snoring noises which had such an effect on Armand that he almost exploded into giggles. Edo warned them to keep quiet and pressed his ear against the door. Only after some time did the friends see a satisfied smile on his face. Quickly he tip-toed back to the other side and gave the others a sign to come and join him.

"No peace and quiet for us tonight," he whispered excitedly, "we've landed right in a new adventure!"

"I knew it," groaned Armand. "Why the hell is it always us? I just want to sleep!"

"Monsieur de Saint Paul is apparently indisposed," whispered Pierre, feeling suddenly wide awake. "But don't worry about Armand, many members of the old aristocracy can be rather indolent. But I'm with you! Tell us what's going on here!"

Edo grinned and whispered back, "I haven't a clue but the butler winked at me when he left the room and he addressed me as 'Signore Edoardo Salvatore'."

"Nice name," grumbled Armand. "I think I have no less than twelve, no idea why my parents were so creative, I'm just a younger son."

"Don't be so thick," protested Pierre. "I'm guessing Edo's name is not 'Salvatore' at all – right? The butler is hinting that you should be his saviour?"

"That's it, exactly, you're quick to catch on." Edo was impressed.

Armand looked positively enthralled. "That's really clever, Pierre! Yes, 'Salvatore' means saviour, I see it now – but what does all of this mean?"

"I can only guess." Edo was frowning now. "The story of renovating the count's rooms is bullshit, the apartments of the count's family were redecorated last year, and I can tell you it cost him a fortune."

"Of course, his banker would know…" murmured Armand.

"I also didn't recognize a single face of any of the male servants, only some of the maids seemed familiar – that's also very strange. In essence, something really wrong is going on here and we ought to investigate. I cannot leave one of my brother's best friends in trouble – and it all indicates that he's in a big mess."

"A big, stinking mess," Armand added.

"Well, that's all very worrying," Pierre threw in, "but what do you propose to do about it?"

"Save him, of course." Edo seemed determined to take action – and he didn't seem too worried as to how to achieve his noble goal.

"How? If I may ask this simple question?" Pierre wanted to know.

"I know the castle inside and out, I spent several summers here. I can go anywhere," Edo went on boastfully.

"Great," said Pierre sarcastically. "So we'll climb down over a hundred slippery steps in a ruined tower in total darkness, walk across the courtyard at our leisure, if need be we'll fight with up to a hundred armed enemies and in the meantime we have no clue as to where to go and find your friends – or even if they're still here! Sounds just great! Anybody here to take note of my last will and testament?"

13

"Does Your Grace have a better plan? Should we let Edo's friends perish and simply walk away?" Armand seemed to have taken sides with Edo, which made Pierre even more furious. Couldn't these simpletons see that they were walking right into a gigantic trap?

While the three opponents were still staring at each other, Jean cleared his throat. "May I speak up, my lords, and make a suggestion?"

Three bewildered and curious pairs of eyes met Jean. In the heat of the moment they had completely forgotten his presence.

"Of course," Pierre answered. "As long as your suggestion makes more sense than guiding us straight into disaster!"

"I propose that I take a torch and walk down to the kitchen, pretending that my master has sent for some mulled wine – this will be credible enough and a mere servant won't bother them. While I'm snooping around I'll try to pick up some information on what's really going on here. This could provide us with valuable information to develop an efficient plan of action once I'm back."

"Excellent." Pierre nodded enthusiastically and beamed proudly at his valet.

"I'll never understand why you throw away your talents serving someone as worthless as your master, when you could stay with me and have a decent one!" Armand cried, but with a wink, as everybody knew that there was no way on earth that Jean could be lured away from his master.

Jean immediately leapt into action and quickly lit one of the torches, but before he left the room he turned back and remarked, "Thank you, my lord Armand, for this generous offer, but I prefer to serve a master who's not only modest but who's in true need of my services!"

The door was closed before Armand could respond.

Pierre laughed. "That was the right reply, my dear friend – and a nice snub!"

"That man is turning into an arrogant fool!" Armand grumbled.

"And I'd love to have a servant like him, I've never met anybody nearly as dedicated as Jean, Pierre's a lucky man!" Edo added with a sigh and a tinge of jealousy.

Meanwhile the unsuspecting object of their remarks descended the slippery steps of the winding staircase in the tower down to the courtyard. Jean was happy that he had chosen to wear a warm coat, as a chill wind was blowing through the dilapidated building.

14

No real surprise, a guard had been placed at the exit that communicated with the courtyard but he swallowed Jean's explanations that his master had sent him on an errand to search for mulled wine – masters, especially foreigners, were known to be demanding and difficult! Jean thanked him profusely for his sympathy and they parted on the best of terms. Jean was secretly astonished that only a single guard had been posted; apparently their intrusion had been regarded as more of a nuisance than a threat.

He strode across the sparsely lit courtyard, rather more slowly than he would have done normally, trying to discover hidden servants and armed men in the corners or doorways. To his great surprise there were none; whoever the enemy was, he certainly had not invaded the castle with a complete army. Jean's mood brightened considerably. Maybe there was a realistic chance after all to help Edo's friends tonight. He knew Armand and Pierre well enough by now – there was no chance that they'd miss a good opportunity to get into trouble!

The great kitchen was normally a busy place, but as it was quite late the cook had been left alone with two kitchen maids. The wooden tables stood scrubbed and deserted, cups and plates had already been cleaned and put away. Copper pots and pans were gleaming by the light of the candles and of the gigantic fireplace, where a warm fire was burning while its huge spits stood idle waiting for tomorrow's roast.

But the peaceful atmosphere was misleading. The two remaining kitchen maids were busy with musketeers who kept groping them under the disapproving eyes of the cook, a stately matron of clear moral principles and Jean could see from the anger burning in her eyes that she detested every single second of the scene that was unfolding before her eyes.

Jean approached her apologetically to find himself snubbed when he asked with a low voice for a jug of mulled wine. Jean didn't give up. "Please, my dear woman, be so kind and prepare me some mulled wine for my master – he's been lodged in the north tower and it's freezing cold up there, have some pity on us poor travellers!"

As soon as the cook realized that Jean did not belong to the bunch of detested musketeers she relented and started to heat up some wine in a big copper pot, adding honey and spices with experienced hands.

The soldiers had darted a quick glance at Jean, but a mere servant didn't seem to be worthy of their attention – especially as they had succeeded in loosening the strings of the maids' aprons. Suddenly the cook exploded with anger. "You sluts, get out of my kitchen or I'll take the poker and have a go at all of you!" angrily waving the red-hot poker at the maids and the soldiers.

"Leave her alone," grunted one of the soldiers. "She's just jealous! Must have been years since anyone's done it with her! " And with a telling gesture he grabbed his crotch and dragged the giggling maid out of the kitchen, to be followed immediately by the second pair.

They were now alone in the big kitchen and Jean saw that the cook had tears in her eyes. Gently he took her hand and whispered, "Tell me what's going on here! Maybe we can help you?"

The cook looked suspiciously at the door that had closed behind the soldiers and then into Jean's eyes. Jean could see that she was fighting with herself, not sure if she should speak or not. Gently he squeezed her hand once more and suddenly the cook's resistance broke down and she started to speak in a low voice. "I don't know if I should be telling you this, but your eyes look so much like those of my dear husband, may he rest in peace!" She quickly dabbed her eyes with her apron and crossed herself. "Our dear master was called urgently to attend his sister's sickbed. He left the castle in the safeguard of the young master and rode away with most of our armed men – he didn't expect any trouble here at home. It all seemed so peaceful. So he left, worrying only about his sister. Only a day later our neighbour appeared all of sudden to make what he called a *courtesy* call." She paused tellingly. "We were never on good terms with him as he's in league with the Spanish bastards, but what could we do? He entered the castle with a good dozen of his men, all looked normal and peaceful enough. The young master received them in the count's dining room and offered them a cup of our best wine when suddenly these bastards produced the weapons they had been hiding inside their coats and took him and his servants as hostages. Threatening to kill our young master, they forced the male servants to abandon their arms and locked all of them up in the old prison." She started to sob. "My poor nephew is among them!"

"But they'll never gain anything by such a bold assault," Jean wondered aloud. "All they'll achieve is starting another family feud that'll last for generations."

"This cursed neighbour has a perfidious plan," the cook answered, still speaking somewhat unclearly, as she was half-sobbing, half-speaking. "He arrived with his only daughter, Lucrezia, and now he's blackmailing the young master to marry her – if not he'll start torturing the hostages down in the dungeon. He'll also make sure that his daughter will spend tonight alone with the young master."

"I imagine the young master won't touch her, even if she were stunningly beautiful – he couldn't be so daft," Jean couldn't help interrupting her.

"That's not what it's all about, you must understand that we have a law here, if a young man spends the night with a virgin, he has to marry her – if the young man refuses, the pride of the young lady's family is tarnished and they have the right to kill him and to claim his land as compensation."

16

"That's truly devious," Jean exclaimed. "So either he marries her – and they get their hands on his land through marriage – or he refuses and by law he's a dead man – and they can claim his heritage."

The cook nodded, she was no longer able to speak.

"It's a good thing that we've arrived," Jean said, in the hope of sounding cheerful. "Sounds like just the challenge for my master and his friends."

"Do you think there is hope?" The cook looked at Jean with wide eyes.

"Of course there is," Jean answered, somewhat boastfully, as in truth he had no idea what to do. "Where are they now?"

"They're up in the count's private rooms."

"And how many?"

"About a good twenty all over the castle, up there maybe six to eight." The last words were whispered as they heard the noise of approaching boots.

The musketeer who had left when Jean had entered the kitchen came back alone, his face tellingly red and excited. He noticed Jean still standing close to the cook and snarled, "What are you hanging around for, get out of the kitchen or I'll make my stick dance on your lazy arse!"

Jean immediately assumed the position of a frightened and submissive servant and wailed in reply, "Oh have mercy, sir, please, my master is already going to be furious because it took so much time. The cook told me the wine has to heat slowly or it's no good."

The musketeer moved closer and sniffed. "It does smell good, give me some of the stuff! Don't waste it on stupid foreigners!"

Jean saw that the cook was about to refuse and was ready to fight. Quickly he bent forward as if he wanted to inhale the delicious aroma himself. Quickly he whispered, "Prepare a good amount for them, and make sure you add plenty of grappa."

"Your lot don't deserve anything of this," the cook grumbled, "but in any case it's not enough. Hand me the big pot over there and I'll make some more mulled wine for you – but promise me to treat the young master well!"

The musketeer spat on the floor. "Better give us the stuff or your little darling might regret it," but he walked to the hook where the biggest pot made of gleaming copper was hanging and banged it down on the table. "I'll be back in no time with my friends and you'd better have some wine ready for us!" the musketeer threatened, before leaving the kitchen to fetch his comrades.

17

"Don't forget: a lot of grappa and loads of honey," Jean instructed her, but the cook had already placed the pot with deft hands on the iron hook hanging above the hearth and had started to fill it with a generous amount of wine.

"Don't you worry," she replied grimly. "They'll see plenty of stars in no time! Now don't stand idle, go back to your master and his friends, you've seen yourself what's going on here, help us to get rid of this vermin!" And in no time Jean found himself ushered out of the warm kitchen back into the freezing cold courtyard, the jug of mulled wine wrapped in a large woollen cloth to keep it warm.

Jean walked back to the north tower, huddling in his woollen waistcoat. After the cosy kitchen the cold outside cut through him like a knife and the damp seemed to penetrate even to his bones. When he reached the door of the tower he greeted the guard who was still standing there, his nose red from the cold while he kept moving his feet in a desperate but futile attempt to fight the biting cold. He kept blowing into his hands, and white mist emanated from his mouth like a cloud of smoke.

"Bloody cold, ain't it?" Jean greeted the miserable-looking guard.

"It sure is," answered the guard with chattering teeth.

"I'm happy to have got hold of some mulled wine, will do us good up there," Jean confided, "but the best thing is, the cook is preparing a big pot with a dash of grappa especially for you musketeers."

"You're sure about that?" asked the guard jealously. "Sure!" answered Jean with gusto. "I saw a fat guy with a dark moustache tasting it, he was slurping it up like a pig."

"That must be our captain," conceded the freezing guard. "But I can't move, I have been ordered to stay here."

"Of course you have to stay here!" Jean looked at him sympathetically. "Although it could be questioned whether staying here in the cold and catching a deadly fever is desirable. I guess having a sip of the stuff would do you good – you look terrible. But I have to hurry, my wine is almost cold by now and my master will surely beat me, he's got a hell of a temper!" He winked at the guard who winked back. They didn't need words to exchange opinions on the craziness of demanding superiors.

Jean climbed the steps back to the room in the tower where the three friends were already awaiting him anxiously. Pierre had spent a difficult hour, tormenting himself and full of remorse at ever having agreed to his valet going on his own and imagining all kinds of disasters that might have befallen him. Thus Jean was greeted with the greatest relief that turned into genuine enthusiasm as soon as the friends discovered that he had been true to his word and brought a jug of mulled wine back with him. The tower room was still freezing cold and the asthmatic fire was close to succumbing to an untimely extinction despite all kinds of resurrection measures that Edo had tried, all to no avail. The warm wine was shared on an equal basis and soon spread like liquid fire through their bones, leaving a feeling of comfort as well as lifting their spirits considerably.

Jean gave a quick summary of what was going on in the castle and it took some serious efforts by Pierre and Armand to stop Edo from rushing down there and taking immediate revenge.

"We need a sensible plan first," Armand insisted, "even if the number of the enemy is not really too daunting. Don't forget that they have the count's son as a hostage."

"And they have firearms!" Pierre added reflectively.

"We can spy on them first," Edo suddenly grinned, full of mischief. "And I know exactly how to do it!"

Three curious pairs of eyes met his own.

"I used to play hide and seek here in the castle with the count's son when we would visit the family," Edo explained. "I know the castle in and out. We can climb up the south tower and there is a doorway leading to the attic above the count's apartments. The oak boards are rather thin; you can listen to every word that's spoken down there – and nobody will ever know that you've been up there!"

Pierre laughed. "Sounds as if some naughty boys must have done this quite often!"

Edo shrugged his shoulders and grinned. "Sure, we did a bit of eavesdropping, especially when they were discussing how to catch and punish those naughty boys... But let's get a move on – and get rid of the guard first!"

"Oh, that should be easy." Armand looked reflectively at his dagger.

"I hope that there won't be any need for such action," Jean commented. "If we're lucky the guard will have joined the rest of the bunch, as the cook was going to invite them for a cup of mulled wine – and she promised to add a lot of honey and a generous dash of grappa," he grinned.

"The mood should then soon turn from jovial to sleepy," Armand commented drily. "Good idea!"

"Tomorrow they'll have a splitting headache," Pierre threw in reflectively. "Yet I'm not going to waste any sympathy on them."

"If they survive until tomorrow," Edo added grimly. "Certainly not, if I get my way!"

Cautiously they opened the door, inch by inch, as the tired hinges were prone to creaking and groaning. Nothing moved, and encouraged by the silence they stepped forward, careful to avoid making any treacherous noise, and keeping close to the cold and damp walls they proceeded down the tricky staircase, feeling rather than really seeing their way. After what seemed like an eternity spent in the darkness they approached the last steps lit by smoking tallow candles and to Jean's great relief his trick had apparently worked. The guard's post was empty, and they could glimpse the empty courtyard through the open door.

"Now comes the tricky part," whispered Edo. "We have to cross the courtyard without arousing any attention."

"Not sure whom you're afraid of," Armand whispered back. "To me this looks pretty empty."

And indeed now as they sneaked out of the door of the north tower, nobody seemed to be around, and all they could hear were some clattering noises and snippets of laughter and conversation wafting over from the kitchen. The cook seemed to have prepared a generous draught of mulled wine! Sticking within the dark menacing shadow of the castle they slowly made their way to the entrance to the south tower. Their nerves were taut; every sound coming from the kitchen seemed to vibrate and amplify in their ears, although to the unbiased listener those noises sounded harmless enough – the clattering of pots and cups, the odd burst of laughter and animated conversation – nothing unusual for a winter night with guards on duty.

The small group reached the solid door of the south tower and Armand lifted the latch. Nothing moved and they looked at each other, speechless and with panic in their eyes. Would their mission end here tonight? Noble knights who had set out to rescue the helpless victims stopped by a simple locked door? But luck seemed to be on their side this latest obstacle didn't really seem to faze Edo, who walked straight to a small window next to the entrance. He hesitated a moment, then he pulled out a brick from the window sill. Underneath the loose brick lay a rusty key. Edo grasped it without further delay. "Unbelievable how old habits die hard," he commented in a low voice while he inserted the key into the lock. "I think this secret cache must have been in use forever." The rusty key screeched in protest as it was pushed hard into the lock but yielded under pressure and the lock turned, the door opened – the way was free!

Armand entered first but turned back almost immediately. "It's pitch black inside – maybe we can manage to climb upstairs, but we won't be able to move in the attic. We need a candle or torches – any ideas?"

They looked around but the only source of light came from the kitchen.

"Let me go and organize something," Jean proposed.

Before Pierre could object he had already left the group. In any case, they didn't have any better ideas.

"Let's hide inside, it's no use lingering around here," Pierre suggested, and so they went inside, prepared for an uncomfortable wait in the cold darkness.

Jean opened once more the door to the kitchen. He was amazed to see how the atmosphere had changed. Almost a dozen musketeers were standing around a pot of mulled wine, laughing and boasting. Jean could see that the cook was busy preparing another batch, a grim smile playing on her face. The men must have been drinking heavily as their collars were undone and their red faces were glistening with sweat.

Jean's entrance was greeted with loud cheers. "The valet again! Look at his skin, his mother must have swallowed a load of coal before she made him!" The fat man who seemed to be the captain looked challengingly at Jean and then at his men, expecting applause for his witty remark. Jean clenched his fist in his pocket. *You vile pig, you'll pay for this*, he thought, but managed to keep his face expressionless.

"What do you need this time for your master, some nice blankets or a kitchen maid to keep him warm?" the fat man continued. "Tell your master all the maids are reserved for us, and anyhow, they want quality, not foreign sissies!"

Jean judged it best to ignore this remark, as he had the first, and answered in a worried tone that he thought fitting for a scared valet. "My master is already furious because the fire and the candles went out, we had a sudden gust of wind. I'm here to fetch a candle and some torches."

Before the captain could answer the cook replied in an angry tone, "These noble sorts know how to keep an army of servants busy, I know their type. Follow me, I'll give you a candle and a torch, but this will have to do for tonight and don't you dare come back again. I'm a decent woman and I'm going to bed now!" She winked quickly at Jean and gestured him to follow her.

The musketeers somehow found her remarks hilarious. "A decent woman!" screamed one of the younger men. "You're so old and fat that you've no other option left!" He took a deep gulp of the wine. "But I'll say this, your wine is excellent, no bedtime for you until you've made another panful!"

21

The cook shrugged off his impudent remark and passed by the group, ignoring the men loftily as if they didn't really exist for her. Outside in the corridor she quickly handed Jean torches and a candle and whispered, "Here you are, better take a solid torch as it may come in handy. Our plan worked – they're almost drunk. Now please hurry and free my master, he's up there with another half a dozen of those beasts plus the neighbour and his horrid daughter."

Jean squeezed her hand to thank her and replied, "Thank you, don't worry, by tomorrow morning this scum will be ejected."

He saw her quickly wipe tears from her eyes. "I trust you, you've given me hope. I'll go back now and serve them another round, another hour or so and they should be sound asleep."

Keeping the burning candle carefully protected against the wind, Jean strode back to the south tower and was just about to push down the door latch when he heard a whistling sound behind him. "Hey, what are you doing here? Your masters are waiting down there in the north tower! It's on the other side."

Jean's heart started to race – this was a complication he could well do without. Jean didn't even dare to imagine what would happen once the guard raised the alarm. But somehow the voice sounded familiar and as Jean was still trying to figure out how to deal with this situation, the guard came closer, swaying rather than walking. Now Jean recognized the guard; it was the same one who had been on duty in the south tower before.

"I – oops – must have had too much of that mulled wine," Jean replied, making sure to slur his voice as if he were drunk. "But I swear, I only had a li–li– liddle sip. O– only a t-taste!"

The guard was now standing close to him, and Jean could smell his breath, reeking of wine and brandy. "Are you sure that it's the other tower?" Jean asked, playing lost. "Can you show me which one, I c-can't see so clearly!"

"Your master will give you a good beating tonight," the guard answered good-humouredly. "You're totally drunk – been tasting a bit too much, mate! Of course it's this tower over there, look!" and turning around he pointed with his not too steady finger towards the north tower.

Jean didn't waste a moment. He raised the torch and brought it down on the head of the unsuspecting guard. A short moan and he was slumped directly at Jean's feet. "Never trust a stranger, my mother used to say," Jean commented, "and right she was!"

Quickly Jean looked around the courtyard – but apparently nobody else had bothered to go out into the cold and damp night as long as the cook was dispensing her mulled wine so freely. Jean pushed down once again on the latch of the door to the south tower and found three freezing and nervous gentlemen who were extremely relieved to find him well.

"You didn't find a torch?" asked Pierre.

"I did, my lord, but it's still outside. First I need some help to get rid of the body of the zealous guard who wanted to send me back to the north tower."

"You killed a guard?" Armand asked curiously.

"No, my lord, I think he's just unconscious, but we need to store him safely somewhere before he can wake up and raise the alarm!"

"No problem, I know where," answered Edo. "Let's go quickly and do this first."

They sneaked out of the door, collected the torches Jean had brought with him and dragged the unconscious guard inside the tower.

"Oh my god, he's heavy," complained Armand. "There seems to be no shortage of food here in Italy."

Edo guided them down to the cellars and unbolted an impressive door that opened under screeching protest.

"What do we do now?" Pierre panted; the guard had been really quite heavy.

"Leave him inside and bolt the door." Edo answered cheerfully.

"What's down there?" Armand asked curiously. "I hope for his sake that those are wine cellars!"

"No idea!" Edo answered. "We never dared to go down there as the housekeeper used to tell us that it was full of rats and bones from the past when the cellars were used as dungeons – but maybe she was only making it up and just wanted to keep us children away."

"Well, he's got a unique opportunity to find out now," Jean commented matter-of-factly and gave a last push to the hapless guard. They saw the body disappearing in the darkness as it tumbled down the stairs and vanished into the cellar. Jean closed the heavy door and bolted it carefully.

"That's been dealt with," stated Edo with satisfaction. "He can cry for help, but nobody will ever hear him. But now we have to move on and climb up to the attic and I have an inkling that the next task will be a bit more difficult."

23

"We don't see problems, we only see challenges," added Armand, trying to sound optimistic. "Until now we've made good progress, especially thanks to Jean. It's about time that we got in on the act as well. Frankly speaking, I wouldn't mind a good fight!"

Eager to move on they raced up the winding staircase and could easily see with their own eyes that Edo had been correct. This part of the building had been renovated only very recently. Whereas the north tower was almost falling to pieces, the staircase here was in perfect condition, no loose or missing steps here!

Edo pulled back the bolts of the door leading to the attic and made a sign to stay quiet. "As I told you, the boards of the ceilings are very thin. This means that we can hear them, as they can hear us of course. So no talking! We'd better leave our boots here and walk in our stockings. Now this is important: take care to walk alongside the joists that support the roof, as here the boards are much thicker and can bear our weight. The living room should be a good thirty yards from here – about where you can see the stanchion in the attic. As soon as we have heard enough, we come back here and decide how to get rid of this vermin."

They nodded to show they had understood the message and took off their boots. Jean nearly had a fit and Armand had to suppress a chuckle as Pierre's left stocking had a huge hole and his big toe poked through. "Monsieur le Marquis with stockings like a pauper," he whispered, grinning broadly. "That's a good one!"

Pierre pulled a face but in reality he didn't care at all. His senses were concentrated on listening – and avoiding making any noises that might give him away.

As expected the attic was totally dark and freezing cold. The light of the candle could barely penetrate the darkness but now Edo lighted the first torch with his candle and with a sudden flare the attic was woken from its slumber – a high vaulted roof and its ancient wooden structure appeared out of the darkness. Patches of damp shimmered on the floor where the roof had leaked and the rain of the previous days had found its way inside.

As Edo had predicted they could hear some noises – and the closer they tip-toed on their stockinged feet towards the spot Edo had indicated, the more easily they managed to distinguish different snippets of animated conversation from below.

"I'm not going to yield to this blackmail!" cried an angry young voice. "I have to defend the honour of our house, regardless of what you keep telling me!"

"Honour, did I hear honour?" screamed a piercing female voice. "Father, did you hear that? Shouldn't we all acknowledge that it's *my* honour that's at stake tonight – the honour of a helpless virgin..."

The rest of the sentence was drowned by her hysterical laughter, accompanied by a deep bellowing sound of laughter from the man who must have been standing close to her.

But their laughter ended as abruptly as it had started and a harsh voice replied, "If you don't listen to reason, you'll have to learn the hard way. After midnight my men will start torturing your servants and you'll spend the night with my daughter – alone, this is what my men will swear. You know our code of honour, either you marry her, or I have the right to kill you and take your property as compensation!"

"Code of honour?" the young voice roared now. "You *dare* to speak about honour? I prefer to die – never will I consent to marry your daughter!" He almost spat the last words.

Despite the glacial cold of the attic, Pierre felt his temperature rising. He almost felt as if he were sitting down there, and in his imagination he could see the count's son, bound to a chair and helpless.

"Father, he's insulting me, your only daughter!" The high piercing voice could be heard in a mock wail, and seconds later they could hear the sound of a leather belt striking an object. Pierre had no illusions what object this was, especially when he heard the suppressed moan of pain.

"This will teach you to insult my daughter!" the voice cried, dripping with sarcasm.

"My lord, please have mercy!" The pleading voice of the butler could be heard. "I'm sure that my master's son will change his mind! The cook sent some mulled wine, please have a sip and calm down, give my lord a chance to think once more about his decision!"

Pierre heard the clattering of cups or glasses and for some minutes the room lay silent. But then the deep voice started to talk again, its tone menacing – and they could hear the proud answer, "No, never, as long as I live!" – and once again the sound of the belt. Every blow seemed to hurt the listeners as well.

"I can't bear this any more," whispered Armand, gritting his teeth.

Edo stood there, his face a mask of utter misery.

"I need to understand more clearly what the father is saying," Armand whispered and before anybody could comment, he started to move.

25

It was indeed most unfortunate that he failed to see the damp spot in front of him. Before he or his friends realized what was happening he had already slipped and almost fallen down. Trying to regain his balance he instinctively stepped aside. The oak floorboard bent slightly but held – Armand sighed with relief – as did his friends. But their relief was to be short lived. Seconds later the board started to crack and before Armand or his friends had fully grasped what was going on he crashed through the ceiling – right in the middle of the drama that was unfolding below them.

Edo looked at Pierre, panic in his eyes. "Pierre, by all the saints, what do we do now?"

Verona

The sulking gentleman sat at his table, legs stretched out, blond hair ruffled, and his expensive lace collar undone and hanging loosely. His slender hands were playing with a goblet of wine, not the first that he had emptied. "Get me more wine, immediately!" His imperious voice echoed through the guestroom and seconds later the innkeeper appeared in person to serve the noble guest.

"With pleasure, my most noble Signore! Here you are, our best, as usual, of course! Is there anything else I can do for you, my lord? We have the most tender goat freshly roasted today – or we have rabbit stewed in a sauce of wine and herbs, a secret family recipe, handed down from father to son!" He beamed proudly at his guest; it hadn't taken him long to assess that the gentleman was a fat goose just waiting to be plucked.

"I guess the art of milking your customers has also been handed down from father to son," Henri snarled in reply. "I'm not hungry. Did you finally get some information about my cousin? He must be in Verona – or at least close to the city!"

The smiling face of the innkeeper quickly changed to a fitting mask of sympathy. "I sincerely apologize, my most noble Signore, but your cousin and his friends have not been seen in Verona, nor in the neighbouring cities."

"How would you know?" Henri answered, his eyes flashing angrily at the innkeeper, yet the landlord was not to be intimidated.

"Giovanni knows," he stated with the outmost simplicity. "Believe me, Signore, there is *nothing* in this city that could happen without my knowledge. Any love affair, a husband straying from his wife, business to be undertaken, a heritage to come – I know," he chuckled, "sometimes even before the people concerned know themselves. I can swear by all the saints of our city, no foreigner of your description has come even close to our city."

Seeing Henri's disbelieving face he quickly added, "I understand, of course that my message must cause you pain, you must have been looking forward so much to embracing your beloved cousin. I do feel for you, maybe he'll come next week, why don't you stay a bit longer? Luckily your room is still free." He nodded enthusiastically to underline his offer to extend the booking.

Henri sat there motionless. He felt his anger rising like a hot wave – but clearly there was no use having a tantrum here. He clenched his fists until they hurt and his face froze with anger. It appeared as if his cousin had – once again – miraculously evaporated. To be sure, he would wait another week, but then he'd travel on to Venice. *It may be more difficult to find Pierre in such a big city, but I'll find him. This is certain. It's my sacred vow, my bastard cousin's destiny is sealed.*

While Henri was deep in thought the innkeeper had continued talking unabashed. Henri let the stream of gossip pass over him until the innkeeper moved his head closer to Henri's right ear and added confidentially, "...I can of course offer some *special* diversion for you, my most noble Signore. I happen to have special connections to a house of quality, offering only the best! Not even in Rome or Venice would you find a better choice – and at the most reasonable prices! And if you tell my friend that you've been sent by Giovanni, you'll even receive a generous discount!"

After he's doubled the prices to pay your commission, Henri thought, amused. *These innkeepers all think that you don't have a brain if you're born into the nobility.*

"Tell me, what's so special then," Henri answered, although he didn't really feel like spending a night in a brothel.

"Dark-skinned girls, girls from the Ottoman Empire, even a girl from China with feet so tiny that she can't even walk on them properly, she has to move her hips back and forth – just imagine," whispered Giovanni with telling gestures, and continued enthusiastically. "And if you prefer boys, there's a large choice as well, they even have a young dwarf – but he's more for the ladies, your lordship would never think how besotted these ladies can get."

"Oh, I think I can, actually," Henri answered, thinking about the dwarf he had seen in action in Nicolas's establishment and who been known to be one of the main attractions in Paris. It seemed such a long time since he had stayed in Paris, let alone Roquemoulin.

"And the latest addition is the most beautiful boy castrato," continued Giovanni proudly. "He's really amazing. Sundays he sings in church – with the face and voice of an angel!"

"Seems a peculiar sort of angel who prostitutes himself at night," Henri added sarcastically, but Giovanni was not to be intimidated, and crossing himself to ward off evil he replied in hushed tones, "even Lucifer was a fallen angel, indeed our Lord's favourite before he fell from Grace."

As Giovanni continued to describe the boy in the most intimate detail, Henri was not only sure that Giovanni himself must have been a customer, it also dawned upon him that this boy must be the very choir boy who had abandoned him in Milan – what a unique opportunity to settle an unpaid account! *I must be careful now*, he thought, adding aloud, "Can you ask your friend to send the boy over to meet me here?" he asked in a casual voice.

28

"I'm afraid that's impossible, he paid a fortune for him and the boy is guarded like a precious treasure. You'll have to go to his villa, but I can arrange this easily, my son will guide you." Giovanni was all smiles; a lovely vision of handfuls of coins disappearing into the depths of his ever hungry purse appeared in front of his eyes.

"Let me think about it, not tonight in any case." Henri wanted to be on his own now; he needed a bit of calm to come up with a plan to get his hands on the boy again. It was out of the question that he would pay anything – this boy was his! The boy needed to be punished, and severely. Nobody should dare to leave Henri de Beauvoir! He felt a pleasant excitement rising when he thought of the various ways he could inflict punishment.

The next day Henri attended Sunday mass, as was expected from every decent human being, unless they were sick or dying. Verona was a stunningly beautiful and rich city, but Henri had no eyes for the richly decorated buildings of the aristocracy, the two-coloured pink brickwork laced with layers of creamy stone used for the churches and palaces. To be sure, the holy service and the interior of the Holy Church of San Zeno had been impressive but as Henri generally regarded church services as a mere waste of time and viewed the priests as a bunch of money-addicted hypocrites, his lips were still curled in disdain when the mass of devout churchgoers flooded out of the arched portals into the square and back into daylight.

Sunday calm and boredom reigned in the city; the pale winter sun could not give any warmth. Henri decided to walk back to the inn with his usual swift stride, ignoring the shrieking voices offering sedan chair rides and cursing the mutilated beggars who had gathered around the entrance of the church in the hope of collecting their Sunday alms like a flock of dark crows of the underworld waiting to be fed.

Some of the beggars were just hovering there, dozing apathetically, emaciated and spent, too weak to chase actively for some coins or their daily ration of food. They represented a shocking array of human sorrow, from missing limbs to festering and oozing wounds, misshapen bodies covered with warts to grotesque growths of all kinds. Although conceivable that their afflictions might be fabricated simply to attract the sympathy of the people who had just attended church, the sickening stench that hovered above them remained silent proof that their misery must be genuine enough. Others were surprisingly agile; a young boy with crippled legs even managed to speed behind Henri, using his twisted legs and powerful arms to move sideways like a crab at surprising speed. He succeeded in grabbing Henri's breeches while shouting aggressively, "Give to the poor as the Lord Jesus commanded! Give to the poor to enter heaven!"

Henri turned around, his eyes blazing, and snarled, "You scum! Get your filthy hands off me or I'll make sure you meet your Lord Jesus right now!" while touching his rapier in a fleeting gesture to underline the fact that his

29

words were by no means an empty threat. The boy didn't understand a word, as Henri had shouted at him in French, but the message was clear all the same, and fearfully he stopped, pleading for mercy.

"Show some sympathy and drop him a coin, I can see that you can easily afford it," intervened a buxom burgess, clad in her best Sunday attire. "He's a poor lad, no family can afford to feed a wretch like him, he has to beg or starve."

But one icy glance from Henri was enough to silence her. While he strode on she shrugged her shoulders and opened her purse silently to drop a coin into the makeshift purse the boy carried tied to his neck as he couldn't use his hands for begging. As she watched Henri disappear she commented in a low voice to her daughter, "What a proud and handsome devil, but a true devil he is!" and she crossed herself.

Henri had braced himself for a day of boredom but at lunch Giovanni appeared – not only to serve the mouth-watering stew but to announce some good news. "I pride myself on being able to detect immediately if a guest is a member of the aristocracy and a man of undisputed quality!" He beamed proudly at Henri. "And I'm aware that your lordship must be accustomed to the best quality only. I have therefore made use of my special relationship with the noble Villa Giusti and organized an invitation for your lordship for tonight's reception. All of the nobility of Verona will be in attendance – which means that you, noble Signore, shall also meet the most beautiful women you can imagine!"

Henri bowed to indicate that he had received the compliment and appreciated the invitation. But Giovanni lingered until it dawned upon Henri that – as a man of undisputable quality – he was supposed to give generous compensation for this service. A silver coin seemed to be adequate but rather less than Giovanni must have hoped for as he thanked Henri dutifully but with notably less enthusiasm than he had shown when he had announced the good news. Henri grimaced but obliged and a second coin – albeit somewhat smaller – found its way into Giovanni's pocket. Now the innkeeper beamed, his good mood restored. They parted on the best of terms, and it was understood that Giovanni's son was to guide Henri as soon as darkness set in.

The noble Villa Giusti was located on the opposite side of the broad river that crossed Verona, right across the Ponte Nuovo – the new bridge. As was customary in many cities the bridge had retained its name although it had been standing there for centuries already – renewed and rebuilt several times. Behind the banks of the river a steep hill rose where the villa was set high above the city and surrounded by magnificent gardens – a location of unrivalled splendour in Verona.

As he approached the villa astride the magnificent stallion that Giovanni had miraculously provided, Henri noticed with satisfaction that the innkeeper had – for once – not exaggerated. No expense had been spared by his hosts as the long winding road leading uphill was lavishly lit by torches, bright flames spreading their warm light into the winter night. As soon as he approached the vicinity of the villa he perceived the sound of music, the noise of conversation, laughter – all those sounds that had been so typical of life at court. Henri felt a sudden pang of jealousy – these people here were enjoying the kind of privileged lifestyle that had been his own, indeed until only very recently, before he had become an outcast. Liveried lackeys were already waiting for their arrival and led Henri and his guide inside with the decorum and respect due a guest of honour. *I wonder what Giovanni has told them about me*, Henri mused. *They seem to think that I'm royalty.*

In no time Henri found himself surrounded by a crowd of elegant guests. Witty, charming, handsome and speaking Italian with an attractive French accent, he was accepted into the highest circles in no time. With his gleaming blond curls he stood out from the Italians – it was impossible for him to be snubbed or ignored, and the ladies attending the party were attracted by Henri as moths to a flame, flocking around him in desperate attempts to catch an encouraging glance from him.

Henri skilfully ensured he kept an aura of secrecy about him, thus enhancing his fatal attraction. Anecdotes of the French and English court were well received and the host congratulated himself on having yielded to Giovanni's insistence that he should invite this unknown guest who seemed to have travelled the world. Not that he really had any choice, he thought. Giovanni simply knew too much…

Time flew by and after a sumptuous dinner the major attraction of the evening was announced: the famous boy castrato who sang every Sunday in the cathedral would perform tonight exclusively for the august assembly. Henri made sure to melt into the background, secretly rejoicing that fate was offering him revenge on a golden platter. No one who abandoned Henri de Beauvoir would go unpunished!

Henri had known, of course, that the boy could sing well, but something must have happened or the high marble ceiling of the great hall was amplifying the ethereal sound of his voice. Even Henri – no lover of music by all accounts – found himself spellbound. The boy's performance was stunningly beautiful.

In no time the first ladies fainted while uttering exclamations of delight. Henri smiled sardonically; he knew only too well that those ladies had as much sense of well-timed drama as they might have for the quality of the music. But if anything were needed to hallmark the boy's performance as truly outstanding and catapult him to the peak of fashionable society, the slightly scandalous behaviour of his female audience would only help. Two more songs were to follow but in the meantime the great ballroom had become as hot as a furnace. Several fires were burning in the marble

31

fireplaces and hundreds of candles had been lit. Now that all the guests had gathered to listen to the boy the heat and the odour of heavy perfume and perspiration became almost unbearable.

A proposal to order the servants to fetch coats for a short stroll through the famous gardens was therefore received with delight and soon flocks of elegantly dressed guests started to stream into the illuminated gardens. Although it was winter, Verona was blessed with only a mild breeze that evening. Acrobats and jugglers had been waiting for this moment and appeared miraculously in the alleys formed by immaculately trimmed hedges to entertain the enchanted guests.

"*Bravo, che bello!*" could be heard everywhere.

The great ballroom was almost deserted when a stout man standing in the corner cleared his throat and addressed Henri. "My lord, I see that you appreciated the performance of my young artist?"

Henri turned around, surprise on his face.

"You are then the …?"

"The Maecenas of the boy…" interrupted the stout man. "Indeed, I have a particular interest in art of all kinds, I worship all things that are beautiful. But I can see we share the same interest. Would your lordship be interested in becoming acquainted with my ward – should I summon him? He's in the kitchen right now."

"Let me congratulate you on having such an exceptional ward. I have never heard such a beautiful voice before!" Henri lied shamelessly.

The stout man flushed. He was evidently extremely proud of his discovery. "Yes, I showed him how to sing properly and especially how to use his chest. From nature he has a beautiful voice, but he only learned from me that a voice is like an instrument that has to be tended to daily. How lucky that he had been castrated – I don't even want to imagine that such a beautiful voice might have been lost!"

Is it really luck to lose one's balls? Henri thought. *I guess this idiot would have a different perspective if I cut off his own balls here and now.* Yet he smiled at the stout man. "Yes, truly remarkable… and as you just said, what luck! I'd love to get to know the boy better, closer – if you understand what I mean. But I imagine it would be better to arrange this outside… in the gardens, perhaps?"

Henri saw a fleeting expression of greed in the eyes of his counterpart quickly replaced by an expression of false modesty.

32

"My lord, I must confess, it's very hard for me to cater for the needs of such a promising ward, he needs good clothes, his education is expensive…"

"And I can imagine that even feeding him is expensive," Henri suggested with a slight tinge of irony. "I guess the boy is very picky when it comes to matters of food."

The stout man wasn't very sure if Henri was being serious or not but he preferred to ignore the irony and nodded. "Yes, even the food is expensive. I wonder if your lordship could envisage contributing to the wellbeing of my ward?"

With an elegant gesture Henri produced three golden coins from his purse and drawled, "I hope you can accept this humble contribution. I'm almost certain that I can support your ward with some more money – but after this meeting. I hope you don't mind that those are French livres, but I guess the language of gold is understood everywhere…"

The stout man's hands shot out like a snake striking its prey and in no time the golden coins had disappeared as if they had never existed. "I think we understand each other perfectly," said the stout man, now very business-like; gone was the submissive tone he had deemed necessary to employ before. "Where would you like to meet my ward?"

"I see that there is a maze formed by the hedges – I imagine it would be a pleasant surprise to meet him there, most of the other guests seem to be heading towards the music pavilion."

"I shall arrange this immediately; in ten minutes you'll be able to meet the boy!"

Henri cleared his throat. "There's actually no need for you to appear as well, I'll be waiting in the centre of the maze, one of the guests told me that there is a simple key to finding it. I hope you understand what I mean?"

The stout man was smirking now and whispered, "I understand – and your lordship will be surprised how skilled he is."

Henri turned in the direction of the double doors that allowed access to the gardens when he noticed that the hostess was eyeing him curiously. Henri was annoyed as he had wanted to leave the room unnoticed but courtesy obliged that he should not ignore her attentions. Sure of himself he strode towards the hostess. "My lady, is there anything I could do for you?"

She answered with a short laugh before she replied in a melodious voice, "There is always something that a handsome young man can do for a woman…"

33

Henri smiled back and scrutinized her more closely. Well into her forties, she was still a very attractive woman, her neckline displaying immaculate breasts, and her chambermaid must have been most skilled as her makeup and stylish wig covered any revealing traces of her age. "I certainly wouldn't mind being of service to a lady such as you," he answered gallantly.

She only laughed and tapped him playfully with her fan and moved on.

Henri exhaled with relief; it would have been impossible to snub the attentions of his hostess, but now it was really time to go and wait for the boy hidden in the maze. Quickly he stepped outside – yet he missed the long reflective glance that his hostess sent after him.

The famous gardens had been transformed into a night-time paradise. Dark clouds concealed most of the stars, yet no rain was falling and the air was mild despite the advanced winter season. The moon was obscured by the clouds but its silver light seemed to be seeping out from behind them, spreading across the sky like a gloss of silver on dark velvet. The alleys and sculptures in the garden had been skilfully illuminated with torches and lanterns and in their mellow light the gardens came alive, shadows moving with the flames and even the marble sculptures seemed to be dancing on their pedestals. Henri inhaled deeply: a peculiar blend of resinous scents from the plants and the hedges mixed with traces of heavy musk from the guests' perfume and the acrid smell of the smoke of the torches. Music, laughter and conversation wafted across the garden from the pavilion where most guests had gathered after a short stroll and where refreshments were being served.

But Henri's mind did not dwell on the beauty of the evening, and as he hurried through the alleys formed by the trimmed hedges he could already see the boy's face in his mind's eye – imagine the boy's surprise and then the fear that would surely strike him. Excitement started to flood through Henri's veins. He would show the boy tonight that it had been a mistake to leave Henri de Beauvoir, indeed a fatal error!

As he was acting on an impulse of revenge, Henri had no real plan of action; what else could he do but kill the boy and this stupid man who had prided himself on being his 'Maecenas'. It all seemed straightforward enough – the challenge was to do it discreetly and to disappear among the mass of guests along the music pavilion before someone stumbled upon the body. *Vengeance is mine!* he thought gleefully.

*****

The boy was sitting in the kitchen, surrounded by a whole army of kitchen maids doting on him, rapt at having a real celebrity among them. News of his successful performance had of course spread with unbelievable speed through the servants' quarters – tonight the boy had become a star. With huge eyes he viewed the mountains of delicacies that had been heaped on the plates in front

34

of him, unable to decide what to sample and where to start. The choice was overwhelming, simply too much – and he loved most of it. Suddenly he spotted a cake covered with roasted nuts shimmering seductively in the candlelight under a thick layer of melted honey. 'Taste me, savour me!' seemed to be the message coming from the delicious dish. Unable to resist, he grabbed a piece of cake, and stuffed it into his mouth, succumbing to the delights offered to him.

Happily chewing a mouthful of the delicious cake he suddenly spotted the man who had exchanged him for some coins and a donkey from the highwayman who had ambushed him shortly after he had left Milan. He supposed his new master wasn't any worse than the men who had owned him before. Besides renting him to the highest bidder he had at least shown him some tricks to improve his singing, which was important to the boy, as somehow he was convinced that his voice would be the only key to bringing him freedom.

His master seemed excited, and was making urgent gestures to come and join him immediately. Obediently the boy stuffed another piece of the heavenly cake into his mouth before he obliged and rushed to his master.

"Don't gobble your food like a pig," his master greeted him sternly. "You'll run to fat and people won't like it, they want boys to be slender, otherwise they can always ask for girls!"

The boy dropped his head in silent acquiescence while he swallowed the last mouthful of nuts. While the delicious taste lingered in his mouth he tried to keep it on his tongue as long as possible.

"I have excellent news," his master continued briskly. "A foreign gentlemen has been so impressed by your performance tonight that he has proposed to meet you right now outside in the gardens – and he's no skinflint, that much I can tell you!"

"He wants me to sing for him?" asked the boy.

His master rolled his eyes in despair. "How can you be so stupid, of course not, he wants to get into your breeches, like all of them. A bit of innocent singing and a nice face gets them going, you should have understood at least that much by now about human nature. But he'll pay handsomely and if you make him a regular, I'll share with you!"

Of course you always share, thought the boy irately. *The misery for me, the money for you.*

But as there was nothing he could do, he just sent a last longing glance back to the table that had been so lavishly set for him and followed his master out into the garden, his shoulders sagging and his head drooping as he knew the routine that was waiting for him. But tonight it seemed a worse ordeal than usual; maybe it was because the beautiful melody of his last song still lingered in his head with its promise of heavenly joy, maybe it was the magical atmosphere of the garden by night, but all of a sudden every fibre of his body rebelled against his fate. Whatever the reason, every step through the maze towards the man he was to meet and entertain seemed like a step closer to an abyss of suffering. *Let it be quick*, he prayed. *If he's old, maybe he'll just want to look at me.*

His master must have got hold of the key to the maze as they went straight to the centre without deviating or hesitating and indeed, the slender figure of a tall man was already standing there. His face was obscured by the drooping brim of a large hat.

He doesn't look old, thought the boy, all hope evaporating.

"I'll leave you now alone with the gentleman," he told the boy in a brisk voice, and addressing the slender figure he added, "I'm sure your lordship will be satisfied, the boy is most obedient!"

The slender figure only bowed in agreement but didn't reply. The stout man hesitated for a second, but then he turned and disappeared from the boy's sight.

The boy was at a loss. The time and place of this meeting seemed extremely odd and not only was he ill at ease, as was usual for him, he was scared as he had never been before. Not knowing what to do or how to react he remained frozen and waited for the strange gentleman to move or start the conversation.

All of a sudden the man leapt forward, and arms of steel embraced him in a vice-like grip. "Good evening, my darling," hissed Henri de Beauvoir into his ear. "Now, I have some good advice for you, my dear boy, cherish every second from now on, there won't be too many left for you, you filthy traitor."

The boy wanted to cry, he wanted to run, maybe he simply wished to be already dead – in his agony he didn't really know what to wish for or think. Like a rabbit in front of a snake he wanted to bolt but was paralysed. Before he could utter a sound or cry for help the hands of the man he knew so well had already covered his mouth and, helpless, the boy felt how the embrace had turned into a deadly crush, an iron grip closing around his neck.

His blood pounded in his ears, as desperately he gasped for breath. This must surely be the end.

Justice From Above

The young man was sitting in the armchair, a heavy throne-like piece of furniture which must have been in his family forever – made of oak, it was polished and richly carved. The chair, decorative though it might be, had always been notorious in the family for being highly uncomfortable, but now the young man was not even aware of the sharply carved decorations poking into his back and could barely feel the ropes that were tying him to the heavy chair, as he was seething with such fury. Helplessly he had to observe as a stranger occupied his father's chair, ate like a pig from his best plates bearing the coat of arms of the house of Salo and washed down the food with the best wine from his father's winery, banging the silver cup on the polished table like a commoner every time he set it down.

The man's daughter was seated next to him. Hands and mouth covered in grease, she kept stuffing down the last morsels of the delicious suckling pig served in silence by the butler. Although the butler's attentions were servile and punctilious beyond reproach, he emanated an aura of disdain that was palpable to everybody present in the room. But father and daughter seemed immune to such sentiments. Both were portly, but where the father was massive yet muscular as a boar, the daughter wobbled with fat, her enormous breasts threatening to burst out of her tight bodice at any minute. Where her father's voice was deep and loud, her own voice was shrill and unpleasant, yet this did not impede her from using it incessantly. Her father was the Count of Monza. Once the lord of an unimportant barony in the vicinity of Milan, he had succeeded in amassing huge wealth and acquiring a vast earldom spreading east by cooperating closely with the Spanish occupiers.

There was another notable difference between father and daughter. Whereas the father was almost bald and his dark beard streaked with grey, the daughter's head was crowned with a mass of curly flaming auburn hair. Her skin had the delicate natural pallor that comes with red hair, yet her face – maybe once attractive – was bloated and disfigured by masses of pimples, and she had the annoying habit of scratching her face while was talking and didn't even stop doing so while she was eating. Her glance wandered around the panelled walls of the ancient room, and still chewing she remarked cheekily, "This castle badly needs a mistress with taste. This room is terrible, like an old wooden box, no golden trimmings, no fashionable paintings on the walls, and the furniture is positively medieval. As soon as I am mistress here, things will change. I wonder why they call this a castle – it's not even fit to be called a hovel!"

Her father only grunted and spat on the floor to show his agreement with his daughter's remarks.

Then her glance went to the butler who was filling the cups anew in silence. "And this sourpuss of a butler will be one of the first I shall dismiss. Even the milk must turn sour when he looks at it!"

Father and daughter burst into peals of laughter, judging her observations to be a capital joke.

"Over my dead body will you become mistress of this castle," rumbled the young man, trying in vain to loosen his ties. "As soon as my father..." but the rest of the sentence was never to be finished as suddenly they heard a creaking noise emanating from the vibrating boards in the ceiling right above them.

"A rat!" shrieked the daughter.

"Don't be so stupid," her father scolded her. "If that were a rat, it would have to be the size of a pig," he added, alerted by the noise.

"What is there above us?" he asked the butler sternly who stood there, petrified.

"Oh... only the c-ceiling," he stammered.

"You worthless, stupid piece of excrement!" bellowed the father. "Of course I can see that this is a ceiling, I want to know which rooms are located above this ceiling! Tell me now, or you'll be whipped."

"Only the roof trusses, my lord, I swear! There are no rooms above us. The only access is from the staircase of the tower that's guarded by your men. Maybe some cats, they like to couple up there."

The count grinned knowingly and made a telling gesture while his daughter broke into a giggle. In the meantime the noise had stopped and, apparently reassured by the butler's answer, the Count of Monza turned again towards the young man. His voice oozing with irony he addressed the young man with a mock bow. "I do apologize, my dearest Viscount Salo, I think your last words were cut short – what will happen as soon as your father comes back? Tell me please, I'm so curious – and maybe it'll frighten me so much I'll wet my breeches!"

His daughter broke into hysterical peals of laughter. "Oh Father, you're so funny, you've such a great sense of humour! Wet your breeches!" and off she went again.

But once again the young man's answer was not to be heard as suddenly the creaking noise came back, but much louder, directly above them. The Count of Monza cast his eyes to the ceiling, as indeed the treacherous sound was located right above him. But before he could move or react, a section of the ceiling gave way and Armand crashed downwards, his full weight like a cannonball directly onto the count. His mouth still open in surprise, the Count of Monza was felled like a tree and knocked out on the spot.

For a second, time stood still, and everyone in the room seemed to be paralysed, such was their surprise at the alien attacker descending from above. To Armand's great luck, his fall had been cushioned by the stout count who now lay motionless beneath him. Instinctively he rolled to the side, and not a second too late, as the captain of the Monza men had woken from his shock and rushed forward to thrust his rapier through him. But as Armand rolled aside, the rapier thrust went right into the count's chest – if he hadn't yet been killed by Armand's fall, the rapier finished the job.

The daughter gasped in horror at her father lying motionless on the floor. Blood seeped out of the wound where the sword had entered his chest and was forming a bright pool next to his body. She threw her hands into the air as if she wanted to appeal to heaven but soon it dawned on her that any help would be too late. Realizing that her father was fatally wounded, she started to scream hysterically, a high piercing cry that seemed to echo back and forth from the panelled walls.

The captain was now fighting like a caged animal. Knowing that he had nothing to lose, he drew the bloody rapier out of the count's body and turned to tackle Armand who lay next to the count, still dazed from his fall. Pierre had been following the scene unfolding below him and without further reflection or hesitation he clutched his sword and jumped down, hoping to land on the raging captain and knock him out as his friend had done before with the count.

Edo wasn't going to be left behind. He spotted a chandelier hanging from the central beam close to the gaping hole in the ceiling and with the agility of an acrobat he managed to jump and grab the chandelier before he leapt to the floor.

Meanwhile the room had turned into a battlefield. Pierre failed to strike the captain hard enough but luckily his own fall was cushioned by the body of the dead count. The captain lost his balance when Pierre jumped down and shoved him hard with his feet but he recovered quickly and drew his sword to engage Pierre in a fierce fight while Pierre was still having problems getting back on his feet. Pierre's situation quickly became desperate as two more of the captain's men joined the fight and he found himself surrounded by three men ready to kill.

Still dazed by his fall, but his will to fight and help his friend unbroken, Armand stumbled to his feet and swaying like a leaky battleship on the high seas he drew his rapier while trying to focus on the people moving around the dead body of the count. Meanwhile the count's daughter kept screaming hysterically.

Edo realized that it was high time to intervene and leapt from the chandelier down to the floor where he immediately engaged one of the musketeers who was trying to attack Pierre from behind. The musketeer was flabbergasted to find yet another mysterious enemy descending from above. Thunderstruck he hesitated – a second too long, as Edo's sword found its way straight between his ribs. Uttering a last cry the musketeer stumbled and dropped down next to the dead count.

Seeing his man stumble and fall the Monza captain became distracted from his own fight, which proved to be a fatal mistake, as Jean had followed Edo and used the opportunity to deliver a heavy blow that sent him reeling to the floor. Not wanting to stay idle, the butler approached the count's screaming daughter from behind. With all of his force he smashed the bottle of wine he had been serving so punctiliously before on her head. "Your wine is served, ma'am!" he pronounced loudly, his refined voice dripping with sarcasm.

The sudden silence was relief beyond imagination. The two remaining Monza musketeers immediately surrendered their arms, as they saw no point in continuing their fight against an enemy who had descended like a divine nemesis from above and seemed to have multiplied in a matter of seconds.

Edo rushed to the chair, cut the bonds of his friend and embraced him. Laughing and shedding tears of joy and relief he exclaimed, "Thank the Lord, Umberto, that you're safe now! My apologies that we had to enter your room in a rather unconventional way without announcing ourselves properly, especially as we find you in the company of such a beautiful young lady!"

Umberto's face was flushed with joy but as soon as his glance swept over the count and his daughter, his fury returned. "You have no idea what perfidious plans these two pigs had in store for me!"

"Well, actually, we do happen to know!" answered Edo. "This is why we're here. We arrived this afternoon. Our plan was to visit your father and stay over for Christmas before we leave for Venice. When we knocked at the gate we had to insist most strongly on being admitted and we found the castle in a strange mood, full of musketeers and servants I had never seen before – the butler was the only one I could recognize. Thanks to the butler we quickly understood that something amiss was going on here and finally Jean found out from the cook what was really going on. Oh, sorry – I'm being impolite. Let me introduce your saviours first!" Edo duly presented Pierre, Armand and Jean, and greetings and congratulations were solemnly exchanged.

"Did you block the door?" Nervous, Umberto suddenly interrupted the lengthy introductions. "There must be a whole army of Monza men in the castle by now. I'm afraid that our ordeal is not yet over!"

The butler cleared his throat. "If I may speak out and reassure you, Signore Umberto, the cook has served extremely generous helpings of mulled wine with grappa, so I don't think that we have too much to fear from them. There was a good thirty of them, but from what I could see when I descended to the kitchen the last time all of them are either asleep or drunkenly chasing the kitchen maids."

Umberto laughed like a schoolboy. Suddenly the stress and anxiety of the last hours seemed to have evaporated. "That was a cunning idea, whose idea was it?"

"My valet's," said Pierre proudly. "He talked to the cook and she must have mixed a mulled wine fit to put a donkey to sleep!"

"It seems that your valet and my butler would make a formidable team in any battle," smiled Umberto, looking at the old butler full of affection. "Although it seems that the wine he served to the lady was a bit too heavy for her liking."

In the best of moods they proceeded to bind the captain, who was still lying motionless on the ground, the count's daughter and the two musketeers who had not only surrendered their arms but beseeched Umberto to allow him to swear allegiance to his cause. "Believe us, my lord, the dead count was a swine, he pressed us into his service." They dropped on their knees, shedding tears and tried to grab his hand to kiss his signet ring.

Umberto was still seething with anger. "You're no better than your perfidious count, you shall be punished, there can be no question of granting pardon!"

Armand touched his arm lightly and whispered into his ear. "I understand that you're upset and have been insulted and must seek revenge, but sometimes it pays to be political, and they're only minions. I'd like to suggest that you should consider granting a pardon if they help us to free your men and arrest theirs – don't forget there's only six of us and the Monza men may be drunk but they have pistols and must be disarmed, so why not use their comrades to deceive them?"

Umberto hesitated and Armand could see that he was fighting with himself. The family's pride had been insulted – there could be no pardoning of such an offence – and yet he immediately understood the common sense of Armand's advice. Like every aspiring elder son of the local gentry he had read and was eager to emulate the teachings of Machiavelli. Umberto turned back to the trembling musketeers. "I guess you know the punishment that will be waiting for you: I'll have you whipped and if you survive this ordeal you'll be hanged, unless…"

As soon as he had pronounced his verdict, the younger musketeer – Pierre reckoned that he was still only a boy – started to choke, and pale as a ghost he fell silent.

The older musketeer was not ready to give up. "Unless what? My lord, please let us know how we can serve you, we're yours, body and soul, from now on!"

"Unless you make sure that my men are freed with your help and lure the rest of your gang into a trap, only then will you be spared!"

"It will be done, my lord, just let me tell you that some of my comrades are good men in their hearts, even if this may seem unlikely to your lordship after today's ordeal. Let me prove that I can fight for you and if I gain your trust, I can show you those that can help you to conquer the dead count's estates. When we set off from our own castle it was left devoid of any protection, it's ripe for the picking. Now that my old master is dead, you can take full advantage – and revenge! None of my comrades will ever swear allegiance to her," and he looked in the direction of the count's daughter and spat.

Umberto looked in surprise at the musketeer who had spoken so frankly – but the man looked back into his eyes, his glance direct and unwavering.

"Prove to me then what you're worth," answered Umberto brusquely, and addressing the hapless younger musketeer he added with contempt, "and you, you coward, show me if you're worth anything."

The young musketeer's face turned scarlet. He gulped hard but then managed to answer, "Yes, sir, I mean, yes, my lord!"

"First, a practical question," Edo interjected. "Where would we find the key to the dungeon to free your own men?"

"These bandits took them," said the butler.

"If you will allow, that's an easy enough answer for me." The musketeer stepped forward and with a swift motion he bent down to the captain who lay on the floor and picked up a large iron key out of the pocket of his breeches. The captain stirred, and Armand quickly checked that he was tied up securely. Satisfied to find all his bonds were tight enough he turned back to the others. The captain only moaned but didn't wake up.

"Now, what's the plan?" he interrogated the musketeer who had volunteered to join their ranks. "Shall we go straight to the dungeon and free our men?"

"There is a risk that the count's men might open fire on us, even if they're drunk." Pierre frowned. "We must find a way to win their trust."

Armand looked at the dead count, whose chest was covered with medals of all sorts. "If you were to arrive with one of these medals as proof that the count had commissioned you to check if everything is going well downstairs, would they pay heed to your orders?" he asked the musketeer. "By the way, what's your name?"

"My name is Luca, Signore, and yes, they would obey me, I'd make sure that I mean business when I talk to them. What do you want me to do?"

"You pretend that you've have been ordered by the Count of Monza to see if all the men are on their guard and sober. Your colleague will assist you and we'll follow, secretly, of course. Naturally they'll be drunk and you can set an example by arresting two or three and taking them to the dungeon. Then we'll appear all of a sudden and help you set our men free. We'll repeat this several times until those scoundrels who're still sober enough to present a danger to us are safely stowed in the prisons."

Luca nodded. He had understood the mission.

"Let me warn you, Luca, if you betray us, you'll join your old master without delay, and I'm pretty sure that this will not be in heaven!" Armand gave him a last stern warning.

Luca grinned quickly. "Yes, my lord, I understand."

Umberto looked amazed at Armand. "You should become a general! Where did you learn to develop such schemes?"

Armand looked rather nonchalantly at him. He loved flattery. "Oh, it comes naturally, I guess it runs in the family."

Their attention was distracted as the count's daughter had woken up and started to scream again.

"Quickly, we need to silence her," commanded Umberto.

Luca took a cloth from his pocket and without any hesitation rammed it into the mouth of the wriggling lady. Seconds later she found herself gagged and silenced.

"Any idea what kind of punishment would be worst for her? What a pity that she's a lady and not a man!" Umberto asked.

"An isolated convent, preferably an order with a vow of silence." Pierre and Armand came forward almost simultaneously with the same proposal and burst into laughter. The gagged daughter wriggled even more. She seemed to dislike this proposal enormously. In vain she tried to speak.

Irritated, Umberto looked at the others. "Any idea what she wants to say? I'm reluctant to take off the gag, but I think she wants to tell us something!"

"I think, I know," said Luca. "I'm guessing she wants to tell us to show pity because she's pregnant."

Umberto looked thunderstruck. "I don't think that's at all funny, the Count of Monza was going to force me to marry her tonight!"

"I'm not joking. I guess that is the reason, my lord, why they were so desperate and came up with this foolish plan. I couldn't help but overhear their conversation when we rode towards your lordship's castle. Her father was still fuming as she had lost her virginity to some minion of his. He had the man executed but now they had to find a way to find a husband, fast – and who'd wed a hideous slut like her?"

Edo gave a long, thoughtful look at the count's daughter. "You're right, nobody of sound mind would do that! To be honest, placing her in a convent is still only a mild punishment!"

Armand was becoming impatient. "I agree that's appalling, but we must move on. We can deal with this slut later. Luca, you know your role, let's test your commitment to your new master. Don't forget, if I'm not happy with you, I'll have no qualms in making you join the dead count tonight," he said, adding a last stern warning.

"It's understood, Signore, but I have a wife and children – don't worry, I have no wish to enter heaven just yet."

Thus they stepped out of the stately drawing room with the gaping hole in its ceiling and left the gagged musketeers and the count's daughter under the surveillance of the butler who had armed himself with another bottle, ready to silence anyone who dared to utter a word or move. A cold draught from the roof cavity made the temperature uncomfortable and the butler was content that he could stay close to the fire.

Jean hastened back up to the roof space to collect the boots they had left up there – they could hardly set out recapturing a castle in their stockinged feet!

"Let's start with the kitchen. The last time I was down there, it was full of Monza's soldiers," Jean suggested after he came back – and thus it was decided.

The kitchen itself was impressive, a succession of huge vaulted rooms that were dominated in the middle by a gigantic fireplace. Huge iron spits were waiting to be turned by tireless servants. The lord of the castle loved to entertain guests and on such days the spits would be turning day and night. But now kitchen and fireplace lay deserted, and even the cook had abandoned her beloved domain. The mood of the drunken soldiers had been swinging from merriment to bouts of rage and the cook had preferred to make herself invisible. Yet for now – as the butler had predicted – the castle was unusually silent. Close behind the kitchen, they suddenly perceived noises of merry laughter and heavy panting. Pierre and Edo exchanged knowing glances; it didn't take a genius to work out what was going on inside.

"Now, show us what you're worth," Umberto whispered to Luca, as he opened the door and pushed Luca and the young musketeer inside.

They entered the room where – unsurprisingly – two of their comrades were having fun with the kitchen maids. Adopting the tone and bearing of the captain Luca bellowed, "What the hell is going on here? Are you mad? Do you want me to report this to his lordship?"

The two men who had been having a good time stumbled to their feet – which was somewhat difficult as their breeches were hanging round their ankles. They hastened to cover their quickly shrinking private parts while the scared maids screamed with surprise and dragged their skirts down and hastened in panic to fasten their blouses.

"Out of here, you sluts!" ordered Luca at the top of his voice. "I'll deal with you later!"

Skirts in their hands, the girls fled the kitchen, expecting the worst to come later.

Luca's glance turned back to the scarlet-faced soldiers who were having considerable problems standing to attention, the mulled wine making them sway like ships on the high sea.

"Shall we go upstairs now and disturb the count or do you accept a night in the prison cell as punishment, and I might just forget this incident?"

The two soldiers looked at each other, unable to suppress a stupid grin of satisfaction and nodded their consent. Who would mind spending a night in the castle prison if this meant that they could avoid being whipped by their brutal captain? This proposal seemed too good to be true, and quickly, so as to avoid any sudden change of mind, they assured Luca they were ready to leave and face their punishment.

Luca led them like docile sheep to the castle's dungeons, supposedly guarded by Monza's men, but the two remaining guards lay snoring on the wooden benches, a strong smell of alcohol emanating from their slumped figures. Luca poked them to see how deeply asleep they were, but as they only answered with an incoherent grunt he decided to ignore them and opened the door of a prison cell to let his prisoners enter. The mulled wine had put them in a happy mood and they entered their cell giggling as if an adventure was waiting for them. Their relief at being safe from the count's judgement was so great that they only realized some time later that they had in fact been chained to the wall and the door bolted – whereas suddenly in the cell next to them they heard strange cheering and quite a commotion.

While Luca took care of the new prisoners, Umberto and the friends had sneaked into the dungeon as well. Gleefully Pierre and Armand gagged and bound the sleeping guards, while Edo, Jean and Umberto used the captain's key to unlock the door of the prison cell where Umberto's men had been detained. From the spy hole in the door they could see a truly pitiful crowd of servants that had been penned into the cell. Umberto's father had left with his personal guard and additional musketeers for protection during his journey, therefore only the regular staff of servants, some young apprentices and those too old to travel had been left behind.

Not much of a crew to defend a castle, thought Umberto, when he looked at his men. Two of the youngest boys seemed to be crying in the cell – he wondered what kind of threats the guards must have uttered to frighten them so.

When the group heard the key in the lock and the bolts being drawn, the older men instinctively crouched together and tried to hide the younger ones. Surely this must be the Monza men coming to execute the first of them as they had promised if their master did not hand over the castle – which meant that they were certain to be condemned. Never would the son of their lord betray the honour of the family! *Let it be quick*, prayed the old groom, with his almost-white hair, stepping forward in order to be the first to be sacrificed.

Their relief at finding the son of their master appear before them instead of the dreaded captain at the entrance to their prison cell was beyond description. "Hush! We've come to free you, but the castle is still occupied by the Monza men, will you help me to catch them?"

Enthusiastic replies followed. "Let's free the castle and kill them, they're worthless vermin!" but Umberto intervened immediately. "There'll be no killing. I insist that my father or I will be the ones to pass judgement – nobody else! Do I make myself clear?"

Although not too content at seeing vengeance delayed, they nodded and kissed Umberto's hands. "Signore, you're our lord, lead us and we'll follow!"

Umberto looked proudly at the small crowd. Of course, he knew all of them. Suddenly he hesitated and turned back the hood of a small, fragile boy. "What are you doing down here?"

"This is my grandchild, Teresa," answered the old groom proudly. "We decided that we would rather see her die than be dishonoured by these villains!"

46

Umberto looked at him grimly. "Let me assure you that she'll be safe from now on, these villains will be sentenced and punished!"

Armand had joined them and plucked nervously at his sleeve. "Umberto, we have no time for noble speeches," he whispered, we must make sure that the castle is safe. There are still a good twenty villains roaming around with firearms!"

Umberto came back to reality and nodded. In the crowded cell they discussed their plans and swiftly groups were created, each of them in charge of arresting the Monza men in the part of the castle that was put under their responsibility.

Pierre, Armand and Jean would be in charge of the north wing. "Let's hope our vigilant guard had a good bellyful of the mulled wine," Jean quipped. "At least, that's what I suggested he should do."

Back they went to the north wing and were unpleasantly surprised to find two guards awake and still waiting there, one of them leaning heavily on an impressive halberd. "I didn't even know that they still use them nowadays," Pierre whispered to Armand.

"It's a dangerous weapon," Armand whispered back. "We'll need to use surprise tactics."

Trying to look as innocent as possible they approached the two guards, both of them reeking of mulled wine.

"*Buonasera!*" Armand greeted the guard, breaking into a hiccup. "We've had too much of this mulled wine and now we want our bed!"

One of the guards grinned sheepishly and returned the greeting with a "Buonasera," but seemed to be having enormous problems focusing on the visitors. "You should be in there!" he added, pointing to the north tower. "We never saw you come down."

"Not my fault, my friend, we were just looking for some hot wine, it's freezing cold up there."

The second guard looked at them suspiciously. "The valet brought some already," he frowned, trying to pull his thoughts together. "You've been spying!" he suddenly accused them, pointing with a trembling finger at the group.

"Spies! What spies? Let me kill them!" cried the first one, swinging his halberd across violently. Instinctively Armand drew his sword but this movement was immediately interpreted by the drunken guards as a declaration of war and with loud cries they jumped upon the three men to attack them. It didn't prove too difficult to disarm the first drunken guard but

47

the second one kept violently swinging his halberd with amazing skill around him and seemed unassailable. Pierre swore as he had left the flintlock pistol upstairs in the tower room; it had seemed too heavy and cumbersome for their original mission, but now it would have come in very handy indeed.

Armand and Jean had succeeded in capturing the first guard and held him in a tight grip, but this was the signal for the second guard to change tactics. Pierre had been distracted for a second when he watched the guard struggle in Jean's iron embrace. It all happened in seconds as the second guard threw his halberd at Armand, who dodged the deadly weapon only by a whisker and like a cannonball he shot forward and grabbed Pierre who was totally stunned by this surprise attack. Now it was Pierre who found himself held in an iron grip and – even more disconcerting – he felt something cold and rough at his throat. There could be no mistake, the guard was pressing his dagger into his neck.

"Help! *Aiuto!*" the guard cried in the hope of alerting his fellow musketeers, his cries echoing across the courtyard. Yet the courtyard remained totally silent – nobody answered, no clamouring or stamping of feet from his comrades could be heard. The guard shouted again, but to no avail.

"I don't know what's going on here!" Pierre heard him exclaim under his breath before he shouted loudly to Armand and Jean, "I'll kill your friend if you don't provide me with a horse and let me leave unhindered. Any attempt to harm me and your friend is a dead man!"

Taken completely by surprise Jean and Armand froze; they didn't dare move a muscle. The blade of the dagger shimmered dangerously in the light of the torches illuminating the courtyard which lay in total silence. Only the heavy breathing of the guard could be heard, a strange sound grotesquely amplified by the close walls around them. Meanwhile the guard had started to reverse cautiously as he had spotted a wall behind him promising to offer protection for his back. Impatiently he dragged the reluctant Pierre with him until they reached the brickwork surrounding the castle well.

Pierre had been shocked to find himself turned into a helpless hostage, but now as the shock abated, he felt a wave of blinding rage sweep through his body. How dare this drunken soldier take him hostage, after all, he was Pierre de Beauvoir, a Marquis of France, a Duke of England. Better dead than have to bear this shame!

Still in the grip of his hot anger, Pierre reacted almost instinctively. Vigorously he stepped with his heavy boot on the guard's soft shoe and as the guard slightly slackened his grip under this unexpected attack, he used a trick he had learned from his Italian fencing master. Pierre could still hear the slightly ironic voice the Italian had used when he explained to them, "This trick is not really supposed to be used by noble gentlemen like you, Signori, but maybe someday you will find yourself not fighting against gentlemen, but villains from the street, then it's as well to be prepared."

Pierre's leg now moved up kicking straight into the guard's private parts. The guard howled with pain and although he somehow tried to drive his dagger forward, hoping to hit Pierre's throat, he missed his target as Pierre had foreseen his reaction and dived downwards. With a swift move he grabbed the guard's leg and made him tumble backwards. Using the wall of the well like the fulcrum of a seesaw he used the impact of his thrust to push both of his legs upwards and the hapless guard's head crashed against the brickwork before he disappeared into the black depths of the well. The blow to his head must have rendered him unconscious as not even a cry could be heard as he vanished into the darkness.

"I think I should inform the cook that she had better use water from a different source," Pierre's voice could be heard. "This well is tainted now."

"I give up, have mercy!" wailed the first guard, who was still in the grip of Armand and Jean.

"You better had give up," answered Jean. "My master is allergic to vermin of all kinds, and that's what you are!"

The guard didn't dare answer. He stared at the ground and bit his lip while Jean bound him, making sure that the straps were tight enough.

"Mission accomplished!" said Armand in a bright mood. "I loved it, you were brilliant."

"It's nothing," Pierre answered, but secretly he was immensely proud of Armand's compliment – it was a rare enough occurrence.

"Though you should have taken better care from the beginning," Armand continued after a short pause. "A mistake like this could cost you your life in battle."

"Yes, I know," Pierre answered meekly. He knew that Armand was right, but he felt that for once Armand could have praised him without having to add some sort of criticism.

To everybody's satisfaction the dungeon filled with amazing speed. Luca kept his promise and lured the drunken Monza men into the trap – the truth was that most of the men had to be carried inside anyhow, and were now sleeping deeply and snoring, happily unaware that Fortuna's wheel had turned against them.

Umberto's offer to have his friends transferred and let them sleep in his rooms was gladly accepted. So it was that a very tired yet immensely satisfied

Jean packed up the last belongings that had been left behind in the north tower in the decrepit, now glacial room.

The next morning brought a new surprise for them. The friends had been sleeping late after celebrating Umberto's liberation until the wee hours of the morning. Glowing with pride and satisfaction, the butler had served the best wines from his secret supply, and consequently Pierre couldn't even remember how he had found his bed. It took a full jug of water and several cups of coffee before he felt able to face the world.

They had just settled comfortably to partake of a late, late breakfast when the news was spread that Umberto's father had arrived. Apparently he had found his sister in considerably better health than announced or anticipated (as usual) and feeling somehow uneasy he had decided to cut his visit short and return to his native shores. Still wearing his travelling breeches and boots he stormed into the breakfast parlour like a force of nature and greeted the friends at breakfast hugging not only Edo but all of them like longstanding and very much cherished members of his family.

He was surprisingly tall for an Italian, with a deep voice that vibrated in the room. Whenever he talked his large hands moved incessantly while his deeply lined face radiated with joy. "*Bravo, bravo!*" he beamed. "Umberto told me how *bravissimo*, how *molto* cunning and intelligent you are!"

Such a deluge of compliments made their cheeks flame red and Pierre hastened to explain that all of this had been nothing but an insignificant service that had been rendered with pleasure.

"I think I will hang all of these villains from the spires of the highest tower!" the old count groaned, his face suddenly flashing with anger. "To attack my castle, keep my son as hostage – and all of this during a period of peace and by means of perfidious treachery – demands a punishment, the most severe!"

"Don't use the north tower then," Edo couldn't help adding. "I think it may need a bit of renovation before it can support the weight of so many corpses."

The count's expression changed from rage to amusement and he answered good-humouredly, "You rascal, you only want to sell me a new loan from your bank! You're no better than your elder brother – always fishing for new business! By the way, I hope Giovanni is well, will he come and join us shortly?"

Edo smiled back, taking this remark as a compliment. "If you will allow, my lord, we would like to spend Christmas here!"

"Consider this castle as your home," the count said simply. "It will be my greatest pleasure – and I hope your friends will stay as well?"

Armand answered for both of them. "It would be *our* greatest pleasure, my lord, to stay here with you!"

"But not in the north tower," Edo added, winking at Umberto who winked back.

"Our pampered banker seems a bit shocked; apparently he's not used to spending the night in rough conditions!"

But then his expression changed and he became serious again. Umberto thought it about time to revert to more important issues. "Father, if you'll allow, I think the Count of Monza has been punished – I hope fervently that he's rotting in hell already! And as for his beautiful daughter..." The untameable Armand suddenly made faces and coughed in the background.

Edo thus corrected his speech. "All right, I mean: as for his hideous daughter, I propose we get rid of her as fast as possible and send her to a convent, somewhere far away, like Sicily."

"You won't need to worry about a maid of honour in that case, she hasn't got any," Armand couldn't help interrupting.

Umberto's father nodded in agreement. "That's true, but what about the rest of this vermin, you won't plead mercy for them? They almost killed my people and they violated the kitchen maids. I heard the full story from the butler and the cook this morning, she was quite out of her mind!"

"One of the Monza men, his name is Luca, yesterday swore allegiance to our house and helped us together with a young comrade to lock up the rest of the gang. He proposes that we seize the Monza estates bordering ours and annex the land as there is no heir besides the daughter. I have given it a lot of thought and I think it's a unique opportunity to get rid of the eternal threat to our territories and take over those castles that have always been thorns in our flesh." Umberto's eyes were bright and he was talking with his hands now, just like his father did before.

"My son, turning into a Machiavellian politician," snorted the old count. "And how does my little Alexander plan to make this happen? How do we conquer the world if we have only a good hundred musketeers armed and ready?"

"That's exactly the point! Luca is absolutely convinced that once we grant pardon to the men, with the exception of the captain, they'll all change sides and we won't even need to get engaged in any heavy fighting. I don't think he's lying, as we all know perfectly well that the Count of Monza was a brute and despised by his own people."

51

"Don't get carried away, Umberto. It's out of the question to close our eyes to what has been going on here – two or three of these villains have even been bold enough to seduce the kitchen maids!" said the count sternly. "I insist, justice must prevail!"

"If I may make a suggestion, my lords?" Pierre suddenly intervened.

The two men looked at him, surprised. In the heat of the discussion they had almost forgotten the existence of their guests.

"Of course, my most honourable Marquis… Your Grace", the count said, suddenly remembering uncomfortably Pierre's superior rank, as Umberto whispered something into his ear.

Pierre smiled his most charming smile. "We're travelling incognito, there is no need to address me by my titles, my lord. What I'd like to suggest is that we invite this Luca and grill him a bit; he seems to be smart, let's see if he's honest and if he has a sound head on his shoulders!"

The count looked quizzically at Pierre, but Pierre returned the look, quite sure of himself. "Let him talk freely and if you still feel that he is dishonest or hiding things, let's forget this whole venture."

The count nodded and Umberto called the guards to fetch Luca.

Luca arrived after several minutes, his look defiant – he must have heard that Umberto's father had arrived and as the guards had bound him he must have gained the impression that his hour of judgement had arrived.

The count examined Luca from his unkempt hair to his dirty boots and snorted to express his disapproval. "What's your name?" he snarled.

"Luca, my lord!"

"I heard that you swore allegiance to my family yesterday; you're thus a traitor to the Monza cause! Don't you have any honour to defend?"

Luca's face became pale but he didn't move. He stood erect and faced the count, his glance steady and unflinching. "I have never been able to detect anything honourable in the tasks I had to carry out for the Count of Monza, my lord."

The count looked at him, surprised at receiving such a frank reply. "You confess thus that you're a traitor?" he roared.

"No, my lord, the Count of Monza is dead and we were led to your castle under the false pretence of defending the honour of his daughter. I only discovered during our journey that this was a blatant lie, as I told your lordship's son. I discovered the truth, that she is with child by somebody else.

I consider myself free from my oath and any obligation to the Monza family – and my lord, I have my own children to consider."

The count was flabbergasted. Luca certainly had no problems voicing his opinion freely. "You would thus betray us for the sake of your children if somebody offered you higher pay. You're a traitor all the same!"

"No, my lord, I said that my oath had ceased to exist as my old master is dead. Unless you choose to imprison me, I'm a free man now and can choose a new master. If I swear allegiance to you and your son you'll not find a better servant in all of Italy! But it's true, I cannot afford the luxury of noble feelings if my children are starving! I would expect that you would pay me appropriately."

The count was speechless for a second, whereas Luca seemed to be at ease, his previous tension gone.

"You pretend therefore that all of you came here on a false pretence and you didn't mean any harm, let's call it a nice neighbourly visit – nothing else?"

Luca grinned. "No, Signore, most comrades wouldn't care why they came here, they just follow orders and hope to make some booty. The captain knew, of course. But the others are just soldiers, they fell into bad habits because we had a bad leader. But nothing that couldn't be solved with a bit of discipline!"

"And you pretend this is also true for the soldiers who violated my kitchen maids? As you seem to have an answer for everything, you'll certainly know how to deal with this?" The count looked arrogantly at Luca, his face flushed with anger, but Luca wouldn't be intimidated.

"I haven't witnessed what was going on, my lord, but I saw how these things started. I personally don't think that you can violate any woman who offers herself like a prostitute and consents. Two of the maids I saw were behaving like shameless sluts. If you punish my comrades – and I agree that your lordship is obliged to do something to keep discipline – you should punish the girls as well – or you might consider..."

"I might consider what?" thundered the count.

"Your lordship might consider forcing the soldiers to marry the maids; that would resolve all the issues."

Edo and Umberto couldn't help themselves any longer, and broke out into peals of laughter. "Some people really do consider marriage as the greatest and longest lasting punishment of all!"

Luca gave a quick smile but continued. "If your lordship doesn't marry them off quickly, their children will have to be brought up and fed at the expense of your estate, my lord," Luca remarked cunningly. "I really would advise that you consider this option most seriously."

The count made a gesture as if he were parrying an imaginary attack. "I think we had better stop here, or soon you'll be proposing to run the whole estate!"

"Before the Count of Monza forced me to join his army, I used to manage a small estate. I'd never have allowed the north tower to fall into such a state of disrepair, my lord. It will be very costly now to renovate it. But I do have some ideas…"

Pierre was amazed. Luca had apparently forgotten that he was being interrogated as a member of a hostile force, and was now totally immersed in his ideas of how to rebuild the north tower.

"Let's change the subject," Umberto intervened quickly. "You mentioned yesterday that we should seize the opportunity and attack the nearest Monza estates. How do you see this happening, why did you propose this idea?"

Luca paused for a moment and seemed to be pondering deeply before he formulated his answer with care. "I'm just a simple man, Signore, please excuse me if my speech is direct and not as polished as it should be. Let me explain what I think though. The Count of Monza was hated by most of us, he took our estates, our money, our harvest – and often enough he would chase our daughters or wives, or offer them to his closest friends. I lost count of how often I had to see my comrades whipped or mutilated." Luca closed his eyes as he recalled the painful memories and clenched his fists. "The truth is that the count was unscrupulous and brutal – may he rot in hell! He was a minor esquire and only became powerful once these Spanish pigs who occupy Milan found out how useful he could be to do the dirty work for them. Cunningly he acquired more and more land and finally became appointed as Count of Monza. But in exchange he had to swear fealty to the Spanish. After the summer the count was called to Milan and ordered by the Spanish commander to levy a small army in order to help defend the border with France. It's nothing unusual – the wars between France and Spain have been going on for years. But this is the reason why most of the Monza soldiers are far away right now under Spanish command."

Umberto looked at his father, his heart beating faster. "Can we believe this story, Father?" he whispered. "That's too good to be true! It's the chance of a lifetime."

His father nodded. "Yes, I've heard this as well. This is why I felt safe enough to leave the castle with only a handful of my people left for defence."

Luca had waited respectfully, seeing that father and son were engaged in a discussion.

Umberto's father waved at him impatiently. "Go on! What else do you want to tell us?"

"This ambush had never been planned, your lordship. I must give this to the Count of Monza: he was a real pig – but he had some balls. When his daughter blurted out the truth that she was pregnant, the unlucky lover was arrested, castrated and slowly cut to pieces, and as news had spread that your lordship had left to visit your lordship's sister, the Count of Monza came up with this bold plan to marry off his daughter to your son – or pretend at least that her child had been fathered by a nobleman."

"That's completely mad!" exclaimed Umberto.

"Mad, but as Luca said, he had balls," said Armand. He couldn't help but feel a little admiration for the count's cunning. "Admit it, he nearly had you trapped!"

Umberto flinched but fell silent.

"As most of the true Monza men were engaged at the French border, the count came here, accompanied mostly by local men. If you'll allow me, my lord, I'd like to plead in their favour. Believe me, most are good men at the bottom of their hearts." Luca took a deep breath. "If your lordship will show clemency I can almost guarantee that at least the neighbouring estates will welcome you with open arms as their new lord and master!"

The face of Umberto's father was inscrutable. "I thank you for your frank words – and advice on the north tower," he smiled. "We'll let you know our decision shortly."

Luca understood that he had been dismissed, and bowing deeply and reverently he left the room.

Umberto couldn't stand still; he was almost dancing around the table. "This is the chance of a lifetime, Father, when do we leave? I shall wear my new armour!"

"You want to play Alexander the Great?" his father asked curtly. "But has my dear courageous son thought about the consequences?"

"The Monza soldiers are tied up at the French border and there is no male heir!" said Umberto truculently. "There'll never be another chance like it, don't tell me that we won't go!"

Armand coughed and said almost apologetically, "I guess your father wants to say that sooner or later the Spanish will either take over the land and titles themselves or grant it as a fiefdom to one of their vassals once they fully understand what has been going on, which means that you risk a lot of trouble in the spring. It's not enough to conquer the land. You have to be sure that you can hold on to it."

Umberto's father nodded enthusiastically. "Fantastico! That's it – exactly. It's not enough to conquer a kingdom – how do we make sure that we can keep it for the house of Salo?"

"Money." Suddenly Pierre's voice could be heard. "The key is money!"

"This should be coming from me!" protested Edo good-humouredly. "I'm the banker here. What do you mean?"

"I understand that the house of Salo is allied to the Republic of Venice. Only the power and the superior military might of Venice can stop the Spanish, so whatever you do, you'll need to negotiate the backing of Venice, and this means that you have to offer money, a lot of money, I would guess."

Umberto's father nodded, evidently unhappy. "My lord, you're perfectly right. But what could I offer? We're by no means poor, but I know these greedy Venetians, if you give them your hand, you'd better count your fingers afterwards! I know that this is a unique opportunity – but I'm afraid we have to let it pass or we'll end up depleting all of our treasury!"

Umberto was outraged. "This cannot be your last word, Father, are we merchants or the noble family of Salo?" he cried out, pain in his voice, his face pale with embarrassment.

An awkward silence ensued, nobody wanting to interfere in a situation that had all the hallmarks of a juicy family dispute.

Suddenly they heard someone clearing his throat behind them. Jean had been standing on duty in the corner. He had been so much a part of this adventure that nobody had bothered to ask him to leave the room when the discussion had started. "May I make a suggestion, my lords?" he asked, keeping the appearance of the dutiful servant.

"Of course, Jean," exclaimed Pierre.

"He'll beat us again," cried Armand. "I can feel it already!"

Jean smiled a quick smile and continued, "I had the opportunity of discussing matters with Luca before he had the privilege of being questioned by his lordship."

"Strange privilege," murmured Armand. "I could think of better things."

Unperturbed, Jean continued. "I took the liberty of interrogating Luca as to why the Count of Monza could afford such a lavish lifestyle. I had noticed that his clothes were made from silk and embroidered with silver and gold – as a valet you notice such things immediately."

"Well, I didn't, but why does it matter now?" Pierre looked curious.

"Luca told me that in the mountains – they are far away to the north but they still belong to these estates – the Count of Monza was the owner of rich silver and salt mines. It was officially kept secret but everyone knew that one of the most feared punishments was to send disobedient servants to toil in the mines. And those who left never came back... Everyone knew about it, but nobody dared to mention it openly."

Armand whistled. "There's your money!"

"You're brilliant, Jean!" Pierre exclaimed. "The Count of Salo could bargain with Venice to share the mining rights – or offer a share of the income to some influential families – they're all desperate for money as they lost so much in the countless wars against the Ottoman Empire and then in the plague, you remember, Julia told us!"

"This changes our plans completely, Father." Umberto rushed to the cupboard and impatiently dragged out a pile of maps. "The mines must be somewhere up here – impossible to attack them or occupy them during winter. At this time of year there'll be several feet of snow up there. We'll have to position guards here," his finger pointed north of Lake Garda, "and strike during early spring, as soon as the snow starts melting and before the Spanish can move in to stop us!" His eager face was flushed with excitement.

"But who's going to bargain with the Venetians? We'll be tied up here!" his father remarked grimly. "Someone has to go immediately after Christmas otherwise we'll never have an agreement in place on time, the Venetians will take some time before they decide to upset the Spanish, nobody needs a war right now!"

"I could do this." Edo's voice was heard. "I have to go to Venice anyhow and I may never become a good accountant, but I'm a smooth talker!"

"Fantastico!" Umberto jumped up and cried out. "That settles it. Oh, Father, please give us your consent!"

Pierre had been sitting in his armchair up until this point. Umberto's enthusiasm was contagious – and yet Pierre had spent enough time close to court to understand that they'd need more than mere money to receive backing for their claim – left to rely on his own resources, the Count of Salo would never be able to withstand the ire of the Spanish. "Who would be the count's heir in normal circumstances?" Pierre asked cautiously.

"His only daughter," the Count of Salo answered, "unless he owns some lands or titles where male succession would be mandatory. Why do you ask?"

"I think that you should play it safe. I propose preparing a contract between the heiress and your lordship. In this contract you'll acquire – for a very modest amount – the estates and mines."

Armand whistled. "Our Marquis is being clever, I think I know what he wants to do!"

"As for those estates close to Milan and the Spanish territories, she'll pledge them to the closest male relative before she takes up the veil..."

"Why should she do this?" asked Umberto. "Why should we give up our claim?"

"Because this will start a family feud that will last for generations and will keep the Spanish busy – Pierre, you're a genius!" Armand cried out.

"Yes, that's right." Pierre looked decidedly smug, and was finding it difficult to hide his satisfaction at becoming the undisputed centre of attention now. "While they fight and discuss details you can strengthen the hold on your new possessions – and gain valuable time to sign a treaty with Venice."

The Count of Salo raised his glass. "To the health of His Grace!" he cried.

Pierre gave a toast in reply. "And to the health of Jean, he gave us the key to all of this!"

Jean's bronze skin suddenly glowed even darker as Pierre winked at him; he was very proud of his valet.

The Journey Goes On

This fatal grip of iron was inescapable! The boy tried to fight – but the more he tried to escape, to breathe or cry out, the more those arms of steel seemed to close themselves around him, without mercy, ready to kill.

"No, my dear, you won't escape me again," breathed the voice he knew so well. "And don't think that I'll make it quick. I'll have my fun before you disappear – forever. There is a river so wonderfully close, I'm sure you'd love to take a dip on a cold night, it's ever so refreshing!" The voice was speaking low, almost dispassionately, yet its effect was ever more chilling.

The boy could feel his heart beating in a frenzy, like a small trapped bird. Maybe his heart would stop beating altogether soon? Fear alone could kill; instinctively he knew that this must be true. And yet it all seemed so unreal! The boy could hear carefree laughter, voices and music wafting through the air scented with the fragrance of the laurel hedges. The high society of Verona was listening to the music playing in the pavilion, glasses were clinking. The warm glow of countless lanterns and torches bathed the gardens in the light of a fairy tale come true.

Not only could the boy feel muscular arms pressing him hard to Henri's body, he could even feel Henri's heart beating against his body, fast and excited – but not in the crazy rhythm of his own heart that was in danger of exploding. And he could feel something different: Henri was aroused, the boy's palpable fright seeming only to be fuelling his desire. Now he felt Henri's arm moving up, pressing hard against his chest, ruthlessly extracting the last breath of precious air from out of his lungs. The boy gave up his resistance, closed his eyes and slackened in Henri's grip, a lamb ready for slaughter.

"Buona sera!" greeted a cheerful voice.

Henri turned abruptly, slackening his grip involuntarily. The boy opened his eyes and gasped loudly, greedily inhaling the fresh night air.

"I hope that I'm not interrupting you." The voice had taken on a mocking note. "I would be ever so sorry, or should I perhaps say: inconsolable?"

A shapely figure detached itself from the darkness. Dumbfounded, Henri watched his hostess approaching him, her arm leaning lightly on her husband's as she walked gracefully towards him on her high-heeled shoes as if she were making a social call.

Henri had no option. Convention obliged him to respect protocol and swiftly he discarded the boy like a useless toy. He bowed deeply and greeted the approaching pair with the perfection and elegance acquired by an experienced courtier.

"I'm inconsolable not to have greeted *you* immediately," drawled Henri. "A lady of such rare beauty lightens up even the darkest corners of this beautifully unique garden!"

His compliment was answered with a short deep laugh and her fan brushed him playfully. "French gentlemen know how to pay compliments," she remarked, looking at her husband. "You should listen carefully, my dear! You could learn a lot!"

Her husband bowed in silent approval but declined to comment.

The lady turned to the boy who was standing there, transfixed, not sure if this was reality or a dream. "You should hurry back to your master," she said, caressing his dark locks. "I saw him searching for you!"

A clap of her hand woke him up, and forgetting to thank her he ran towards the figure of his master who had indeed appeared out of the shadow of the high hedges. Now that the boy had left, an uneasy silence reigned.

"I think you owe me a service. I saved you from doing something very silly, especially as the Cardinal Benevenuto told me this evening that he intends to acquire the boy as a gift for the Holy Father."

Henri remembered the Cardinal. Seated like an oversized fat scarlet toad in his sedan chair he had been carried into the reception room by six muscular servants. A poisonous toad – if appearances were not deceiving...

"And the Cardinal wouldn't appreciate it *at all* if his plans were disrupted," Henri's hostess continued. "A single remark from His Eminence and you would risk being banished to the dungeons of the Inquisition forever. We're uncomfortably close to Rome in such matters."

She approached Henri and he saw her face close to his. "It would be such a pity to see a man like you disappear forever," she said in a hoarse voice, yet still mocking him. Her hand started to caress his chest and before he had understood what she was going to do or could react, her hand dived down right into his breeches. "Hard as an iron rod," she cooed and squeezed him.

Henri was stunned. He had met many women in his life – ladies, duchesses, simple barmaids or artful sluts – but never had a lady of the highest breeding taken command, talking like a lady yet acting like a whore – and all of this in the presence of her husband.

"Haven't you forgotten somebody?" Henri managed to say, trying to ignore her curious hand.

Her melodious laughter could be heard once more. "Not really, my dear friend. Maybe I should mention that we share only a few things in life, but we do share a passion for young and handsome men!"

Before Henri had fully digested her casual remark she had already continued. "Luckily our guests seem to be well entertained and won't miss me during the next hour. You may lend me your arm to walk back to our house now, I think we can spend our time better than conversing out here in the freezing darkness. At least I have some ideas…"

Henri masked his astonishment and bowed elegantly, extending his arm which she took with all the decorum of a lady attending a social event. While she continued chatting, totally at ease, they strolled back to the villa until they reached a back entrance where her servants were already waiting. Henri found himself ushered upstairs into a bedroom of truly royal proportions. He was not really astonished to find the walls covered with paintings of amorous scenes, little cupids shooting their arrows at an amazing diversity of nude gods and goddesses. The paintings must have cost a fortune; they were surprisingly tasteful and the painter must have been a master of his art. Silken bed sheets embroidered with threads of pure gold shimmered in the light of the numerous candelabra that had been placed by attentive servants.

"Do you like my bedroom?" she asked him with her seductive smile.

"It certainly serves its purposes," Henri answered drily.

She dropped her pose and broke into laughter. "It does! You'll discover!" And she winked at him.

While they were conversing she had been standing in the centre of the room, motionless, while two exceptionally beautiful maids had started to undress her. In next to no time she stood there, completely naked, and Henri had ample opportunity to admire her. Although past her prime she was still an exceptionally beautiful woman – and she knew her worth. The mellow candlelight played with the creamy complexion of her skin and her lustrous black hair – impossible to tell if the dark colour was natural or owed its lustre to the secret skills of her maid.

Henri stood close to her. A young black page – as was the height of fashion – suddenly materialized from the shadows and made signs that he wanted to undress him. Like his hostess, Henri didn't move. Like a statue he stood still – yet very much aware of the appraising glances of his exciting hostess and her strange husband who had slumped into a comfortable armchair in a corner close to him. His host hadn't deemed it necessary to exchange a single word with Henri, but Henri had seen the thrill in his eyes as soon as the pageboy had removed his silk shirt.

61

It was a bizarre situation, somehow unreal – but it aroused Henri with an intensity he had rarely felt before in his life. In no time he tumbled into the huge bed to discover with delight that she was not only a lady with the soul of a whore, but also one who possessed such skills.

Moaning with pleasure she grabbed him hard. "I knew that we were from the same mould from the moment I set my eyes on you, walking this evening into the ballroom, handsome and proud like a peacock. I vowed to tame you with lust, to break your arrogance!"

Henri laughed, and sure of himself he embraced her hard. "First, my darling, I'll tame you – but I'll make sure that you'll love every second of it!" and before she found the opportunity to answer he started to show her that he was true to his word.

They made love as if the world was going to end, but soon, far too soon, the page and maids made them come back to reality. "My Lady Sophia, your guests are waiting!" the maid was pleading.

Quickly they dressed her and Henri so they could join the waiting guests. Sophia's husband had left the room discreetly – immersed in their own world they hadn't even noticed – but now he came back into the room and unperturbed his wife accepted his arm with all due decorum to walk downstairs to entertain once again her waiting guests. Henri followed at his leisure. The incident with the boy was long forgotten, and a satisfied smile played around his lips – what a surprising yet most pleasant evening!

The next afternoon the same page who had undressed him the night before knocked at the door of Henri's room above the tavern. Bowing reverently he handed Henri a precious fur-lined coat and a beautifully crafted chain. Henri took the gifts, thinking he must indeed have left an excellent impression.

He almost grinned but knowing enough of human curiosity, he was convinced that Sophia must have given precise instructions to her page to register any of his reactions and report it to him. Therefore he kept his face non-committal and dropped the gifts nonchalantly on a chair. He didn't even bother to look at the gifts that not only must have cost a small fortune but probably had been chosen with a lot of care in order to please him. Yet behind this cool façade Henri's heart was jubilant. Bored and frustrated by his hitherto fruitless efforts to track down his bastard cousin, this promised to become an enticing diversion, a most pleasurable way to spend some time!

The precious gifts were accompanied by a letter. Henri glanced at it as the page looked expectantly at him and was clearly waiting for his answer. Though formal in its tone, the message was clear: Henri was invited to come tonight back to the villa; a coach would be at his convenience, waiting for him after dinner.

The night came but this time Sophia received him alone, with no sign of other guests, let alone her husband. Skipping all unnecessary formalities Henri found himself back in bed with her in no time. He was content that she received him alone; her husband with the sagging shoulders and the mournful eyes wouldn't have added any spice to their night.

From this day on the black page would knock at his door almost every day. During the day Henri continued to interrogate the owners of all post stations around Verona, and the nights were taken up by Sophia. Yet the troubling fact remained, there was no trace of his cousin, nor of his companions. The group had disappeared without a trace.

But fascination soon turned into dull familiarity. After a fortnight Henri's enthrallment with Sophia and her impressive array of amorous tricks started to wane, and her summons became a tedious routine. Yet Sophia seemed to become more and more besotted with Henri – to be point of staging a hysterical scene one night. While the pageboy was still undressing Henri, Sophia suddenly started to slap her flabbergasted maid. "Out of my room, you slut!" she yelled. "I'll have you whipped!"

"Signora, what did I do wrong?" sobbed the girl, dissolving into tears.

"You dare ask *me*?" yelled Sophia. "Don't you think that I noticed you almost devouring my guest with your greedy eyes!"

Eyes sparkling with anger, Henri brutally seized Sophia and forced her arm down.

In panic the maid fell to her knees. She could easily imagine her ladyship's wrath once Henri was gone. "No, sir," she wailed, "let me have my punishment, I deserve it!"

Henri ignored the maid's intervention. Looking deeply into Sophia's eyes he snarled, "Don't forget, my darling Sophie, I'm the master of this game here. If ever I should decide I want her, I'll have her – and together with you, if I fancy it. And you'll do exactly what I wish, or tonight is the last time we make love. Do I make myself clear?"

Henri could see furious lights flashing in her eyes and her arms flexed as if she wanted to slap him. But Henri's grip was too strong for her, she wriggled in his arms but he only laughed at her. Locked in stalemate they stood frozen like warring statues until Sophia realized how ridiculous they must look. All of a sudden she relented and like a playful cat she withdrew her claws and started to snuggle in Henri's arms.

"I hate you," she sighed, "yet I like you too much, you'll have your way," and with an impatient gesture she sent the trembling maid away and

63

whispered something into the pageboy's ear. Henri could see his big eyes widen in astonishment and briefly wondered what Sophia had said to him, but the pageboy withdrew, and they were alone now.

In a voice hoarse with excitement Henri commanded, "Undress me!" and demurely Sophia followed his order, yet not without letting her hands linger at his thighs, stroking him slowly, knowing exactly how to render Henri mad with desire. Once more Henri marvelled as to where she had learned these tricks – certainly not from her tepid husband.

That night Sophia was truly insatiable. Worn out, Henri returned to his inn in the early morning, right on time as the city gates were being opened to let the first farmers and peddlers enter the city. His coach and the coat of arms were well known to the guards and as usual he entered the city without having to endure any interrogation or lengthy searches. Henri went to bed totally exhausted and only woke up when the winter sun was standing high in the firmament.

A servant from the inn must have attended to his room already while he was sleeping as water, a fresh towel and a clean shirt were waiting for him. Henri grimaced as soon as his fingers touched the water, as it was already cold. He felt a brief pang of jealousy when he thought of his previous life where a personal valet ready to fulfil any whim had been a natural part of his daily life.

While Henri freshened up, his thoughts turned to Sophia. It was true enough, he had rarely encountered a woman like her; even Marina had seemed tame compared to Sophia – Sophia was like a hungry tigress. But Henri knew this type of woman. *She'll eat me alive if I don't pay attention,* he mused. *She's starting to get on my nerves, soon she'll bore me to death with her demands and tantrums.*

For a second he considered spicing up the relationship by inviting the pageboy. Only yesterday he had been tempted to invite the young page to join in their amorous play. A crooked smile appeared on his face as he imagined Sophia and the pageboy. *I imagine she'll kill me afterwards. I think I had better stop this now! Anyhow my dear bastard cousin seems to have disappeared, maybe he's in Venice already. I must go there urgently!* It felt good to have made a clear decision.

His mind made up, he opened the chest that contained his clothes and arms. The heavy lid opened smoothly on well-greased hinges. In Giovanni's tavern all was impeccably maintained! But as soon as the sunlight lit the contents of the chest, Henri felt hot and cold at the same time. With the exception of some carefully folded woollen blankets, the chest was empty. All of his personal belongings were gone! Quickly he dived underneath the bed where he had deposited his horde of gold, spices and jewels, well hidden underneath a loose floorboard. But not so much as a bit of fluff could be seen; the floor was as clean as his secret hiding place was empty.

Fuming with rage he put on the fresh shirt and stormed down to meet Giovanni who was – as usual – supervising the taproom at this hour of the day.

"If you son of a bitch want to live to see tomorrow you'd better give my belongings back to me, and I mean all of them!" Henri yelled across the taproom. There were only a few guests waiting for a late lunch to be served but they fell silent immediately; this promised to be an unforeseen entertainment!

Giovanni held a tin cup in his hands and unperturbed he continued to polish it slowly to gleaming perfection. His calm gaze rested on Henri and he made a tutting sound. "My lord, you can be assured that nothing has been stolen! Of course not – something like that would never happen in *my* establishment."

All of a sudden his attitude changed. Giovanni's chest swelled and he became the very picture of humiliated indignation. "Yesterday evening my Lady Sophia sent a messenger commanding to deliver immediately all of your belongings into her personal safe keeping – which I did, of course. The young black page collected it all. He also informed me that her ladyship would pay for your stay here, so please don't worry, all will be taken care of."

Henri gasped and sent silent curses in the direction of the villa he had learned to know so well. Sophia had outsmarted him – now he knew what she had whispered into the pageboy's ear the previous night.

"I suppose my horse is gone as well," stated Henri grimly.

"The pageboy said that there is ample stabling at the villa and that it would be more convenient!"

Two young and well-built guests seemed to be following their discussion with special attention and Henri was no longer surprised to see Sophia's coat of arms on their livery.

"I'm a prisoner of her ladyship then," Henri said in a low tone, pointing to her ladyship's servants.

"Of course not!" protested Giovanni. "Simply under her special protection, it seems that your lordship must have impressed her greatly!"

"Oh yes, I understand this now, and I guess all of Verona knows about this as well, right?"

"My Lady Sophia is extremely well connected," answered Giovanni, apparently concentrating again on the task of polishing his cups. "Let me put it this way: it would be extremely foolish for anybody here to ignore her wishes." He put the gleaming cup down and looked straight into Henri's eyes and whispered, "Rumour has it that the Inquisitor himself" – he quickly crossed himself – "is... ahem... a close friend. Nobody would dare to interfere with her in any way, Lady Sophia is the law in this city."

"And she pays handsomely, I imagine?" replied Henri, flushed with rage. "Giovanni, you scum, you knew all of this when you got me the invitation up there!"

A quick smile flashed across Giovanni's face. "I do happen to know her ladyship's tastes, and that she is rather – how shall we say...? – neglected, by her husband. I was convinced that you'd match perfectly; two very attractive persons..."

For a second Henri reflected that it would be immensely satisfying to strangle Giovanni here and now, and some of these thoughts must have been visible in his eyes as Giovanni quickly moved back to the shelter of his counter. "My lord, please be ever so careful now!" Giovanni exclaimed. "Every single move of your lordship will be observed from now on," and he pointed towards the servants who had risen from their table.

"I'm not daft, Giovanni, I understand this," Henri replied, restraining himself. "But your scheming Lady Sophia will find that I'm not the tame lapdog she may have hoped for!"

"It's far above my position to judge her ladyship's desires," Giovanni answered with a hypocritical expression, "yet I imagine that she hopes for the reverse. I'd wager that she's looking for a wild tiger more than a lapdog."

Henri didn't bother to answer. Abruptly he turned and went back to his room. Nothing had changed – and yet his room had become a prison cell, and he was trapped.

Versailles

"Your Eminence!" The secretary entering the sanctum of the most powerful man in France, probably in all of Europe, looked flustered. "I apologize for the disturbance, but one of our brothers arrived early this morning from Versailles – and he has expressed his urgent desire to speak to Your Eminence immediately!"

Cardinal Richelieu looked up from his papers. He held a quill in his hand but so abrupt had been the interruption that a large drop of dark ink had splashed on the letter he had been writing. Quickly he strewed sand across the page to soak up the ink, but the stain couldn't be removed. He sighed. He'd have to write the letter again. Annoyed, he looked at his secretary. "Will you ever understand that this is a study and not a courtyard where I rear chickens? Can't you learn to enter a room discreetly and with the dignity we owe to our position?"

The secretary stood to attention, pale and trembling. The Cardinal was known to be choleric and visions of being bundled off to a mission to the remotest parts of the new colonies flashed before his eyes and didn't do much to put him at his ease. But from experience he knew that insisting on the fact that he had knocked several times at the door to announce his entrance would just worsen his case, therefore he kept his mouth shut and prayed silently that the thunder would pass.

The quill now started tapping impatiently on the desk. "I'm waiting..." remarked His Eminence in a bored tone. "When may I expect to be honoured with further explanations?"

The secretary hastened to reply and burst out, "It's His Majesty, Your Eminence, his condition is worsening by the hour and Brother Antoine would like to see you immediately!"

The Cardinal's face remained expressionless. Over many years he had refined the art of keeping his thoughts secret and maintaining the face of a sphinx. Yet inside him a cold hand seemed to be gripping his heart and squeezing it. *By all the blessed saints, this cannot, this may not, be true!*

France might be the most powerful nation in Europe by now, but its power was far from being consolidated. If the King died now, his Spanish widowed queen and the infant princes would become mere pawns in the huge game they called politics. Furthermore the Cardinal could feel that his own health was failing quickly, and if the King expired now, his country would face the abyss of civil war.

"Let the brother enter, then," he answered. "Why are you waiting?"

His secretary bowed reverently and as fast as protocol would allow he disappeared to fetch the brother who was waiting outside impatiently.

"How's his mood today?" asked Brother Antoine. He looked full of sympathy at the pale and trembling secretary.

"Sometimes I think it's getting worse every week!" answered the secretary with a deep sigh while he started mopping his face. "Better go in quickly, we can talk later."

Brother Antoine winked at him to show that he had fully understood the message and entered the inner sanctum.

Reverently he fell on his knees and kissed the large ring of office on the Cardinal's hand. The big ruby gleamed malevolently in the light of the numerous candles. Although the grey winter daylight seeped through the opened curtains, the Cardinal needed the light of the candles to plough through the stream of documents that seemed to arrive day and night.

"I have bad news, Your Eminence!" Brother Antoine had decided that it would not help to beat around the bush.

"The King?"

"Yes, His Majesty's health is failing and his physicians fear the worst!" Quickly he crossed himself, as even from his position he could easily understand that the death of the King would spell disaster for the country.

"And you're sure that it's not just one of his usual bilious attacks? I try to tell him to eat and drink less, but he never seems to listen!"

Brother Antoine nodded knowingly. The King's penchant for heavy drinking was no secret in court circles.

"I'm afraid, Your Eminence, it's worse this time. As Your Eminence knows, I managed to befriend one of the physicians. He told me that it all started as usual, but by now the physicians simply don't know what to do, they say that the King has melancholia and as his body has no strength left, they fear that he might simply give up the struggle!"

The Cardinal's face remained expressionless. The merest raising of a single eyebrow would indicate to people who knew him well that he did not appreciate the behaviour of kings who wallowed in bouts of melancholia when their kingdom was at stake.

"You did well to inform me, these idiot physicians are capable of bleeding him to death if I let things slip."

Energetically he rang a bell and only seconds later his secretary opened the door.

"Brother Antoine and I are leaving for Versailles now. I'll also need my personal valet and ask him to prepare the usual case with the medicines. Cancel all audiences, tell any visitors that I'm in, but am feeling unwell today and most probably tomorrow. Nobody is to know that I've left to see the King in a hurry, is that clear?"

The secretary bowed reverently. "All will be arranged as you command, Your Eminence!"

Suddenly the Cardinal gave him one of his rare smiles. "You may not know how to enter my office correctly, but at least you never talk too much!"

About an hour later the Cardinal's coach was already speeding towards Versailles. The blinds had been pulled down to keep the cold air outside therefore they were sitting in almost total darkness. The Cardinal had been wrapped in fur-lined blankets and heated stones warmed his feet, but Brother Antoine had refused such luxuries as his holy order had sworn him to a life of poverty. If he regretted his decision in the cold coach, he wouldn't say so.

The coach made good progress as long as the roads were paved. The Cardinal's musketeers mercilessly chased off all farmers, merchants and even the proud coaches of the minor aristocracy to make way for what was announced officially as a messenger of his most noble and mighty Eminence, the Cardinal, Duke of Richelieu.

Once they had entered open country they had to cover sections of road that resembled muddy wallows as the winter drizzle had completely soaked their slippery surface. Potholes filled with water were an ever-present danger, and there were times when Brother Antoine feared that the wheels must be breaking, they could hear such moaning and squeaking of the wood grinding against gravel. But the Lord seemed to have blessed their journey, as the coach grumbled but kept on speeding towards Versailles.

From time to time the valet peeped out of the windows to monitor their progress, but all he could discern were endless shady forests looking as grim and grey as the thick clouds that hovered above them. *No wonder the King suffers from melancholia,* he thought, but some inner voice told him not to raise this issue with the Cardinal, who had closed his eyes. As usual Cardinal Richelieu was not sleeping, but he was suffering. The bumpy road was sheer torture for his frail body and all he hoped for was that this ordeal might terminate as soon as possible.

In the early afternoon Versailles came into sight. Although more a hunting lodge than a castle it was the King's preferred refuge as King Louis XIII hated the Louvre, a place still haunted by vivid memories of his tyrannical mother. He also hated the rigid protocol which governed his day from waking in the morning to his last prayers at night in Paris – here in Versailles he could feel almost human.

The Cardinal descended from his coach; stiff from the long journey, he had to be supported by Brother Antoine and his valet. As a regular guest he had his own rooms and it was there where he could be seen interviewing the King's physicians soon after his arrival.

The interviews did not yield any new information. Brother Antoine had given him a clear picture – clearer than the information proffered by the learned doctors of medicine – the only difference being that the physicians' speech was loaded with Latin expressions and – the Cardinal noted this with alarm – they had almost given up hope of the survival of their King. Scared stiff of becoming the scapegoats in this affair, they spent most of their time in preparing their defence and calling on the Almighty.

"I understand that the cause is not one of his usual bilious attacks?" The Cardinal insisted on getting some clarity from their somehow confusing statements.

The physicians looked at each other and the youngest took courage and answered, "Yes, Your Eminence, it started as usual. To be frank with you, we don't know why things look so bad this time, it looks as if…"

"As if?" the Cardinal insisted.

"As if His Majesty has given up the fight!"

Aware that such a statement could be interpreted as treason, his older colleagues immediately intervened with full force. "Not at all, our young colleague has chosen his words ill, of course our gracious Majesty is fighting his illness as vigorously as a King is supposed to do, a glorious example for all of his subjects, indeed!"

The young physician turned scarlet with embarrassment and quickly joined the choir of denial of his more experienced colleagues.

The Cardinal had heard enough and dismissed the embarrassed physicians. "You may leave now. I understand that you have done all that is humanly possible; the rest will be in hands of our Lord!" Solemnly he made the sign of the cross and three very much relieved physicians left his room.

"Let the young doctor know that I appreciate his honesty!" the Cardinal said to Brother Antoine, "but warn him in future to be open to you and me only, never to say the truth in public, it could cost him his head!"

"Now let's all go and visit our great King who's fighting so vigorously!" The Cardinal added, his even voice hiding the irony of his statement.

70

"And prepare your secret weapon," he ordered his valet. "I hope that we can use it once again."

"Your Eminence, give me fifteen minutes and I'm ready!"

His Majesty, Louis XIII, the glorious King of France, lay in his huge bed, the canopy above showing the embroidered lilies of France and his coat of arms on a background of a rich blue velvet. Heavy blankets made from the finest furs kept him warm, and the air was heavy with the expensive incense that the physicians must have been burning. Candles were shining brightly and a golden cross and a painting of the Virgin Mary with her Child had been placed close to his bed so that the King could see and pray to them.

It looks like a rehearsal for his funeral, the Cardinal thought. It would have been verging on the ridiculous yet Richelieu didn't feel like joking. Reverently the Cardinal kneeled at the bed and immediately a feeble voice could be heard from the bed.

"Richelieu, we have told you so often that there is no need to kneel!"

"Your Majesty is too kind, I simply pay my respects to the greatest king of this world!"

"A king who will soon leave this world," Louis whispered with a sigh. "Have you come to take my confession and perform the last rites, will you console my poor widow?"

"I shall do whatever Your Majesty requests, but initially I came for some other reason."

"Richelieu! Do not dare to bother me with affairs of state when I have to concentrate on the purity of my soul, only the purest hearts may enter heaven!" He paused. "Our life seems to have been so empty since my dear friend Cinq Mars was proven a traitor. I have detached myself from the vanity of life and I've had much time to concentrate on my spiritual wellbeing."

Time you should have spent governing your kingdom, the Cardinal thought irately, his hands itching to box his King's ears. "I was really not intending to bother Your Majesty in the least," the Cardinal protested. He had settled in the meantime in a more comfortable position in a large armchair and now deliberately changed to a brisk tone. "Your Majesty's greatness in history is assured, the matters of state run smoothly!" The Cardinal cleared his throat. "The reason why I wanted to see Your Majesty is that I received an urgent letter from the Marquis de Beauvoir," the Cardinal lied shamelessly. "It seems his affairs in Venice have been progressing much more smoothly than planned and the Marquis yearns to come back far earlier than foreseen!"

The King, who had lain as still as a corpse, suddenly started to stir. With a voice much stronger than before, he enquired, "The young Marquis, the one

71

who's always accompanied by his dashing young friend, the youngest son of the Marquis de Saint Paul?"

"Yes, Your Majesty, I'm amazed how you remember all of these details – Pierre de Beauvoir and Armand de Saint Paul, they seem inseparable!"

"But why should he write you a letter, of course de Beauvoir can come back at any time!" the King responded, his curiosity awoken.

"As Your Majesty may recall, your dear cousin, the King of England, urges Pierre de Beauvoir to join his cause. Your Majesty is aware that I'm not very hopeful for King Charles's situation…"

"We know," sighed the King. "My poor sister, it seemed such a promising marriage."

The Cardinal was not willing to spend more sentiments on the Queen of England. "The fact is that the Marquis is requesting if we can find an elegant way to keep him in France, without of course upsetting King Charles greatly. He'd rather attend the court of your glorious Majesty; my personal opinion is that he loved his stays here in Versailles and would prefer to hunt with Your Majesty rather than chase insolent roundheads in England…"

King Louis's face suddenly lost its deathly pallor and irately he snarled at his surprised valets, "No wonder we're convinced that we must be dying with all these heavy blankets that you have heaved upon our person! Take some away!" Turning back to Richelieu with eyes full of longing, he continued, "We'd love so much to organize a huge hunt, when will they be back – in spring? What a pity that we're suffering so badly, we don't think that we'll ever be strong enough to ride again!"

The Cardinal sighed softly to show his sympathy. "The young lords should be back in the early spring. If Your Majesty would permit it, my valet has a secret recipe – a broth that has often enough brought me back from the gates of Hades to life – would Your Majesty condescend to taste it?"

With the gesture of a conjurer, Richelieu made room for his valet who held a shining silver chalice full of steaming broth. Deliberately the Cardinal had chosen a chalice to render even more great the effect upon the King and was purring like cat when the King's eyes opened wide.

"Like the holy chalice of our Lord Jesus," he breathed and took a first careful sip. In no time the broth had disappeared and the King heaved a satisfied sigh followed by a royal burp. "How extraordinary!" the King exclaimed. "We feel reborn! Let us have some more of this delicious soup – and what's the secret?"

72

"I suggest that Your Majesty should have only a little more, and then Your Majesty should rest a little; please don't forget that Your Majesty has been very ill indeed!"

"Without you, my dearest Richelieu, we would have been dying! But now tell us the secret!"

"My valet obtains some special herbs right from the heart of the Orient, the same that King Solomon used to consume!" the Cardinal invented shamelessly, *and, of course, we added a goodly amount of brandy to cheer you up*, he thought.

The King looked suitably impressed.

"But please keep this secret between Your Majesty and your humble servant, otherwise all of your nobles will be queuing up to have some – and my valet has only a limited supply – just enough to cure Your Majesty!"

The King nodded enthusiastically and chuckled. "Yes, this will remain our little secret, let the others die at the hands of my physicians!"

Day by day the King's health improved steadily. The third day the Cardinal celebrated a mass to thank the Lord for his miraculous cure and returned to Paris. Not even the worst potholes could erase the satisfied look on his face.

Barely a week later, the Cardinal decided to return to Versailles for an extended visit. The Cardinal's valet suggested that some fresh air and a little exercise might be indicated and therefore the King and the Cardinal took a short stroll through the garden, now covered in light snow.

Suddenly the King came back to the subject of the Marquis de Beauvoir. "Richelieu, we have been thinking about the letter of the Marquis de Beauvoir!" he exclaimed, cheeks flushed and eyes animated. "We shall appoint him master of the horses, this will make his stay in France mandatory!"

The Cardinal looked at his King as if he had seen a ghost; he was flabbergasted.

"Now you're surprised!" The King was delighted. "Admit that this idea is brilliant – it resolves all diplomatic issues – even my sister won't be able to reproach us for anything!" He paused a moment while the Cardinal remained silent. For once the Cardinal didn't know if he could trust his voice.

"And we'll also find a satisfactory position for Armand de Saint Paul at court, this will certainly please his father, for sure."

The Cardinal bowed and replied with a weak voice, "As always, the analytical strength of Your Majesty's suggestions is compelling, I'm sure that they will be delighted and most grateful!"

"This time, my dear Cardinal, we have beaten you!" The King laughed, now in the best of moods.

Let's see who's beaten whom, but this much I swear – I'm not going to let you install an offspring of the Marquis de Saint Paul right under my nose in the centre of royal power. All my work will be for nothing if the old families can usurp the royal power once again. I vow that I shall never let this happen! Out loud, Richelieu said, "If I keep telling Your Majesty that Your Majesty is the greatest monarch on earth, it's not pure flattery, it's the simple truth." The Cardinal could see in the King's eyes that he devoured this compliment as a hungry dog would seize a juicy bone and in harmonious mood they went back into the castle.

The discipline of the Cardinal's household was such that even during his absence the machine of the Grand Palais worked with the precision of well-oiled machinery. Musketeers, secretaries and all servants carried out their duties as if the feared Cardinal were breathing right down their necks.

Thus the Cardinal's secretary was on duty immediately as soon as the Cardinal had come back from Versailles and rang for him. To his astonishment the Cardinal, who had been in an excellent mood when he had left for Versailles, came back in the foulest of moods – not even the usual cup of spiced cocoa could appease him.

The Cardinal dictated rapidly an even more surprising letter, insisting several times it must be kept secret.

"Seal it immediately with our special seal, you understand that I can't use mine – and only the brothers we trust may carry it. Do not hand it over to any official messenger or musketeer," the Cardinal insisted and the secretary hastened to confirm that he would – of course – comply with all of these requests.

It seemed that the visit this time had greatly exhausted the Cardinal. In a tired voice he continued, "I will dine alone only with my niece and go to bed early tonight; please inform my niece, the major-domo and the cook!"

The secretary bowed and hastened to follow all requests. Those seemed to be more difficult to fulfil than foreseen, as no brother could be found immediately to carry the secret message, the cook was having a row with one of her maids, the Cardinal's niece had gone out and the major-domo was supervising the delivery of a cart loaded with large barrels of wine that had arrived from the Cardinal's estates and cursed the hapless secretary that he should be so rude as to interrupt him.

"You look utterly worn out," an elegant voice addressed the secretary from behind. "Has the old toad been chasing you again?"

There could be only one musketeer who dared to call the august Cardinal Richelieu an 'old toad', and when the secretary turned around he looked right into the laughing face of François de Toucy. They had become friends when de Toucy had been in the services of the Cardinal – and even today he was still employed by the Cardinal for special missions. The secretary therefore was happy to have a sympathetic ear and gave a short summary of his tasks, omitting of course the true nature of the secret message.

"Don't worry," François tried to comfort the secretary. "You know His Eminence, he's always barking, but he only bites when there is a true reason to do so!"

The secretary's face brightened. "I guess you're right, but he can reduce me to a bundle of nerves. Now let me try once more to speak with the cook!" And with these words he stood up and hastened to the kitchen. He had almost reached the door when a young pageboy suddenly popped out of the entrance and collided with him. Heartfelt curses were exchanged on both sides and the secretary left the room, sure by now that it was not going to be a good day for him.

On his own now, François stood up to walk to the stables when his eyes fell on a document that the secretary must have dropped. Nothing is as interesting as documents that are labelled 'confidential', and glancing quickly around him, François unfolded the document and read it – while he strained his ears to detect any approaching footsteps.

Silently he whistled through his teeth. Never trust and never underestimate the Cardinal, he thought. In his hand was a note to draft a letter withdrawing all protection for two travelling Frenchmen, proposing to the unknown receiver an important amount in gold, payable at a certain bank in Venice, if these Frenchmen were detained secretly in jail for at least a year – or indeed should vanish forever (in which case proof was requested). It was signed by a codename; the Cardinal – as usual – had been careful to cover his tracks.

François had just enough time to fold the message again and slide it back to the floor when he heard running footsteps and a puffing and sweating secretary almost jumped into the room.

"Dear Lord, you look ghastly!" exclaimed François. "What's the matter?"

"Did you see a letter?" gasped the secretary.

"No, I'm sorry, should I have?" asked François, all innocence.

The secretary had been scanning the room and with a deep sigh of relief he seized the letter that lay abandoned on the floor. "It's nothing," he breathed. "I just lost a letter for my parents and I had promised to send it today!"

"Now you can send it," François smiled at him, "and I must leave as well, I think I may just have received a new mission!"

"From His Eminence?" asked the secretary with wide eyes.

"Sort of, but it's so secret that nobody must know about it!"

"I promise, I won't breathe a word!"

"You'd better not, you know that the old toad can become really nasty if his secrets leak out!"

The secretary shivered. "Oh yes, I do know!"

Back in his own dwellings – thanks to Pierre's generous gift, now much more luxurious than anything he had ever owned before – François sat down to analyse the situation. He was greatly puzzled though. Why had Cardinal Richelieu suddenly changed his mind? The description of the two noblemen journeying to Venice had left no doubt that he was targeting Pierre and Armand. But his most pressing thought kept haunting François: *I must warn Pierre and Armand urgently – but how?*

My Lady Alessandra

Julia looked out of the tiny barred window of her room, although she had long since abandoned calling it a room. It had become her prison. She had no idea of the time of the day as a thick layer of dirty grey clouds had wrapped Venice in a shroud of sorrowful darkness. Gusts of wind beat relentlessly against her window and Julia was watching the raindrops running down the pane – she had nothing else to do. Her room had become freezing cold and Julia sat hunched beneath the window, wrapped in the only blanket that had been given to her by a servant in a rare display of sympathy.

The raindrops gathering on the window pane behaved like human beings; some were downright lazy, some pretended to be busy and important, some bumped blindly into others, embracing them to become a larger trickle of water running down the window, following the curves of the rough glass, gathering strength to cross the lead fittings and drip into the canal flowing below.

Suddenly Julia jumped – she was talking to raindrops as if they were human beings! Scared she clapped her mouth shut with her right hand – was she becoming mad as a hatter after all? Had her ever-so-young and ever-so-beautiful stepmother won the fight?

Her only friend, the mouse, hadn't shown up for several weeks. Julia didn't know if it had found a new home, or if the mouse had been careless enough to fall into the paws of the large white cat with the black spot that reigned on the lower floors. Having no one to talk to, nobody who cared about her, Julia suddenly dissolved into tears. She wanted to live, she wanted to laugh, to have friends, eat decent food – for once – and dance. Yes, she wanted to dance!

Soon the carnival season would be in full swing accompanied by endless balls where the golden youth of Venice would have fun, flirt and do all kinds of things that later would be either deeply regretted or (hopefully) forgotten. *I give up. I can't fight anymore. The odious Claudia has won, I'll marry whomever they present to me, sign over my heritage – but I must get out of here and breathe again or else I'll become mad!*

Claudia and Julia's father were still in Rome, but the servant who brought her daily miserable dinner had dropped a hint that they were expected to return any day now.

"Let's see if this despicable Claudia managed to get pregnant – our groom seemed to be eager enough to fulfil those duties! Oh Lord, why did my father

77

have to marry a slut?" Julia's voice was bitter – she found herself talking out loud. But it didn't matter, nobody would be listening here beneath the roof – and as long as there was daylight, no servant would make the effort to climb the steep steps until the church bells were ringing and it was time to serve dinner. *Time enough to be miserable*, she thought.

Listlessly she picked up the prayer book that was her only entertainment and companion. It almost fell to pieces, but there was no other distraction. "I need something to keep my mind busy and cheer me up," she said to herself. It felt good to talk. Finally she started a game. She picked a word from the prayer book and tried to invent new words from it by using its letters. Julia was busy with her game when she detected a faint noise emanating from the staircase. The noise grew more distinct and she could hear the sound of creaking steps under the impact of a heavy body and the puffing noises of heavy breathing that came with it. Julia tried to stay calm; there was only one person she knew who would cause such a noise – and this was her confessor. It had been some time since he had dared to show up as most probably Julia's insistence on remaining firm had dimmed his enthusiasm to come and pray with her.

Julia braced herself for this confrontation. She had made up her mind now. The truth was that she had given up hope. She would have to give in, but she wanted to give the news to her father, and to her father alone. She didn't want her confessor to know and boast that he had been able to convince her to change her mind.

All of a sudden Julia could hear the person talking. This voice – chiding a hapless servant most likely – was definitely *not* the voice of her confessor. Julia knew this voice – but could it be true? She fell on her knees and prayed fervently, "By our blessed saints, please don't disappoint me – I think I simply couldn't survive it!" And although she tried to keep calm, scared of disappointment, her heart beating like hammer in her chest, a tide of joyful hope swept over her with an intensity she had long forgotten existed.

The familiar voice came nearer; she could hear it shouting, "You silly idiot, unbolt this door immediately! Don't be so clumsy or I'll make my major-domo's whip dance on your back until your skin has peeled off!" Her aunt was practically snarling on the other side of the door.

Julia could hear the noise of sliding bolts and a key turning in the lock – it sounded like the most beautiful music she had ever heard in her entire life. *I'll be brave and calm*, Julia commanded herself, *dignified like a true member of the noble house of Contarini!* And then she dissolved into tears.

It was therefore a small and very unhappy girl that her aunt set eyes on, unkempt and clad in clothes that hung loosely around her bony figure, almost falling to rags. Her disbelieving eyes surveyed the tiny room with its shabby furniture, two chairs that were almost falling to pieces and, her eyes glittering with fury, Lady Alessandra turned to the butler of the house and breathed, "This can't be true, *you* dared to hold my niece, a member of the noble house of Contarini, a shabby prisoner in her *own* house?"

Her aunt wasn't yelling. She didn't even have to shout, but the effect of her words made the servants' skin crawl. If ever they had dreaded setting their eyes on their nemesis, here she was.

The butler was the first to fall to his knees. Kissing the hem of Julia's aunt's dress he stammered, "My Lady Alessandra, have mercy, we were only following the explicit orders of our lord and master and the new mistress Claudia. They told us that a demon had possessed the Lady Julia. Her confessor came and spoke to Lady Julia regularly, so we believed it must be true and didn't dare object!"

"A demon? Does this poor child look like a demon to you?" Alessandra was indeed shouting now. "I can tell you who the demon is, it's the demon of money and greed! It has possessed all of you, including my Lady Claudia, but not my poor darling. But from now on I am taking things into my own hands and you had better follow my orders! And I warn you once and for all; I don't give orders twice, and I won't hesitate to have you flogged in public!"

As she spoke she was already drawing Julia into her soft embrace and for the first time since her mother had died, Julia felt safe, protected and loved. Her aunt was as stout as she was small, but never had Julia met someone with a personality like hers. No member of the Venetian aristocracy still alive had ever dared to speak up against her as, apart from owning a substantial fortune, she had countless doges in her ancestry and could swear like a fishmonger if she so desired. Rumour had it that her husband had passed away just as quietly and inconspicuously as he had lived with her, never a match for her personality or her sharp brains.

"My poor lamb!" she cooed at Julia. "Let's go downstairs and make you feel like a human being again. You look terrible, like a skeleton! I'll deal later with this worm of a butler, don't you worry!" and with a last scornful look she turned her back on the trembling butler and ushered Julia towards the staircase and into liberty. Julia could barely walk down the staircase but proudly she refused all help until she collapsed into the helping hands of her aunt's servant as soon as she had reached the main hall, situated on the first floor as was customary in Venice to avoid flooding during the frequent high tides of autumn and winter.

Now Julia could see why her aunt had not encountered any resistance. She had arrived accompanied by a small army of her personal gondolieri, all of them exceptionally tall and muscular. It was clear at first sight that they could wield arms as well as they wielded their oars.

Soon Julia found herself tucked comfortably into her aunt's stately private gondola while her family palace disappeared into the misty light of a rainy winter afternoon. But only when the familiar shapes of her family home dissolved into blurred shadows, did Julia finally loosen her gaze on the building. What had been her cherished family home for many years would forever remain tainted by painful memories of her imprisonment. She turned her head and looked behind the gondola that moved swiftly towards her aunt's palazzo. The lanterns of her aunt's gondola shone brightly, leaving a trail of molten light behind them, golden reflections that shimmered like sinking stars in the dark waters of the Canal Grande. Like the train of a princess's gown, studded with golden stars, she thought wearily.

Unable to suppress the tears in her eyes Julia turned her head and looked at her aunt, but was incapable of finding the words she wanted to say. Finally she managed to utter a simple, "Thank you, my dearest aunt, I think you not only saved my life, you also saved my sanity. I was only days away from going mad."

"You tell me all about it later, my dear," her aunt replied softly. "Now be a good girl and snuggle into my arms and close your eyes, you're safe and you can be sure of this: I'll never let this happen again to you, my love! This nightmare is over forever, I promise by all the blessed saints!"

Julia inhaled greedily the fresh salty air and sighed deeply, then she closed her eyes and listened to the rhythm of the oars touching the Canal Grande with the precision of a well-oiled machine. Julia hadn't realized how tired and worn out she must have been, but soon the warmth of her aunt's Siberian furs and the monotony of the oars sent her to sleep.

She must have slept for almost a day, a deep sleep, unperturbed by the terrible nightmares that had been her constant companions during the past months. It was the pleasant and delicate sound of a porcelain cup clinking on its saucer and the smell of freshly brewed coffee that finally woke her up. Julia opened her eyes, still reluctant to leave the realm of slumber. She noticed a young maidservant waiting for her orders, and anxious to please, she offered Julia the kind of breakfast Julia had long forgotten could exist.

After breakfast a tub filled with perfumed hot water was already waiting for her and stretching her limbs Julia suddenly started to doubt that paradise could be any better than the kind of pleasures that earth was offering up to her right at this moment. The maid dressed Julia in her old gowns of silk that her aunt must have had brought over – far too loose for her now – and yet Julia couldn't stop marvelling and wondering at the luxury and refinement she had taken for granted for so many years. *I shall never forget those months I spent in that miserable attic room. Whenever I risk becoming arrogant and selfish, I hope I shall remember how quickly the wheel of fortune can turn!*

80

"I think I'm presentable now!" she smiled at her maid. With satisfaction she studied her reflection in the large mirror that was hanging in her luxurious bedroom. Her eyes seemed unusually large and bright in her shrunken face. But her maid had fixed the gowns with some rapidly stitched alterations and after a hearty breakfast Julia felt fit to receive even a king. "Let's go and look for my aunt!" she cried, now in the best of moods.

"Her ladyship is waiting downstairs," the young maid answered timidly. Like all members of the household she had heard about the terrible fate that had befallen her young mistress and was full of awe at having been selected to serve Julia.

Her ladyship was sitting in the large reception room. Lady Alessandra was writing a letter but when her niece entered she jumped out of her chair to embrace Julia. They settled comfortably on a low sofa and her aunt took Julia's hands in hers.

"You look much better!" she stated with satisfaction in her voice. "One could say: almost human!" She smiled, and continued with a brisk voice, "Now, you have to tell me everything, even if it's painful, but I need to know what has been going on! I came several times to visit you at home and every time I was informed that you were ill, a rare illness, something contagious and necessitating a long convalescence. Then I must admit something really stupid happened, I fell ill myself! Immediately I felt better I returned to see you – only to learn that your father had left Venice for Rome – but without you, my dear, as you were still known to be suffering. Now, I'm not *that* gullible, this sounded really suspicious! I visited your house once again under the pretext of bringing you some grapes from my glasshouse and the butler's story sounded more and more fishy. In short, I decided to return with my gondolieri." She chuckled. "You may have noticed that I selected them carefully, they're especially well-built specimens! You can't imagine your butler's face when I entered your house with my men, asking to see you immediately; he almost wet his breeches!"

Julia imagined the stuffy butler's surprised face the moment her aunt had set foot in the hall, accompanied by an army of muscular young men who meant business. Imagining the stunned expression of the butler she had learned to loathe, she had to smile.

"The rest of the story, you know already," her aunt concluded. "Now you tell me yours!"

As Julia prepared to tell her story, all colour seemed to drain from her face, and only her eyes shimmered bright with unshed tears in her pale face. Then Julia started, first not knowing really how to begin and with a faltering voice, but as her narration went on she started to feel more sure of herself, even relieved. It actually felt good to have a sympathetic listener after so many months of solitary confinement.

81

Julia decided to start her story back in London. Accompanied by both parents she had been looking forward to the journey back to Venice. Their journey had been smooth and uneventful until – out of the blue – disaster struck, swift and without warning. Her mother fell violently ill and helplessly Julia saw her perish in no time at all in some forlorn place in the South of France. Wrapped in her sorrow she couldn't help but notice all the same her father's remarkable haste to bury her mother and move on quickly, his eyes cold and without a tear. As soon as they set foot on the island of Venice Julia's growing suspicions were confirmed – a replacement for her dead mother in the form of a young and beautiful future stepmother had been waiting already!

Her situation worsened as soon as Julia discovered that her father had speculated on the financial markets and in due course had managed to lose the family fortune. By chance Julia was due to inherit a fortune, money her father needed desperately in order to be able to pay off his pressing debts. Julia was now transformed into the only remaining and very precious asset her father still possessed – an asset to be traded on the marriage market.

"You cannot imagine my shock when I set eyes on the husband that father had chosen for me!" Julia shuddered.

"People of our class rarely marry for reasons of love," remarked her aunt. "Could it be that my niece set eyes on some dashing man during her stay in London?"

Julia turned scarlet. Her aunt must indeed possess a sixth sense! "I know that I'm expected to marry someone who'll help our family to prosper. But never had I expected to be married to a mere commoner, older than my father. A man without manners, a hideous peasant who had just bought a title. I'm not a horse to be traded on a whim!" Julia protested hotly.

"You have a point there," conceded her aunt. "I understand your father auctioned you off like a prize cow!" The last remark was accompanied by a belligerent sparkle in her eyes. "We'll teach your father, don't worry!"

Julia continued her story, even mentioning how she befriended and tamed a mouse. It was supposed to sound amusing but tears started to run down her cheeks when she recalled those lonely days and interminable hours. It was certainly no coincidence that she could see her aunt dabbing her eyes with her sleeve.

"So I understand that your charming stepmother threatened to make you disappear forever into a convent? And she had the impertinence to boast that the next heir of the noble house of Contarini is to be sired by a groom?"

Lady Alessandra jumped to her feet and strode up and down until she suddenly stopped, snatched a highly decorative jug that was standing innocently on the marble table and smashed it furiously against the wall.

"That felt good." She sighed. "I never liked that stupid jug anyhow!"

Panicking servants rushed into the room, expecting to witness yet another crisis.

"Stop staring!" Lady Alessandra commanded her gawping servants, herself unruffled. "Clean this up and make sure you don't serve water in jugs that offend my eyes!" Having made her point she majestically dismissed the servants and addressed her niece. "I think I have a plan of action! What does the holy scripture say: Vengeance is mine! So be it. But I need you to be a very brave girl and help me, are you ready to this?"

"I don't know..." Julia hated to hear the echo of her own voice. It sounded too timid and thin. "What would I need to do?"

Making sure that no curious servants were listening in, her aunt explained her plan. She was not surprised that Julia refused categorically, but her aunt was not one to give in. Slowly, patiently, but very firmly, she persuaded Julia to play her part. "I know it will be hard for you, my dear, but we must stop your father and his new wife. I've known your father for many years, I still remember how proud my sister was when this marriage was arranged by our parents. You know, your father certainly was one of the most attractive men in Venice! Very attractive indeed, rich and, like us, from one of the best families in Venice..." She sighed. "But he always had a weakness in his character, therefore I warned my sister, she could have chosen somebody else, she had enough admirers. But she wanted your father, nobody else would do. But as weakness now turns to evil, my darling, it's our holy duty to act! We must avenge your mother, my sister. And I vow by all the saints that I'll do it!"

Julia nodded, but she couldn't speak. Her feelings and thoughts were in turmoil. Until this moment she had never dared to formulate clearly her suspicions, to admit openly that her father might have tried to get rid of her mother, might even have poisoned her. And yet Julia had seen with her own eyes how besotted her father had been with his new wife. For her aunt, apparently there wasn't even a shadow of doubt. In her aunt's eyes, her father was a ruthless killer.

"Do you know that your father is on his way back to Venice?" Julia's aunt's voice drew her back into reality.

"I do, actually one of the servants dropped me a hint, but I have no clue as to how soon he'll arrive."

"I'll know soon enough, as I have positioned my people on the mainland. As soon as your father prepares to sail across to Venice, I'll be informed – and we must act!"

Julia looked at her aunt with fear-stricken eyes, and yet she knew that she had no choice, she owed it to her mother.

*****

Had she only dreamed of her aunt's sudden appearance, of leaving her miserable prison and being a free person? Like a small, frightened child Julia looked around her tiny room, her prison of so many months that she had almost lost count of them. Time seemed to be frozen up here in this attic – she seemed to be locked in a bubble, invisible and yet unyielding. Her gaze continued to wander, first down to her ragged dress, and then she tried to peep out of the dirty window panes.

"Don't panic," she thought. "It's not reality, it can't be!"

And yet here she was, sitting on her shabby chair that creaked and sighed dolefully under every move as if even her chair had given up hope of deliverance. From time to time muffled noises of shouting voices of the boatmen on the Canal Grande would seep through her window, echoes of a free and colourful world she was forbidden to see or live in. A feeling of boundless sadness took hold of her – and before she fully realized what was happening to her so she could fight it, big tears started to fall from her eyes, tears that ran down her cheeks until they rolled down her dress, leaving a trail of dark stains.

Julia must have been drowning in this dark sea of sadness as she almost failed to pick up the noise of approaching steps. The steps were light and energetic, the hallmark of a young person who knew her way in life. Impatiently bolts were pushed backwards, the key was turned and finally the door was thrust open. The stage was set for the appearance of her oh-so-young and oh-so-beautiful stepmother. Claudia entered, radiating beauty and the kind self-confidence that almost made Julia vomit.

Arrogantly Claudia examined her stepdaughter. "I'm sooo glad to meet you here!" she chirped. "How *fortunate* for me that you haven't gone out for a walk, and how *kind* of you to have waited for me here for so many weeks, I feel absolutely honoured!" and she gave a forced laugh. "But as your doting stepmother, I think I should tell you that your appearance hasn't really improved during the past months, my darling Julia, so to speak. Actually you look positively awful, maybe it's about time you made up your mind and came to your senses?"

Claudia scrutinized Julia's face and discovered the tell-tale signs of reddened eyes and tear-stained cheeks. Delighted she suddenly changed her tone and cooed, "Oh, my little *darling*, have we been crying? All alone, aren't we? You can leave this room at *any* moment, just tell your father that you have changed your mind!"

Julia clung to her chair, her hands clenching onto the rough wood until it hurt. *Don't show her how much you hate her, don't show your true feelings!*

Claudia came so close that Julia could smell the sickening scent of her perfume; sweet and heavy, it clung to her like a disgusting cloud. Julia tried to breathe and fought an intense wave of nausea while Claudia whispered into her ear, "Today is your last chance, my sweetie, to change your mind. Either you relent and stop being a stubborn and naughty girl or I'll have you bundled up and locked forever in a convent on a damp island. The abbess and your father will share your dowry, your father only has to sign the document and you're a bride of Jesus, buried alive for the rest of your life."

Julia clenched the chair so hard that she could feel splinters of rough wood driving into her flesh. She looked up, right into the cold eyes of her stepmother. "You've won," Julia said flatly. "But I want to tell my father myself what I have decided!"

Claudia laughed triumphantly. "Finally, do I detect a sign of commonsense? The proud Julia Contarini – giving in to reason! And I almost thought that you'd never come to a reasonable decision."

Julia looked calmly at her stepmother. "You've hated me from the beginning, am I right?"

Claudia looked at her, eyes sparkling with malice. "Not only did I hate you, my dear Julia, I detested you, and I still do!" she spat out. "You walk into the room as if the whole world is yours. Oh yes, we are well bred and well educated, aren't we? Of course you greeted me when we met for the first time, but you had your subtle ways to make me understand that I was inferior by far, you would never accept me as your relative, you would never accept that I carry the proud name of Contarini now!"

"So you decided to destroy me?" Julia asked softly.

Claudia snarled. "I married your father, only to discover that behind the façade of the famous Contarini name there was nothing, only emptiness, pretention and stupidity. No money, only debts. And yet you all behaved as if the world was yours!"

"Therefore you looked for revenge?"

"Call it revenge, I call it justice. I convinced your father that your money should be his in truth and that your inheritance was nothing but a blatant case of injustice – something that cried out to be corrected." Claudia snorted deprecatingly. "He's so easy to steer. I open my legs, I moan a bit and he thinks that he's a hero!"

"How smart," Julia whispered. "You found a way to destroy my pride and get my money at the same time."

"I am smart..." Claudia asserted. "One should never underestimate me. Most men think that beautiful women are stupid, but later they pay dearly for their error! At least I make them pay."

Julia raised her voice. "And finally you decided to crown your revenge by making a stable groom sire your first child, the heir of the Contarini name?"

"If I had waited for your father, my dear Julia, to make me pregnant, I'd become an old woman. And the groom, you remember, the one with the curly hair and the fiery eyes, he's a real man, a dream. He took me in his arms – and I knew immediately that it would happen that night. I screamed with pleasure like never before. I can only recommend his services – well, once you've taken a bath, my dear. With your new husband, you'll need someone..."

But Claudia was never to finish this sentence as the small door leading to an adjacent room burst open. Claudia's eyes almost glazed over as she recognized the figure of her husband rushing towards her.

"You abominable slut!" he shouted at the top of his voice. "I heard every single word and you'll pay for it!"

But Claudia was not to be intimidated. She stood erect and shouted back, "You'd better shut up, or shall I tell everybody that you poisoned your first wife? If I'm a slut, you're a murderer, you lusted for me and seduced me before you went to London, tell your daughter what kind of rotten man you are!"

Julia watched the scene in trepidation; her worst nightmare had come true. Helpless, she witnessed her father lunging forward and before Julia fully realized his intentions she could see the deadly gleam of a blade in his hand. Violently he raised his arm and thrust the blade forward. The dagger plunged into Claudia's chest. Julia's stepmother was taken completely by surprise. A first shock gave way to fright, she started to scream and raised her arms to protect her chest but like a maniac her husband thrust the dagger into her, until she dropped down, blood gushing out of wounds like small fountains of bright red.

Julia turned around. She needed to vomit, urgently. Of course she had seen murder being performed on stage with comedians dying a noisy death smeared all over in animal blood. She had found these performances either thrilling or funny, but the reality was so different, simply horrendous! The small room was quickly filling with the sweet smell of spilt blood mingling with the scent of Claudia's heavy perfume to form a disgusting, overpowering odour. The moaning and gasping of the dying victim lying close to Julia's feet was almost unbearable, as Claudia gurgled helplessly and tried to breathe, desperately trying to cling to a life that was deserting her fast.

Only minutes ago Julia had prayed fervently that heaven and earth should move to make justice prevail and God strike down her tormentor – but had she really asked for this to happen? Julia turned abruptly and her eyes met the eyes of her father, a sight she would never be able to forget. Her father's shoulders were sagging, he was crying. Awkwardly he turned towards Julia and stuttered, "Will you ever... be able to forgive me?"

Instinctively Julia stepped back, scared of being touched by this strange man covered with blood. Her father made a strange moan and suddenly raised his arm, but this time he thrust the dagger into his own chest.

Julia was still in shock when her aunt entered the room. Gently she took Julia into her arms. "Poor lamb, let's get out of here, don't look at them any more. Justice has been done. Your father was no gentleman in life, at least he knew how to die like a nobleman."

Tears were streaming down Julia's face and she tore herself violently from her aunt's embrace. "You never told me that father would listen to our conversation, we only agreed that I should make Claudia talk!" she accused her aunt, and with a trembling arm she pointed to the two corpses, closer in death than they had ever been in life.

"You're angry with me, my dear, and I fully understand that. But if I had told you my plan from the beginning, you'd never have consented. I simply couldn't live with the fact that your father destroyed the life of your mother." The Lady Alessandra cleared her throat. "Julia, you and I are members of the oldest and most noble family in Venice, we have to defend our family's honour, never forget that! Your father had become a murderer, a disgrace, he betrayed all the principles of our noble blood!"

Julia looked at her aunt in awe. Her aunt's personality seemed to fill the room. Still uncertain how to react, she answered, "I understand, but it's a cruel world that asks for such a sacrifice!" and she started to cry. Angry at her own weakness she wiped her tears away with an abrupt move of her hand and continued, "But you talk about our family's honour – this will create an enormous scandal, have you thought about that?"

"Of course I have." Lady Alessandra was unruffled. "Downstairs are waiting a physician and an official of the Republic to certify that your father and his wife have become victims of a violent type of food poisoning."

Julia looked at her in shock. "You knew beforehand that Father would kill himself?" she exclaimed.

"If he hadn't killed himself, I would have used this," and calmly her aunt took a dagger out of the folds of her scarf. "I vowed to avenge your mother, and I'm *always* true to my word. But we've discussed this enough; let's leave now." Her aunt took her hand. "The sooner you forget what has happened up here, the better it will be, and never forget: your father and his far too young wife have been victims of food poisoning, and both of us will be shocked and show all the appropriate signs of sadness and mourning!"

"Yes, I understand, dear aunt, an extremely violent form of food poisoning, I understand... we have to defend the family honour!" Julia answered meekly.

"That's a good girl," her aunt answered resolutely. "I can see the female members of the Contarini have more balls than the male side."

All Roads Lead To Venice

François de Toucy sat on the highly uncomfortable chair that was customarily reserved for visitors of rank; the lesser ones were expected to remain standing while they waited to be granted the favour of an audience in the sanctum of His Eminence, the most noble Duke de Richelieu and Cardinal. Not being of a timid nature, François had seated himself without waiting for an invitation. But now he shifted his weight on the hard seat, and his buttocks started to hurt as if they had been set on fire. He had been sitting here for almost an hour already if the golden clock on the mantelpiece wasn't lying.

"Busy today?" he casually asked the secretary who had been scurrying in and out of the Cardinal's library, red spots of exhaustion showing on his face.

"Sheer madness," answered the secretary breathlessly. "His Eminence is preparing a treaty with the Holy Roman Empire and you know him, everything must be perfect, every detail checked and revised not only once, twice minimum, before we receive the Emperor's ambassador and his delegation."

François suppressed a yawn. This didn't sound like he would be granted a quick salvation from his uncomfortable chair, more like further hours of waiting – one more hour at least.

The hands of the clock had crept forward by about three quarters of the hour when the secretary hurried out of the Cardinal's library with a conspiratorial smile. "I've been able to convince His Eminence to receive you now, otherwise you might as well have prepared your bed, we're far from being finished."

François winked back and answered, "I owe you a tankard of ale, remind me!"

"A big one and not that peculiar stuff they serve in the inn around the corner," answered the secretary. He might have taken his vows, but this didn't mean that he had forsaken all earthly pleasures.

François smoothed his sleeves and made sure that his lace collar was straight, but the secretary secretly thought that he could have spared this effort; never had he seen François anything else but immaculately dressed. Not showing any nervousness, François waited until the secretary had announced him officially and strode blithely into the library as if he had come with the sole intention of making a random social call.

The Cardinal sat behind his desk and François wondered – not for the first time – if he had shrunk. His head rose up out of his scarlet robes more like the head of a tortoise than that of a human being, he looked frail and his pallid complexion was witness to his failing health. And yet his eyes shone as brightly as ever and scrutinized his visitor with his usual shrewd glance.

François sank on bended knee and kissed the ring of office that sat loosely on the bony finger. The Cardinal didn't invite him to be seated, which in this case was a good sign – the audience was to be a brief one.

"You have asked for an extended leave?" The Cardinal opened the discussion without wasting time on any social niceties. "My secretary told me that you wish to visit your mother until early spring. This seems to be a rather … ahem… unusual display of filial duty?"

Not for the first time, François had the feeling that those eyes could see right through him. The old fox was suspicious, it would be difficult to fool him! He tried to display his most casual smile before he answered. "Your Eminence is right, as usual. I have a specific reason for spending some more time at home!"

The Cardinal looked at him and made an impatient gesture to indicate that he was waiting for a more detailed explanation.

"I admit that my request is slightly unusual," François continued, "but my mother is worried that my youngest sister might be tempted to accept the courtship of a young man that she deems to be highly unsuitable and she is counting on my support to avoid what she views as potential disaster!" The vision of his obedient and demure youngest sister floated briefly in front of his eyes and he hoped fervently that she'd never get wind of his fabricated story.

The Cardinal nodded sympathetically. "Young sisters… I had one myself."

With a swift and yet meticulous movement he signed a paper and handed it over to François. "This is your leave… but your family originates from the northern parts of our realm, if I remember correctly?"

"As always, Your Eminence has an excellent memory." François bowed shortly. "Indeed my mother lives close to Reims."

"That's excellent," beamed the Cardinal. "You surely won't mind delivering this message," and he withdrew a sealed envelope from a large pile, "in person to our envoy in Liège?"

François gulped. Of course he had never had any intention of passing via Reims, let alone Liège. This would cause a delay of at least a month! The old fox had won again – was anyone ever able to get one up on the Cardinal?

"I'm delighted to be of assistance to Your Eminence," he hastened to say.

"I'm sure you are!" answered the Cardinal, and as François took his leave and left the room, he was almost sure he heard an asthmatic wheezing. His Eminence was laughing.

"That was a very short audience," marvelled the secretary.

"Very short indeed," answered François still in shock at being sent across all of France to deliver a letter.

"Did His Eminence entrust you with a new mission?" asked the secretary curiously.

"Oh yes, he did!" exclaimed François bitterly. "And the devil only knows why His Eminence always has a sixth sense when it comes to his affairs!"

The secretary crossed himself quickly and protested. "You should never mention the devil when you speak of His Eminence!"

"Shouldn't I?" answered François unabashed. "But both are clad in red if I remember correctly, so how to tell them apart?"

The secretary looked at him speechlessly as François stormed out of the antechamber and crossed himself once more. This was sheer blasphemy – better to be forgotten immediately!

Once François arrived home he retired to his study with a bottle of wine. He needed to think. He wasn't sure if he should loathe or admire the Cardinal who had destroyed in a second his careful planning. The Cardinal was certainly someone to be reckoned with. If he followed the orders and delivered the letter in Liège he'd lose at least four to six valuable weeks – and he'd even risk a prolonged stay in a cosy prison as the Spaniards were not known to have a great liking for the Cardinal's spies. And as there had been one or two occasions where François had drawn the ire of the Spanish enemy on his person, he could not hope for any leniency. *And yet it's out of the question not to deliver the letter, Richelieu will never forgive me!* he muttered furiously under his breath.

He looked around his study. It was tastefully decorated and furnished with the best Paris had to offer – Pierre's generous gift had made this possible. Yes, it was definitely nice to have some money to hand, he mused. Suddenly he banged his hand on the table. Money was the key! He rang for his manservant and ignoring the subtle suggestions of his valet he ordered his horse to be prepared at once, not even bothering to change into the correct riding attire.

"He must be in a real hurry, anything amiss?" commented the young groom, only to find himself being stared at with total disdain by the superior valet. This treatment was crowned by a last blistering remark: "I cannot remember ever having invited you to share confidences with me!" The groom blushed and sped off in order to get the horse ready.

François was lucky; his friend was at home. "Jerome, I need you to do me a small favour!" he greeted his old mate from the musketeers.

"The last time I did you a 'small' favour I was almost massacred by an army of lunatic Spanish bandits," his friend answered good-humouredly.

"Excellent!" François exclaimed, a smile full of mischief. "Your knowledge of the Spanish will be very helpful! Trust me, it's not a big thing, I just need you to take a letter to Liège in the Spanish Netherlands, so it's not a big thing at all!"

"No!" said his friend. "No, no, no! I simply know you too well, I could bet a month's pay that the old toad Richelieu has his fingers in this pie! I can smell trouble, I prefer to stay here in Paris, alive and happy."

"You can't bet a month's salary!" protested François. "You owe me several already!"

"Do I?" His friend was visibly shaken. "I tend to forget it, somehow I never seem to have any money anyhow, so how should I be able to pay you something, if I don't possess anything?"

"Your logic is brilliant and compelling as always." François took the envelope out of his waistcoat, placed it on a table and put a small bag with coins on top of it. "What a pity that you're not interested, this bag would have been yours," and he moved it slowly to make the coins clinks.

"With friends like you, who needs enemies?" complained Jerome, but his hand reached out greedily, snatching the soft leather bag.

"All right, you win. Consider your letter delivered already!"

"There is a small insignificant detail, I need to add," said François. "When you deliver the letter you have to pretend to be me!"

Jerome looked at his friend and grinned broadly. "I don't even want to know what you're up to! Better if I don't, but if I have to pretend to be François de Toucy, you'll need to spit out some more livres. I'll need a better horse and new clothes!"

François sighed but he had to admit that Jerome's attire was far from the kind of clothing he'd ever wear. "You're a cut-throat!" he exclaimed, but added some golden coins.

Jerome laughed and slapped François's shoulder. "Our deal is done; now you're free to invite me for a decent meal and let me know why the hell I have to ride to a place nobody ever wants to visit and why I should pretend to be you. It sounds like quite an adventure!"

"All right, let's try the new tavern, L'auberge du Roi; the place seems to be the height of fashion right now. And on the way I'll explain to you why I need to disappear for some time..."

Thus they walked in the best of moods to the auberge and François quickly fabricated a story of a friend who needed his help – but in an affair of such delicate nature that no publicity was desired.

"Got himself involved with the wrong kind of girl?" Jerome commented wisely. "I never understand why most of our mates can't keep their sticky fingers away from young ladies of good families; there is plenty of choice here in Paris, but no, they have to go and get themselves into trouble!"

January

"Hey, stop staring at my friend!" shouted Armand good-humouredly. "Look at me instead! I have so much more to offer!" This last statement was followed by an inviting wink.

The pretty maid who had greeted the travellers giggled but had difficulties tearing her eyes away from the handsome blonde stranger who had arrived together with his two friends. They were accompanied by several footmen and a dark-skinned valet – no shame in hoping that they would be spending money freely.

The maid was proud to serve in the best inn in Mestre, a small town that was the last mainland inhabitation and thus a natural bottleneck for all aspiring travellers bound for the famous city of Venice, or La Serenissima, as the city called itself. The guesthouse was a large brick building dating a long way back, its origins so obscure that once a guest had told her that the old Romans must surely have stayed there. But she didn't believe such fairy tales, certainly no house could ever have stood firm for such a long time! Anyhow, who cared about old Romans, long dead and forgotten, when good-looking and seemingly affluent visitors were there to be welcomed!

The maid glanced from under her long eyelashes back at Armand, making sure that her glance was demure and yet slightly provocative at the same time. She liked what she saw; Armand was well-built, muscular, with long curly hair and a dashing smile that displayed a row of white teeth. But when it came to his eyes, she found them simply adorable as they had the kind of dangerous sparkle that promises adventure as well as nightly pleasures. A man her mother would have commanded her most firmly to stay away from – which made him even more attractive! But men – however attractive – with brown hair and brown eyes were regular patrons of the tavern; a young man as handsome as he was fair, however, certainly presented a rare opportunity. She would need to give this some serious thought, a subject best to be discussed in detail later with her best friend!

The pretty maid was interrupted in her day-dreaming as the landlord bustled onto the scene. Word had reached him that three potential well-to-do customers had reached his establishment and a short yet very experienced glance at their expensive clothes and manners and their well-bred horses had been sufficient to make his heart beat faster. Bowing so low that he almost touched the ground, he invited the friends to enter his inn. "Welcome, most honourable Signori, you've chosen well! In all modesty, I can assure you that this is the best establishment in town, I dare say that you'd have problems finding anything better, even in Venice. I imagine, that you noble Signori are on your way to Venice?"

94

Edo stepped forward. He had seen the familiar signs of greed in the landlord's eyes and thought it time to intervene. "A nice inn this surely is," he answered jovially, "and yet I saw another very nice place when we entered the city, the guide told me that they serve good food at excellent prices there," he added with an air of innocence.

The landlord shot an angry glance at the guide. Quickly he hastened to explain, "Oh indeed, the Golden Lamb enjoys a decent enough reputation, the rooms are a bit noisy and damp, but all the same they enjoy good business. Yet I would say this: when it comes to accommodating visitors of rank, my house is the only choice, we serve only the best wines and food here – and our rooms are airy and clean. And all of this at very reasonable prices, of course."

Edo entered into an animated bout of negotiations and soon the innkeeper discovered that he had met his match. *This can't be a nobleman,* he thought angrily. With his experience of many years he managed to hide his true feelings behind a mask of immaculate politeness. *He haggles like a merchant!*

In the end he had to accept a price that was much lower than he had hoped for, but he was consoled by the news that his guests were intending to spend several days in Mestre and not only the usual single night before moving on. He would make sure that the maids served only the most expensive food and wine. This line of thought improved his humour vastly and after he had shown the guests to their rooms in the sprawling building he sped back to the kitchen to make sure that a vast array of delicacies would be ready to tempt them at dinner.

"What's the plan now?" asked Armand after he had settled comfortably on the bed. "Isn't it good to stretch out after riding for those endless hours!" he remarked with a deep sigh.

"You're getting spoilt," Pierre looked at his friend critically, "and fat – I think we'll have to take some fencing lessons once we arrive in Venice to get you back into shape! Endless riding – it barely took us a week!"

Armand looked down at his figure but – as usual – couldn't really find any fault. "It's all muscle!" he protested vigorously. "But I must admit, a bit of fencing practice will do us good! The Italians are supposed to be the best, so let's look out for an accomplished master of the art."

"That's one clear plan then, but as for the rest, I have no clue." Pierre looked troubled. "I mean, we cannot simply ride into the city and shout, 'Has anybody by chance seen a century-old sapphire ring that matches mine!" He looked doubtfully at his grandfather's ruby ring.

"Even worse!" Armand cut in, "we won't even be able to keep our horses, it's gondolas or walking in Venice," he finished gloomily.

95

Therefore it was in quite a sombre state of mind that Edo found the two friends. "What's the matter?" he asked briskly.

"Can't you ever be anything else but good-humoured?" muttered Armand. "I mean it's not normal. We have a serious problem to solve!"

It took more than that to intimidate Edo and, seemingly at ease, he dropped into an armchair close to the door and gobbled down some nuts he had brought along.

"You could propose sharing some of your nuts at least!" Armand's mood had not improved.

"Only if you let me know why both of you look so gloomy!" Edo answered, and savoured the next nut. "Quite delicious, these nuts, by the way!"

"We've been talking about those damned rings," Pierre explained. "You know that we have to find the third ring here in Venice to solve the riddle and have any chance of finding the hidden treasure, but we have no idea where to go from here. We can't really walk around the city and ask for an ancient sapphire ring, can we?"

Edo didn't seem to be too bothered. "Pierre, if you'll allow me a remark: you're far too serious, no Italian would ever be so bothered about anything! You told me that the deal was that you accept the quest to *search* for the ring; you never actually promised to find it! I think it's fairly simple. We ferry over to the city as soon as I have set up our accommodation there – and we'll get acquainted with the city. Believe me, it's the ideal time, remember it's carnival now, there will be balls, dinners, all kinds of festivities. In no time we'll know everybody who is anybody in Venice – and then you can start making your delicate enquiries."

Armand jumped up and embraced Edo. "Let me call you my brother, you're absolutely brilliant. There will be no excuse for us to stay at home; I see now that we're genuinely and irrevocably obliged to immerse ourselves in the festivities of carnival, fraught though it may be with danger and adventures!"

Pierre had to laugh. "Yes, all in the interest of the Templar brotherhood, of course!"

"Of course! No sacrifice to be spared!" Edo beamed back.

"We'll dedicate our bodies and souls, especially the body, I vow it! But let's stop talking and pass me some nuts!" Armand pleaded, with puppy-dog eyes. "I'm so hungry, I could turn into a cannibal!"

Edo shoved the nuts towards Armand. "Here you are, but listen to a friend's advice: Don't eat too much at dinner. I have an inkling that tonight some entertainment might be waiting for us."

"Did the pretty maid mention anything to you?" Armand suddenly forgot about the nuts.

"Yes, after both of you had left, this slimy toad of a landlord wanted to give me what I consider to be his worst room. I guess he didn't appreciate my bargaining for better rates. But as soon as he got distracted by a new guest, the girl quickly warned me that this room was located far too close to the stables, it's known to be noisy and it stinks. I quickly thanked her and she dropped a hint that she might have the opportunity to wait on us tonight, together with her girlfriend."

"That sounds fabulous." Armand closed his eyes in rapture. "Two girls at once!"

"Not really, and don't expect too much. I bet she's determined to become acquainted closer with Pierre, didn't you notice she only had eyes for him the whole time?" Edo warned, "but let's wait till tonight! I mean, I dropped a hint, that there are actually three of us..."

"Can you ever talk about anything but girls, what about Julia?" Pierre didn't know if he should be upset or laugh.

Armand only waved nonchalantly. "You really should have stayed in that stupid monastery! If you're not careful, you'll turn into a stuffy bookworm. I, personally, don't have any vocation to live like a monk. Of course my heart beats faster whenever I think about Julia – but why should I remain chaste tonight? I don't even know if I shall have a chance to meet Julia in Venice, so don't be a killjoy and let's have some fun!"

"I think Armand has a point here," Edo intervened cheerfully. "None of us has been trapped in wedlock yet, so in case her girlfriends are as pretty as she is, as far as I'm concerned, I certainly won't object..."

"I see... moral lessons are not very popular tonight. All right, I promise, I won't spoil the evening."

"I'm moved to tears." Armand's voice dripped with irony. "The sacrifices my friend is willing to make for the sake of our friendship."

Pierre kicked Armand with his booted leg; there seemed to be no other suitable answer left.

It was therefore with joyful anticipation and a general sense of agreeable suspense that the three friends – dressed in their finest attire – sat down for their dinner to be served in a private room that had been eagerly provided by their landlord. A bright fire had been lit in the fireplace and the flames seemed to be dancing to the tunes of the gay flute melody that could be heard from the neighbouring guestroom. The room was cosy and warm, a nice change after the long hours of riding through drizzle and cold.

Yet when the first course was served, only an aged waiter showed up. Armand pulled a face and Pierre couldn't help quipping, "I didn't know that you were into bald men?"

"She promised she'd come!" Edo was all annoyed disappointment. "Women!" he spat out. "You simply can't rely on them!"

They sampled the mouth-watering starters, but not surprisingly their mood was far from upbeat and they did not really do justice to the cook's attempts to rise to new culinary heights. Edo tried his best to jest and keep the conversation going, but Armand was no help. He had become downright sulky.

Starters finished, they waited in uneasy silence for the numerous main courses they had chosen in the hope of entertaining the girls when the door opened slowly. "Don't get excited," Pierre whispered. "I bet it's the mummified old waiter again, maybe this time he's brought his eighty-year-old mother to help him!"

But his words had barely left his mouth when the pretty maid appeared, followed by two others, each girl as pretty and adorable as the first. Armand jumped up as if a wasp had stung him and rushed towards them gallantly. "Let me help you, my pretty ones, these silver dishes are far too heavy for delicate maids like you!"

He earned a long glance from the girl they knew already, sent from beneath long black lashes before she demurely thanked him, but firmly refused to let him help her. Her two pretty friends were dressed as soberly as she was and as by now the bald waiter had appeared on the scene in order to supervise the serving of the dinner, there was no occasion for Armand to continue his efforts to get closer to her or the other girls.

The three friends looked at each other, stunned. Somehow they had anticipated the evening would take a very different course. Even Pierre had warmed to the idea of not sleeping alone in his bed that night and felt a pang of disappointment.

Dinner, though, was excellent. The proximity of Venice had left its influence and Pierre tasted spices and dishes unheard of before. Even Armand's mood had brightened considerably. Relaxing in his chair he sighed, "That was really excellent, I'm afraid I may have eaten far too much!" He looked at Pierre. "What you think? Is she playing cat and mouse with us?" He moved on his chair to find a more comfortable position. "She probably thinks we'll be more excited if she plays hard to get. You know, the don't-touch-me-I'm-a-decent-girl strategy."

"And are you feeling more excited?" asked Pierre curiously.

"Hmm, I must admit… it does work," Armand stated reluctantly.

"Let's hope for dessert then," sighed Edo. "I must admit, it works for me too!"

Dessert arrived in due course and to the delight of the friends it was served by the three maids only. The door was closed with no sign of the bald waiter showing up, not that he would be missed, by any account.

Strangely enough the girls were no longer dressed in their previous sober attire; they were wearing coats now, and masks that covered the upper part of their faces. Impossible to tell which girl was which! Armand's eyes sparkled with excitement. He loved a bit of drama – an evening that had started with disappointment promised to become entertaining after all.

Now one of the girls dangled a key out of her pocket and locked the door. Immediately Armand jumped up. "I think those coats must be terribly warm in this suffocating heat. Allow me to help you to get comfortable," he suggested smoothly.

Pierre rolled his eyes. He thought that his friend was overdoing it. Yet Armand met no rejection and the coats were gone in no time, giving way to light muslin gowns, with appealingly low necklines, but Armand's attempt to loosen the girls' masks was firmly rejected.

Pierre didn't really need to see the girls' faces as he had noticed a small mole on the neck of their maid earlier that day and – as Edo had predicted – she was the one to approach him now.

In the meantime the mood had undergone a remarkable change in the dining room. Armand had become the undisputed life and soul of the evening. In his funny mix of Italian and French he managed to make everybody laugh until the party was in full swing and in the gayest of moods. Desserts and numerous bottles of wine finished, Armand's proposal to withdraw to their rooms earned some nervous giggles but no serious objections. The friends left in the best of spirits, each of them accompanied by one of the girls. Pierre sensed a tinge of excitement; feeling light and slightly tipsy from the intoxicating wine, any qualms had long since evaporated.

In the intimacy of their bedroom he found his girl to be surprisingly timid, almost shy. Gently he took her mask away and kissed her lips. "What's your name?" he asked curiously. "You never told us!"

"Paola," she answered, her voice shaky.

99

"Paola, my love, you're trembling. If you don't like me or don't want to share the bed with me, please tell me! I would understand, don't worry!" he pleaded.

She didn't react immediately, therefore he gently took her face in his hands and smiled down at her. Through a treacherous curtain of tears Paola saw a row of perfect teeth and eyes seductive and blue as the sea in summer. Those eyes seemed to speak to her, to urge her: "Plunge into me, discover a love and pleasure you've never experienced before!" *Why are men always so stupid? The only reason why I'm here is that I fell in love with you this very morning when I saw you for the first time. I'm only a simple girl. I know that it's a stupid hopeless love without any future. And yet I want you to make love to me, I want this night to be perfect, so that I can store it like a precious jewel in my memory forever.* Aloud, she answered, "I wouldn't have come if I hadn't wanted it, I'm not one of the tavern girls who entertain men for money. I like you very much, do you like me as well, at least a little bit?"

Pierre looked at her earnest pleading face, bent upwards, watching him like a curious little bird. He couldn't resist drawing her closer. "Paola, you're simply adorable. The man who marries you later will be a lucky man, I truly envy him."

Quickly Paula lowered her eyes. She had to hide the stupid tears that were welling up. Rapidly she started to kiss Pierre with an intensity and passion that took him completely by surprise. They tumbled onto the bed, and as their clothes ended up in all four corners of the rooms, Pierre felt as if a secret fountain of desire had been unleashed. Their lovemaking was genuine – she knew none of the tricks or routines of the maids they had encountered from time to time in taverns during their long journey, maids happy to serve a customer for a little money.

"You are still a virgin?" he couldn't help exclaiming, but she silenced him with a long kiss, exploring every corner of his mouth with her tongue.

Pleasurably exhausted, Pierre fell asleep after they had made love – far too quickly for Paola. She kissed her sleeping lover a last time, a single tear falling onto Pierre's lips, as she knew that her fairytale was over now. Making sure not to disturb Pierre she dressed in silence. She had almost walked out of the room, ignoring the golden coins Pierre had discreetly left for her on the dressing table – but then she stopped and turned back. Swiftly she grabbed the coins. *If I end up being with child after this night, I'll not go to the wise woman to get rid of it. I want his child as it will keep the memory alive forever. This money will be for his son!*

Paola went back to the servants' quarters, making sure to avoid the watchful eyes of the guards that were on duty at night. She went into her bed and not much later her friends arrived, still giggling and whispering excitedly. "Look at Paola," she heard her friends whisper, "she's already sleeping.

Apparently her night was not as stormy as ours...!" and another conspiratorial giggle followed.

"My Armand, he was dreamy. So strong and passionate..."

"I can't complain, the Italian one had a lot of fire too," the second voice cut in. "Once wasn't enough... and we've already arranged that I should be waiting in his room tomorrow evening again. I must have pleased him!"

"It will cost us a fortune to keep Giuseppe sweet, he'll want his share..."

"I don't mind, he was really generous."

Paola could hear the faint clinking of coins.

"Pity for Paola really, she seemed so keen to get to know this Pierre closely; Edo told me that he's not just a gentleman, he's a sort of big shot in France, he even seems to know the King of France in person!"

"Imagine, a real baron or even a count, whatever – and here is Paola sleeping like a baby. I'll tell her tomorrow how stupid she is, I mean, as her best friend I have to open her eyes, this is an opportunity she won't get again soon!"

The excited whispering went on for some time until it died down and Paola could hear the regular breathing of her room-mates. But sleep wouldn't come, memories of Pierre's kisses, his smile, his laughter – even the scent of his skin – kept haunting her. She couldn't hold back her tears, the dam broke. Tonight Paola had tasted love but slowly she understood that she'd have to pay dearly. She could only hope that time would help. *Oh Lord, why must it hurt so much?*

The next day Pierre looked in vain for his pretty companion. He felt somewhat disappointed but rapidly convinced himself that most probably she had been given some tasks in the kitchen and might only be free later to serve lunch.

Yet by noon, no Paola showed up and Pierre decided to take the initiative and find out where he might be able to find her. The night before he had been a bit tipsy, but not utterly drunk, and he remembered that they had spent a very agreeable night. Clearly this adventure was something that merited being repeated, and listening to Edo and Armand, it was clear they were already looking forward to spending another night with good company.

Casually Pierre approached the landlord. "Would you know where I can find the kind girl that waited on us yesterday evening?" he asked. But even to his own ears the words rang false and hollow.

But the landlord didn't seem to notice, he seemed upset to the point of feeling that he had been personally insulted. "Oh, please don't speak of her, my lord!" he grumbled. "This girl has totally disappointed me, she's a snake! I gave her everything, decent pay, a bed, even Sunday mornings off to go to church. But what do I get in return? Only impudence and ingratitude! She left this morning and just gave word that she had to leave urgently to nurse her sick aunt!"

He almost spat the words out and sneered, "Sick aunt, my foot! I could swear that she's on her way right now to Venice, trying to find a place in a noble house, that's all these young maids think of. A decent house like mine won't do, a *noble* house it has to be! But she'll find out, wait till she sees how they treat her! She'll regret it and come back on her knees, crying, but I won't take her back, never!"

Pierre felt a sharp pang of disappointment as soon as the landlord started his litany. *Why did she go? I could swear that she liked me at least as much as I did her!* He shrugged his shoulders – who would ever understand women? Abruptly Pierre turned and left the grumbling landlord. He went in search of Jean, after all, what else could he do but plan an evening of playing dice together? Armand and Edo would surely be busy, they were the lucky ones!

*****

An unhappy girl with sagging shoulders sat on the cart that was slowly travelling forward on the road north. Paola knew that she had been extremely lucky to find this elderly couple on their way home back to the mountains. The cart was pulled by an ox that seemed to be as old as his owners and they talked to him like a human being. The ox obviously had no intention of moving any faster as it loftily ignored whatever efforts its owner made to encourage it to go any faster. Paola didn't care; she knew that nobody would pursue her, neither the landlord of the tavern, nor her lover of last night. Her future seemed as grey as the horizon that was stretching in front of her. If only she could stop crying!

******

"We've got it!" Edo was shouting, while excitedly waving a document in his hand.

"What have you got?" Armand stretched his legs like a lazy cat. He looked far too content and self-assured for Pierre's taste.

"The council of the Republic of Venice has accepted our request to enter the city and we may stay at our bank's palazzo, the Ca' Piccolin!"

"Why shouldn't we be allowed to enter?" asked Pierre astonished, "don't they want strangers? That would be silly for a city that depends on trade!"

102

"I admit it does sound silly, and yet the Government of Venice doesn't allow any competition that could hurt Venetian business," Edo explained. "As you're applying to enter the city on the pretext of working in our bank, it was really difficult to obtain permission. Our family is from Milan, we're considered outsiders."

"You mean it cost you a lot of money..." Armand made as if he were greasing the palm of an imaginary official.

"Sure, it did," Edo laughed. "It always does. That's the system not only here, but over all Italy."

"It's the system in France as well," sighed Armand, "and if Cardinal Richelieu gets involved, there are no limits to how much you'll need to pay! He gives a whole new dimension to the word 'greed'."

"I must pay you back then!" Pierre gripped Edo's hand. "I cannot let you pay on our behalf, don't forget it's our quest to find this bloody ring."

"I know, your most noble lordship, I'm just a minion in this noble adventure!" Edo quipped, "but may I remind your lordship that my bank will make good money because we'll be representing the mining rights of the Count of Salo – thanks to your intervention that saved his son!"

"That seemed only the natural thing to do." Pierre suddenly started to giggle.

"What are you laughing about?" Armand asked suspiciously.

"I still remember your face when the ceiling suddenly gave way and you disappeared right into the scene below, just like in a theatre. It was hilarious!"

"Well, somebody had to take the initiative," Armand replied, unperturbed. "If I'd waited for one of you to make a move, we'd probably still be sitting there and talking."

Clearly Armand was not amused. Both friends assured him immediately that only his brave intervention had saved the young Count of Salo. Pierre, though, could detect a tell-tale sparkle of amusement in Edo's eyes.

The next morning after sunrise three enterprising young men were ready to embark on a sailing boat that was to ferry them with their retinue to Venice, la Serenissima. Fog greeted them, which fitted the general mood perfectly.

Jean shivered, was it just the fog, or was it a premonition?

A Journey With A Surprise

François de Toucy looked at the few things his valet had packed and grimaced. In order to travel fast he'd need to travel light; some fresh shirts and the bare necessities would have to suffice. "Oh Pierre, I hope you appreciate the sacrifices I have to undergo for your sake!" he said aloud to himself. Even his proud hat with the plumed feathers had to remain at home. A simple leather one with a large brim would offer better protection against the winter rain.

"I look like a peasant," he sighed when he looked one last time in the polished silver mirror.

"I don't think that I have ever seen such an elegant peasant, my lord, if you will allow me this remark," his valet replied.

"So there is hope!" François answered, his good mood restored.

His groom was ready and waiting, as they were to ride together. François was aware that every day counted if he was to warn Pierre and his cousin, but after some reflection he had decided to call on his mother first, even if this meant stretching the journey by several days. Cardinal Richelieu was simply too cunning and too dangerous an enemy to have. François would need to be seen leaving Paris in the right direction; furthermore, he'd need to brief his mother if any of their numerous relatives popped up for a surprise visit – she'd need to invent a good excuse as to why he wasn't there.

As could have been expected, the weather was cold. But the light drizzle of rain, so typical for the north of France at this time of the year, luckily changed into a light snowfall, with crystals so tiny that they were almost invisible. François closed his eyes; he liked the feeling of the melting crystals on his lips.

Like a thin layer of white powder, large patches of snow had gathered on the roads and the endless rolling fields. François knew this landscape by heart; it was the landscape where he had grown up before he had moved to Paris. It had always had a disconcerting effect on his soul, a landscape plain to the extent of being boring and yet by the simple means of its empty vastness was imposing and impressive at the same time.

Normally not given to profound philosophical thoughts he started to contemplate all of a sudden how insignificant mankind must appear compared to the size of the world, not to mention the universe. The endless fields were studded with sorry-looking trees, dark and naked, as they had long since shed their leaves and were now merely dark skeletons dotted with bizarre clusters of green, as mistletoe thrived in the region and clung tenaciously to the bare branches. Memories of druids living in ancient times long forgotten floated through his brain, stories full of mystery that were handed down from generation to generation. This was a strange landscape indeed, so empty and yet so full of imagination.

From time to time they passed a forlorn forest but either the local bandits had no interest in attacking a well-trained young man accompanied by his armed groom or they simply preferred to stay close to their hearths during the cold. The frozen roads made for easy riding and François reached his mother's home a day earlier than he had reckoned.

His heart beat faster as he approached the relatively small but well-kept estate that had been his home for many years. The road and the brick buildings were meticulously maintained. He had to smile – there was to be no laxity where his mother was concerned.

His welcome was all he could have hoped for: the prodigal son could not have wished for anything better. The servants, many of whom had known him from his youth (and had often saved him from the wrath of his father, as François had displayed a particularly adventurous spirit from early on) flocked to the courtyard, laughing and chatting and trying to be helpful with his horse to the extent of creating complete chaos.

As soon as his mother appeared the chaos miraculously stopped. Merely a few words spoken in soft but determined tones were necessary to allow the grooms to calm the nervous horses down and to have order and quiet restored. If she was astonished or maybe even apprehensive to see her son arriving without prior notice, she didn't show it. She greeted François warmly and he found himself ushered into the building.

Inside she embraced him. "What a nice surprise to see you home! Maybe a word or two in advance would have allowed us to greet you with more decorum. But now go to your old room and freshen up, I've given orders to have the fire lit and some hot water will be brought up. We'll get comfortable and talk as soon as you're ready!"

François grinned; he knew that he must be a sorry-looking figure in her eyes as he hadn't shaved for several days and his leather breeches were stained from the journey. "I must look like a peasant," he admitted, "but I thought it better to travel like a peasant than look like a wealthy man ready to be picked off by highwaymen."

"You did indeed succeed remarkably well in creating this illusion, but it's time to become a gentleman again," his mother answered firmly. Only a slight wink betrayed her amusement. François got the message and obediently went up to his room.

Some time later, washed, shaved and now dressed in immaculate breeches and a fresh shirt, he joined his mother in the intimate drawing room that was her favourite place on the estate. Although it was furnished according to the prevailing fashion with dark panels, oil paintings and heavy furniture of darkened oak, somehow she had managed to add a lighter and feminine touch to it and it never appeared stuffy.

A glass of sweet wine, tempting small pastries and nuts were waiting for François and, suddenly realizing how hungry he was, he dug his hand into the nuts and started to crack the shells, offering his mother the first ones. It felt good to be home.

His mother chose a nut with a grateful smile and opened the conversation. "Now tell me, my boy, why have you popped up without a word in advance, is there anything important you wish to tell me?"

François saw that his mother was slightly uneasy and couldn't help teasing her a little. "Could be… what's your guess then?" he challenged her.

She cleared her throat. "Well… I imagine that it would be only normal for you to be planning to get married, now that our financial situation has improved. In any case, I want you to know that I'm ready to hand over the reins of this household to your bride immediately after you marry and move to the dower house, this has always been my intention. I'll not be one of those mothers who cling to their sons like a leech."

François smiled and his grey eyes looked warmly at his mother. There couldn't be a single girl on this planet able to resist her son, she thought proudly.

"For once, you guessed wrong!" he laughed. "No wedlock for me for the time being, I'm really very comfortable being a bachelor and who could do a better job here than you? This household runs like clockwork!"

He saw with satisfaction that his mother flushed lightly; apparently she wasn't immune to his praise.

"It's a bit more complicated than that, I'm afraid. I urgently need to help a friend, Pierre de Beauvoir, to be precise."

Quickly he explained to his mother that Pierre's old foe, Cardinal Richelieu had, once again, chosen to change sides.

"Of course you must go and warn him!" his mother exclaimed. "The Marquis de Beauvoir has been most generous towards you, it's our obligation to help him now! What can I do in this regard?"

"I asked leave from the Cardinal's service under the pretext that you appealed to my help because my sister might be about to choose the wrong

106

husband. But he must have suspected something because – just before I left his study – he suddenly produced a letter for me to deliver up north in the Spanish Netherlands."

"How will you manage that, then?"

"A good friend of mine will go there, pretending to be me when he remits the letter, that's been dealt with!"

"Excellent!" she exclaimed and with a sharp glance she continued. "So you'll expect me to pretend that you rode north but will come back any minute if someone should come round asking curious questions?"

"Exactly, I knew that you'd understand immediately, but can you make sure that our servants and my sisters stick to the same story? By the way, is my sister already contemplating marriage?"

"Don't worry about the servants, they're all loyal. Even after your father died and for several years when I had his creditors harassing me daily and not a penny to spend, they stayed, although I couldn't pay them. It was most embarrassing as I felt indebted to them. I remember doing the inventory one autumn in the pantry and the wine cellar. I was really worried about how to survive the coming winter – and I found much more than I had ever counted before. Each of them must have secretly brought either some food, some wine, I found even cider, which most certainly I would have never ordered." His mother had tears in her eyes. "All the same, they treated me with all the respect due to the mistress of a house, they never let me feel that I depended on them to survive."

François gulped. "I never knew that it was so bad, I could have sold some land!"

"Nobody wanted this to happen, you know they love you, they feel deeply attached to the family. They were so proud that we managed to keep your inheritance!"

François made a mental note that somehow he must later repay this debt to his servants. "I think we can be very proud of them, but what about my sister?"

"I'd like to marry her to our young notary in the town," she confessed. "Your sister is far too serious, she's still contemplating taking the veil."

"If this is what she wants, I can certainly pay her a decent dowry and find a convent fitting for a lady." He furrowed his brow. "I think I can make use of some of the Cardinal's connections."

107

His mother didn't look particularly pleased. "I don't think that she should take her vows. Your sister is far too soft-hearted and naïve to survive in a convent."

"You make the convent sound a very harsh place!" François was astonished; his mother had always been very religious.

She sighed. "A convent remains a place on earth where real people live, and frankly speaking, you need to fight your corner in such an environment. People can be nasty, that's a simple fact. Your sister would arrive there, thinking that heaven is close and would soon be very much disappointed to find herself closer to hell. It needs guts to survive there, you need to lead and manipulate people – and this she can't do. You have no idea how bitchy women can be when they're cooped up together!"

François looked at his mother with respect. Every word she spoke seemed to convey the wisdom of her own experience. "Let's look at the notary then. Why are you so sure he'd be a good match?"

"Whenever he sees your sister he turns scarlet and starts talking total nonsense!" she laughed. "Poor lad, he's head over heels in love with her!"

"But he's not an aristocrat, she'd be marrying far below her station." François still felt scandalized. "Don't forget that we carry royal blood on both sides of the family!"

"Hogwash!" his mother answered curtly. "Times are changing! It's money nowadays that rules the world. Our kingdom is run by an upstart priest who comes from a low-born noble family. Our famous royal blood… where has it got us, are we running the country? If you want to survive at court you must bow to Richelieu, and if the next man to govern us isn't that horrible Italian upstart, Mazarin, then I'm not your mother! Don't think that we're buried deep in the provinces and don't get any news. See what's happening in England right now – they're even talking about a republic!" and she almost spat the last words as if they tasted disgusting.

"Filthy *canaille*, wanting to make their sacred king dance to their tunes – so this is our wonderful new world! Let me tell you, if my girl marries a decent man with a reasonable amount of money, it's the best I could want for her!"

François was shocked. He had never expected such a rebellious speech from his mother of all people – her line of ancestors must reach back to the first kings of France! An uneasy silence reigned until François sighed, "Let it be the notary then, if money can make her happy."

His mother laughed. "Don't be so stuffy, money only comes as a welcome addition, believe me. He worships her and they'll make a wonderful couple.

And it'll save you a lot of money as he won't ask for an impressive dowry. Be prepared though, your other sister has her sights set on becoming nothing less than marchioness! I'll be compelled to introduce her at court soon and use all the connections of my sister in Paris – this is going to cost us a lot of money!"

"Let me know in good time then, so we can rent a house, hire servants!"

His mother was right, it would indeed cost a fortune. She nodded guiltily. "I know, it will be very costly, but frankly speaking, it'll be wonderful to spend a season in Paris. It's been such a long time since I stayed in town and although I love it at home, from time to time I long to be back. I think I shall cherish every minute – just imagine, we can have conversations on topics other than the next harvest or whether the pigs are fat enough. I hope by spring I can marry Jeanette to her notary and then we'll be ready to go to Paris!"

François spent an agreeable dinner in the company of his mother and sisters; they beseeched him to tell them about life in Paris and happily François obliged by sharing the latest gossip from the Parisian salons (at least the less daring stories) until the last candles had burned down and it was time to go to bed.

The next morning François left at sunrise. He didn't want to lose any time, and yet his mother had gently but firmly insisted on a detour. "I know that you're pressed for time and I understand the importance but please do your mother a big favour: I need you to ride to Reims and pay back some old debts I have with the Montjoie family which are weighing on my conscience. Marie's mother is not only a relative but an old friend and she was so kind as to lend me some money when I faced severe problems. It's time to pay her back!"

"When was this?" He looked at his mother critically.

"You remember when you were invited to join the musketeers?"

"Of course I do, I was so proud!" he smiled warmly.

"Well, you needed to have a uniform and a horse, and I didn't know how to pay for it! I'll always remember how tactful and kind she was to me, I found it so hard asking for this favour!"

"Of course we have to pay her back, it's a question of honour!" François exclaimed; scandalized, he scrutinized his mother. "Any other debts I need to settle? Better tell me now!"

She laughed. "No, believe it or not, it's the only one. Thanks to Pierre de Beauvoir we've no more debts to settle!"

The family and servants waved good-bye while the grey shadows of the early morning dissolved into the subdued colours of the northern winter. The weather showed no mercy, the light snow turned into a drenching rain and François was more than happy when a day later the turrets and spires of Reims appeared on the horizon.

The guards at the gates quickly understood that François was one of their own and standing to attention they let him pass – it was not every day a high ranking officer of the musketeers from Paris came along, better to leave a good impression!

It didn't prove difficult for François to locate Marie's parents' house as everybody in Reims seemed to know the Montjoie family. Arriving during the late afternoon he was welcomed warmly and invited to stay for the night.

With the diplomacy and tact he had acquired in the Cardinal's service, François de Toucy approached the subject of the outstanding debt. To his surprise Marie's mother adamantly refused to accept any money. "You must have totally misunderstood the situation, it was a gift, so don't let's talk about this again!" she countered loftily in the face of his attempts to hand over the money.

But François was not inexperienced in dealing with the female sex. In no time he had Marie's mother eating out of his hand and to her own surprise she heard herself agreeing that even if it had been intended as a gift, returning the money was simply a question of respecting his mother's honour. François was relieved; at least one mission had been accomplished successfully! Yet he couldn't help but notice that Marie was very quiet. She barely participated in the conversation and only nibbled at the excellent food. Her lustrous amber eyes glowed large and far too sad in her pale face.

An uneasy tension was reigning in the Montjoie household – clearly the members of the family were not on the best of terms. When Marie's father announced that he was retiring to his room, courtesy compelled François to do the same and he went to bed, feeling slightly ill at ease. "Something is wrong here, I wonder what it is – Marie and her mother definitely seem to be at odds!"

The next morning François expected to be on his own as Marie's mother had dropped hints during their conversation that she rarely partook of breakfast and Marie's father had apologized, saying that he needed to leave Reims early in the morning in order to inspect some vineyards in the east. François therefore was already dressed in his riding attire, prepared for a leisurely breakfast. Still pondering about the strange atmosphere of yesterday's dinner he was chewing on the excellent fresh bread when the door suddenly opened and Marie slipped into the breakfast room.

Quickly he rose and greeted his cousin. In reality they had given up figuring out the exact relationship as their family trees seemed to have kept meeting and intertwining so often that it needed an expert to figure out if she was a fourth, fifth or maybe even sixth cousin – or maybe all of these.

Marie looked with disgust at the mountain of food François had piled on his plate, although she realized that he'd probably need to skip lunch during the long journey that lay ahead. A servant brought a cup of chocolate and silently Marie started to nibble on a piece of bread. As soon as the servant had left the room she opened the conversation. "François, you'll become fat in no time if you make a habit of gobbling so much food so soon in the morning! It's disgusting!"

François just grinned at her, far from being intimidated. "Had a bad night, my darling? Don't worry, I'll be gone in no time and will spare you any further disgusting sights."

"That's typical! You come, you eat and you treat us as a tavern! Would you call this good manners or showing any consideration for your relatives? I might have wanted to talk to you." Marie was visibly upset.

François contemplated that her excitement was certainly very becoming to her; always a beauty, with her slightly flushed cheeks and sparkling eyes she radiated a vividness which made her look simply stunning. And yet François was in no danger of falling in love. She hisses like a poisonous viper, he thought, poor Pierre, he'll have a hell of a time trying to tame this one!

"Marie, please believe me, I would love to stay and spend some time with you. I promise I'll stay longer next time. I get the feeling you've had a slight disagreement with your mother – if I may be so bold?"

"A slight disagreement?" She laughed coarsely. "There isn't a single day when she doesn't harass me because there is no news of Pierre! The first weeks she was all sweetness and understanding that I should marry him – but now she's warming up the old idea that I should marry the neighbour's son to make us the biggest owners of vineyards in the Champagne region! I'm going mad! And now you turn up, I hope to get a bit of support, consolation and distraction, and what do you do?"

"Finish my breakfast and take my leave?" he answered meekly.

"Exactly, but what else could I have expected from a cousin whose only interest is in fighting, gambling, chasing girls and… eating!"

"Oh Marie, please have mercy, I'd really love to spend some time here, but in actual fact I have most pressing things to do!"

"I can imagine, probably the most pressing matter has long dark hair and wears gowns with low necklines!" Marie answered darkly.

111

"Oh come, on, I have to help a friend who'll be in deep trouble if I don't act quickly. So don't be awkward, I really must leave today, it's no joke! And it's in your interest as well!"

How you wish you could turn back time sometimes! François had just uttered the last sentence when he realized that he had made an enormous mistake!

"It's Pierre, then, who's in trouble," she breathed and the angry snarling tiger turned into a frightened kitten.

"No, why do you think it should be Pierre, I have many friends!"

She made a gesture to show him that any further explanation would be futile, a simple waste of breath. "What do you intend to do?" she cried. "Sit here, eat and waste precious time?"

"Hey, a moment ago you wanted me to stay for several days, now you're literally throwing me out of the door!" he protested. "I shall leave immediately after breakfast but I'll need to buy some provisions for my journey. But don't worry, you won't see my face anymore after a matter of minutes!"

The frightened kitten changed once more and a purring Marie suddenly took his hand. "Don't be angry with me, I was just scared because you mentioned Pierre!"

"I did *not* mention Pierre!" he cried.

She gave him a long reflective glance. "If you need to buy provisions, you're planning to join him in Venice, I guess. That's a long way from here."

"Yes, I'll be away for some time, but I'm not going to rescue Pierre, however often you repeat this idiotic suggestion." He was incensed now.

Marie gave in; meekly she folded her hands in her lap, and looking at them, she apologized. "I'm sorry, you know, I'm simply so worried. I sit here, without any news, my mother keeps pestering me day and night – maybe I'm seeing phantoms. I'll leave you now, have a safe trip and don't worry, I won't keep you any longer from helping P–, I mean, your friend."

François felt slightly uneasy. He was still cursing himself for his slip of the tongue. But finally he consoled himself that Marie seemed to have given up pursuing him on this matter. Formally taking her leave, she invited François to kiss both her cheeks as was customary in order to say good-bye and with a swirl of her silken gown she was gone.

Quickly – hoping that she wouldn't change her mind and return with further annoying questions – François finished his breakfast and went in

112

search of his groom. He found him downstairs in animated conversation with Marie's maid; it didn't take much imagination to understand that he would have preferred his master to be elsewhere.

"I'm sorry to disturb, but we have different priorities on our minds," he commented good-humouredly.

His groom grinned. "Nice, ain't she, my lord?"

"Yes, she surely is, but you'd better keep your mind on our trip, it might be a bit farther than you imagine."

"Yes, I know, my lord, we'll have to ride up north to the Spanish bastards, I guess we'll need a good fourteen days."

"You might discover that we'll be away for some more time than you imagine, let's get going and buy the stuff we need for your journey!" François de Toucy answered lightly, but refused to go into detail.

His groom shrugged; he didn't really care – what difference did it make if they rode for a week or two more? Had François told him that he was to accompany him to visit the heathens of Africa, he'd have followed him anyhow.

Their venture into the city centre took longer than anticipated as François made the basic mistake of haggling too long with the first merchant. Not succeeding in negotiating the price he had in mind for the felt coats they needed to defy the winter rains he loudly voiced his opinion about greedy merchants who spent their lives ripping off unsuspecting customers and moved on to the next stall – just to find that prices there were even higher. A very frustrated and unusually taciturn François returned to the first stall and bought the coats, trying to ignore the satisfied smirk of the salesman. Therefore they rode through the gates only long after the cathedral bells had chimed noon. To the surprise of his groom François chose the gate leading to the south – he was no expert in geography but he knew perfectly well that the Spanish Netherlands were located north-east of Reims!

The roads, soaked by the relentless rain, were slippery and muddy and riding was no fun. The dark clouds were becoming even more menacing as they approached the hours of the late afternoon and François was calculating whether they could reach the post station before darkness enshrouded them. He was still deep in thought when all of a sudden his groom whistled.

François reined in his horse and looked attentively in the direction his groom indicated. Softly he swore to himself. Their journey had been simply too smooth until now! The shadows of two galloping horsemen were approaching them fast. The shadows detached themselves quickly from the blurred background and came closer.

113

"Merde, merde, merde!" he said to himself. "Richelieu must have been informed of my real intentions, no ordinary highwaymen would chase us here in the open, they'd have waited for darkness or ambushed us in the forest."

Aloud he said, "Prepare your pistols, it looks like a fight is waiting for us… and I'm afraid it's against people who know their job."

The groom only shrugged; he had full confidence in the skills of his master. He took out the flintlock pistols and the powder flask and with experienced hands prepared the weapons they had brought along.

In no time they were ready to fight.

Lady Sophia

Whenever Henri bothered to look out of his window he had the most beautiful view, and not only onto the famous gardens – he could even see the tranquil, silvery ribbon of the river and the spires and roofs of the city of Verona in the near distance.

His room had been decorated with all the elegance and refined luxury that had made Italy famous all over Europe and murals depicted mythical characters playing their eternal games of love and seduction. A luxurious prison, but a prison all the same. After fourteen days Sophia had invited him to move from Giovanni's guesthouse in the city centre over to their villa located on the opposite side of the river. Henri knew immediately that the invitation was a command by any other name, although he was treated with all the decorum due a guest of honour. Henri had become nothing more than Lady Sophia's prisoner, her private toy.

It hadn't taken long to piece together Lady Sophia's history. A woman of simple origins, but exceptional beauty and a sharp wit, she had managed to become the mistress of the powerful Archbishop of Verona. His Eminence – in appreciation of the exceptional and extremely satisfying services rendered – had arranged a marriage of convenience to a son whose family was desperate to keep up appearances as he had never showed any interest in the female sex. Sophia had immediately grasped the advantages of such a marriage and in no time had become the true mistress of the house, ruling her husband and her household with a will of iron – Lady Sophia had in fact become the secret queen of Verona.

Night had fallen and the brocade curtains had been closed. A bright fire was burning in the fireplace spreading comfort and warmth. Several candelabra cast their bright light into the room, making the golden decoration glow vividly. The wall paintings seemed to have come alive, the cherubs playing their enticing games, almost floating in the air.

Henri lay naked on the huge bed, his legs spread apart, the golden hair of his body glistening in the candlelight. His eyes were closed while the young black pageboy was caressing his thighs – an exciting change from Sophia's lovemaking, a routine that had lost its fascination for Henri long ago. Now the young page lowered his head to plant kisses on Henri's body as Henri shivered with delight. The black boy's head was hovering right above Henri's belly when the door was flung open and Lady Sophia stormed into the room.

"I can't believe my eyes!" she shrieked. "When my maid told me that I should watch the two of you, I thought that she was just making up stories, being the jealous bitch she is. But I've seen enough, you perverts, I'll teach

115

you never to betray me, I'll have you flogged, I'll have the pageboy skinned alive!"

Her piercing voice filled the room. Henri jumped up and walked towards Sophia, and even though she was seething with anger she couldn't help but admire his athletic body; he looked like a Greek statue come alive.

Henri saw the maid standing in the entrance. Her satisfied smirk said it all, she was revelling in this scene. Without undue hurry he took Sophia in his arms and although she tried to wriggle out of his embrace, his arms of steel held her tightly.

"Sophia, calm down, I always do what *I* want, you had better get used to it!"

She laughed, a spiteful sound. "You'd better get used to *my* rules, Henri, your noble pretensions, you can stuff them up your arse!" she answered rudely, forgetting her position as a lady.

Only a quick tightening of Henri's arms showed his reaction – but then he released Sophia from his embrace. "What do you mean?" he drawled.

"I mean, either you stop groping my servants and be an obedient boy, or I'll have you flogged and you'll disappear forever in the dungeons of the archbishop. I happen to have a very special relationship with him – as you might know already!"

Henri's eyes widened in anger but he kept himself under masterful control. "That would be a great mistake," he answered.

"Why?" Again the spiteful laugh. "You think you can scare me?"

"If you get rid of us," and he pointed to the young page who sat on the bed shivering with fright, "You'll miss something my dear, you'll regret it forever!"

He lowered his voice and whispered into her ear. "I needed the boy to get me in the mood, but now I want you, I want you badly. You can feel it already!" and he pressed himself tightly against her thin nightgown. "But I want you together with the boy. Just imagine, the two of us, lusting for you at the same time! Sophia, my darling, I'll make you scream with delight."

His glance went to the maid. "Send her away and let's make love like you've never experienced it before, just the three of us!" He saw the flicker of desire in her eyes and gently he started to rub himself against her.

Sophia turned towards her maid. "You may leave us now, but stay in the antechamber, I'll call you when I need you!"

"She'll be there, the second I need her," Sophia hissed. "I'm not stupid."

"You're all I desire!" he whispered back while he watched the maid closing the door behind her, unable to hide her disappointment at the sudden change in her mistress's mood.

Slowly Henri undressed Sophia and carried her like a precious treasure to the bed. Sophia had dropped her silken scarf carelessly on the floor but Henri took the scarf and started to caress her thighs and belly with it, moving up to her breasts. Soon Sophia started to breathe faster and wanted to drag Henri down to her, but he refused to be pulled into her embrace.

"I've promised you something unique for tonight, we'll take our time, you won't regret it, my darling little slut." His voice was hoarse and made her shiver with delight.

"I'm a lady, don't call me a slut or you'll regret it!" she protested, trying to regain the upper hand.

"You're a slut in your heart and I love it, it excites me."

She relented and smiled lazily. The soft scarf caressed her breasts, her nipples… and it felt so good!

"Now close your eyes," Henri commanded. "The boy will join us and you'll not know who is doing what, just feel and savour every second!"

He made a sign to the pageboy who immediately came closer. "Feel his young and smooth skin, feel mine?" he whispered.

Sophia only sighed with delight and closed her eyes. The silk scarf moved higher, and now she couldn't tell any more how many hands were caressing her. *Yes, he's right, this is absolutely wonderful.* The silk scarf moved higher again, caressing her neck and throat. Henri made a sign to the pageboy to move his hand between her thighs and when she started to moan with pleasure she probably never even noticed that the scarf was being drawn tighter, merciless and swift, until her head lolled to one side.

"You went too far tonight, darling Sophia," Henri whispered. "Nobody ever insults Henri de Beauvoir without paying for it!"

He dropped her on the bed. "Not even in death do you manage to look like a lady," he said, his voice dripping with contempt. He quickly looked at the boy, expecting to find him frozen with terror, in any case, Henri was ready to silence him as well if need be.

"Neatly done," commented the boy. "I have been longing to do this for a long time. What is the plan now?"

"It's 'my lord', and don't you forget it!" If Henri was astonished at his reaction, he didn't show it.

"What does my lord plan to do now?" the boy asked, only a light flickering of his eyes betraying his emotions.

"Get out of here, of course," Henri answered loftily.

"May I propose a deal, my lord?"

"Go ahead, but make sure it's a good one."

"I know every single room and door in this villa and all the secret exits from the garden. I can organize horses for us – and I know where my Lady Sophia has hidden the coins and jewels she took from you."

"Go on." Henri was becoming curious. "What's my part of the deal then?"

"I want to travel under the protection of your lordship to Venice, where your lordship has to release me so that I can find a ship and return to my native country – and I want you to give me enough money to pay for the passage."

"Agreed," Henri answered loudly. "Anyhow," he thought, "if I don't give him the money voluntarily, he'll steal it from me sooner or later."

The boy only nodded and flashed him a quick grin as if he had read his mind. "One more condition though, your lordship won't request that I share your bed again!"

Henri shrugged; he had more important things on his mind at present. Anyhow, not for a second was he in any doubt that the boy could seriously resist him.

"First things first." Henri looked at the boy. "How do you propose we get rid of this stupid maid. I'm sure she's been eavesdropping behind the door and will enter any minute to check what's going on!"

The black pageboy frowned, then grinned, full of mischief. "I know her well, she's Lady Sophia's private chambermaid, quite prudish actually. If I rush out naked to tell her that she's dismissed for the night, she'll probably be so confused and upset that she won't really check to see what's going on!"

118

Henri smiled, but it was not a nice smile. "Let's then offer a last favour to our dear Lady Sophia and make it a realistic scene." Before the pageboy had fully understood Henri's intentions he saw him mounting the naked body. "Now rush out!" Henri ordered curtly, "or do you seriously think that I enjoy lying on top of a corpse?"

Henri started an impressive performance; sounds of ecstatic moaning echoed through the room. The pageboy swallowed hard but obeyed. Quickly he opened the door and – as Henri had predicted – the curious maid almost fell into his arms. When she realized that the pageboy was stark naked she was flustered, not knowing where to look. In the background Henri's moaning was increasing in speed and loudness, filling the room.

"Her ladyship is allowing you to retire." The pageboy looked into the maid's eyes.

She looked back astonished. "But…"

The boy didn't let her finish the sentence. "Sweetie, if you prefer to join us, you're welcome," and he pointed to his manhood. "I'm ready and willing!"

The maid shrieked as he made to draw her into his arms and fled out of the room.

Smiling he walked back into the room and immediately Henri stopped his macabre performance. "That's one problem solved," the pageboy commented, content with his own work.

"And about time, too. Making love to a corpse is not my style." Henri frowned critically at the body. "But it was just the kind of weird scene she would have appreciated – once a slut, always a slut!"

"Let me give you a hand," offered the pageboy, and started to move the corpse into a more natural-looking position. With the swift gestures of an experienced servant he covered Sophia's naked body with a blanket and arranged her hair. Now she looked as if she were sleeping on her tummy, her dark hair spreading across the pillow and covering her face.

Henri watched critically while he dressed. "I admit, that looks far better now! It'll take them some time to discover that our sleeping beauty is never going to wake up again! By the way, what's your name?"

"Mustafa, my lord!"

Mustafa searched in Lady Sophia's dress until he found a golden key chain, then he quickly dived into his clothes as well and in no time both of them were ready to sneak out of the room. Secretly Henri could only congratulate himself on the pageboy accompanying him. He had killed Sophia

119

under an impulse of hot rage, not considering the consequences or how to escape from this well-guarded household. Mustafa skilfully navigated his way through dark and empty hallways, avoiding the busy servants' quarters and in a matter of only minutes they had already entered the cavernous cellars, guarded only by a single servant who was sleeping peacefully. The servant's end came quickly; Henri could barely see the flash of a blade before the boy cut his victim's throat.

"You seem to have some experience..." Henri remarked drily and made a mental note to pay more attention when alone with the boy in future.

"I learned my trade when I was fairly young, and I had an old issue to settle with him," Mustafa commented evenly, but kicked the dead guard with his foot as a last gesture of contempt. Then he turned away and directed Henri towards a big wooden chest with wrought-iron hinges and lavishly decorated fittings that stood among several similar-looking chests. He fumbled with the key he had retrieved from Lady Sophia's dress and Henri heard a clicking sound, and the lid swung open on its hinges, well greased and in almost total silence, to display the treasures of the Orient in front of them.

"Are all of those chests filled with gold?" Henri couldn't help asking curiously.

"No, my lord, most are filled with clothes and furs – you can smell the camphor, it's really effective at keeping the moths away."

Now Henri noticed the slightly nauseating scent of camphor in the air. It wouldn't only keep the bugs away, he reflected; it would repel any creature. Henri grabbed whatever he could take quickly – he didn't bother to distinguish between his own belongings and those of Lady Sophia. "Where are the spices she took from me?" he asked the boy, "any idea? They are much lighter and would be ideal to carry."

"Oh, she sold them. I heard her laughing that she'd be spicy enough for you, my lord."

Henri only shrugged. Sophia had laughed too soon... Once his pockets were almost bursting he invited the boy to serve himself. "That will pay your passage to Africa!"

"And it will buy me a bride, I may look young, but I'm of an age when I should marry, according to our tradition." The pageboy dug his hands into the gold and jewels and filled his pockets.

They continued their escape until they reached the stables. A lone elderly groom was on watch there, at least he was supposed to be keeping watch, especially to make sure that no fire ravaged the stables. But as nobody had ever dared to steal anything from Lady Sophia, and the tallow lights were hanging safely on wrought-iron holders, the groom had emptied his customary bottle of wine and was sound asleep when Henri and Mustafa arrived. Henri shook him, but the groom only protested feebly in his sleep, eyes firmly shut.

"Let him sleep," whispered Mustafa, "I know him quite well, he'll sleep like a baby until tomorrow morning, he's harmless!"

Thus the sleeping groom escaped the fate of the other guard while the two intruders calmly saddled the best horses and stored their booty. Mustafa knew a secret gate that would lead them out onto the road, and well hidden by the bushes and the darkness they embarked on their journey to Venice.

Henri followed Mustafa's lead; he had no idea which direction to take.

"Any idea how many days it'll take to reach Venice?" he asked Mustafa. "Should be two or three maximum, if I remember Giovanni's explanations correctly!"

"Yes, my lord, but if you agree, I propose making a detour to the northern lakes first, as it is generally known that your lordship was bound for Venice, and Lady Sophia's husband will send soldiers from Verona to search for us!"

Henri gave this suggestion some thought. "Are you sure, I would have said that he'd be eternally grateful to us... it didn't look like a very passionate marriage to me."

The pageboy flashed him a quick smile. "My lord is correct, but he'll have to pretend, especially as the archbishop will be out of his mind! Her ladyship was very skilful..."

"Oh, I forgot His Eminence..." Henri drawled. "I agree, his feelings of deepest Christian charity will be hurt! Let's go north first, it's safer, you're right."

They sped forward on the well-paved road north. The road, an efficient legacy left by the Romans, was illuminated by unusually bright moonlight as a gigantic moon hung like a glowing lantern low and close in a night sky of darkest velvet, studded with sparkling stars that guided them safely. Henri felt the tension of the past hours abate and a sensation of joy and freedom spread like an exhilarating elixir through his body.

Sophia, my darling, he thought triumphantly, you chose the wrong lover. Nobody will ever be able to tame me!

La Serenissima

Pierre listened to the rough cries and curses of the sailors answered immediately by the even ruder replies of the stevedores who were busily stowing all sorts of merchandise, barrels of wine and bags of grain onto the sailing boat that was to ferry them the short distance to Venice. The boat was still moored in the port. Like an army of ants, everybody was bustling around, chaotically at first glance and yet part of an organized master plan all the same. Pierre's glance wandered to the jetty where he spotted Armand and Edo saying good-bye to the girls they had befriended in the tavern. Involuntarily Pierre's glance searched for the figure of his own girlfriend. For a second his heart beat faster as he saw her silhouette standing there, close to the sailing boat, a slender figure wrapped in a woollen coat with a large hood.

But the girl turned and immediately a wave of disappointment swept over Pierre. She was not the girl he had been searching for. You're a sentimental idiot, he chided himself, I should be like the others, just enjoy the fun and forget this adventure!

His friends were in the best of moods; snippets of animated laughter and jokes reached him, and he could see their smiling faces. His friends were looking forward to visiting Venice, just as mice must look forward to sneaking into a well-filled pantry!

Pierre couldn't help but wonder if their journey would be crowned with success. It sounded so easy to immerse oneself in the social activities of carnival – but how to proceed further? His position in England had been recognized by King Charles II, but the Knights of the Templar were very powerful, they certainly wouldn't brook any failure! And how to find and acquire the missing sapphire ring? No owner would ever voluntarily sell such a rare jewel! Most probably they'd be compelled to steal it.... Pierre swallowed. He had heard that Venice boasted the most terrifying jails in the entire world, with their lead-roofed chambers, places of hell on earth.

Such thoughts will get you nowhere! Pierre tried to think about more cheerful things but despite his previous resolution to forget about the girl, a vague disappointment remained; why had she left him so quickly, never to turn up again; had he disappointed her that night? Suddenly he felt a firm hand on his shoulder. Armand was standing behind him.

"You're brooding again! You should join us and have some fun!" his friend scolded him.

"I'm not brooding! I'm being very cheerful, excessively so!' Pierre hotly defended himself.

"His Grace is not brooding…! Pierre you're probably the worst liar I've ever met; by the way, that's one of the reasons why I like you so much. Of course, you're brooding, I've always thought you were born into a constant state of worry."

Armand slapped Pierre's shoulder encouragingly. "Everything will be all right, don't mull over things that might happen, life is too short to worry. With our help, you'll manage. Nobody will be able to resist us, you'll see!"

Pierre relaxed and had to laugh; Armand's optimism really was irresistible.

"That's much better!" Armand hugged his friend. "We'll have the time of our lives, believe me!"

The sailing boat had left the port and now Pierre started to feel the cold as a steady wind was blowing from the north, an uncomfortable reminder that the snow-covered Alps were not too far away. The boat started to sway as the wind created small waves and foaming spray, nothing too dangerous, but the boat was pitching and rolling on the heavy sea like a tossed nutshell.

"Let's go down to the cabin, Jean is already making it comfortable for us," Pierre suggested and Armand had no objections. Although both of them were wearing fur-lined waistcoats, the damp cold was becoming most uncomfortable.

"I hope Jean has a good brandy ready for us," Armand said with chattering teeth. "I could do with one!"

"So could I, let's go!"

They found Jean inside the cabin surrounded by chests of clothes they had acquired in order to conquer Venice. Under the expectant eyes of the two friends he produced a flask with a transparent fluid, almost like water – but its aroma filled their nostrils and immediately sent a wave of fire through their bodies.

"That's excellent!" Pierre sighed with satisfaction. "Tell me your secret, Jean, what is it?"

"They call it grappa here in Italy, it's strong stuff, please be careful, my lord!"

"Jean, I'm not a schoolboy, I can take care of myself. Another one, please!"

Jean added a mere dash. Apparently he didn't share his master's belief that he was capable of looking after himself.

Pierre made a face but changed the subject. "Where's Edo? I guess he'd like a glass of grappa as well, this stuff is really excellent!"

Hopefully he moved his glass in the direction of the bottle, but Jean pretended not to notice the gesture and stored the bottle back in the chest. In any case, Pierre's mood had brightened considerably, as the grappa began to have an effect.

"I'm afraid, Monsieur Edoardo is highly indisposed," answered Jean and made a telling gesture.

"I think I'm starting to feel it as well." Armand's face had taken on a greenish tinge. "Maybe I should not have tasted the grappa…" These were his last words as he stormed out of the cabin and just seconds later Pierre and Jean heard the choking sound of desperate vomiting.

"Didn't he say that I could count on him whenever I needed him?" Pierre asked Jean. "Doesn't really look like it…!"

"I guess his lordship meant whenever his feet are on firm ground," Jean added with a smile.

Pierre giggled. The grappa had blown his sorrows away, and suddenly everything seemed easy and he felt light hearted, ready to take on the world. "Please tell the captain that it's my wish to go out and see Venice when we start to approach the city. Ask him to send a sailor to remind us on time so that I can go out to the railings and have a good view!"

Jean looked sceptically at his master. "The weather is not really *that* good, my lord, there will be a lot of mist, I'm afraid your lordship will be disappointed!"

Pierre was still in an optimistic mood. "I don't care. Everybody's been talking about Venice, Jean! A city that is so special and proud that it calls itself La Serenissima, the serene city. I don't want to miss the chance of seeing a skyline that is so famous, even Monsieur Piccolin raved about it – and he has seen a lot in his lifetime!"

Jean bowed and went outside to give his instructions to the captain.

Neither Edo nor Armand turned up again and while the ship was gently rocking him Pierre fell asleep, comfortably snuggled in a fur blanket that Jean had provided for him. Pierre was convinced that he had only slept for a second or two when a young sailor was already knocking at the door of the cabin.

Gruffly he bade the intruder enter. A young lad stuttered and swallowed nervously, saying his captain had ordered him to inform the high-born stranger (rumour had it that he was nothing less than a genuine count) of their approach, but he was doubtful that this was true and feared it might just be a bad joke. Who would want to leave a warm and cosy cabin and stand in the cold if he was of sound mind? The young sailor had been pondering this question and was almost sure by now he must have committed a major stupidity in following this order. But the high-born stranger now opened his big blue eyes and smiled at him.

"I know it sounds a bit strange to go out in this weather, but thank you very much for reminding me!" Pierre threw off the blanket and prepared to leave the cabin. Maybe it was still the effect of the grappa, the refreshing nap or the spirit of adventure, but Pierre felt strangely elated as soon as he was up on deck leaning against the rail.

The wind was not only freezing cold, it had freshened up while Pierre had been sleeping inside the cabin. Gusts of wind were now chasing thick clouds across the sky like a sheepdog chasing a flock of overweight reluctant sheep. The fact that the city was still shrouded in a layer of mist should have put a damper on his mood, but Pierre looked at the thin grey veil covering most of the buildings and felt thrilled all the same. A thought flashed through his mind: *Venice is being coy, like a seductive woman, not willing to reveal all of her secrets to me at once.*

Inhaling the fresh air Pierre watched the foaming sea, then his eyes followed the intricate patterns that the tireless seagulls painted across the sky. The wind started to dissolve the mist, as minute by minute the blurred silhouette of the city's skyline became sharper and more and more detailed. Suddenly Pierre had to gasp as the wind broke the grey clouds apart and a single beam of light descended onto the city, illuminating the top of the Campanile tower and the domes of what he believed to be the Cathedral of Saint Mark.

Edo had already painted vivid pictures of the beauty of this city during their journey but only now did Pierre understand how truthful he had been. This must be a sign from heaven, Pierre thought; he felt blessed and elated. The beam of light broadened and hit soft-coloured tiled roofs, then moved on to the spires of the numerous churches and further to the cathedral and the canal. Pierre had to hold his breath; touched by the sunlight, the purest gold gleamed from the spires and the dome of the cathedral, and even the surface of the lagoon shimmered with gold as if a magic wand had touched them. Venice looked like a heavenly city that had appeared on earth.

But the magic spell was short lived, as all of a sudden the dense curtain of clouds closed over again, the beam of light disappeared as rapidly as it had materialized before. But Pierre still felt as if in a trance. Venice had welcomed him, the Serenissima had offered him a glimpse of her eternal beauty.

125

"It's time we prepared for landing, my lord." Pierre could hear the voice of his valet, bringing him back to reality.

"How are Edo and Armand?" Pierre asked curiously.

"Surviving, my lord!" Jean answered laconically.

Pierre laughed. "I guess our heroes will be restored to their former greatness as soon as they strike terra firma..."

Now, as the sailing boat approached the port, the crew of the ship started to stir into action. The army of ants was bustling once more, on the ship and on the jetty. Surprisingly rapidly they were able to disembark, but it felt odd to be back on firm ground! Pierre had the impression that the whole city was swaying around him.

Once their chests of clothes had been unloaded, Pierre looked with a questioning expression at Edo (still taciturn and looking unusually pale); he could not see any coach waiting to pick them up.

"Where are we going now? You mentioned that we'd most probably be staying at your bank? And how are we to get there?"

Edo smiled and pointed at two luxuriously decorated gondolas that were moored nearby. "We have to take those," he grinned ironically, "but I must admit that Armand and I decided to give it a moment until we feel that our stomachs are back where they belong!"

Pierre grinned back. "You don't seem like natural sailors to me!"

Edo closed his eyes and shuddered. "I couldn't imagine anything worse, to be honest. Even accounting must be better! But let me answer your question as to where you're going to stay. As you know, my brother is no friend of luxury or unnecessary spending, when it comes to my humble person or his employees, at any rate..."

Pierre didn't comment on the last statement, but he could indeed imagine that Edo's brother had precise ideas about spending money that were not necessarily compatible with Edo's.

Edo now beamed with satisfaction. "Yesterday I made sure that I could rent several rooms in the best albergo here in Venice. It's called the Albergo Leon Blanco. In fact it's an old palace in the Byzantine style that belonged to a noble family, but they have moved to a newer and bigger palazzo and now it serves as a guesthouse for noble and especially wealthy guests."

In the meantime Armand had appeared, looking less lively than usual. Eagerly he snapped up the last bit of the conversation and whistled. "A guesthouse in a palace, I like this! But let me guess, Edo, we'll end up leaving this city as paupers?"

Pierre put on a hypocritical face. "It's all for a good cause, we're here on a sacred quest and if this means spending my grandfather's well-guarded treasures, we'll just have to sacrifice them!"

Edo laughed. "Indeed, it's ludicrously expensive, but Pierre can afford it, don't forget, we're his bankers, and we should know! And didn't we discuss that you two must look like well-to-do gentlemen, eager to spend money in order to mix quickly with the nobility here?"

Armand breathed in the fresh air and cried, "All right, I'm ready now to face the gondola. Edo what about you?"

"I'm with you, let's face the inevitable!"

Pierre was amazed how practical it was to live in a lagoon. In front of every house brightly painted poles had been driven deep into the water, serving as moorings for the boats and elegant gondolas that replaced horses and coaches. From the gondola they entered directly into a spacious hall, which was surprisingly sparsely furnished and served apparently more as a warehouse than a guesthouse. But what Pierre really liked was that unlike Paris, there were no traffic jams, no muddy streets in winter, no time wasted in waiting.

"Strange setting for a palazzo," Armand commented. "Edo, you've been pulling our leg, the truth is, we're all going to be sleeping in a warehouse!"

Edo laughed. "All palazzi in Venice are built like that! Remember they can't dig any cellars here and as there is frequently *aqua alta* during the winter season, this floor must be evacuated quickly.

"What is *aqua alta*?"

"In winter the winds often push the high tide back into the lagoon and all of Venice is flooded. It happens so frequently that people have learned to live with it."

They followed the servants upstairs and now they entered a different world indeed: opulent decor, high ceilings with tall windows, a house fit for a noble family and noble guests. Later when Jean was overseeing the unpacking of their belongings, Pierre and Armand stretched out on the luxurious bedstead and Armand sighed from the bottom of his soul, "I have been dreaming of this since I stepped on that swaying nutshell that passes for a sailing boat here. Give me a few hours of sleep and I shall be ready to conquer Venice!"

"The female half, I guess?"

127

"Of course," Armand said, his voice already drowsy. "I leave the rest to you."

"Oh thank you so much, that's what real friends are for!"

Armand answered Pierre only with a sleepy giggle followed almost immediately by the noise of satisfied snoring. Pierre tweaked his friend's nose – sometimes it helped. But today the snoring only stopped for a second and then resumed even more loudly as if his friend were mocking him.

Pierre lay on his bed, unable to find sleep. He still felt this strange feeling of being excited, almost elation. This can't be the grappa any more, he mused, it must be the effect Venice is having on me. Something will happen here to me, I can feel it!

The Louvre And Beyond

Cardinal Richelieu came out of the room where a private council with His Majesty, King Louis XIII of France, had just taken place in the royal palace of the Louvre. He was still in deep discussion with the finance minister, an obstinate donkey if ever he had met one. Richelieu had suffered a humiliating defeat when he had pleaded to open the chests of the treasury to invest in new warships, a defeat that was as unusual as it was deeply vexing.

But today the King had taken the side of his finance minister and there would be no additional warships built. Spain was in decline, England on the brink of a civil war and who – being of sound mind – cared about the insignificant Dutch, a nation with a strange language nobody could understand? Richelieu tried his best to convince his King that the English weakness was an opportunity not to be missed, but it was in vain, His Majesty had remained obstinate, like a mule.

We're being governed by a donkey and mule, Richelieu fumed inwardly, *maybe I should be running a farm!* But none of these treacherous thoughts were visible on his face – being an accomplished courtier, the Cardinal would never show his cards.

Later his carriage sped through Paris, traffic jams or delays unknown to the Cardinal. A cavalcade of private musketeers rode in front warning unsuspecting passers-by to get out of the way: "Make way for His Eminence, the most noble Duke, Cardinal Richelieu, by appointment of his most gracious Majesty the King, Prime Minister of the kingdom of France!" Richelieu was aware that pride was considered a major sin for a son of the Church but no human being could listen to those cries, watch the musketeers in their uniforms adorned with his ducal coat of arms speeding ahead of his coach with blazing torches that lit their way in the dark winter afternoon and not feel proud.

Back in his study the Cardinal sank into his favourite armchair. Never would he tire of touching the jewelled bible or the golden candelabra, nor the delicate Chinese porcelain cup that stood there, ready with the steaming herbal brew that seemed to be the only beverage that could calm his stomach and soothe his pain, a pain which lingered in every corner of his body like a fierce caged animal, just waiting to break out again. His glance swept over the piles of documents that lay there waiting for him and he sighed. He now regretted that he had ever asked for the council to be scheduled. He'd have spent his time more efficiently working in his office.

Richelieu sifted listlessly through the piles of documents, trying to sort them by importance when his glance fell on a letter awaiting signature, addressed to his colleague, the Patriarch Archbishop of Venice. The Cardinal started to read the first lines and couldn't believe his eyes! He seized the silver bell that stood on his table and rang impatiently. Almost immediately his secretary arrived, slightly alarmed as he had – of course – noticed the angry tone of the ringing.

"Your Eminence rang?" he asked, slightly out of breath.

"Of course, I did!" answered an irate Cardinal. "Did you think that I was playing with the bell?" The question was of course rhetorical; the Cardinal didn't expect any answer. "You wrote this?" Another rhetorical question.

The secretary gulped and nodded. Feverishly his mind went through all the various terrible mistakes he might have committed – the Cardinal would spot them all, from wrong titles to faults in his Latin spelling or grammar. The Archbishop of Venice was one of the revered Patriarchs of the Catholic Church – should he have been addressed differently compared to an ordinary cardinal?

"What did I ask you to write?" asked the Cardinal, his fingers drumming on the desk.

"Your Eminence told me to write to His Eminence, the Patriarch of Venice, to make sure that Pierre de Beauvoir and Armand de Saint Paul would be arrested on their arrival in Venice and that Your Eminence would offer to reward him appropriately."

The Cardinal looked at him as in pain, but didn't react. Encouraged that no tirade was being unleashed on him, the secretary proudly added: "I even added your last remark, that their disappearance would please Your Eminence!"

The Cardinal closed his eyes in pain, then opened them again and looked unbelievingly at the young monk. Was it really possible that people could walk, talk, write fluent French and the elegant Latin of the Church – and yet be utterly brainless? He'd need to find a new secretary, for certain. This specimen would sooner or later cause major diplomatic havoc. The Cardinal hated those changes, as training a new secretary could take weeks and months... He sighed and decided to concentrate on the work that lay ahead of him.

"What I say and what we put into writing are, of course, two different issues and you should know this by now," he admonished the secretary. "I will now dictate the letter to my colleague in Venice and I expect the letter to be ready tonight, as Brother Fabrizio is ready to leave for Venice and he wants to depart as soon as possible!"

The secretary checked his quill and dipped it into the ink, just in time, as the Cardinal had already started to dictate the letter to the Patriarch of Venice.

130

"To His Eminence, blah, blah, my brother in Christ, blah, blah... make sure that we mention *all* of his titles, the Patriarch of Venice remains the Patriarch of some strange and long forgotten dioceses in the Mediterranean, but he jealously keeps those titles, so we had better mention them!" The Cardinal sipped at his cup before he continued. "Dearest Brother in Christ! Now add all of the formalities with our wishes for his wellbeing etc." The Cardinal waited until his secretary had scribbled down his remarks. "It has been brought to our attention that two imposters are intending to visit the city of Venice, assuming different identities but most probably pretending to be the most honourable Marquis de Beauvoir and his friend, Armand de Saint Paul... Now you add the detailed description of the two, is this clear?"

The secretary nodded diligently. "Yes, Your Eminence!"

The Cardinal continued. "It is our aim to protect our well beloved cousin, the true Marquis de Beauvoir, from those imposters and we ask you, dear Brother in Christ, to spare no effort in supporting us in this quest. Please accept this small gift from my messenger as a token of my devoted obligation to Your Eminence." The Cardinal paused. "Now you now add the usual flowery greetings and blessings, please use our most formal and elegant Latin, don't forget the Patriarch is one the highest members of our Church, only His Holiness, the Pope, is of higher rank."

The secretary bowed reverently and hurried out of the study, knowing that several hours of hard work were waiting for him; nothing else but a letter written on the most expensive vellum in his most beautiful script and without a single error would be expected from him.

The Cardinal watched his secretary disappear, then he took the first letter and walked to the fireplace where he burned it. He watched the flames devour the treacherous letter greedily and only when the last words had disappeared did he step aside. "I can't be careful enough," he whispered to himself. "If the Marquis de Saint Paul were to have seen the first draft, I'd be a dead man. No army of this world could protect me when it comes to taking revenge for his youngest son. Even the latest version is risky enough, the Marquis would smell danger immediately!"

The Cardinal stood near the marble fireplace and his hand caressed his coat of arms that crowned the mantelpiece. He cherished the heat that seemed to spread through his body like an invigorating potion. Oh, dear Lord, why am I surrounded by idiots? he pondered. Why do I seem to be the only person blessed with a mind that can analyse properly and draw the right conclusions?

Suddenly he seemed to hear a voice answering. "Because, my Son, I wanted you to be unique, you were destined to become the greatest prime minister France has ever seen!"

131

The Cardinal looked suspiciously around him, but as expected, nobody else was inside the room. He walked back to his armchair; lately he had heard the voice on several occasions. Either he had been blessed by the Lord or he'd need to be more careful with his herbal potion... He fought for several minutes, but then his hand stretched out as if it had acquired a will of its own and greedily the Cardinal swallowed the by now tepid liquid that would help to bring him sleep and keep his pain at bay.

Before Brother Fabrizio was dispatched to Italy the next morning, Cardinal Richelieu met him for a private audience in his study. Brother Fabrizio was a man of average height with a nondescript face. He possessed hair the colour of a mole, his eyes were brown, but not the brilliant brown that could melt female hearts; slightly short-sighted, they lacked the lustre that would generate any interest. In short, Brother Fabrizio was the ideal agent and messenger; nobody ever remembered having seen him, and he seemed to melt into any given background, never to be remarked upon. The Cardinal gave him some instructions regarding the message he was to deliver, for the eyes of the Patriarch of Venice only together with the written message and a precious jewelled cross.

The Brother only nodded. He had worked often enough for the Cardinal to have stopped wondering about the strange content of messages he was to deliver. He received a bag of coins to ensure a rapid journey from the Cardinal's secret reserve and after the Cardinal had blessed him, Brother Fabrizio kissed the Cardinal's ring of office and was gone, as noiselessly and unobtrusively as he had entered the room before.

Reims **And Beyond**

François de Toucy watched the two highwaymen galloping at full speed towards him. If he was nervous he didn't show it. Calmly he squinted to see if there were any additional shadows coming up behind; knowing the Cardinal, François was certain that he wouldn't take any chances and even more villains must surely be waiting in hiding to join the ambush. Apparently they were still invisible, as the two horsemen speeding towards them were alone so far.

"Deterrence often works wonders," he said more to himself than to his groom and raised his arm to shoot into the air. The reaction was indeed immediate, but different to what François had expected in his wildest imagination.

He heard a loud shriek and then a voice screamed at him, "Lower your weapon immediately, you bloody idiot!"

The voice made his flesh creep like no villain's could have done. The voice was not only familiar, it was of the wrong gender, the voice of a girl. François made a sign to his groom to stop all hostile action. The groom answered with a bewildered glance, as he too had noticed that the highwayman had answered in a surprisingly high voice.

Only minutes later, the two horsemen had joined them, wearing breeches and greasy and slightly worn leather waistcoats, their heads covered by large hats. François, however, had no problems recognizing his cousin Marie behind this masquerade. Even in a man's disguise she still looked beautiful. The second horseman looked like a young boy, but on closer inspection showed a great likeness to Marie's maid.

"What a pleasure and coincidence," he drawled, "to meet my beloved cousin out here in the wilderness!"

"No coincidence at all," Marie answered, "as you must surely know!"

"You'll certainly not be under any illusion at all that I'll finish our meeting here, we'll turn right back and you, like a good girl, will accompany me back to Reims, to your parents and you'll have time enough to invent a credible story for your mother. She'll be raving mad by now!"

Marie smiled, but her smile did not comfort François. Immediately he sensed that trouble was brewing, big trouble.

"My dearest François, there can be no question of returning to Reims. I waited deliberately for our cosy meeting until dusk; as you may have remarked, you with your supreme intelligence, it'll be dark soon. As the sky is overcast there won't even be any moonlight to guide us and it would be far

133

too dangerous to stay on the road, and anyhow the gates will be closed and we won't be able to enter the city before sunrise."

François had the impression that he had been punched in the stomach; Marie's logic was chillingly obvious.

"Therefore you have no option but to ride with me to the next auberge, dearest cousin, and stay there before we can ride any further!"

François pressed his lips tightly together. From his expression it was obvious a thunderstorm was brewing. This expression was well known by his subalterns and normally a single stern look from his blazing eyes was enough to make them shit their breeches with fear. But apparently Marie was made of sterner stuff, she didn't budge. Restraining himself hard, he managed to answer, "We shall *not* ride on together, Marie! If necessary, I'll ride tomorrow back to Reims with you, but don't – not even for a second – believe that I'll let you accompany me to Venice!" he barked.

But if he had hoped for a maidenly reaction of submission or to intimidate Marie, he was entirely wrong. Marie rode her horse alongside so that the servants couldn't overhear their discussion. Her eyes blazed back at him and in chilling tones she replied, "François, you're totally mistaken; you have no choice. Either you let me accompany you to Venice – or we'll indeed go back to Reims. But I swear by the virgin Marie, my namesake, that once I'm back home I'll tell my parents that we stayed together tonight and that you must marry me. Mother will be delighted, she somehow doesn't believe any more in Pierre turning up and although I personally think that you're a bit pompous and conceited I imagine my parents would love the idea of finally seeing me married off to a suitable bridegroom! You don't look too bad either, everybody will think I've made a good catch."

François felt as if someone had just knocked him off his feet. "You wouldn't do that!" he croaked, more than he cried. "In any case, it would be easy to prove that you're still a virgin!" he added triumphantly, trying to find a last resort in a situation that seemed as unreal as it was nightmarish.

"Are you so sure?" Marie answered in her sweetest voice. "Maybe your friend Pierre has not behaved in so saintly a manner after all...?" Suddenly she changed her tactics and like a miserable little girl she added in a small voice, "François, I'm sorry to put you in such a sordid situation. But believe me, I have no choice. I know and I feel that Pierre is in trouble and I'm on the verge of going mad. I simply cannot stay in Reims, sitting there and doing nothing. Please, let us find an auberge for tonight and sleep on it. I promise, I won't be a nuisance!"

François looked at her face and before he could continue to argue he saw two large tears slowly rolling down her cheeks. He knew when he was beaten. He turned to his groom who was trying his best to keep an impassive face and barked, "Don't smirk at me or you'll regret it. We'll ride on – and not a word that our companions are not real men, you understand me?"

"Yes, my lord, but may I make a suggestion?"

"You may!"

"I suggest rubbing a bit of dirt onto the ladies' faces, they look too clean to pass as real men…"

"That's an excellent idea!"

François dismounted from his horse and with glee he rubbed some dirt into the faces of Marie and her maid. But Marie didn't shy away as he had secretly hoped, she didn't seem to mind.

Now a group of four, they continued on their way together, while François continued to observe the surrounding fields in order to look out for any villains out on a late foray. At the same time his brain was working feverishly: how could he get rid of Marie without creating a major scandal? Marie was undoubtedly a beauty, but François had no inclination to become married to a female tiger in disguise! François wanted a home where peace would reign – just the thought of being wedded to Marie sent waves of panic through his body.

Night started to fall, and quickly the leaden sky turned almost black until they could barely see the road ahead. It was therefore with considerable relief that they detected a faint glimmer of light ahead. As they rode on they spotted the silhouette of a house and stables and soon they were reassured that they had indeed reached the auberge that had been recommended warmly to François by the musketeers who had been on guard at the city gates.

Freezing and tired they entered the taproom where they were greeted at once by a stout innkeeper who was delighted to take in four more surprise guests at this late hour. Immediately the landlord assessed that François must be of noble rank and bowed until he almost touched the floor.

"What may I do for your lordship?" he asked, rubbing his hands in delight.

"We need rooms for tonight, would you have anything suitable?"

The innkeeper beamed at his noble guests. "Of course, my lords, with the greatest pleasure. I can offer you a large room, suitable for the four of you, it's clean but maybe a bit simple for your refined taste. I could speak with some other guests to see if they wish to move and offer you two rooms, one for my lord and your noble companion", he bowed elegantly towards Marie, "and one for the grooms. I think this can be arranged as the other guests are of lesser rank than your lordship and will understand my request."

Hastily François intervened. "The room for the four of us will be absolutely fine, anyhow it's just for one night. If you could bring us a decent dinner and a tankard of ale, I'd be grateful enough."

While Francois's groom, accompanied by Marie's maid acting as second groom, went to the stables to make sure that their horses would be taken good care of, Marie and François found themselves alone in the room that the innkeeper had reserved for them. He had left them, apologizing profusely for the simple furniture but pointed out proudly that the two beds were larger than the average to be found in inns of lesser reputation, and they would find it very comfortable to sleep at night.

"We even offer two chamber pots," and he pointed to the objects of his pride. "As your lordships can see, we provide every amenity imaginable. I'll ask the servants immediately to bring you a carpet, you'll see the room can be made very agreeable!"

Marie looked at François who had watched the innkeeper waddle out of the room heading back to the kitchen in order to supervise the dinner preparations for his noble guests and started to giggle.

"Every amenity imaginable," she repeated, smiling broadly.

If François had hoped that the shabby furniture and the knowledge of having to share her room with him and her bed with her maid would put an immediate damper on Marie's travelling plans, he was to be disappointed.

"You won't see anything better, indeed, probably much worse, for the next weeks if you insist on coming with me," he said in a tone he hoped would discourage her. But his efforts were in vain.

"Oh I couldn't care less! I'm just happy that I had my hair cut, it will be so much easier for Antoinette to get rid of the lice if the hair is shorter." She took off her hat and with a shock he realized that Marie had cut her wonderful hair according to the fashion of a young gentleman, barely shoulder length.

"I presume Antoinette is the unlucky maid you dragged along?" François couldn't help asking.

Marie giggled again. "She's definitely *not* unhappy, so far she's enjoyed every minute of our adventure. She's always dreamed of getting out of Reims and seeing the world, and she would have hated me if I had left her behind!"

François gave up. It seemed useless to try to convince Marie that this was not an adventure; he knew far too well that his mission was dangerous enough and didn't even want to think what could happen to them if he had to drag two inexperienced girls along. But Marie didn't seem to care. Frustrated, François decided to concentrate on the next task first: order a decent dinner. He couldn't fight with his stomach and a stubborn girl simultaneously.

136

The innkeeper had done his best to please his guests and the rabbit stewed in his homemade beer would have pleased the palate of a king. After a copious helping of Madame's compote with cream, followed by cheese, François felt fortified enough to contemplate further action to get rid of his unwanted companions – at least this should have been the plan. Maybe it was the meal, or the excellent brandy served afterwards but as soon as François's head touched his pillow he sank into a deep slumber.

It was Marie who couldn't find sleep for a considerable time. The decision to leave home had not been an easy one at all. She loved her parents dearly despite their recent disagreements and daily petty quarrels. Marie knew perfectly well that they must be mad with anxiety and anger by now. She felt extremely guilty. It was difficult to forget her fear of being caught at the last minute, of sneaking through the well-guarded city gates: were people so blind as not to recognize a girl in disguise? Once they had been on the road, doubt had set in: had she made the right decision? Had they chosen the right direction? She had been almost desperate until she had spotted her cousin, as the sky had become darker and darker and she had had no idea what to do if she missed meeting up with him. But Marie was sure of one thing: never would she yield, as Pierre needed help badly; there was no doubt, come what may, she would go to Venice!

The next morning Marie and François continued their argument. When François, his face red with anger, threatened to leave her behind and ride away alone with his groom, Marie answered, "Just try and you'll see what I'll do!"

Fuming with rage he turned to the stables, ready to give orders to pack his belongings when he heard a piercing scream. He turned back and saw Marie standing in the courtyard, screaming like a pig ready for slaughter. Immediately the servants of the auberge streamed into the courtyard from all directions. The cook held his ladle like a weapon, ready to defend himself against unknown attackers. Finally the landlord appeared, panting, as he must have run to see what was causing such a stir.

François turned back, and aware of the curious glances of the servants he tried to mollify the irate landlord who addressed him. "What's going on, my lord, this is an honourable guest house, may I know what is the cause of this turmoil?"

François seized the landlord's arm and manoeuvred him into a corner where he could speak confidentially. "My travelling companion is not feeling exceedingly well," he whispered and made a telling gesture towards his head."Nothing serious, a bit effeminate if you ask me, this is why I didn't want to share the bedroom alone with him… If you understand what I mean!"

A very cold glance met him, and the innkeeper quickly crossed himself. Of course he had heard about such people, didn't the priest warn them every Sunday that the devil was lurking everywhere in disguise? "My lord, you must understand that an establishment like mine cannot tolerate such people under its roof, may I invite you to settle your account and leave with your... travelling companion... as fast as possible?"

"Running the gauntlet must be fun compared to this," François thought furiously while he watched his groom and Marie's maid packing their belongings. The account was settled and like a group of lepers they took to the road, southbound. If Marie was satisfied with the effect of her little scene, at least she possessed the decency not to show it.

François had managed at least to wriggle one concession from Marie; she promised to write regularly to her parents to let them know that she was well and was under the protection of a relative during her travels. Under these humiliating circumstances a ceasefire (or perhaps indeed a straightforward capitulation on François's part) was established between Marie and her cousin. As they were in agreement that no time should be lost, the small group rode south as fast as possible, covering impressive distances daily.

If Marie or her maid were suffering under the strain, at least they were too proud to admit it openly and didn't complain. François exchanged knowing glances with his groom when they noticed Marie and her maid walking with a wide gait like sailors after the first day of riding; their bottoms must have been on fire. But François – with dismay – also couldn't help but notice that his groom and Marie's maid had become a team, working closely together, far too closely for his liking.

Their daily routine barely changed during their travels. They mounted their horses as soon as daylight permitted and sank into a deep slumber after a hasty dinner at nightfall. Although François had decided not to tell Marie about the Cardinal's message she skilfully managed to extract the details out of him. Immediately François could have kicked himself for having opened his mouth but Marie took it with surprising calm. "You see, I was right that Pierre is in danger, I simply knew it, it was no use lying to me!"

As they approached the city of Avignon, still an important stronghold of the French crown, François decided to avoid any risk of running into any old mates or musketeers that he might know from Paris and to stay in an auberge well hidden in a forlorn place, only surrounded by silvery olive groves that stretched to the horizon and beyond. The ancient stone building looked as if had been built by the Romans – and then almost forgotten by mankind as no other buildings could be seen for miles to come.

It was already late afternoon and they decided to settle here overnight, as François was quite pleased at their progress. He calculated that they could reach Venice by late January, if all went smoothly; it was unlikely that

Richelieu's messengers would be much faster. In view of the secrecy of the mission, François was convinced that the Cardinal would rely on his network of travelling monks and avoid sending any official messenger.

Their routine now established, they agreed with the landlord that they would share a room between the four of them and sank down tired on their beds – they had seen better, but it would have been useless to complain. When dinner was ready they pulled themselves together and walked to the taproom where rough wooden chairs and tables were waiting with a steaming bowl of broth for them.

"I feel born again!" François sighed happily, and wiped his blonde beard clean after he had emptied the bowl filled to the brim with a surprisingly delicious soup. There could be no doubt that the landlord was particularly thrifty (rarely had they seen such a collection of miserable furniture and thin blankets) but apparently his wife – who reigned in the kitchen – wouldn't accept any false economies when it came to her side of the business.

"So do I!" agreed Marie and ignored the loud belching from their neighbours' table. The days when she been the sheltered daughter of a wealthy noble family must have seemed long ago. They savoured the fresh bread served with tiny black olives and plenty of strong red wine, accompanied as usual by a local cheese. Dinner was finished, night had fallen and they were ready to go to bed.

Maybe it was the effect of the strong wine, but only one or two hours later Marie woke up with an urgent need. Not wanting to use the chamber pot in the presence of her cousin and his groom, she decided to go the lavatories that were located most probably close to the stables. During her journey Marie had discovered that most inns regarded their guests as welcome contributors to their dung heaps, and the lavatories seemed to be a mere extension of the latter. She therefore tried to ignore her bodily weakness but she couldn't get to sleep, so finally she gave in and woke up her maid, keeping in mind her cousin's stern warnings never to go alone and never to go unarmed.

Putting on their overcoats they had to pass through the taproom that was surprisingly busy. It only needed a short look to realize that the night visitors were the kind of guests that probably avoided daylight, and certainly any contact with the authorities. Marie kept her eyes down; even if she was dressed and had learned to walk like a young gentleman, she didn't want to be drawn into any conversation – or worse – into a game of dice or cards .

Having successfully navigated around those pitfalls the two girls sneaked out of the main building, crossed the poorly lit courtyard and now Antoinette took the lead. "How do you know the way?" Marie asked curiously.

139

"It's not too difficult," Antoinette answered. "Michel showed me the way earlier," she giggled. "Basically all one needs to do is to follow the smell of the dung heap."

Marie didn't comment that her maid seemed to have become very close to her cousin's groom, as it was probably inevitable under the circumstances.

They stepped into the stable and Antoinette led Marie straight to the lavatories, a room that was composed of a simple brick wall that separated the stables from a rough wooden bench with large openings in it from the rest of the stables. A small, stinking gutter glistened in the dark and led directly from the lavatories to the dung heap.

Marie tried to ignore the nauseating stench and entered the lavatory with long strides, eager to get down her breeches and alleviate her most urgent need. But as soon as she had entered the small room she stopped, as the room was occupied by two men, most probably belonging to the group they had seen before in the taproom.

One of the men had his breeches hanging down to his knees and was peeing noisily into the gutter while his mate sat on the bench busy emptying his bowels, or at least the noise and stench in the small room could only lead to that conclusion. In a friendly manner they greeted the newcomers. "Come on in lads, we've got enough space for the two of you!"

Marie stood frozen with shock and it was Antoinette after a long pause who answered, "This is very kind of you, but my master is from a noble household, he's used to having his private seat, he'll wait until you've finished!" She had tried to speak with her deepest voice and as convincingly as possible, but the effect was not what she had hoped for.

The man who had been urinating turned round abruptly and scrutinized the two newcomers from head to toe while he calmly shook off the last drips before storing his private parts back into his breeches. Marie tried to keep her glance steady but inside she was panicking – how stupid not to have used the chamber pot!

The man spat to show his contempt for young pampered gentlemen who judged themselves to be above common folks but didn't bother to answer. He now addressed his mate. "Finished shitting? His noble lordship wants to have a place of his own for his tender arse! Make sure you keep it warm for him."

Now it was time for his mate on the bench to spit in order to show his contempt for the spoilt brats. After a last orgy of noisy farting he slowly pulled his breeches up and the men left the small enclosure. Desperately Marie hurried to the bench – she was almost bursting!

"This is the part I'll never get used to!" she confided to Antoinette as she fastened her breeches and prepared to go back to the room they shared with François and his groom. Antoinette declined to comment. The lavatories in the servants' quarters back in Reims weren't any better...

They stepped out into the courtyard and although it still held the stinging odour of the dung heap, the fresh air seemed to smell sweet compared to the disgusting stench inside the lavatories. They were just about to return to the main building when Marie detected the movement of several persons inside the courtyard. One of them held a torch and in the flickering light she could see his scarred face with an unkempt beard and a mouth with gaping holes where there should have been a row of gleaming teeth.

"Hey, there are the two sissies who didn't want to lower their breeches as long as us normal folks were close, I think we should teach 'em good manners!" She suddenly heard a voice in the background, which sounded uncomfortably familiar. Marie's stomach contracted. She didn't like this opening line and could sense the group's hostility.

"Oh, our noble guests have lost their voice!" jeered the man.

The group moved menacingly closer. "Let's have a look and see if these cowards have any cocks at all!" continued the malicious voice. "I bet there's nothing at all between their legs!"

"Just some shit!" another voice interjected, to the general delight of the others.

Marie saw them moving closer and closer. "I must be valiant now," she spoke to herself and at the top of her voice she cried back, "If you want to pick a fight, just come on and we'll show you that gentlemen know how to fight!"

As she was speaking she drew her rapier and held it in the defensive position that Pierre had shown her before. Antoinette saw the movement and as rapidly as she could manage she tried to follow Marie, but her movements were clumsy, betraying the fact that she had never fought with a heavy sword in her life. Marie continued to shout as loudly as possible, praying fervently that François might hear her. But to no avail, the small crowd of men drew closer, and she could already see the excitement in the eyes of the men. Like bloodhounds following a scent, she thought.

Marie was close to despair.

141

A Sad Dinner

Dinner was being served in the comfortable town house of the Montjoie family, opulent and of exquisite quality as usual. But the two persons sitting at the table had scarcely any regard or interest at all for any of the wonderful dishes the cook had prepared in her desperate attempt to cheer up her master and mistress.

Generous candlelight, silver candelabra, chased silver bowls and polished trays, none of this splendour could lighten the depressed mood that reigned at table. The fact that the two servants serving the dishes and later taking away the almost untouched plates kept sighing melancholically to express their sympathy didn't really help to improve the atmosphere. A cloud of sadness had settled on the noble house since Marie had left it.

Refusing to taste even the smallest morsel of one of the tempting desserts, Marie's mother dismissed the servants. Finally she was alone with her husband and they could talk openly. Her husband looked at his wife; she seemed to have aged several years in a matter of days, but he was under no illusions, so had he. He cleared his throat. "Let's go into the library, I think I could do with a glass of cognac." His wife nodded and rose silently from the table.

Each of them had their favourite armchair in the library. Like so many old couples they had developed set habits and would rarely break them. Silently Marie's mother walked towards her chair and sat down while her husband filled two glasses with the cognac that the diligent butler had already put out on the low table close to the fireplace. It was a cosy room and the fire gave off an agreeable warmth, and yet Marie's mother rubbed her hands as if they were ice-cold.

She accepted the glass although it was highly unusual for a gentlewoman to drink such strong liquor but she knew that her husband meant well and dutifully she took a sip of the strong amber-coloured liquid. *Almost the colour of my daughter's eyes*, she couldn't help thinking, and tears filled her own eyes.

To her surprise her husband didn't choose his usual chair opposite hers. He settled on a less comfortable chair that stood close enough so that he could take her hands in his. She looked into his eyes where she read sorrow, but also love and understanding. I'll never understand what I did to merit finding a husband like him, she thought. Aloud she chided him gently. "You should be really upset with me, you should be scolding me! There is no question that Marie's disappearance is entirely my fault, I was far too obstinate in pursuing my plans for a marriage that must have appeared repulsive to her. I curse my terrible temper, and the worst of it is, she has inherited it, for sure!" and she almost sobbed the last words.

"Stop blaming yourself, *ma chérie*, I must blame myself, I was far too soft with Marie!" her husband replied, while he continued to rub her hands mechanically. "If you were too rash, I was far too lenient with her, I truly must blame myself!"

"She's gone!" Now Marie's mother couldn't hold back her tears anymore, "my little one is gone!" she wailed. "I don't know how to face each day, how could she ever do something like this to us?"

Her husband continued rubbing her hands. He didn't know what to say or do, any reply that came into his head seemed either stupid or utterly inadequate.

Wrapped in their grief they almost failed to notice the faint knocking on the door. But the knocking was repeated, becoming insistent now. Angrily Marie's father rose from his chair and shouted, "Come in!"

The butler almost fell into the room, such was the haste of his entrance. "I have a message for you, my lord!" he shouted jubilantly, "from your lordship's daughter!" The last words were uttered in triumph.

Forgetting all decorum and restraint, Marie's father grabbed the letter, tore it open and started to read while his wife jumped up as if she had been stung by a wasp.

"What does it say? Is she well, my little darling?" and she grabbed her husband's arm and shook it violently.

Marie's father didn't know if he should be annoyed or laugh at his wife, but he was a prey himself to a mix of emotions he had rarely experienced in his life before: relief, as if a millstone had been removed from his soul, vexation and fury at his daughter's impossible behaviour, and yet a feeling that he could embrace the world and wanted to fall on his knees and praise the Lord. Suddenly he realized that the butler was still standing close to him, obviously burning with curiosity to hear more news.

"She's fine and sends her regards!" Marie's father managed to say before he grabbed the glass of cognac like a pillar of support and downed the liquid in one go. It burned his throat but the fire spread through his body and with renewed energy he embraced his wife and cried to the butler, "You may go now, fetch wine tonight for all the servants, tell them to drink to my daughter's health!"

"What has she really written?" insisted Marie's mother after the butler had left the room. Her cheeks flamed red – it was difficult to tell if this was the effect of her excitement or of the glass of cognac that she had just emptied, following her husband's example.

"Marie apologizes that she has caused us great grief."

143

His wife's colouring deepened to scarlet, as close to hysterics she cried, "There can be no question of granting any apology, we've been in hell, she nearly killed me!"

But she was stopped by her husband, who continued without paying attention to her outburst. "Marie's on her way to Venice to rejoin Pierre, accompanied by her maid…"

"I'll kill Antoinette, the moment she crosses my threshold, but before that I'll have her whipped! How could she ever consent to this crazy adventure?" Marie's mother shrieked and started to wring her hands.

"*Chérie*, please calm down! It was certainly the wrong thing to do and she should have confided her stupid plan to us, but let's be honest: Marie would have left us anyhow, you just mentioned five minutes ago that she's as stubborn as you must have been when you were young. Under these circumstances it's much better that her maid should travel together with Marie!"

Marie's mother took the hint and swallowed hard.

"And…" her husband continued.

"And what? Come on! It's not a game, what else does she write?"

"She met her cousin, François de Toucy, shortly after leaving Reims and he's promised to protect her during the journey!" he added, unable to hide his satisfaction.

Marie's mother fell into her armchair, bowled over by this news.

"May the Lord be blessed! We're saved!" she cried. "There's no doubt about it, he'll have to marry her!"

Her husband looked at her; they didn't need to talk, their glances said it all.

"Yes, tomorrow I'll go to the cathedral and offer a donation, the Lord has truly answered our prayers."

"The Lord may have done His work, but that doesn't dispense us from doing ours," Marie's mother commented after a short pause and a smile played on her lips.

"What do you mean? We should follow her? God alone knows where she is at this moment!"

"My dearest husband, I mean that I feel an urgent need to go and travel to meet my old friend, François's mother…"

144

"Not willing to leave anything to chance now, are you?" Her husband looked at her with admiration. "You never give up!"

"I may have lost some battles in my life, but I'm willing to win this war!" she declared. The letter and the cognac had put her in an exuberant mood, and she suddenly felt that no obstacle would ever be able to stop her. An evening that had started like a funeral had suddenly become full of hope!

Suddenly they heard another knock at the door. "Didn't you dismiss the butler?" Marie's mother stated, rather than asked.

"Of course, I did!" Her husband looked puzzled.

The knocking was repeated, so he cried 'Come in!"

The door opened and Marie's father found himself shoved aside gently by the gigantic person who entered the library.

"Charles!" squeaked Marie's mother. "What a pleasant surprise, did you bring Céline along?"

Charles grinned while executing a surprisingly elegant bow to greet his host and hostess.

"I didn't! She sends her kindest regards but she's tied up with the baby tonight." His deep voice seemed to make the candelabra dance on their feet – he could barely hide his pride at the recent addition to his family. "In fact she sends her love to you and Marie and hopes to see you soon, we intend to rent an estate close to Reims and wait for Pierre's return before we travel back to England. I apologize for disturbing you so late, but I need to speak with your husband as a property has been offered to me and I would like to have his advice before I visit it tomorrow morning."

Charles didn't look it, but he was a keen observer with quick wits, and not only had he sensed the strange mood in the library and the household when he had entered, he also noticed the strange reaction from Marie's mother as soon as Marie had been mentioned and her nervous twitching as soon as Pierre's name was uttered. *Something fishy is going on here!* he thought, while accepting his host's invitation to settle down in an armchair close to the fireplace. Charles looked suspiciously at the elegant piece of furniture offered as a seat to him before daring to sit on it. The armchair only sighed in despair but it held, and Charles stretched out his long legs, happy to be sitting comfortably despite his reservations.

"Where's Marie, by the way?" he asked casually.

Maybe it was his comforting deep voice or his broad chest but it didn't take long for Marie's mother to confess to him the details of Marie's adventure. Although he personally judged Marie's behaviour to be quite

145

scandalous, he hid his true feelings behind his usual mask of politeness, a social skill perfected over considerable time, but which he found most useful on occasion. Still wondering secretly how a gentlewoman could forget her manners to the point of eloping with a distant cousin, he decided to put this riddle to his wife. Céline would probably be able to understand – and shed some light on this strange story.

He therefore kept his visit as short as possible without vexing his host and hostess before riding back to the small house Céline owned in Reims where they had settled with their baby, waiting for their move to the small castle he intended to rent in the valleys of the Champagne.

His wife had been waiting for his return for some time and as soon as the servants had left the salon, Charles quickly recounted to her the strange scene and the events he had witnessed in the Montjoie household. He was voicing his displeasure at Marie's elopement but was cut short immediately.

"Oh Charles, don't be so thick!" protested Céline, but as her fingers were busy caressing his curly hair, the reproach was mild enough. "Of course she hasn't eloped! She loves Pierre, and only Pierre, forget all those ridiculous stories! I always thought her mother a bit dim, she thinks that Marie's as ambitious as she probably was when she was young. I could bet Marie's using this poor François to get to Venice, but the poor girl must be desperate indeed if she is forgetting about all conventions!"

Céline paused before coming to a conclusion. "I think I'll call tomorrow on Marie's parents, it's time I asked for some advice about the baby…"

Charles tried to get more information out of his wife, but she only laughed absent-mindedly. Charles gave up. He knew his wife well enough to know he might as well spare himself the effort.

146

Avignon

François de Toucy was sleeping peacefully and deeply, in fact he was dreaming. It was a particularly pleasant dream, as he saw himself standing in the public audience room of the Louvre palace, ready to receive a medal of distinction from the King. His Majesty now rose from his throne to present the shining medal when the dream took a strange turn of events. The King opened his mouth, but François heard a screaming voice instead – the voice of a girl! Annoyed François tried to ignore the disturbance and bent his neck forward in his dream to receive the medal he had been hankering for, but the screaming voice didn't stop. Worse, it became more urgent and more intense – and now even worse: not only did he recognize the voice, he seemed to know the owner of this particular voice very well.

As soon as François realized that it was his cousin Marie who was screaming outside, he woke up. The practise of numerous years of having been assigned to night duties made him jump up, wide awake and ready to think and act instantly. It only took him a few seconds more to kick his sleepy groom into action and to push the window open to see what the hell was going on. As their room gave straight onto the courtyard, François enjoyed a chilling view of their companions being molested by a bunch of ragged-looking scoundrels, about seven as far as he could see. And yet when he addressed his groom, François seemed unruffled.

"It seems that a determined intervention on our part will be needed to rescue our enterprising ladies," he drawled, as he started stowing two loaded pistols into his overcoat. "You stay here at the window and use this if necessary." He pointed to a rifle and handed two parcels to his grooms.

Michel grinned. "Looks as if we'll be having some fun, sir!" he remarked and looked enthusiastically at the parcels.

"Could well be! Use them wisely!"

And with these last obscure words he was gone. Only seconds later Michel heard his swift footsteps on the staircase that led down to the taproom.

Soon the groom could see his master walking with long strides into the poorly lit courtyard. The group of thugs had already seized Marie's maid and although she was fighting like a furious cat, her fate seemed inevitable. Michel's heart beat faster as he saw her frightened face in the flickering light of the torch. François had reached the men, and could see the lust gleaming in their eyes. How often had he witnessed such scenes during his career as a soldier! François had had no illusions about mankind for some time.

Marie had still managed to keep her pursuers at a distance as she was swinging her rapier in circles around her. One of the men held a bleeding arm as he showered curses on her. François couldn't help but be impressed – rarely had he seen a girl handle a sword with such dexterity. But it wasn't difficult to see that it was about time to take things into his capable hands and with the piercing voice of an experienced officer he shouted, "Stop this immediately or I'll have you hanged from the next gibbet!"

Instinctively the men reacted and let Antoinette go, but their leader was made of tougher stuff. Furiously he turned to scrutinize the intruder who dared to oppose him. His furious glare met an impeccably groomed young gentleman, well dressed with gleaming blonde curls falling above his collar. The thug smirked; this looked like an easy fight and promised rich pickings to boot.

"Looking for a fight, are you? I know your type, bullshitting around but wetting your breeches as soon as it gets down to business. I'll give you a good piece of advice: piss off or you'll be the next one to lose your breeches!"

His mates broke into rough laughter. They grabbed Antoinette's arm once again and bent it backwards until Antoinette wailed with pain.

"Stop that, you miserable cowards!" François shouted angrily and drew his sword.

Immediately his opponents responded and stormed forward. François fought with the elegance of an experienced officer and it didn't take him long to put the first enemy out of action. Their leader had by now understood that he had completely misjudged his opponent; quickly he ducked the dangerous sword and lunged forward to grab Marie who had committed the fatal error of lowering her sword while François was fighting. He had almost succeeded in seizing Marie when the sound of an explosion echoed through the courtyard. The thug stopped, swayed and fell down. Michel had seen the sign from his master and used his rifle with deadly precision.

For a moment the men in the courtyard seemed frozen until one of them suddenly howled in fury and in pain. "Kill them! Avenge my brother! Let's skin them alive, the filthy bastards!" and he stormed forward, not even waiting to see if the rest of his gang was going to follow. His rushed action broke the spell, and shouting and cursing they stormed as one man towards François and the two girls who retreated quickly towards the stables. The fast advance of the furious mob made it impossible to use the pistols that François had brought along; all they could do was to raise their rapiers in defence.

But then – once again – something strange happened. A second but much louder explosion echoed through the courtyard, followed by a blinding light and yet more deafening sounds of explosions. The group of villains who had been storming forward in formation stopped in panic, all thoughts of revenge forgotten.

148

"Help us, Lord!" François heard the first cries.

"This must be the workings of the devil, flee!" another thug could be heard.

François took advantage of the general confusion and drew the first of his pistols. The dead man's brother had no chance, and seconds later a bullet hit his chest and he joined his brother – a family reunion that most probably was not going to take place in paradise.

A second shot from the window felled the next thug. Amazed, François noticed that Marie hadn't hesitated to make good use of her rapier and saw her plunging its blade with grim determination into one of the men who had been careless enough to stand in her way. The remaining villains realized that the game was up, and crying for mercy they fell on their knees. The landlord who had watched the scene wringing his hands with trepidation now rushed forward to embrace François in a show of true Gallic exuberance while his servants came out of their hiding places and finally dared to show up in the courtyard turned battlefield.

"Praise all the blessed saints!" the innkeeper cried. "Your lordship has delivered us from a true curse of mankind, a scourge if ever there was one!"

"Delighted to be of service to you!" François grinned. "But I propose that you have them bound, and tomorrow we'll deliver them to the constabulary!"

"We'll bind them well, my lord, don't worry! But I propose to ask the lord of our village to judge them!" the landlord answered. "Our master is a good man and will dispense justice, the constabulary..." He stopped, embarrassed.

"The constabulary might be open to accept some gifts and leave the prison door open?" François finished the sentence instead. The landlord only nodded unhappily.

Immediately his servants rushed forward to obey their master's command. In no time the three men were bundled and dragged into the deepest cellars where they would wait for their fate to be sealed.

François's glance now fell on the wounded man who was lying on the ground, writhing in pain. Marie had inflicted a deadly wound, and François could see the blood seeping out of his bowels. From experience he could tell that it would take the man painful hours to die.

"If you're a true Christian soul, finish him off!" he remarked to Marie. "Look how he's suffering!"

"I can't, but he doesn't deserve any better," Marie commented, still fuming with anger. "This swine had his hands all over my poor Antoinette!" she hissed in a low voice.

François looked at Marie's maid who stood there. Still in shock, she was hiding away from the light of the torches, but François knew that she must be crying silently. It'll take Michel to comfort her, he thought, but I guess he won't mind. Without further comment François stepped forward to the suffering man and with a swift gesture he cut his throat.

If he had expected a maidenly outcry from Marie he was to be disappointed. Respectfully Marie looked at him. "I didn't know that you had such skills," she remarked, trying hard to keep her composure while she saw the blood spilling on the ground as soon as François stepped aside. Her anger had abated and suddenly she had a queer feeling in her stomach.

"My father died when I was quite young and someone had to slaughter the sheep," François commented drily. "You get used to it!"

"I'm not sure I would." Marie turned her face away. She had seen enough violence for one night, and suddenly she felt terribly exhausted. "Let's go upstairs," and she grabbed the arm of her maid, who still seemed to be paralysed by the shock, and they returned to their room.

Upstairs they met a very buoyant Michel who had difficulty remaining modest as Antoinette looked at him with adoring eyes and declared that he was her hero.

"What did you throw down into the courtyard?" Marie asked curiously. "It nearly frightened me to death!"

"Chinese fireworks, my lady," he answered proudly. "My master bought them in Paris, he told me that they would probably come in handy sooner or later!"

"They cost me a fortune," François interjected, laughing. "I'm happy that Michel only needed to use one!"

Marie looked at François who grinned complacently. "Come on, Marie, tell me that I'm a genius!" he challenged her.

"Pffft!" Marie answered. "Real men fight face to face, they don't use tricks!"

"If they're stupid enough to ignore the fact that they're outnumbered, maybe!" François still grinned, sure of himself. He knew his worth.

Strangely enough Marie slept like a log, and no images of villains marred her dreams. And thus they continued their journey to Venice the next day.

"Are you sure you don't want to ride back to Reims?" François teased his cousin.

150

"Of course I'm sure!" Marie replied, after a second's hesitation. "I won't be intimidated by a gang of stupid villains, I know that Pierre needs me! And you know very well that we need to advance fast, there can be no question of returning home!"

François was only too well aware of the truth of her words. He was not easily given to feelings of anxiety but whatever thoughts he had in his mind of what might happen if they arrived in Venice too late to warn Pierre and Armand was something he didn't dare share with Marie. Yes, she was right, they needed to travel fast now! Grimly he spurred his horse on and if Marie wondered about his change of mood, she didn't comment and just concentrated on the task of following her cousin who sped down the road southwards as if the very devil were following him.

Carnival In Venice

Jean lovingly patted the silk doublet that gleamed a rich plum blue. From time to time the candlelight caught the silver threads that had been woven by a master of his trade and made them come alive. Finally, sure that it fitted impeccably on his master's shoulders, Jean stepped aside. Secretly Jean was convinced that his master would outshine any of the gentlemen that would be present at tonight's ball, an event all of Venice was talking about and which would certainly bring together members of every noble family inscribed in the Golden Book.

"Thanks, Jean!" Pierre smiled at his valet while critically scrutinizing his picture in the glass mirror. "I can't help feeling a little conceited, but you have done a marvellous job, it looks simply perfect to me!"

Jean was still glowing with pride at this unexpected compliment when Armand burst into the room, dressed in a striking combination of white and black silk that matched his dark curly hair. His hands played with his mask as he gently chided Pierre."We'll be late because of you, I'm sure you overslept! Jean, you should have dragged your master out of his bed at least half an hour earlier!"

Pierre protested. "It's fashionable to arrive late, nobody is ever on time here! And by the way, I was utterly exhausted. I think we've attended at least ten balls or receptions during the past fortnight, it's killing me! Don't you ever get tired?"

Armand shook his head. "Why should I be tired? I'm simply loving it!" he confessed. "Paris is a mere village compared to Venice, if you ask me, and don't even mention Lausanne." He shuddered. "You remember drab Lausanne?"

"Of course I do, I almost got killed by that crazy Calvinist maniac!"

"Well, nothing Calvinist here in Venice for sure," Armand laughed. "I couldn't imagine a greater contrast, actually!"

"To be honest, I'd love to stay home tonight," Pierre confessed and eyed his latest book longingly. As languages came naturally to him, he was fluent in Italian by now and had started to discover a wealth of local literature – so much more entertaining than the boring books written in the stilted Church Latin that had been his daily staple in the monastery school.

"You're becoming an old bore without ever being young!" Armand frowned at his friend. "Have you ever seen any better carnival balls than these, or any better looking girls? You have it all – and still you complain, like a doddering old grandfather!"

"I don't remember there being many balls at our monastery school," Pierre answered acidly, "but I'm not complaining. I just feel so tired, I think we only came back this morning at eleven o'clock, as your noble lordship insisted on playing cards with the boys after we had left the masked ball!"

"Indeed I did! And didn't I win more than a hundred ducatos? It made my day!"

"The night before you lost more than that…"

"Don't be such a damn bore, you're behaving like Edo's brother, sitting at home and spending his time counting money!" Armand was starting to get upset. Suspiciously he looked at Pierre's open book. "Maybe that's the reason," and he pointed his finger accusingly at the book. "It's probably full of some stupid boring stuff that sends you to sleep!" He took the book in his hand and studied the cover. "'Decamarone' it says, strange title, must be Italian!"

Pierre laughed. "You have no idea, it's really fascinating!"

Armand shrugged. "I'll bet it's just some fancy stories about monks and a bunch of dull holy saints; I had more than enough of those when Brother Hieronymus used to chase us around daily with his damned scriptures."

"It's about real life, a story of young people, each of them telling a story, some funny, some tragic, some about love and some shockingly daring, actually…"

Armand looked at the innocent-looking book with renewed interest. "Now you're talking! Maybe I'll oblige you and have a look at it later when I find some time. But for the time being, let's go – Edo's waiting downstairs and will be freezing to death if you don't shift your arse, Your Grace!"

Pierre made a telling gesture but slipped into the overcoat that Jean held ready. He knew that he had no choice; once Armand had made up his mind, he'd move heaven and earth to get his way. They walked downstairs and found Edo, splendidly dressed in shining silk as well, waiting in front of an open fireplace, trying to warm himself up. Rumour had it that Venice boasted wonderful weather during spring, early summer and autumn but until now winter had been damp, cold and miserable. The dampness seemed to linger everywhere, even inside the rooms and seeping into the clothes and bed sheets.

Edo embraced his friends in the Italian way to greet them. With obvious pleasure he received Armand's compliments on his elegant costume.

"It's really nice, isn't it," Edo beamed, and caressed the soft gleaming fabric.

"I'm not sure if your brother will share this enthusiasm if he ever sets eyes on the bill," Pierre laughed.

"Oh, Giovanni will have a fit, no doubt about that!" Edo answered good-humouredly.

"You don't seem particularly bothered?"

"Why should I? I'll simply explain to him that we urgently needed some formal court outfits to present all of us to the Doge and his government – he can't possibly criticize my diligence in helping you to be presentable!"

"You mean, you'll make him understand that you paid for our clothes as well?"

"Oh, not explicitly of course, but if he reads this into my words, I can't help it, can I?"

Pierre was speechless whereas Armand exploded into peals of laughter. "Edo, never become a banker, you'd be wasting your talents; you should go into the diplomatic service!"

Still grinning, they stepped outside. In front of the albergo a gondola was already moored, ready to bring them to the palazzo, or *Ca'*, as a palatial home was called here in Venice, where one of the highlights of the season was supposed to take place.

"Tonight we've been invited by one of the most influential families, the famous Giustiniani. They're part of what the Venetians call the 'old families', you can't find anyone of more exclusive nobility in all of Europe," Edo explained, visibly proud to have organized invitations for such an exclusive event.

"Besides Pierre's and my family maybe." Armand's tone made it more than obvious that he was slightly offended; nobody was ever allowed to question the superiority of the august de Saint Paul family, even the King of France was a parvenu of questionable background in their eyes. Edo realized his faux-pas quickly enough.

"I was talking about the nobility of lesser degree! Of course you can't compare a French Marquis with a mere Italian count," he added smoothly, hoping that Armand wouldn't know that the list of noble titles held by the Giustiniani was legendary. It seemed to work as Armand looked mollified but Pierre only grinned. From time to time he still found it hard to believe that fate had catapulted him from the poverty of a monastery into the highest ranks of European aristocracy.

In the best of moods they climbed into the swaying gondola and soon enough they were gliding smoothly along the Canal Grande towards the Ca'

154

Giustinian. The lanterns of their gondola left a shimmering trail of light on the dark water, to be united soon enough with the lights cast by the lanterns and torches announcing the arrival of a whole flotilla of gondolas loaded with elegantly clad guests, all of them streaming towards the Ca' Giustinian from all parts of Venice as if drawn by a magnet.

Edo had consulted the clock in Pierre's hotel and with satisfaction in his voice he remarked, "We're arriving just at the right time. It would have been grossly impolite to arrive at the time mentioned on the invitation, we're about two hours late, the perfect delay according to the current fashion."

"You see, you didn't need to harass me to get a move on, I know the rules better than you do!" Pierre couldn't help throwing in, but his friend didn't really care or listen. Excitedly he tugged at Pierre's sleeve and whispered, "Did you see the gondola right over there? No, not that on, the other one on the left! At least five beautiful young ladies and I can only detect one elderly gentleman to guard them – this promises to be an entertaining evening!"

"Probably their father, in which case he has my full sympathy," Pierre answered, as he saw one of the girls casting inviting glances towards his friend.

Edo now started to point out the various faces or coats of arms that he recognized and soon it became clear that the crème de la crème of Venetian society would indeed be attending tonight. During the past weeks Edo had done an excellent job of introducing the two friends into the highest circles of society. Young, handsome and spending generously, they were welcomed with open arms even if they hadn't disclosed their true identities yet. He had also discreetly inquired about Julia Contarini and had been informed that she wouldn't be attending this year's carnival balls as a terrible tragedy had befallen her family. In a single day she had lost her beloved father and stepmother by some terrible food poisoning. But if Pierre had expected Armand to be disappointed, his friend seemed strangely unmoved. Although he still claimed to be in love with Julia, Pierre had the impression that Armand preferred to remain a free man during carnival.

Only the illustrious matrons of Venetian society still eyed the good-looking bachelors with suspicion, not sure if they presented welcome marriage material or were to be regarded as potentially dangerous for their sheltered daughters' reputations. But in the meantime a gang of young and enterprising gentlemen had already adopted the strangers and after only two weeks Pierre and Armand had become part of a boisterous group of fashionable gentlemen and found themselves showered with invitations from all sides.

The arrival of so many gondolas at the same time created a major traffic jam at the jetty and it took some time until they had disembarked and set foot in the palatial building where the masked ball was to take place. Thousands of candles were burning and illuminated the great ballroom and the adjacent salons with their bright light. Swathes of gold cloth had been hung from the ceiling to create the atmosphere of an Oriental tent, an illusion that was enhanced by the fact that they were greeted with drinks by young pages of dark oriental or African skin dressed in Turkish costumes and slippers.

"Have you seen, their servants are wearing diamond- and ruby-studded brooches on their caps?" Edo whispered. "Everybody will be talking about this tomorrow!"

"Pffft! Looks like nouveaux riches showing off to me," Armand commented, pretending hard not to be impressed.

"Not if your family tree goes back at least seven hundred years," Edo answered but Armand had already moved on and Edo was spared another lecture on French superiority.

When they had arrived Turkish music had been playing to greet the guests and add a finishing touch to the oriental set-up but soon the first merry dance tunes could be heard. In no time Pierre had completely forgotten that he had ever felt moody and tired. The inhabitants of the Serenissima knew how to organize a truly memorable ball, and their joy and laughter were simply contagious.

Armand meanwhile was pursuing his own plans – shamelessly flirting, he danced with a succession of young ladies. Being an accomplished dancer and with his handsome looks, Armand was rarely informed that the lady of his choice was engaged already – and if this was the case, he could hear true disappointment in her voice. And yet choosing a dancing partner was a difficult task tonight for Armand as beauty was in abundance all around him. The young ladies looked like birds of paradise in their colourful silk gowns worn with seductively low necklines, faces hidden behind beautifully painted masks, adorned with feathers and gold. Excitedly Armand could see their eyes sparkling invitingly behind their masks; each one seemed to be more attractive than the last. He decided that he simply loved carnival!

Having danced twice in a row with a young girl (at least he guessed from her voice and her delicate figure and arms that she must be fairly young) dressed in a dashing turquoise gown with a matching feather mask, he enquired politely if she would like him to organize some drinks as the temperature inside the great ballroom had risen to a tropical heat – the cold and damp winter seemed forgotten and far away.

Demurely the girl accepted and eagerly sipped at the cool wine Armand brought her only minutes later. Of course the Giustiniani had their own ice house, the ice being supplied from the Alps on a regular basis.

"That was lovely!" he could hear the girl's voice chirping. "I really needed that – but it's still very hot in here, don't you think?" and as if to prove her statement she started to fan herself playfully with her turquoise feather fan.

Armand couldn't help noticing that her bosom moved up and down as she breathed faster and he had to do his utmost to remember his manners and tear his eyes away. The girl seemed to notice his confusion, her sparkling eyes mocking and challenging him at the same time. Armand cleared his throat and quickly agreed that it was indeed extremely hot inside the ballroom.

"Are you interested in paintings? The Giustiniani are known to have one of the most valuable collections here in Venice!"

Armand was still distracted by the fan which by now seemed to be caressing the girl's chest. Pulling himself together he answered truthfully, "I must confess that I'm not a big admirer of paintings, I mean, if I have the good fortune to see perfection in front of me, why should I bother to look at some musty old paintings? I think they're rarely interesting, mostly hideously religious. It's supposed to be edifying, I know, but I've seen hundreds of them in my life and I never understand why people go crazy about them! Dull and boring, if you ask me!"

The girl laughed softly. "You're fascinating. Most young men would lie and tell me how interested they are in art and paintings! It's fashionable to be interested in those subjects!"

"They must be idiots, why waste their time on silly paintings if they have beauty right in front of them?"

They had started to dance once again and as soon as their hands touched during one of the elaborate dance moves, Armand had the sensation of a hot flame shooting straight through his body. As the girl in the turquoise dress moved closer to him he heard her say, "Maybe you would care to see some paintings after the dance if *I* showed them to you, it's too hot in here anyhow!"

The next dance move meant that they were separated immediately but as soon as they were reunited Armand whispered back, "I'll go and look at the paintings with pleasure, I'd follow you anywhere!" but now *he* was feeling really hot, and this was not only the effect of the temperature inside the ballroom!

As soon as the dance was finished the girl in the turquoise gown led him out of the ballroom and then upstairs into the private apartments. "The paintings are very valuable," she explained as she extracted a key from the folds of her gown. "This is why they are kept locked away!"

Armand was quite amazed; this girl really had managed to surprise him like no one before.

Not waiting for his comment, she took a candelabrum from the brightly lit hallway as they entered the room that lay in darkness. Diligently she closed the door and Armand heard the key grating in the lock as she locked the door – he felt more excited than he had in a long time.

The candles now cast their light into the room, surrounding the girl like a halo, but as Armand looked around him, all he could see were several paintings of mediocre quality, showing morose-looking ancestors of the Giustiniani. One thing was sure, none of the famous Giustiniani paintings was to be found here! He turned around and looked at the girl, who slowly removed her feathered mask. Armand held his breath, as she was quite beautiful, probably of a similar age to him.

"I hope I didn't disappoint you, my lord," the girl said, still mocking him. Surely she knew that she was breathtakingly beautiful.

"How could I be disappointed, my lady? I'm here with the most beautiful girl in all Venice!" he answered gallantly. "But I'm surprised, with your beauty your parents should have locked you away or had you married already and your husband should be waiting outside to challenge me, raging mad with jealousy!"

She giggled as she seemed to be picturing the scene but then her mood become more serious. "Nobody has ever managed to lock me away for more than five minutes! I've been betrothed to a wealthy gentleman for almost two years now, but luckily the date of our marriage hasn't been fixed yet. He's an important ambassador of our Republic, still assigned to some extremely important and most probably secretive mission on the island of Crete for the time being, something to do with the Turks!" she answered with a shrug. "But I'm not sure he'd ever challenge you, my future husband seems more interested in politics and counting his gold! He just wants to marry me because he needs a fitting noble wife who comes with a respectable heritage."

She moved so close that he could smell her perfume and while Armand was still hesitating how best to answer her frank words and make the next move, she once again took the initiative and sank down to her knees. Armand felt delicate but experienced hands opening his breeches and while he briefly wondered how the daughter of a noble house had gained the experience of a lady of easy virtue, soon his brain had no more time to spend on useless reflections as waves of pleasure extinguished all reflection.

*****

Pierre had seen his friend dancing with several partners and soon he too was drawn irresistibly into the unique atmosphere of gaiety and feasting.

Dancing until his feet started to hurt he felt light hearted and cheerful as rarely before. Handsome, strikingly blonde and in high spirits he was most popular with all the ladies. As soon as Pierre approached them they cast inviting glances through their masks, promising favours that surely wouldn't end with a dance.

The next time Pierre looked up to search for his friend, Armand had disappeared. Pierre grinned; he had not failed to notice that plenty of couples were making convenient use of the long and heavy brocade curtains and the dark balconies to exchange secret kisses, and had no doubt that Armand had steered the lady of his choice to the same destination. But in fact his mind was on different matters: he now regretted bitterly having chosen new shoes, as his feet were on fire!

I need to sit down, pause for a moment and get a drink, or I'll die, he thought desperately, while executeding all the same a punctilious bow to take leave of his last dancing partner. He could read the disappointment in her eyes, but there was no way he could survive another round of a lively country-style dance. He smiled at her and unknowingly broke another heart as he turned and left the ballroom in search of a chair and a glass of cool white wine.

This undertaking proved to be more difficult than anticipated as it took Pierre considerable time to wander through the crowded rooms with their high wooden painted ceilings. Tonight the entire aristocracy of Venice seemed to be present; either his progress was blocked by groups of chatting or flirting people, or worse, he was recognized by friends and greeted warmly while being drawn into a conversation.

With great relief he suddenly discovered Edo standing with a bunch of his friends in a corner, laughing and exchanging animated remarks. Pierre used the sight of his friend as a welcome excuse to take leave of a sticky young gentleman of nearly his own age, a fleeting acquaintance who seemed to have heard of the young stranger's wealth and was trying hard to convince Pierre to invest a fortune in a new vessel that was bound for trade with Africa. Excitedly he shouted, fighting against the noise of the ballroom, "Pierre, listen! You'll never regret your decision, it's a business that will yield the highest profits with literally no risk at all, and in no time!" He grabbed Pierre's sleeve to underline the importance of his words and it took Pierre all of his diplomatic skills to get rid of the young man without upsetting him too much.

"Sailing to Africa with no risk!" Pierre muttered to himself as he made his way to Edo's group. "Does this guy really think that I'm a total idiot when it comes to money or business?"

Pierre was still shaking his head in disbelief when a servant miraculously appeared with a tray loaded with delicate glasses filled with cool white wine.

Forgetting all about Africa and even his noble manners, Pierre grabbed two glasses at once; he felt as if he were going to die of thirst on the spot – if his feet didn't kill him first.

Clutching the two glasses firmly in his hands he limped forward to greet his friend who was standing in animated discussion with a large group of young gentlemen. Pierre was about to nudge him with his elbow to announce his arrival when he heard a low voice saying, "How considerate of you to bring me a glass of wine, this is exactly what I need now!"

Pierre stopped in his tracks and turned his head. He now discovered the reason why the group of young men was hovering here in the corner, far away from the music and the action in the ballroom. Comfortably half-sitting, half lying, on a low sofa was a young lady of striking features, her laughing eyes directed at Pierre, challenging him. Almost mechanically he stretched his arm out and offered one of the glasses to the beauty who took it with slender fingers and toasted him. "Thank you, *santé!*" Eagerly she sipped at her glass while she continued to speak. "You wouldn't believe that none of these cavaliers was able to anticipate the needs of a delicate lady, I might have perished here right under their eyes and they probably wouldn't even have noticed."

A storm of protest went through the group of men. Pierre could hear comments such as, "This is soooo unfair, I asked you several times, my goddess!" whereas a second young gentleman tried to outdo him by falling on his knees: "I would sacrifice my life for you, my dearest lady, my treasure! Command it now!" But she only laughed and tapped her admirer teasingly with her fan.

Pierre ignored this playful display of refined courtship; he was still spellbound by the apparition in front of him. Older than Pierre, in her mid-twenties, she was dressed in a velvet gown the colour of ripe cherries – lush dark curls fell on her snow-white collar made from Flemish lace. This striking combination of a carnival costume would probably have looked cheap and out of place on most women, but Pierre was sure that perfection, sinful perfection, was sitting right in front of him. She looked like the very incarnation of forbidden fruit.

"You seem to like to keep secrets – is this why you haven't introduced yourself?"

Was she teasing or was she challenging him again? Probably both, Pierre concluded, as he looked into her eyes, the colour of blackest coal, laughing at him. His knees seemed to turn to jelly. Pierre desperately wanted to answer, but somehow his tongue had managed to tie itself into a knot, and it was impossible for him to utter a sentence although he knew that a witty reply was expected. His brain seemed as empty and dry as the Mongolian desert he had been reading about recently in the stories of Marco Polo.

Edo was watching Pierre's confusion with growing amusement and thought that it was about time to intervene and rescue his friend. "May I present my friend, the noble Pierre de Beaulieu." He kicked Pierre to make sure that he wouldn't betray his true name but his friend was apparently on a different planet. Without a further word, Pierre sank automatically into a not very elegant yet acceptable bow.

Looking amused at Pierre, Edo continued, "And may I present to you the beautiful Contessa de Montefiori!"

"Pierre de Beaulieu!" Pierre heard her answer in a melodious voice. "Welcome to Venice! Your name seems to suit you perfectly, I have rarely seen such a handsome man! Please excuse my bad pronunciation; I have only a very basic command of your beautiful language." She was speaking in fluent French now, with a charming Italian accent, well aware that her French was almost perfect.

Pierre blushed like a teenager as he saw her eyes appraising him, at the same time hating himself for being so awkward. *I must look like a total idiot*, Pierre chided himself.

Edo laughed. "Oh, my dearest Contessa, Pierre doesn't care at all for his looks, your compliments are lost on him!"

Pierre was still trying to find a fittingly smart reply when the Contessa suddenly jumped up and shouted in high spirits, "I wonder if someone would care to invite me for a dance, I simply love this piece of music, it's a country dance, it reminds me of the time when I was a young girl in Sicily! I used to dance till I dropped!"

The Contessa had risen and now looked straight into Pierre's eyes. Immediately all other young gentlemen were swarming around her like excited bees, pleading to be the chosen one. But the Contessa only smiled like the sphinx and simply ignored the men around her. Without any hesitation she presented her arm to Pierre who took it as if in a trance while he stammered some words, knowing that his reply must sound utterly inadequate. Under the jealous and spiteful glances of the other gentlemen Pierre led the Contessa into the ballroom, but had he looked at Edo's face, Pierre would have detected a slight frown on his face; obviously his friend did not like what he saw.

Aching feet forgotten, Pierre seemed to float above the ground as if some magic wand had transformed him. He didn't know how it happened but in next to no time he found himself laughing and chatting with the Contessa as if they had been best friends forever. Pierre suddenly felt witty, charming and elated; her admiring eyes seemed to be telling him that he was her hero, the only man in this ballroom capable of capturing her interest.

161

As the Contessa had predicted she proved to be a tireless dancer, but Pierre didn't mind – on the contrary, he was sure that he would never get tired of watching her slender body moving to the rhythm of the music. Every time their hands or bodies touched during the dance his heart almost stopped beating. He seemed to be caught in a dream, but a beautiful dream that should never end.

And yet, Pierre's dream ended soon, far too soon. They had finished the third dance when a dragon of a matron appeared, dressed in sober black silk. She didn't bother to wear a mask to hide her wrinkled face, and her only concession to the masked ball were some long black feathers worn as part of her hairstyle which made her look even more like a crow. She approached the couple with a sour face: "Eleonora, may I remind you that you promised me to go home early, it's been a tiring day and hopping around until the early morning will be no good for your health!"

The Contessa tilted her head in the most charming way, almost like a flustered bird, and looked at Pierre. "I'm so sorry, dear sir, it's been such a pleasure to dance with you, but I dare not upset my aunt. I must go home and take some rest or she won't speak to me for a whole week!"

Before Pierre fully realized what had happened she was gone. He kicked himself mentally as he had failed to ask her when they could meet again, but he comforted himself quickly with the reflection that Edo would probably know her whereabouts. He absolutely must see her again, that much was certain!

Pierre walked back to the room where he expected to find Edo, but the Contessa's magic had disappeared and suddenly his feet seemed to hurt like never before. Therefore a very much astonished Edo saw his friend limping more than walking into the room where he was still standing in animated discussion with some fellow gentlemen.

"What happened?" Edo commented good-humouredly. "Did the divine Contessa tread on your feet?"

Pierre sighed. "It's these new shoes actually, they've been killing me, right from the start!"

"I didn't notice you limping when you abducted the gorgeous Contessa, you seemed to be floating towards the ballroom rather than walking…"

"I was," Pierre admitted with a broad grin. "Let me tell you, I have never met such a woman before. She's divine, she's pure magic!" Pierre rolled his eyes in ecstasy. "When shall I be able to meet her again?"

"Is she gone? Why didn't you ask her?"

162

"I forgot, I was still in shock when this dragon in a black gown appeared to take her home. Don't tell me, I know that I'm an idiot!" Pierre answered.

"There is a good chance we'll meet her next Saturday. That will be the last ball of the season, and everybody is excited as to how the hosts will try to outshine the Giustiniani. It's not going to be easy, as this ball has been such a success, you can see it's been a grand triumph for the hostess, and although her husband is serving as ambassador in London right now, everybody turned up!" Edo answered soothingly.

Pierre looked around at the opulent set-up and he could only agree; outdoing the luxury and especially making sure that once again all the leading members of the Venetian aristocracy were present would be an enormous challenge for any host.

"And what's your bet then?" he asked Edo.

"I think they'll manage, as rumour has it that the Molin family who are hosting the next ball are frontrunners to take up the position of Doge of the Republic of Venice – even if the present Doge has to die first, nobody will dare to snub the rising star!"

Edo hesitated a second and cleared his throat before he continued. "Would you allow me to give you some personal advice, Pierre?"

"Of course, you're my friend, you don't even need to ask me!"

"The Contessa is regarded as the most beautiful and most charming woman in Venice, there is no other woman to match her!"

"You tell me!" sighed Pierre. "I never met anyone like her before, even at court in Paris she'd easily outshine any other woman!"

"But the number of broken hearts she has left behind is legendary and I know of at least two men who committed suicide as they couldn't face living without her. She's got the reputation of driving men insane and the circumstances of her husband's sudden death have never been clarified. Her family and past are also very shady – conveniently there are no known relatives, and the Conte de Montefiori saw her, was besotted and married her on the spot!"

Pierre only saw laughing eyes of darkest coal and a slender figure swaying to the rhythm of the music. What did he care about some senile count who had died, didn't they all die when they got old?"

"Why is she being received in society then, if her reputation is so bad?"

"Nobody knows, either she has more money than we know about, or..."

"Or?"

"Or she knows too much..." Edo finished. "In any case this woman is dangerous, you must know that!"

"Thanks for telling me!" Pierre smiled politely at his friend, but in truth he didn't see Edo, he saw a figure dressed in a gown the colour of ripe-red cherries, moving seductively to the sound of the music...

Pierre was spared further admonishment as a cheerful voice cried from behind, "Why are you both looking so serious? It's the most entertaining ball I've attended for a long time and you stand there far from the action, probably discussing all kinds of serious philosophical problems!"

Armand had arrived and was radiating cheerfulness all over. Never a person to be gloomy, tonight he seemed to glowing with satisfaction. Pierre looked at his friend and grinned. "You seem to be having the time of your life!"

"I cannot complain!" Armand answered with false modesty. "I had a most interesting lesson in art tonight, paintings actually."

Pierre couldn't help it, he almost exploded with laughter. "You must be kidding!" he spluttered. "I've never seen you interested in art at all! The last time I saw you looking at paintings was in Hertford when you tried to figure out which out of all my dowdy-looking ancestors might resemble me most!"

"This is exactly how I am misjudged. I can assure you, I'm an intellectual at heart, it was very entertaining tonight and I gained a lot of insight into skills I would never have expected here in Venice. But I do remember the gallery of paintings in Hertford, a strange bunch of relatives you have indeed!"

Pierre ignored the last remark and couldn't help boasting, "While you were looking at boring paintings, I was dancing with the most beautiful woman in Venice! I have no idea why she chose me, but she did. She only wanted to dance with me and I must confess, I'm still in heaven..."

"Maybe she had promised her confessor to do charity work tonight," Armand commented, skilfully avoiding a kick from his best friend.

"It seems we all had a great time then, let's go and have a last drink and play cards to finish the evening, unless you want to return to the dances?"

"No way!" answered Pierre quickly, "my feet are killing me. I should never have put on new shoes for this ball!"

Thus they decided to spend their time playing cards at one of the tables set up by their hosts and were considerate enough to lose enough money to make the other players happy. As the time was approaching four o'clock in the morning, Edo suggested going home, and everybody agreed that it had been a long and eventful day.

The next morning Pierre looked worn and tired, whereas a fresh and cheerful Armand entered Pierre's bedroom to share a cup of early coffee with his friend, served by the faithful Jean.

Pierre hadn't been able to get any sleep. He was torn between feelings of elation whenever he had seen the face of the Contessa in his imagination, then tormented by terrible pangs of guilt as soon as his thoughts wandered towards Marie who must be sitting in Reims now, desperately waiting for him to come back.

Jean looked thoughtfully at his master. Edo had given him the low-down on Pierre's encounter with the Contessa and immediately Jean had been worried as he could sense that his master was walking straight into a trap, but seeing Pierre this morning told him that things were far worse than he had imagined. Pierre looked quite haggard and Jean steeled himself for a difficult time ahead.

As soon as Armand had left the room, Pierre asked Jean, "By the way, could you please try to find out where the Contessa di Montefiori lives?" Pierre stopped and wondered if he should add further explanations, as his valet might find this request strange but finally he came to the conclusion that there was no need.

"Of course, my lord, I will do this immediately!" Jean bowed stiffly, the incarnation of the correct and faithful servant.

"Oh, there's no urgency!" Pierre added lamely. "The Contessa is an acquaintance of Edo's and I'm wondering if I should send her a small present as seems customary here, every gentleman must be able to court a lady of his choice, it's simply a question going about it the right way."

An uneasy silence prevailed. Pierre had the impression that not only did Jean not believe a word of his carefully prepared speech, as usual he seemed to be able to read his mind, normally an excellent quality in a valet, but this morning an unsettling thought.

Actually Jean was content that Pierre had given him this order, and as soon as his master was dressed he took leave to start his own investigations. Jean was burning with curiosity and being able to find out as much as possible about the famous – or according to Edo's comments – infamous Contessa would help him to judge if his master was only committing one of his usual follies or if real danger was on the horizon. Jean couldn't count on Armand. The latter had caught a cold and had retreated to bed with a large brandy, having steadfastly refused to swallow one of Jean's effective but evil-smelling potions.

Human nature being what it is, Jean was sure that the hotel servants would be open to a bit of gossip. He therefore descended the stairs and headed to the back of the building where the kitchen was located. His gut feeling proved to be right, as he found not only the fat cook who ruled over his small empire with an iron fist, or more precisely with an iron ladle, he also saw a fellow valet who was spending some free time here in the kitchen, probably in the hope of getting his hands on some leftovers or being invited to taste some of the mouth-watering dishes that were simmering on the big stove.

"Do you mind if I take a seat?" Jean opened the discussion. "It's been a tiring day, my master has been most demanding today."

"Sit down, mate!" replied the valet invitingly. "I know them well enough, these noble folks are all the same if you ask me! Our bishop says that the Lord created masters and servants – easy to say if you're a bishop and a master, if you want my opinion!"

Jean quickly made some clucking noises to show his sympathy, and encouraged to have found a fellow sympathiser, the valet continued, "Take this horrid spinster who resides on the floor above you, she's sent me up and down the stairs five times already today! 'The coffee was too bitter'," the valet now imitated the whining voice of the spinster, "then she needed a hot brick for her feet, but the first was too cold, the second burned her feet – has the Good Lord really thought about those masters when he commands us to obey them?"

But Jean wasn't really interested in discussing holy scripture or the order of the world; he had more pressing issues on his mind. Thus he decided to change the subject. "Have any of you heard of the Contessa di Montefiori?" he said, going straight to the heart of the matter. The reply was unambiguous. The cook dropped the ladle with a loud clatter, the valet whistled.

"Why do you want to know? Has your master become her latest victim?" asked the valet, eyes burning with curiosity. "All I can say, there is a lot to tell, but talking makes my throat so dry." He looked expectantly at the cook and at Jean. Jean got the hint and put his purse on the table. "I'll let you choose the wine, three cups please!"

The cook was happy to oblige. Quickly he fumbled at his apron and produced a key. Then he waddled off to the cupboard he kept locked for good reason and lovingly chose a sealed jug of red wine. "From Tuscany, let me tell you, 1638 was an excellent year!" he explained, while he served a cup of wine to Jean and the valet. "Those wines are the best, lots of sun there to produce great wines, I have my secret connections!"

Jean ignored the fact that the cook had poured the most generous portion into his own cup, anyhow, he wasn't interested in discussing the pros and cons of wine, he needed to find out more about the Contessa. "Cheers, and good health to you!" Jean toasted and resolutely cut short the discussion on wine from Tuscany. "Now, tell me about the Contessa, a friend of my master seems to be totally besotted by her!"

"Suicides, and plenty of them," answered the valet darkly.

"Where does this female monster live then, and what does she have to do with suicides?" Jean was alarmed, but tried to keep his expression as calm as possible.

"The Ca' Montefiori is only a small palace, but of course the Contessa chose a palace directly on the Canal Grande, wouldn't settle for less."

"You're too quick for me!" Jean became impatient. "Is she married, why did she choose the location and not her husband?"

His two companions exchanged telling glances. The valet sighed. "I see you know nothing about her. Let me tell you then!" He took a large gulp of wine and started. "The Contessa di Montefiori is the most beautiful gentlewoman of Venice, lustrous curly hair, dark eyes that promise the temperament of a volcano, lips like cherries, a perfect figure – and I should know, as I have served many women of quality in this establishment!"

The cook nodded to underline the fact that the valet was an expert.

"The Contessa arrived about two years ago here in Venice, recently widowed, wanting to find a new home. Nobody had ever heard of her before, her husband was an elderly count from Tuscany who possessed large estates in the middle of Italy, really wealthy, if you understand what I mean. The count met the Contessa in Paris, fell in love with her and married her straight on the spot! But their marriage was not to be blessed, a short time after they married the count *all of a sudden* succumbed to a high fever..."

The valet drew out the last words. It was clear that he didn't believe that the sudden death had been a natural one.

"Why didn't she move to Tuscany?" Jean asked curiously. "If her estates are located there, wouldn't it be natural to move there?"

The valet and cook only snorted in unison. "She inherited everything, not a single denarius was left to the count's relatives, I guess she was scared to show her face there!"

The cook sniffed. "They would have wrung her pretty neck, no wonder she never dared to set foot in Tuscany." His comment was accompanied by a telling gesture; Jean could imagine that numerous birds had found their way into the cooking pots that way.

"Now I understand," Jean resumed the conversation. "She left Paris and came straight to Venice where she bought a palace. What about her own family?"

"Dubious, if you ask me," the valet said. "These cups are really small, mine is already empty!" and he looked accusingly at the cook.

Apparently the cook liked a good gossip and to Jean's surprise he filled the cups once more without too much discussion. "Alright, it's on me this time!" he sighed, while making sure that his cup once more received the most wine.

"You mean, the wine is on the house," giggled the valet before he continued his narrative.

"The Contessa arrived with her aunt, who plays her chaperon, but nobody has ever met any other relative of hers. She claims to be of Sicilian noble origins, but Sicily is far away and we all know that you can buy all kinds of documents there. And finally, she's got plenty of dough!"

"Dough?" Jean was not sure if he had caught the right word.

"Money, you idiot!"

Jean swallowed but this was not the right moment to pick a fight. "What about the suicides then?"

"Nobody knows exactly how she managed to get received by the leading families and sneak into high society, but we all know that even our high-born masters need money, plenty of money, actually – I could tell you some stories!"

Jean was alarmed. The valet was becoming too talkative, soon he'd be discussing every Venetian family secret in detail. Quickly Jean inserted, "Oh, I can imagine that! All broke, I guess. But tell me more about those suicides, this sounds worrying!"

"Makes them crazy," interrupted the cook all of sudden. "She makes them wild and then drops them like a hot iron."

"Oh, yes," the valet added. "She drives them really wild, they believe they have a chance with her, and then…"

"And then?" Jean was close to panic; he could already see his master in the clutches of this heartless female monster.

"And then – all of a sudden – she goes cold, won't receive them any more, dances with other men. One of them couldn't take it any more, he came one evening to the Ca' Montefiori with gondolas loaded with musicians who played the most romantic love songs; but when she even refused to show herself to him on the balcony, he shot himself right off the gondola. It was a major scandal!" The valet radiated satisfaction; he loved to tell a good story.

"And then there was the young and handsome marchese – heartbroken, he poisoned himself, leaving a letter," the cook added quickly. He hated to be outshone by the valet. "Those are two cases that are generally known of in Venice, but there are more... hushed up by their relatives."

"Plenty more!" the valet added darkly. "I'm sure!"

"And the worst is..." the valet added triumphantly.

"What's the worst?" Jean uttered impatiently, close to strangling the valet.

"The worst is that both men bequeathed their whole fortune to her, leaving letters that they would leave every single lira to her!"

"She must have refused!" Jean was shocked. "No woman would ever accept an inheritance under these circumstances! That must have set all the tongues in Venice wagging!"

The cook and the valet laughed at Jean. "You foreigners are so naïve! The Contessa put on a magnificent show, how heartbroken and distressed she was, hadn't she acted with the best of intentions and only stopped seeing her gallants as she possessed the highest moral standards? But now as they were dead she – obviously – had to respect their last wishes and accept the inheritance."

The valet made a dramatic pause before he added, "Since then her fortune has been growing every year!"

Jean emptied his cup with one large gulp. *Typical for my master to walk blindfold into the biggest and most dangerous trap Venice has to offer. I should have known it, now I'll have to visit the Ca' Montefiori and see for myself.*

Jean was trying to think of some more questions that might be important for his mission but suddenly the kitchen bell started to ring furiously. The services of the valet were demanded urgently and as the aroma of burning meat was already wafting through the kitchen the cook was reminded that he had to turn his roast immediately to avoid a calamity.

*****

Armand looked in the mirror. The face he saw in the expensive mirror of Murano glass was pleasing to him – as usual. By nature not given to feelings of mediocrity or humility, Armand was convinced that the Good Lord had endowed him with a pleasing face and a nice body to make the most of it. And yet this morning he frowned at his reflection with disdain and talked loudly to himself. "Armand, you're a coward!"

The Armand in the mirror flinched. He didn't appreciate these blunt words.

"You have been procrastinating now for weeks with the excuse of keeping your liberty and doing whatever pleases you, but it's time to be a gentleman, a true de Saint Paul, and finally make the effort to find Julia and visit her!"

The Armand in the mirror nodded. Yes, it was time to get a grip on himself, do honour to the family name, and go and see Julia.

Armand turned around and sighed. "I'd better tackle it now, before I change my mind; Venice is simply too alluring!" and his weak mind – ever so open to temptations – wandered immediately to his extraordinary art lesson in the Ca' Giustinian until he told himself sternly to be serious for once and stop pursuing those thoughts.

It proved fairly simple to find where Julia was living at the moment. Everybody in Venice had been talking about the catastrophe that had befallen the famous Contarini family; the fate of Julia who had lost her beloved father and stepmother on the same day due to a vicious case of food poisoning had kept tongues wagging for several days – there had even been some voices (the usual gossips) who had dared to question such a bizarre occurrence. Hadn't it been known that Julia had never accepted her young and lovely new stepmother?

But those who had spoken to Julia's aunt and offered their not always very sincere condolences to Julia and to her impressive aunt, the Contessa Alessandra, could only ascertain that this version of an accident must be true. The Contessa had said in public that Julia's father had always been a fool, hadn't she advised him never to eat any oysters unless they had been tasted first by his servants? Well, he had known better and had paid for it!

Those words might sound unfeeling, but the Contessa Alessandra had never been known to mince her words. In any case this statement had been straightforward enough to kill all rumours of a potential scandal. Venice being Venice, and carnival with its carnal temptations and usual infidelities being in full swing, the scandal-mongers soon found new and juicy gossip and the death of Julia's father was soon forgotten.

Armand found out from the keeper of the albergo (who enjoyed the best connections) that Julia was still staying with her aunt, and was rarely seen in public as it would have been unfitting for a young lady to visit balls or receptions during her period of mourning. Armand therefore decided to send a messenger with his card offering his condolences and some flowers. Only one day later an invitation to call on the Contessa Alessandra and her niece for an afternoon visit was forthcoming.

Armand accepted with mixed feelings; never had he been in love as much as when he had set eyes on Julia last year in London, and yet time had passed, would he still find her so fascinating, would she still like him? Hadn't she played cat and mouse with him in London, making him mad with desire? Therefore it was an unusually nervous Armand who set foot in the gondola that was to bring him to the palace of the Contessa Alessandra. Dressed in his usual splendour, the young gentleman would do justice to any demanding hostess and the Contessa immediately understood why Julia had been so excited when she had received the card of a French stranger. Armand de Saint Paul was certainly a suitor to be reckoned with.

While Armand bowed and greeted both ladies with his usual aplomb and decorum, the Contessa Alessandra scrutinized him in detail. Her conclusion was clear after two minutes, a charmer, handsome and intelligent – a danger for any unmarried girl! But one look into his soulful brown eyes told the Contessa as well that his charms would be lavished on every good-looking young lady, for Armand de Saint Paul was a ladies' man.

If I were thirty years younger, she mused, *I'd drag him into my bedchamber – immediately!* She almost had to giggle at the thought of it. *But I'm afraid he's not marriage material, although Julia told me that his best friend procured him an earldom and a good income. I'll have to keep an eye on Julia – luckily she doesn't need to chase money, she needs a decent husband! I don't want her to marry a man who'll never be fully hers and who breaks hearts wherever he goes. She needs a broad and dependable shoulder to lean on after this nightmare!'*

Nothing of these thoughts could be read in the Contessa's face as she started a polite but meaningless conversation with Armand while offering him some sweet wine and candied fruits. Julia sat next to her, behaving as correctly and with as much restraint as might be expected from the daughter of one of the leading families in Venice, and yet she was glowing, her eyes were sparkling and her cheeks – so pale lately – had taken on a healthy rosy tint.

The Contessa saw with glee that meeting Armand was probably the best cure she could have imagined and decided to allow Julia to continue meeting her friend – but the Contessa also decided to keep a very watchful eye on those two – she might be old, but she was no fool!

Armand knew the rules of a first visit and took his leave after only thirty minutes as the unwritten rules of society prescribed. He noticed a tinge of disappointment in Julia's eyes as he prepared to leave but she knew the rules well enough and simply raised her hand to allow him to kiss it before he left. The Contessa did the same but added that she would be delighted to see him again soon, which allowed Julia to add that she, too, would be pleased.

Armand walked out of the palace in deep thought and with mixed feelings. To be sure, Julia was still as beautiful as he had remembered her – and yet she had changed profoundly. She had lost weight, she looked almost ethereal now. But what puzzled him most was the fact that Julia was no longer the self-assured and celebrated beauty of society. Armand was normally not given to deep reflections about others, but he could have sworn that Julia must have gone through some rough times during the past months and if Armand was truly frank with himself, he preferred the light-hearted Julia to the new one.

But yes, stunningly beautiful she still was, even more than he had remembered! When Armand thought about her beautiful face, her slender figure and her melodious voice, he was certainly looking forward to his next visit. Hopefully this dragon of an aunt would leave them alone for some minutes! Being a born optimist, Armand soon convinced himself that time would surely tell how to handle this relationship best.

Carnival season was still in full swing and all of Venice was whispering that the Molin family would do everything possible to outshine the luxury of the ball given by the Giustiniani. Even if the Doge was the Prince of Venice by name only, the position still held so much sway that every great family wanted it badly. As the present Doge was ailing, the Molin had decided to throw a ball all of Venice would remember – especially when it was time to go to the ballot!

*****

In the meantime Jean had decided to tackle his task without further delay. To be on the safe side he opted for a disguise, as experience had taught him never to put all his cards on the table at once. He finally opted for a dark outfit, simple yet elegant enough to pass as the servant of a noble but not too wealthy master. Then he chose a hat in the Spanish fashion and carefully applied a false moustache. He hoped that his dark skin would be acceptable for a Spanish servant. Satisfied with his appearance in the polished silver mirror he hired a small boat – a more fashionable gondola with its customary two oarsmen would have been too expensive. He was equipped with a small box and a small bouquet of flowers.

As soon as Jean announced his destination the owner of the boat looked at him with suspicion – apparently the reputation of the Ca' Montefiori was not the best.

"Any comment?" Jean interrogated the boatman.

172

The man looked at him and spat into the water. "No-good folks," he answered curtly.

"Row me over there, all the same!" Jean answered, "but please stay and wait for me, I'm pretty sure it won't be too long."

"You pay in advance?"

"Half – and a good tip if you wait."

The boatman nodded in agreement; Jean found him unusually taciturn for a Venetian.

About twenty minutes later they were approaching the Ca' Montefiori, a small but neat palace built in the prevailing Byzantine style with its typical curved bow windows and decorative marble pillars. Jean disembarked onto the private jetty and was led to the first floor where he was greeted by a haughty butler who demanded arrogantly to know his business.

Jean answered in a tone that matched the butler's arrogance. "This is not of your concern, my master is the most noble Duque de Salamanca, Grandee of Spain, and His Grace has instructed me to remit these gifts to her ladyship, the noble Contessa di Montefiori, personally!"

But the butler was not to be easily impressed, as in reply he snorted, "Everybody wants to meet her ladyship, it's out of the question that she will find the time to meet anyone today. Tell me more of your master and I'll try to put in a good word for you!"

"The Duque of Salamanca," (Jean fervently hoped that such a title did exist) "is of the purest and most venerated Castilian blood, his family dates back to the illustrious Queen Isabella!" Jean quickly invented a fitting family connection.

But once more his speech apparently failed to impress the butler, as unmoved he replied, "My mistress, the Contessa, can choose from the highest born admirers, prince of royal blood, duke or marquis – she has the choice. I've never heard of a Queen Isabella, but tell me, is your master wealthy?"

Jean made a good show of trying to avoid a straight answer. "A Grandee and Peer of Spain doesn't need to bother about trivial things like money." He paused briefly and reluctantly he added, "but lately His Grace has suffered from some misfortune, the terrible Dutch have captured his galleons."

The butler looked at him with disdain. "Forget your flowers then," he answered curtly. "Her ladyship only receives men endowed with a fortune, a mere title won't do!"

He gestured towards the door; Jean's audience was finished.

"Oh, please have mercy on me!" Suddenly dropping his arrogant airs, Jean adopted a pleading tone. "My master is brutal and choleric; he'll beat me to death if I have to confess that I didn't even succeed in seeing the Contessa. His Grace saw her ladyship at a masked ball and he cannot think about anything else since, he's deeply in love!"

Jean thought that he saw a glimmer of sympathy in the butler's eyes and quickly he produced some silver soldi. "Can I at least see the reception room? At least then I can describe the room and tell His Grace that I met her ladyship, but he's suspicious, and he'll grill me for every detail!"

It must have been the silver coins that did the trick, as the butler gave in. "You're lucky, most people are having their siesta right now. I can show you up to have a quick look at the salon where the Contessa normally receives her more intimate visitors."

"Thank you so much, you've saved my life!" Jean moved forward to shake the butler's hands to show his gratitude but the butler quickly stepped back – he was not keen to be touched by a stranger.

"It's a pleasant palace that your ladyship owns, maybe a bit small compared to the ducal palace my master owns in Valencia." Jean now changed to a gossipy tone.

"Didn't you say that His Grace is the Duque of Salamanca?"

"Oh, we own several palaces, of course, but costly to maintain…" Jean lied quickly, he must be more careful!

The butler looked impressed and added, "The Ca' Montefiori is much more spacious inside than it looks when you approach it from the Canal Grande," and added with condescension, "Her ladyship has been most astute and has acquired most of the houses around us and her garden is a true gem, you won't find many of those in a city that has no space and where the price of a piece of land is far beyond the reach of less fortunate people."

They had reached the reception room situated on the first floor and Jean looked around, pretending to be full of awe. The room was well decorated; he could see that no expense had been spared, and although Jean had already taken an intense dislike to the Contessa, he had to concede that she did have taste. The typical Venetian floor made from polished broken marble pieces set in concrete was mostly covered with expensive oriental rugs, and the room emanated an air of expensive elegance. The usual scent of winter, a mix of acrid smoke from thousands of chimneys and the smell of the lagoon was masked by an agreeable scent of flowers, inviting without being overpowering.

Jean had seen enough of the room. "Thank you so much, if I could bother you for five minutes more of your precious time, you made me terribly curious with your mention of the beautiful garden; may I ask you the favour of granting me a quick look?"

The butler hesitated but finally gave in; apparently he was very proud of the garden. He guided Jean to the back of the palace and indeed directly behind the building was a lush garden; even now in winter it was easy to see how beautiful it must be in spring or summer. Jean made the appropriate admiring comments but his real interest was focused on the sprawling buildings that surrounded the garden. As the butler had indeed mentioned, full of pride, all of these buildings now belonged to the Contessa.

Why does she need so many houses, so much space? Jean was perplexed. It somehow didn't make sense that a widow would acquire so many buildings. He thanked the butler profusely, hoping that his Spanish accent had been credible enough and embarked on the boat that had been waiting for him patiently as agreed. The boatman looked at him with raised eyebrows, but still didn't say anything, he didn't need to.

"You were right," Jean replied. "Strange people there, very strange indeed!"

The butler watched the boat rowing slowly away. "Spanish Grandee, pah! Peer of Spain... but not enough money for a gondola with two oarsmen or a decent yacht, heaven forbid that I should disturb my mistress for a penniless suitor," he mumbled. "Let this Spanish fellow find a widow stupid enough to be blinded by a title, there are plenty of those available in Venice," and satisfied that he had shielded the Contessa from a most unsuitable suitor he went upstairs to the servants' rooms. Finally it was siesta time and silver coins were clinking pleasantly in his pocket...

Pierre was delighted that Jean had already found out the address of the Contessa. Somehow he hadn't dared to bother Edo for further details. "I would like to send the Contessa a small gift and some flowers," he told Jean, eager as a schoolboy, "and I'd like you to take it to her with a personal message!"

"May I suggest that your lordship instruct one of the parlour maids to carry out this errand? I think for such a delicate task a female messenger would be a nice touch and much more fitting."

Pierre hesitated, but accepted Jean's proposal. Maybe he was right, Jean would probably know best.

"All right, the parlour maid it is then, and Jean, please send for a jeweller, but one with the best reputation here in Venice, I need to choose a fitting gift!"

175

Jean bowed. Even if he didn't like his master's request, it came as no surprise. With his usual efficiency Jean announced the arrival of the jeweller already organized for the next day.

To Pierre's great surprise the jeweller was quite an old man, in his late sixties, he guessed. A small figure, bent by age, he wore a simple black costume, his grey hair covered partially by the cap usually worn by followers of the Jewish faith. But as soon as the strange visitor opened his bag, Pierre knew that Jean had sent for the right man. The inconspicuous leather bag contained rings and necklaces of outstanding quality; precious stones of unusual size and purity sparkled in the light of the candles that were kept burning even during daytime in winter.

Carefully Pierre chose a necklace with a sparkling ruby the colour of blood set among precious oriental pearls – an expensive rarity, as he discovered when the jeweller named the price. Pierre flinched but paid – it simply seemed to be the perfect gift for the most beautiful woman he had ever set eyes on.

The gift now ready and chosen, Pierre laboured over the text of the accompanying message until he almost despaired and opted to keep it as short as possible. There seemed to exist no way to express his feelings in writing – and the possibility that the Contessa might reject his love if he put down his feelings in words written too crudely made him cringe with shame and fear.

After yet another night spent in turmoil and restless sleep, Pierre decided that he couldn't endure the tension any longer. He rang for the parlour maid who was to deliver the gift and the message accompanied by a small bouquet of red roses. The bouquet proved to be ludicrously expensive as they were out of season and the flowers had to be brought to Venice at great cost.

The parlour maid who entered seemed to be an excellent choice, a pleasant girl with a kind nature. Not only did she seem to be awed at having been chosen for such a delicate mission, she also seemed greatly inspired by the fact that she should be the carrier of a love letter from a high-born guest of the albergo.

Eager and willing to please she listened to Pierre's lengthy explanations and promised solemnly to fulfil her mission at once. When Pierre insisted that she should hire a luxurious gondola with two oarsmen for the short distance her eyes nearly popped out of their sockets; never had she envisaged such a luxurious form of travel as being suitable for herself.

During the next two hours, Pierre behaved like a caged lion. Restlessly he walked up and down in his room, opened and closed his books, but his mind was unable to concentrate on the content of any of them – had he ever thought that the Decamarone was interesting? Jean brought his dinner, but Pierre barely touched the delicious risotto; in his mind he pictured the maid presenting the flowers to the Contessa, then he saw her offering his precious gift, but then – what would happen then?

The more Pierre tried to imagine the scene that must be unfolding in the Ca' Montefiori the more he was torn apart by feelings of elation (in his mind imagining the Contessa crying out with joy and immediately trying on the necklace) and total despair as he envisaged the Contessa rejecting the necklace, even throwing it with a dismissive gesture to the ground. How could a nameless youngster dare to offer such an intimate gift to a widowed lady of rank who could choose freely among all of the eligible bachelors of Venice! Finally – before Pierre succumbed to the advanced stages of lunacy – Jean announced the arrival of the parlour maid. Jean had been a nervous wreck too as he had watched his master becoming increasingly desperate.

Pierre watched the maid enter the room and his heart nearly stopped beating. The girl, so happy and confident when she had accepted the mission, had dissolved into tears, her eyes red and puffy; obviously she must have been crying for a considerable time already.

Pierre sent an angry glance to Jean who pretended not to notice. Not such a great idea to send the girl, Pierre thought, enraged, before he rushed towards the distraught girl.

"Sit down!" he commanded gently. "Stop crying and tell me what's happened."

The girl was still sobbing but calmed down, realizing that the foreign gentleman was not going to beat her or shout at her. Slowly and reluctantly she produced the flowers and the gift, the flowers starting to tilt their heads, a fitting match to the girl's sorrow.

"I met the lady as your lordship instructed me to do," she managed to utter, "and I handed the gift, your message and the flowers to the beautiful lady." Now she started to sob again and although Pierre would have loved to box her ears to bring her back to her senses, he knew better and simply waited until she was able to continue talking.

"Her ladyship looked at the flowers, then commanded her maid to open the gift and while her maid was still opening the box, her ladyship read the message."

"And then?" Pierre couldn't help asking.

"I don't understand what happened!" The girl was clearly at a loss. "Her ladyship had seemed quite happy to receive me and quite curious to see what I had brought. But suddenly she changed her mind, dropped the flowers on the table, asked her maid to give me back the necklace and said: 'Tell your master that I cannot be bought. Take everything back and tell him my name is

Montefiori, not Rose. If your master understands my message, he may see me again!'" The girl repeated the message quite carefully; evidently she had rehearsed this speech again and again during her journey back.

Pierre looked crestfallen. The Contessa had rejected his gifts – she had answered only with a riddle. How could he decipher this strange message – or was she only joking? Joking at his cost, or was there a ray of hope?

Pierre suddenly realized that the maid was still looking at him, terror-stricken, obviously convinced that she had failed in her mission. Although his mind was totally occupied with the strange riddle, he smiled at her reassuringly and handed her a golden coin, after all, she had done exactly as he had asked. The parlour maid nearly fainted when she saw the golden glimmer in her hand; never in her life had she had touched a real gold coin. Forgetting all her sorrows she sank to her knees and kissed Pierre's hand before she hastened out of the room – you could never tell with these noble gentlemen, they were capable of changing their minds at any minute!

Pierre looked at Jean. "Did you understand the message?"

Jean shook his head; he understood of course extremely well that the Contessa was playing games with his master. She was apparently as clever as she was beautiful, that made her an even more dangerous enemy to have. But as his master was infatuated beyond any reason, Jean knew instinctively that he had better keep his mouth shut.

"I have really no idea, my lord!"

"Not Rose, I'm called Montefiori..." Pierre repeated. "Montefiori... Rose..."

Suddenly he smacked his hand against his forehead. "I'm so stupid, it's so obvious!" he cried.

"What's so obvious?" asked Armand, as he entered the room. "The fact that you're stupid?"

"*Montefiori* means 'mountain of flowers'," Pierre cried excitedly. "The Contessa doesn't want a rose, she wants me to show my true feelings by sending her a mountain of flowers!"

Armand looked at his friend as a benevolent teacher would look at a pleasant but rather dim pupil. "I have no idea about mountains of flowers, although at this time of the year, you'll pay a mountain of gold for it, but I do have the very clear notion that our dear Contessa has you wrapped around her tiny but admittedly very beautiful fingers! Pierre, I can only warn you, this woman is dangerous, don't be a fool!"

178

Jean could have embraced Armand – at least one of the friends had kept a sane head on his shoulders.

But Pierre wouldn't listen. With shining eyes he repeated, "A mountain of flowers, if this I what she wants, this is what she shall have!"

The news that a gondola loaded with bouquets of roses had appeared and delivered its precious cargo to the Ca' Montefiori spread like wildfire in Venice. During carnival season all kinds of extravagances could be seen and heard of, but who would be crazy enough to spend a fortune to send enough roses to the infamous Contessa to decorate her entire palace – was she secretly preparing a ball and had one missed the invitation? Rumours spread like wildfire – the number of men known to admire the Contessa was impressive and Pierre was probably lucky that he was spared from hearing most of it.

Pierre was walking on a cloud of happiness; not only had the beautiful Contessa graciously accepted the flowers, she had even retained the necklace he had sent once more with a short message that true love could never be bought.

Armand had tried to get some reason into Pierre's head, but Pierre, normally always kind and reasonable, had behaved like a stubborn mule – and maybe for the first time since they had left the monastery school together, the friends were seriously at odds.

The night – finally – had arrived when the Molin family had invited the aristocracy of Venice for a masked ball in their sumptuous palace. Venice was humming like a beehive, and the wildest speculations were heard across the city.

Edo had come to the Albergo Leon Blanco in order to pick up his friends. Despite their disagreement regarding the Contessa, Pierre and Armand were in good humour today, Pierre because he fervently hoped to see the Contessa (and be finally rewarded for having sent his daring gifts) and Armand as he secretly hoped to meet once more the girl who had given him a most entertaining lecture on art in the Ca' Giustinian.

Outside the Ca' Molin the scenery was no different from the Giustinian ball; gondolas and other boats were fighting for space in front of the palace in order to let their noble passengers disembark as a priority. Torches lit the entrance with bright flames and huge candles had been placed to light up the windows. The Byzantine palace looked elegant and inviting while the sound of music could be heard outside.

But it was inside the palace that the guests were crying out in pleasure and in awe. The Ca' Molin had been transformed into a palace of the Roman Empire, all the servants were dressed in short tunics (even the female ones, as

Armand noted with satisfaction) and an amazing number of palm trees had been placed inside the room to create the illusion of a green oriental oasis. Fountains of wine were gurgling with their precious liquid. Later on, strong gladiators appeared, their well-oiled bodies gleaming in the light of the numerous candles. They carried a table loaded with rare delicacies from all corners of the world, but instead of the usual decorative centrepieces, dwarfs were standing in the middle, dressed in the garb of a Roman emperor. There could be no doubt that the Molin had succeeded in surpassing the Giustiniani – surely the host of such a ball was worthy to be considered the future Doge of Venice.

Pierre had other things on his mind. He had been wandering from room to room, but no Contessa could be seen – at least he hadn't been able to recognize her. His task had been rendered so much more difficult by the fact that not only were there several ladies dressed in red costumes (would she wear red tonight?), there were many slender ladies wearing face masks – but whenever Pierre looked hopefully at them to catch a glimpse of their eyes, never had he been able to detect those laughing eyes the colour of coal that he had been dreaming about since he had met the Contessa for the first time.

He saw Armand dancing with several partners, as usual having a great time. Of course, being his best friend, Pierre did not really begrudge the fact that his friend was having a lot of fun, but all the same he felt that Armand could have been a bit more sensitive and caring about his best friend who was decidedly unhappy…

"Good evening." A melodious voice greeted Pierre from behind.

Pierre turned around as if he had been jabbed with a needle. Standing just in front of him he could see a lady dressed in pearl-white silk, dark curls falling on her delicate shoulders but the mask showed the same laughing eyes he had been dreaming about. And then Pierre noticed that she was wearing a necklace of pearls with a ruby, his necklace!

His knees went weak and once again his tongue seemed to be tied in a knot. Pierre hated himself for his awkwardness. He managed to utter some form of incoherent greeting which she found apparently amusing as he could hear her delighted laughter.

"I remember that you like to dance," she said in the tone of one making light conversation, "and so do I. Maybe we can make the best out of this?"

Pierre bowed and offered his arm as he led the Contessa to the dance floor. Was he walking, dancing or was he floating? How long had they been dancing? He couldn't tell! Pierre only knew that he was in heaven, knowing that she was close, touching her skin, feeling her curly hair tickle his hands, smelling her perfume, sweet and alluring as the lady wearing it. Time lost all significance; Pierre danced and laughed, and whenever the complicated figures of the dances made them meet or dance together, whenever Pierre was able to touch the Contessa, a shock went through his body, a powerful mixture of pleasure, combined with a yearning that was so strong it was almost overpowering. If only he could be alone with the Contessa!

Of course the other guests remarked that the handsome stranger was dancing only with a single lady of his choice – it needed nothing more to start the tongues wagging. Pierre noticed that people were looking at him and starting to whisper, but he didn't care. He had fallen head over heels in love. The musicians paused for a short while, but very soon the flutes and the mandolins started to play their merry tunes again. Pierre bowed to invite the Contessa to join him for the next dance, but she refused laughingly.

"Have mercy, dear sir!" she exclaimed and started to fan herself elegantly. "It's so very hot in here, I really must pause to breathe for a moment, please forgive me – I am but a weak female!" she explained in her charming French.

Pierre immediately felt a pang of guilt. "It is I who should apologize, my dearest Contessa, my behaviour is unforgiveable. Please allow me to lead you out of this ballroom, it's as hot as a furnace. Let me fetch a drink for you!"

He led the Contessa into the next room where the air was bit cooler, but as it was almost as crowded as the main ballroom, the improvement could barely be felt. Pierre searched the room for a servant; he felt quite parched. He had just got hold of two glasses of wine when all of a sudden a murmur went through the crowd. It started as a whisper, ending in a crescendo. Pierre turned his head curiously to see a new spectacle, a group of Roman-style dancers coming in, led by a drunken, half-naked Bacchus. Slowly, under the cheers and jeering of the bystanders they made their way towards the ballroom.

Pierre was fascinated by this spectacle, but the Contessa tugged at his sleeve. She led him straight towards one of the large French windows standing ajar and opening onto a balcony, half hidden behind long brocade curtains. A second later he found himself standing with the Contessa behind the curtains she had drawn shut. In the intimacy of their confinement the Contessa removed her mask and shook out her hair, greedily inhaling the fresh air. Blazing torches had been placed outside to light up the palazzo façade. Their light, mellowed by the darkness and reflected by the thick glass of the window panes, allowed Pierre to discover the unmasked face of the Contessa for the first time. It was perfect, beautiful – just as he had imagined it in his dreams. Her full lips smiled at him as she said, "I think it's time to say thank you for the flowers and this lovely necklace, I've never received such a beautiful gift before!" She laughed. "And I was impressed that you understood my little riddle. I detest stupid men."

There was no way to describe the elation Pierre felt as his arms closed around her delicate shoulders. She was anything but shy, he could feel her body pressing against his own, her heart beating against his chest – and then her curious tongue tickling his mouth. Close to delirium, time seemed to stop for Pierre, but he was sure of one thing: he wanted more, he needed more! Pierre was still in heaven when she withdrew all of a sudden from his embrace.

"Don't!" Pierre moaned with exasperation, "I want you!"

"It's not for long!" the Contessa answered and gave him a quick kiss on his cheek. "But I must go and powder my nose, stay here my darling and wait for me, I'll be back soon, I promise!"

Pierre let her go, but not until he had kissed her again, greedily, as if there would be no tomorrow. Seconds later she had disappeared, but her perfume still lingered in the air, as intense as if she were still present. Pierre inhaled the seductive scent but then he pushed the balcony door open, he needed to cool down. In his mind he imagined how they'd leave the ball to spend the night together, how he'd hold her in his arms in the gondola, then later he'd undress her, slowly, tenderly…

As the time passed Pierre grew more and more impatient. His daydreams were interrupted by a curious couple who had detected the secluded balcony door and peeked through the closed curtains. But Pierre was not ready to give up this hiding place – the Contessa had promised to come back any minute! Time ticked away slowly, the musicians finished the third or fourth dance since the Contessa had left. Pierre, already nervous, started to become annoyed. He knew that women always took a considerable time to powder their noses, but what if the Contessa had failed to go back to the right room? Women easily got lost; this was common knowledge, after all.

By the time the musicians had started to play yet another piece, Pierre's patience had evaporated and he decided to check all the rooms – an upsetting exercise as his peeking behind the curtains was ill received by those who had sought the intimacy of the shelter of the balconies. His disappointment turned into utter frustration as he walked from room to room, trying to find his Contessa among the crowds – but nowhere could he spot the woman who had kissed him so passionately and promised to come back soon – had it happened only half an hour ago?

Close to despair, Pierre entered the central ballroom, hoping to find her here; surely she must be waiting for him here! But as soon as he discovered that the grim and imposing figure of her chaperon aunt had disappeared as well, the truth dawned on Pierre: the Contessa had left the ball.

Pierre was still fighting with a disappointment that cut into his heart like a dagger when a heavy hand fell on his shoulder. "Why are you looking so gloomy, my friend, isn't this a great ball? I've never seen anything like it!" a tipsy Armand shouted into his ear, himself in the best of moods, and nudged his friend vigorously in an attempt to cheer him up.

Pierre stared furiously at Armand. The man was supposed to be his best friend, but he could quite easily have murdered him.

Travelling With Marie

François de Toucy had been satisfied with the speed and smooth progress of their journey – until today. Travelling with Marie and her maid had been a lot easier and faster than he had initially feared. After their adventure with the gang of scoundrels south of Avignon, Marie had avoided any repetition of such a dangerous situation; she had learned her lesson. Secretly – and somewhat reluctantly – François had to admit that he had underestimated Marie's tenacity. She rode and fought almost like a man and would never complain, even when they had to spend a night in rooms or locations that made even François turn up his nose. He hated bed bugs – yet the tiny beasts loved his body and never failed to find him. He had never understood why he would wake up covered all over by bites whereas his groom never seemed to have more than one or two. "The beasties love blue blood, my lord," grinned Michel while he applied an evil stinking pomade onto his master's bites that was supposed to soothe the irksome itching.

Yesterday it had happened that the travellers had been surprised by rough weather. A damp and unfriendly morning hadn't taken long to unveil its evil character, transforming into a disgusting wet afternoon, including tantrums of cold winter rain and hailstorms. Far away from any shelter, a real deluge had relentlessly followed the hapless riders and by the afternoon their felt hats and coats were totally soaked. The cold rain glued their clothes to their bodies and their skin, men and horses freezing like rarely before. Seeing the blue lips of Marie and her maid, Michel had stopped to light a fire under some fir trees. The result had been unsatisfactory, only a meagre fire with bluish flames, far too miserable to yield enough warmth to dry them or their coats. They had been thankful to find a room in the first inn that lay on their route but their room was as cold as the grave. The miserable bedsteads were only covered with worn, stained sheets and threadbare blankets. François had obtained some more moth-eaten rugs after a loud and animated argument with their stingy landlord, but their night had been anything but comfortable.

The next morning Marie started to cough, at first only from time to time, but as the afternoon approached she wouldn't stop coughing. Marie refused to listen to all suggestions to stop and take a rest, and stubborn as a mule she insisted on riding onwards. They were still a good fifty miles away from the city of Torino but as the sun started to set, François was in a state of extreme apprehension. He could see that Marie was holding onto the reins of her horse by sheer willpower alone. It became clear they must urgently find a decent inn, or albergo, as it was often called here in the Duchy of Savoy where a mixture of French and Italian dialect seemed to prevail most of the time.

Regardless of what Marie might be saying, they needed to rest and warm Marie up. *You're a weakling and a coward*, François chided himself, not for the first time cursing himself that he had given in and allowed Marie to join him. Finally, heaven appeared to show mercy on his plight and answered François's prayers. Not only did they spot a small hamlet on the horizon, as they approached the buildings they could make out a small post station. It was a neat building, apparently quite busy, as during the winter months all Alpine passes were closed and the traffic between France and Italy had no option but to use this road.

Heaven still seemed to be smiling on François, as his question of whether a room for four tired and frozen travellers (accompanied by the discreet appearance of some silver coins) was favourably answered by the old groom who ruled over the neat and well-kept stables.

"You're really lucky sir, this morning a party of Flemish wool merchants returned for France, one of our best rooms is now free tonight!"

Invigorated by what he considered a stroke of luck, François entered the taproom. If the stables had made a good impression already, the inside of the post station promised even more luxuries, such as good food and a warm room with a clean and decent bed. The proposed price was certainly at the high end and for a second François considered bargaining as his reserves had been shrinking fast – it certainly made a difference if two or four persons had to be fed! The innkeeper noticed his hesitation and added in a patronizing tone, "If you can't afford such a price, son, there is a small inn some miles further up the road, it's certainly not as well kept as our establishment, but it caters for guests of... ahem... limited means..."

François didn't appreciate being addressed in a confidential tone as 'son', nor did he appreciate being labelled poor or thrifty. He stared back at the innkeeper with the look he usually reserved for junior subalterns and immediately the innkeeper seemed to snap to attention.

"I can afford to pay for the room, don't you worry," François answered curtly. "Now show the room to me and I'll ask my companion and our grooms to join me – if I judge the room to be good enough!"

"You won't be disappointed, my lord!" The innkeeper had smoothly changed his tone and given François a title. "All is fully equipped to satisfy the most demanding guests!"

François followed the innkeeper to inspect the room and indeed, not only did it offer plenty of space and a rare window with diamond-glass panes, to his delight the room was clean and – what luxury – all was set so that a fire could be lit in the open fireplace. François could already imagine how the room would become comfortably warm. Exactly what they needed for Marie!

The innkeeper had followed his examination of the fireplace and added proudly, "We use only dry wood, you won't find the chimney smoking because of cheap inferior pine or brushwood! And we only charge a modest fee to keep it burning."

"We'll see quickly enough if this is true," François answered curtly. "Have it lit, I want a warm room!"

Silently François sent a small prayer of gratitude to all the saints in heaven that he could call to mind and strode to the stables to search out his companions. It was not difficult to locate them as he could already hear Marie's coughing before he had even passed the stable doors. As soon as he entered the stable, he sensed that something was amiss. His groom looked frightened, and tears were welling up in Antoinette's eyes. Marie was leaning heavily on a bale of straw, her breathing difficult and rough. François had to suppress a wave of panic – Marie was glowing hot with fever, and there was no doubt that she had become seriously ill. Losing no time, he lifted her up and carried her like a fragile bird inside the post station. They had almost made it to the stairs when they had the bad luck to run into the landlord who eyed him suspiciously.

"You're not trying to smuggle a sick person into my *respectable* house, my lord?" he asked, rolling the 'r' to underline his suspicion.

"Of course not!" François quickly lied, while he smiled at the landlord with the dashing smile he usually reserved for his superiors – or members of the female sex he wanted to impress.

"My young relative is very tired from our long journey, he's not used to travelling . Tomorrow he'll be as fit as a fiddle!"

But his famous smile didn't work tonight. The landlord gave him a long reflective glance and remained silent. Unluckily Marie chose this moment of silence to sneeze loudly and to cough; François was certain that the trumpets of Jericho couldn't have been any louder. Not waiting for any further comment, François grabbed Marie firmly in his arms and fled towards his room, shouting behind him, "Maybe he caught a slight cold as well, a drop of brandy and bit of sleep will do him good!"

Inside his room he placed Marie on the bed that stood closest to the fireplace. The fire was burning as brightly as the landlord had promised and gentle warmth was already spreading through the room. And yet François had the impression that a cold hand was gripping his heart and squeezing it. He looked down at Marie; her face was burning, she was sweating – but worse, her breath was rattling. Forever he'd remember this scene, the sobbing of her maid Antoinette, so much at odds with the comforting sound of the crackling fire, and the terrifying rattle of Marie's breathing. François had heard this sound often enough on the battlefield with his men. This heavy breathing was the herald of death, time to call a priest for the last rites. François prided himself on being a man of great resources; cool-headed, he had faced and

186

survived many situations that would have driven lesser men to despair. But this evening he learned the meaning of true fear and it took all his resolve to keep up appearances – he knew that Michel and Antoinette were relying on his strength.

Should he call a doctor? But had he ever met a doctor who had been able to heal a patient? Furthermore Marie's masquerade would become known to everybody – if the innkeeper didn't eject them from their room for bringing a sick guest into the house, the scandal of bringing a woman in the disguise of a man would be the last straw. Helpless and close to tears himself, he watched Antoinette wrapping her mistress in blankets while she kept crying and softly calling her mistress's name – but Marie didn't answer. Only the unsteady and rattling sound of her breathing filled the room.

In the grip of his fear, François missed the fact that the door of the room had been flung open. He almost winced as a sharp voice addressed him from behind. "May I know what's going on here, Signore?"

François turned around and faced the lady of the house. A quick glance sufficed to tell him that she was a formidable opponent, and that no dashing smile or boyish excuse would save him now. Whatever the wife of the innkeeper might lack in size, she made up for in personality. A stout person of undefined age, she was immaculately dressed, her white apron spotless, her eyes as sharp as the points of her starched lace collar. A human bull dog, if ever he saw one.

François was still going through all the options that came to mind: should he lie to her, throw himself desperately at her starched bosom and appeal to her sympathy, or play the haughty French aristocrat and simply command her to fetch a doctor? Nothing seemed to be adequate though. The sound of Marie's heavy breathing filled the room and made it impossible for him to think properly. His brain only seemed to repeat the same plea: *Don't die, Marie, please don't die!*

The landlady didn't bother to wait for his reply – maybe she hadn't really expected any reasonable excuse from her guest. With surprising agility she stepped forward, looked at Marie's face, and gently she caressed her burning forehead. Then she opened Marie's collar and shirt with experienced hands. Suddenly she gasped and gave a sharp exclamation. "Can you explain to me, *Sir*, why this man is in fact a young girl?"

François couldn't help it, he blushed like a schoolboy caught cheating by his teacher. But before he could find a suitable answer, Antoinette took over. She fell on her knees and sobbed, "Please help us, ma'am. Have mercy on us! The sick lady is my mistress, her parents are noble folk from Reims in France and I'm her maid. We were persecuted and had to flee from Reims, we feared for our lives, therefore both of us had to dress as men, but I've been with my mistress together ever since and I swear to the Holy Virgin that no harm has been done! Please help us to find a doctor, my mistress is going to die if nobody will help her!" The last words were uttered in a desperate appeal as she dissolved in tears and kissed the apron of the landlady as if she were the Virgin Mary herself.

"You and your groom get out of here, leave us alone!" the innkeeper's wife ordered curtly, not without adding darkly, "We will most certainly discuss this later, but first I have to see if we can rescue this poor girl. Tell my husband to send a maid with hot water and a clean nightgown – what a disgrace to keep her in this filthy riding gear, she's totally drenched in sweat, why are men always as incapable as they're blind?"

Meekly François promised to ask for the maid and added, "Shouldn't we send for a doctor?"

The landlady replied with a sharp snort; clearly she thought that this request was a waste of precious time. "The last time we saw our doctor was two years ago when the French recruited him for their army. Mind you, it hasn't been a great loss! But tell my husband to call the wise woman from the neighbouring village, I can certainly do with some help, we must get the fever down or she'll die!"

François and his groom left the room; they had received their orders. He looked at Marie, hesitating as to whether he should really leave her. But somehow he believed that he was now leaving Marie in the best hands he could imagine, and all he could do was to ask the innkeeper to rush and fetch this wise woman… and wait for a miracle to happen. The landlady might have spoken curtly, but François had seen the fear in her eyes.

They stayed in the taproom until the early hours of the morning. Numerous candles had burned down and had been replaced by the servants; all of the servants and even the few remaining guests had been strangely silent, as if all were aware that Marie was fighting for her life upstairs in her room.

In the meantime the wise woman had arrived. François had expected an old hag with a wrinkled face and the usual bag containing strange and disgusting ingredients. But the woman who presented herself was still quite young; neatly dressed, she carried a bag from which emanated the agreeable scent of herbs, one of them being rosemary, François was sure. She had been rushed upstairs and since then, François had lost track of time.

Suddenly the door opened and the landlady entered the taproom. Her apron was still spotless but he could see the tell-tale signs of worry and fatigue on her face now; she had wilted like the points of her lace collar.

"I think it's time we called for the priest," she said calmly, trying to remain composed, but there were tears shimmering in her eyes. "I've done my best, but the Lord seems to be calling her home, I don't think she'll make it to tomorrow!"

"I know that you did your best..." but François couldn't say any more, his voice broke, the world seemed to stop. He suddenly felt something warm and wet on his hand; François de Toucy, the aloof and elegant musketeer and gentleman, had started to weep.

Some Time Ago In Reims

"Why are you so restless, my dear?" Céline was sitting comfortably in her favourite armchair. It still felt strange to be back in her old house in Reims, so small and confined after all the sumptuous castles she had been living in during the past year. It felt even stranger to be here in Reims together with a husband and a baby that was sleeping peacefully (she hoped) with its wet nurse upstairs. Céline sighed, but it was a sigh of contented happiness.

She glanced at her husband and he looked back, rather guilty that she had been able to read his thoughts so easily. Charles moved uncomfortably on the chair that squeaked in protest. Not for the first time, Charles thought that French furniture was simply not built to accommodate people of his size. "I can't forget tonight at Marie's house," he confessed. "Something really strange must have been going on! You saw Marie's mother as well – and you're sure that Marie hasn't eloped...?"

"Yes, I'm sure. Something is wrong with Pierre, that's the point. All I can say, my dear Charles, is that you've never been prone to hysterics. If you feel that something is amiss as well, I'm afraid we'll have to take the matter seriously!" Céline laid her embroidery aside – she had only been stitching halfheartedly; Céline had never understood why gentlewomen were supposed to do needlework for charity. Critically she looked at what should have become a work of art and sighed. Clearly her embroidery would never live up to expectation.

She looked at her husband and challenged him, "What do you think is going on?"

"I agree, it must be something to do with Pierre," Charles admitted reluctantly. "If François de Toucy left at full tilt and Marie has joined him – against all conventions – there can be only one conclusion!"

"Pierre's in difficulties?" Céline stated, rather than asked.

"Knowing that de Toucy is stationed in Paris, he must have received some warning or some information, maybe Richelieu has changed sides again."

"That's speculation, Charles, as far as I remember, the Cardinal even gave them a letter of protection!" Céline protested.

"You're right, maybe I'm seeing phantoms. It happens if you're close to politics, finally you become paranoid. I'm so happy that I don't have to take sides in England at present; poor King Charles, I wonder how long he'll keep his head on his shoulders!"

"Come on Charles, you're becoming really gloomy tonight, the King might lose his kingdom, but he can always go into exile to France!"

Charles declined to comment. He knew the King very well and how stubborn he could be; he didn't see the King choosing exile.

"But we've strayed from the topic: you think that Pierre is in trouble?" Céline quizzed her husband.

"There can't be any other conclusion; if not now, he's about to be. François de Toucy is no fool," Charles admitted unhappily.

"What are you going to do then, don't beat around the bush, Charles!" Céline knew her husband well enough by now; he wouldn't sit in Reims waiting for disaster to happen.

"I envisage a short trip to Venice," Charles answered and added hastily, "I'll be back soon enough, you won't have to wait a long time, don't worry!"

Céline looked at her husband; how much she loved him! There could be no question of letting him leave for Venice – alone. "You're wrong Charles, I won't have to wait at all! I'm going to travel with you!"

Resolutely, and ignoring his protests, she opened the cupboard in the hope of finding some maps that her father or some long forgotten ancestors might have stored there. Suspiciously she pulled a rather old map out of a pile that must have been gathering dust for decades. "It doesn't look very accurate to me," she remarked.

Charles scrutinized the old map and agreed. "More artistic value than accuracy, I agree, but at least it'll give us some idea!" His finger traced some lines. "I think the fastest way will be to use a coach to reach the Saône river and then sail down to Marseille via Lyon, then we'll have to ride to Italy but the weather will be much better down there!"

He turned and embraced his wife. "You're sure you want to come with me? It means you have to leave our baby alone?" he asked.

"I hate the idea, but I have a wonderful nurse, my cousin and my aunt will love to help out as well – and I have a bigger baby to look after," she said lovingly. "When do you want to leave?"

"Tomorrow?"

Céline swallowed. "All right, tomorrow sounds ideal, that leaves me plenty of time to arrange everything!"

191

"You're a darling!" Charles kissed his wife. "Most women would have thrown a tantrum and insisted that I stay at home!"

"There's at least one advantage to marrying an old spinster," Céline replied drily. "We know better than to throw useless tantrums!"

All Roads Still Lead To... Venice

Henri de Beauvoir felt tired, frustrated, and almost frozen to death. The biting cold was penetrating through his clothes, seeping from his flesh into his bones, spreading through his body, paralysing his limbs and even his mind, a mind that seemed to be detached from his body. He didn't know what was worse – the numbness of his limbs or the fact that he could barely keep his eyes open.

They had been playing hide and seek to avoid being tracked by the dreaded soldiers of the Archbishop of Verona. For two weeks they had meandered through boundless forests until they had reached the steep mountains. But by now Henri had come to the conclusion that Mustafa was overdoing it. No soldiers had been spotted since they had left Lady Sophia's villa; in fact they'd rarely seen anybody at all, with the exception of tongue-tied peasants, scared to death by the appearance of a white stranger and his black servant. Sometimes it appeared to Henri as if Verona, as if even Lady Sophia and her sallow husband, had been a mere anecdote, if not a bad dream.

Since yesterday their horses, worn out and tired as their riders, had been ploughing through ever deeper layers of fresh snow. A sudden spell of cold weather had transformed the damp, unfriendly dark forest into a glitteringly pristine landscape. The sad skeletons of winter trees, their dead leaves shed long ago in autumn, and their miserable companions, the dark foreboding pine trees, had been covered overnight by crystals of ice and snow, a glittering fairytale landscape, pleasing and different to the dark woods they had crossed before. The sun was shining out of a blue winter sky and their way seemed to be littered by a trail of sparkling diamonds when Henri heard Mustafa exclaiming full of awe, "Isn't this beautiful?"

Henri half-closed his eyes, squinting at the glaring sun's rays reflected on the snow. He huddled even deeper into his fur coat and muttered, "My vision of beauty is a warm fire and a decent glass of wine!"

After they had escaped from Verona, they had slept mostly under the roofs of farmers, poor devils willing to accommodate guests without any curious questions as long as they paid some copper coins. Would he ever get used to sleeping not only under the same roof, but often enough in the same room as their hosts, shared with their numerous and noisy offspring as well as with animals of all sorts? Henri had turned his nose up at this to begin with, but somehow he must have got used to the pungent smell of dirt, animal excrement, smoke and sweat that was only masked from time to time by the sickening scent of the winter staple of the poor – cabbage soup – sometimes refined by some chicken bones. For the poor, a pot with soup boiling on the open hearth meant times were good, people were not starving. But the smell turned his stomach – on the first few occasions he had refused to it eat it, but later he had given in, having had no choice.

At first their nightly escape had appealed to Henri's sense of adventure but after two weeks he had started to hate their daily routine of sleeping on makeshift mattresses of dirty straw and eating the unavoidable cabbage soup, accompanied by a piece of stale bread if they were lucky.

The relationship between Henri and his guide had undergone a subtle change since they had escaped from the golden cage of Verona. Although Mustafa still addressed him with the respect that was due to Henri's position, Henri soon detected a note of irony, even thinly veiled contempt in Mustafa's speech. Of course the boy knew that Henri depended fully on him if he ever wanted to find his way out of these endless woods; all Henri could do was to pretend that he didn't notice.

"I must stink like a goat," he muttered, more to himself than to Mustafa.

"Not only that, my lord, if you don't pay attention you'll also start bleating like a goat," answered Mustafa, skilfully avoiding Henri's whip.

Henri considered for a minute if he should challenge the boy here and now, but of course he couldn't, he had no idea where he was, whereas Mustafa seemed to know the region like the back of his hand.

As soon as we arrive in Venice, I'll show you what it means to laugh at Henri de Beauvoir, you'll pay me back for this impertinence!

Mustafa must have sensed Henri's fury as he quickly added to mollify his new master, "We'll be starting our descent today, in a matter of three days we'll be back to civilisation, my lord." He paused before adding, "And I apologize for the remark about the goat, my lord!"

Henri didn't bother to answer; he wouldn't forget, and he *never* forgave.

Mustafa remained true to his word. Two days later the woods started to thin, the snow receded and soon they entered the first forlorn scattered villages followed by a busy small town where they could stay in a comfortable inn. Henri's spirits started to rise. To the surprise of the innkeeper Henri ordered a hot bath to be prepared. The innkeeper repeated the strange request to his wife and crossed himself; he was sure that only a heathen would think about such a strange thing in winter. But as soon as Mustafa rubbed Henri dry, Henri – for the first time in weeks – felt like a human being. Clean clothes, the hot bath and a decent meal accompanied by dark red wine restored Henri to civilisation. He also discovered that Mustafa could not only handle his knife to perfection to cut a throat, he made a surprisingly good valet and barber. Chatting with the landlord in the dining room Henri understood that they had reached Venetian territory. He was out of the reach of the Archbishop of Verona, he was a free man now. Obviously the next step had to be to search for the best tailor in town, not a very difficult task in a small town that boasted only three tailors at best.

"Giuseppe will be the only tailor suited to the taste of a true gentleman," the innkeeper concluded after long reflection and intensive scratching of his head. Henri had already remarked that the inhabitants of this region were not fast thinkers, to say the least.

Giuseppe proved to be a rare pearl amongst tailors and as soon as he had understood that this strange gentleman who spoke Italian fluently but with an undeniable French accent not only thought that it was far below his station to bargain about negligible details such as prices but expected him to choose only the best quality fabrics, he delved deep into rarely opened chests and drawers to search for lace and the finest wool from Flanders, silk from the Middle Kingdom and buttons made from silver and exotic mother of pearl while he secretly sent a prayer of gratitude to the Madonna and vowed to make a special offering this coming Sunday.

Mustafa steadfastly dodged Henri's orders to share his bedroom, continuing to sleep in the servants' quarters. Henri was furious but – after giving it some more thought – wasn't certain if he ought grudgingly to accept this rejection, as he still remembered how easily Mustafa had cut the throat of the guard in Verona, a skill that could only have been acquired with practice.

In early January they arrived in Mestre, a small town serving as the gateway to the sprawling lagoon of the city of Venice. A freezing wind was blowing from the north and with a shudder Henri remembered the ice and snow they had just left behind. Henri had thought finding a boat to cover the small distance between the port to the island of Venice would be the easiest part of their journey, but it soon became apparent that the Venetian authorities painstakingly controlled all traffic between the mainland and the city – and Henri had no intention of making his identity and his arrival in the city known to the authorities.

He therefore dispatched Mustafa to the port with the task of finding a boat willing to smuggle them inside the city. A new, depressing routine ensued: morning after morning Mustafa left for the port in order to hire a boat, only to be seen returning frustrated and disappointed with sagging shoulders in the evening. Henri – unused to not getting his way immediately – grew more and more impatient as the days ticked by.

A new day had dawned and as usual Mustafa rode to the port in order to hang around in the sleazy wine bars in search of an owner of a boat, a man willing to turn a blind eye to his passengers. It was raining heavily outside, so Henri decided to stay inside the taproom and not to roam around the city; instead he'd read the new French book he had acquired from a peddler, a rare find. To his dismay he discovered too late that the intriguing title had been misleading, and the author was nothing but a damned philosopher, inspired by a burning desire to improve the morals of his fellow men. Henri stifled a yawn; exercises for improvement of the mind or lessons of a moral nature had the effect of boring him to tears.

195

Henri had almost fallen asleep over his reading when he noticed the arrival of a new guest. He would probably never have bothered to look twice at this particular guest, as he was nondescript on all accounts, if it hadn't been for his noticeable, decidedly well-schooled French accent, that is. *A scholar or a gentleman*, mused Henri. But the guest's clothes were simple in the extreme, the drab, dark-brown robe spoke of meagre means, and yet Henri's eyes were not deceived: the quality of the fabric was smooth, this robe had not been woven from the scratchy cheap wool used for the poor. The man moved and spoke with a quiet demureness Henri had seen many times before... He looked at the guest with renewed interest and immediately it dawned on him: *This must be a man of the church, but why is a member of the French clergy travelling disguised as a poor merchant?*

The guest vanished as noiselessly as he had arrived and Henri was still trying to solve this riddle when Mustafa suddenly appeared, much earlier than usual. He was dripping wet from the rain, but was beaming with satisfaction. Henri's heart beat faster: this could only mean that – finally – Mustafa had found a boat!

"Did you find a boatman willing to take us to Venice?" Henri shouted, more than asked, as soon as Mustafa came face to face with him. Mustafa took in the smells of approaching lunch with satisfaction; he was always hungry.

"It's arranged, my lord, but it was really difficult!" Mustafa did not hide his pride. "The Venetian authorities seem to be very strict, it took me a long time to convince a boatman to smuggle us into the city, my lord – I mean a boatman who wouldn't just throw us overboard as soon as he left the port – that would have been easy enough to find!"

"What you mean is that I'll need to part with a lot of my gold to get both of us to Venice?"

"That's certain, my lord, most men didn't even want to discuss it with me, it seems the Venetian prisons are hell on earth!"

You've no idea, how right you are, just the place for you, my friend, as soon as we get there!

Unaware of Henri's thoughts Mustafa continued happily, "But the owner of the wine bar helped me after I left a small fortune there and introduced me to the captain of a fishing boat today. I invented a story that we were forced to flee from France because my master killed his opponent in a duel, a question of your lordship's honour. I told them that we need to stay incognito until the issue is forgotten in Paris."

"Don't they say time heals all wounds?" Henri commented ironically. "But I appreciate that you didn't make me a petty criminal in your story: a duel, now that, I can live with!"

Mustafa flashed him a rare smile. "Tomorrow afternoon we must be at the port and pay in gold, my lord, the boatman wants to arrive in Venice when it's dark and he can enter the city without being detected. We can sleep for one night in his house. I had to promise that we'll be gone afterwards, though!"

"Of course! I'll probably stink like a barrel of salted fish after staying a day on his boat and in his house, did he seriously think that I'd remain there voluntarily?" Henri made a contemptuous gesture. "But I agree, the important thing is to get to Venice, there's time to arrange the rest later! You've earned yourself a meal, my boy, come and sit down, there is plenty for the two of us!"

I'll make sure that this is your last decent meal, Henri thought, as Mustafa eagerly watched the servants heaping the delicious meat and freshly baked bread onto the table and dug his fingers and dagger with delight into the food. *I'll find a way to get rid of you in Venice, nobody shall ever know what happened to me in Verona!* Henri finished his thoughts and smiled like a wolf as his gleaming teeth tore into a juicy piece of mutton glazed with honey, spices and rosemary. How entertaining to watch Mustafa savouring his last supper!

Time seemed to be creeping at a snail's pace as Henri waited impatiently for the next day to arrive. If the young girl who'd shared his room from time to time had hoped to earn some more silver coins tonight she found herself bitterly disappointed. Henri waved her away like a troublesome fly when she approached him in the taproom, hips swaying, a moist smile on her lips. His mind was focused on more important issues: How would he find his cousin? How would he establish himself credibly in the city?

He couldn't come up with a satisfying plan, but it was comforting to know that his pockets were heavy with the treasures stolen from Lady Sophia's chests. Henri was confident he would be able to bribe or spend his way into society. From his own experience he knew that many noble families were as poor as church mice behind their carefully maintained facades of tradition and splendour – easy prey to be plucked, once you promised to take care of their ever mounting debts. Henri reached for the jug of heavy red wine that would be his chosen companion for the night and as the warmth of the wine spread through his body his eyes closed and he fell asleep.

The great day had come! Henri sat on a coiled rope, covered by some rags, his makeshift seat for tonight's crossing. Wrapped in his fur coat and additional blankets he sat facing the cold night, but for no gold in all the

197

world would he stay inside the grimy cabin with its penetrating stench of rotten fish. He felt excited, almost elated, confident that the time of his revenge was finally approaching. He had never harboured any doubts that Pierre might not be in Venice, Nicolas's informants had never failed. His thoughts wandered to Nicolas; it seemed so long ago that they had met! Had Nicolas survived that terrible night in Paris when the cursed Pierre and Armand had destroyed Nicolas's house in a blaze of flames?

Henri heard the subdued cries of the sailors as the first distant lights of Venice came into sight. He could see them moving close to the ship's bow like bodiless shadows. Mustafa must be among them, invisible, as his dark skin melted into the blackness. Henri smelled the salty water. He could hear a random seagull crying – or was he just imagining it? The rolling movement of the boat started to lull him to sleep, and he had difficulty keeping his eyes open. How long until they reached Venice and he could disembark? Henri gave in to the temptation of fatigue and closed his eyes.

As he was nodding off, strong hands, cold and hard as steel, closed around his neck and a familiar voice whispered into his ear, "Good evening, my noble friend, maybe you should be more careful when you travel in unknown company!"

A Messenger Arrives

The unknown traveller had reached the port. Politely he asked to be shown the way to the guards but among the ragged urchins who had gathered around him like dirty sparrows in the expectation of coaxing him into throwing some morsels of food or coins, his question – harmless enough – had the effect of dispersing them as if a buzzard had landed among the flock of sparrows. Only one of them, apparently the toughest one, remained and challenged him. The traveller had difficulty understanding the boy's broad Italian accent, but – of course – he wanted to know how much there was to be gained for guiding him to the dreaded authorities. A deal was struck and only minutes later the traveller found himself confronting a member of the Venetian coast guard. Tall and fat, sporting an imposing moustache, he was resting comfortably on his halberd, his colourful attire heralding the importance and wealth of the Republic of Venice.

"May I speak to your captain?" the traveller enquired politely.

The guard scrutinized the foreigner who stood in front of him. Clad in brown, unremarkable clothes it was obvious that this man was just another insignificant individual in the endless row of callers, probably troublesome – the guard knew this type. With no money for bribes, these people would try to get their way by sheer tenacity. The guard knew his duty, he had to shield his captain from this sort of penniless customer.

"The captain is very busy today!" he answered. "You can leave a message and come back tomorrow, maybe he'll have time to meet you then!" knowing perfectly well that this would never happen.

"I do understand that your captain is very busy," the foreigner answered smoothly with his slight French accent. "This is a very important port and you have very important tasks to fulfil!"

The guard's chest swelled slightly; at least the foreigner had understood the importance of his assignment.

"I'm really sorry though to have to insist that your captain receive me immediately, and I mean now!" the polished voice of the foreigner had suddenly changed, cutting like a knife. He had opened his waistcoat and produced a document. The guard suddenly had an uneasy feeling, as he was not very literate, but it didn't take an accomplished clerk to see that the heavy seals affixed to the documents must signify something important.

"I think you had better go and see your captain now, I guess you don't want to get into trouble with your superiors in Venice!" The voice was smooth again.

The guard knew he had been beaten and retreated hastily to inform his captain. As he had expected, the captain had retreated to his private apartment. Not surprisingly, his captain wasn't using his siesta for sleeping. Through the closed door the guard could hear the giggling voice of a woman and the captain's cajoling answers. The guard breathed heavily to steel himself against the insults that would inevitably be forthcoming once he was to enter the captain's sanctum, but the document had looked official enough to demand immediate attention. He knocked at the door, once, twice, until finally he could hear the gruff answer of the captain. "Get lost, don't you dare to disturb me!" a voice yelled from behind the closed door. The guard was perspiring now, but diligently he knocked again. Seconds later the door opened and his captain appeared, his shirt hanging loose, hair tousled, standing in the doorway ready to strike.

"Didn't I order you *not* to disturb me!" he roared.

"You did, sir, but there is a messenger downstairs, he insists on seeing you immediately, sir!" The guard stood to attention and tried to ignore the naked woman who had stepped out of the bed and embraced the captain from behind.

"You dare to disturb me for a bloody messenger?"

"I cannot read very well, Sir, but he's got an urgent message for His Eminence, the Patriarch of Venice, I saw the seal of the Church!" The last sentence was added with awe.

The captain tried to digest this information. Still irate, he barked at the woman, "Get dressed until I come back, you stupid whore. I told you never to show yourself naked to my men!"

Then he turned back to the guard. "I hope for your sake that this is true, otherwise you'll be assigned to Crete!"

But he had already returned to the bed to put on his breeches and stockings. Minutes later the strange messenger found himself received by a hastily dressed and decidedly bad-humoured captain.

"Can I see your credentials?" he barked at the foreigner who had noiselessly entered his office. "And may the Lord save you if you have made up some fancy story! We've got very nice dungeons here!"

"This is a letter from His Eminence, the Duke, Cardinal Richelieu, addressed to his beloved Brother in Christ, the Patriarch in Venice, and I'm supposed to meet His Eminence, the Patriarch, *immediately*." The foreigner handed the document and the captain immediately recognized the heavy seals and the expensive vellum. There could be no doubt about the importance of this message.

"What do you wish me to do for you?" he asked in a more polite tone.

"I need a boat, now, as I want to meet His Eminence today." The foreigner answered as if his request were nothing extraordinary.

"I have no boats available until tomorrow," the captain answered curtly, "come back tomorrow and I'll see what I can do!"

"If I said today, I mean today!" The messenger's tone had changed, and he suddenly had become a person of authority. "I can only recommend, my son, that you follow my orders without further discussion, or I'll make sure that His Eminence will take care of the salvation of your soul by the means we have at our disposal within the holy institution of the Inquisition. It seems that your dedication to the Church might need to be tested, at least it seems to be in urgent need of improvement."

The captain swallowed and reflected for a second if he should wring the neck of the impertinent messenger or drown him here and now in the port. But this tempting prospect only held for a fleeting moment, before he came back to reality; the methods of the Inquisition were as terrifying as they were legendary. "You'll have your boat in one hour at the latest, of course, I'm an obedient servant of His Eminence and our Holy Church!" he choked more than he answered.

"This is what I expected!" the messenger answered, his voice suddenly smooth again and devoid of emotion as if nothing had happened. "I'll recommend you to His Eminence for your obedience to the cause and the efficiency of your service!"

The captain of the guard bowed and strode out of the office. He'd need to find a boat ready to set sail; if need be, he'd recruit a merchant's boat. While he was still wracking his brains over which merchant to approach, ugly pictures of the torture chambers of the Inquisition lingered in his head. Once in his career he had been compelled to attend such an interrogation. He still remembered the cries of the victim and the burning – almost ecstatic – eyes of the priest who had conducted the interrogation to its gruesome end. The captain shuddered. He vowed to find a boat for this strange and dangerous messenger, and the faster he could get rid of him, the better!

A boat ready to sail for Venice was found almost immediately, thus the messenger arrived in the late afternoon that same day in front of the palatial buildings of the Patriarch of Venice. From here he was ushered into the antechambers of the episcopal offices as soon as the clerks had ascertained the authenticity of his letters. Their initial arrogance was soon replaced by an almost comic show of reverence, as a formal message sent by the highest prince of the Church in France to the Patriarch of Venice must signify some special event – of course His Eminence would be informed immediately, as soon as His Eminence returned from his meeting with His Grace, the Doge.

The French messenger thanked the secretary and sank into the upholstered armchair embroidered with the coat of arms of the city, the Lion of Saint Mark holding the holy scripture. He let his gaze roam around the room, a room with high vaulted ceilings, covered all over with gigantic paintings depicting saints in various stages of their martyrdom. The effect was as awe-inspiring as it was depressing, but the messenger didn't seem impressed. His eyes closed as he recited the rosary.

He must have been waiting for almost two hours when the secretary opened the winged doors ceremoniously and announced in a low voice, almost a whisper, that His Eminence was prepared to receive the foreign visitor. The messenger stopped praying and entered the huge office. He noticed that the Patriarch of Venice was standing close to the fireplace, rubbing his hands. Having just returned from his visit to the Doge, he must still have been feeling cold. The messenger's steps were muffled by the thick oriental carpets that covered the floor and as soon as he reached the Patriarch, he fell on his knees and reverently kissed the Patriarch's ring of office. Punctiliously they exchanged the appropriate forms of polite greeting until the messenger bowed once again and handed the letter of the Cardinal de Richelieu addressed to his Brother in Christ, the Patriarch of Venice.

The Patriarch took the letter and held it close to his eyes. Apparently His Eminence was severely myopic. He took the trouble to read the letter carefully, twice, before he lowered his arm and asked incredulously, "It is always a pleasure to assist my Brother in Christ, the Cardinal de Richelieu, but I can hardly believe that this affair should be so urgent as to demand our immediate attention?"

The messenger bowed reverently in order to show that he accepted the mild reproach. He looked behind his back to make sure he would not be overheard, as it was time to deliver the Cardinal's secret message. "His Eminence, the Cardinal de Richelieu, sends Your Eminence his brotherly greetings and asks for a favour that Your Eminence might be well disposed to carry out. If Your Eminence can use Your Eminence's undeniable influence to have both men arrested immediately and let them 'disappear', either by means of an accident or imprisonment, the Cardinal de Richelieu will feel indebted to Your Eminence and show you his special gratitude!" And like a conjurer he produced a bag of golden coins and placed it on the low side table.

The Patriarch of Venice had well understood the gesture but he looked very critically at his visitor. "Please tell His Eminence that I cannot be bought. Arresting members of the high aristocracy of France does not only seem a very odd thing to do, it will also cause an enormous stir if ever our involvement were to be known; I know the situation in France well enough to understand that the de Saint Paul family exerts a lot of influence at the royal court. I think I may even be related to them by some distant cousin. I'm afraid that I must decline this request!" The Patriarch frowned; he was displeased.

And yet the messenger didn't seem to bother, he didn't even look irritated. He bowed again and replied, "We fully agree that this is a very delicate matter indeed and that it must be handled with the greatest diplomacy and care. Never would it be known that Your Eminence could have been involved. Any move from the authorities must be done in utter secrecy and appearances must be maintained that Your Eminence is trying to shield the genuine holders of the title by arresting those imposters. The Cardinal de Richelieu will still have the greatest respect if Your Eminence should come to the conclusion to refuse his small request, but in the meantime he would like me to offer you a second gift!" The messenger now unwrapped the precious jewel-studded cross: diamonds, emeralds and rubies sparkled like a rainbow in the light of the candles. The monk fell to his knees and while he offered the cross to the Patriarch he said in a low voice, "The Cardinal de Richelieu is offering this small gift reverently to the man he fervently hopes to see elected as our next pope. All votes of the French clergy will be yours when the next conclave gathers. Any service rendered to the Cardinal de Richelieu will not only be remembered, it will bear fruit once the time of papal election has come!"

The Patriarch seized the cross as if in a trance and drew it close to his short-sighted eyes in order to study the intricate pattern and the precious jewels. The messenger had seen the flicker of greed as soon as he had mentioned the papal elections – once again the Cardinal had assessed his opponent correctly. The messenger still remembered the words of Cardinal Richelieu: "To a Patriarch of Venice we must offer much more than money or some fancy jewels, he probably has more of those than we can imagine. But the Patriarch is the second man in the Church's ranks, and I've rarely met a second man who didn't burn with desire and ambition to become the first!" He had chuckled and added, "Just look at our dear Mazarin!"

The Patriarch cleared his throat and answered slowly, "I can see now... we must protect the Marquis de Beauvoir from those imposters. Please tell my Brother in Christ, the most noble Cardinal-duc de Richelieu, that I will use my humble influence in this city to further his cause. As for the next elections, let's pray that that date is far away and may the Lord grant a long life to His Holiness. I'm certain that the Good Lord will guide and enlighten us all in order to choose the best shepherd for His flock when the time is due!"

The messenger stood up. It was about time, as his knees had started to hurt abominably. He bowed rather stiffly but reverently, kissed the ancient ring of office of the Patriarch and took his leave. His master, Cardinal Richelieu, would be content; the messenger had accomplished his mission smoothly and successfully, and as always, would not have disappointed the Cardinal! The two men would disappear now, their fates having been sealed.

Time To Fast, Time To Repent

Pierre sat at a small table, clad in his favourite brocade dressing gown, opposite Armand who had joined him for a late breakfast. Sunlight was streaming into their room, a pleasant change after a miserable week with barely any sun. And yet the change in weather failed to lift the mood of at least one of the two gentlemen sharing their meal in silence. As usual, the faithful Jean was serving his master and his friend, but he rolled his eyes in despair.

It was no secret that his master had fallen head over heels in love with the infamous Contessa. Since they had left the last ball, Pierre de Beauvoir had become extremely moody and taciturn, and he'd barely touched any food despite Jean's efforts to please him. Pierre had become a true burden to his friends and even more so to his loyal servant.

"I think I'll go out this afternoon, Edo has discovered a new Turkish bath, he's heard that it's very invigorating – and the massage is apparently excellent. I think I can do with a bit of a massage, my back has been hurting lately!" Armand reached for another piece of flaky pastry and spread a generous helping of honey on top of it – he didn't look at all like a person who was suffering from a sore back.

"I'm not surprised your back is hurting, you've been sitting in this new gaming parlour until the wee hours of the morning!" Pierre couldn't help answering. "Our fencing teacher keeps telling you that you should take more exercise!"

Armand made a face and took a large bite of the flaky pastry. "He's always complaining," he mumbled with a full mouth. "He would do better to show us some new moves, at least that's what we're paying him for! But in any case, he won't object as a massage will make me more supple!" Armand swallowed the last delicious morsels and resumed his initial idea. "Want to join me for the Turkish bath? I think it'll be fun! Edo has promised to come as well if he can make it!"

Pierre was undecided. Since the Contessa had disappeared from the ball without any trace or excuse, nothing seemed to attract his interest, nothing seemed to matter. While he pondered if he should join his friend, he sifted listlessly through the small pile of sealed envelopes and messages that Jean had prepared for him on the table. Apart from the random bills for new clothes, most of those would be invitations. Since the Carnival season had ended and the official period of fasting before Easter had started, there would be no more invitations to masked balls or public gatherings; all activities were confined to private invitations or intimate dinners, as the secret police would report and punish any deviation from the rules. But they had been flooded with invitations for card parties as word had spread that the foreign gentlemen were keen players and exceptionally generous.

Stifling a yawn, Pierre opened the second envelope in the pile. It bore only his name but no sender, a plain envelope, nothing special. He opened it and unfolded the paper when all of a sudden he felt as if a bolt of lightning had struck his body.

Pierre, chéri!

Please forgive me for leaving you so suddenly! Something dreadful happened, I had no time or opportunity to explain, my aunt dragged me away from the ball. Before I have to leave Venice forever, I simply must see you again, and wrap my arms around you... Come to the Ca' Montefiori this afternoon, I shall be waiting for you, alone.

Eternal love,

Eleonora.

Pierre read the short message several times, wondering what kind of dreadful event might have affected the Contessa; his heart was bleeding for her. Suddenly he realized that Jean was standing close to him and addressing him: "Anything I should do, my lord?"

Pierre realized that two curious pairs of eyes were fixed on him. Armand was remarking that his friend's thoughts were far away, his behaviour seemed very strange!

"Thank you, nothing, oh yes, maybe, a fresh cup of coffee!"

Jean didn't comment on the fact that he had poured a fresh cup only minutes ago. Silently he removed the cup of finest Chinese porcelain and set off to the kitchen to fetch a pot of fresh coffee. Armand cleared his throat. "Anything special, Pierre? Don't tell me that the Contessa is up to her tricks again, I told you to forget about her, she's got the most shocking reputation and seriously – she's driving you mad!"

Pierre turned scarlet. He felt awkward, he hated lying to his best friend. Trying to save the situation, he improvised, "No, it's a just stupid reminder, I forgot to pay the jeweller; it's most upsetting, if I'm not careful, news that I'm broke will spread through Venice like wildfire!"

Armand seemed to be mollified. "You're right, better pay him quickly, here you never know. In France they wouldn't dare to be so impertinent as to send us reminders, but here in Venice we're just treated as any other stupid foreigner!"

"Well, this is exactly what we're pretending to be!" Pierre answered, happy to have diverted his friend's thoughts.

"What about this afternoon then, you'll join us?" Armand insisted again.

"No, I'm really sorry, it's tempting but I just remembered I have to go to the tailor, I ordered a new silk suit and this afternoon I have a fitting!"

Pierre was happy that Jean had not yet returned to hear this lie. He'd surely know that the fitting had been scheduled for tomorrow.

Armand looked disappointed but as he attached the greatest importance to being impeccably dressed, he immediately accepted the logic of Pierre's excuse. "All right, I'll go on my own, I hope that Edo will join me at least!"

After breakfast they parted as best friends again. Pierre's mood had suddenly improved, and they had been joking and chatting just as in old times. Armand left Pierre, hoping that his friend had finally started to overcome his obsession with the Contessa.

Now, I need to get rid of Jean, he's behaving like a clucking hen and will never let me go on my own to the Ca' Montefiori! But once again, fate seemed to be smiling on Pierre. As Jean poured the fresh coffee, he cleared his throat nervously. "May I ask for an afternoon off, my lord?"

"That's unusual, Jean! Of course, you may, but tell me, have you met a nice girl?"

Jean's bronze-coloured skin deepened in colour, and he looked positively embarrassed. "She's one of the parlour maids... and she's offered to show me the city..."

Pierre laughed. "I hope she shows you even more! You have my blessing, just prepare the blue velvet waistcoat, I might go out this afternoon and join Armand, and you know he always wants me to be dressed my best!" *I'm becoming an accomplished liar*, thought Pierre, not sure if he liked his new skill.

The sun was shining brightly in a pristine sky of pale blue. Luckily the lining of Pierre's velvet waistcoat was not too thick – how embarrassing it would have been to arrive at the Contessa's house bathed in perspiration! It was one of those lovely days that February can produce. The dark shadows of winter were quickly forgotten, a general mood of spring-to-come had set in. Soaking in the sunshine, Pierre sat in his seat with mixed feelings. Was the boat going to bring him now to the Contessa, to the fulfilment of his dreams – or to the end, their final farewell? He had read her hastily written letter again and again, hoping to decipher a hidden message, a reason why she had to leave Venice so fast. Her letter seemed straightforward enough and from whatever angle he had looked at it, it didn't yield any additional information. So here he sat, his heart beating like a hammer, his chest filled simultaneously with hope and trepidation, a bundle of nerves.

The boat moored at the jetty of the Ca' Montefiori and Pierre inhaled deeply the weird but wonderful smell of Venice, a strange perfume made from the ingredients of sun, salt water, the smoke of thousands of chimneys, a slight tinge of mould and the ever-present scent of the exotic spices that were stored in the warehouses along the Canal Grande, mixed from time to time with a more unpleasant note of drying fish. He heard the shouting and cursing of the sailors on the Canal Grande, echoed by the furious cries of a gang of ever-present and watchful seagulls competing to get the best bits of rubbish or the rare delicacy of a rotten fish head.

Pierre wanted to hold this moment in his memory forever, but there was no reason to linger on the boat. He stepped forward and a haughty butler received him as soon as he stepped on the ground. His arrival must have been expected. "Signore de Beaulieu?" the butler stated rather than asked. Not expecting a denial he continued, "Her ladyship is expecting your arrival."

The butler walked composedly towards the staircase that rose in easy flights and Pierre followed him to the first floor. The formal attitude of the butler reassured Pierre; maybe the situation after all was less dramatic than he had imagined. Didn't women always like to create a bit of drama? They crossed a gallery, covered from floor to ceiling with a myriad of paintings. Although Pierre had his mind on more pressing matters he couldn't help noticing that all of those paintings must have been painted by true masters of their art. Whatever terrible disaster had befallen the Contessa, it couldn't be poverty.

As soon as they had reached the end of the gallery, the butler opened a door and led Pierre into a room that lay in almost total darkness as the curtains were still drawn. The air of the room was unpleasantly damp and Pierre wondered why their rendezvous was to take place in this dark and disagreeable room. Since this morning he had imagined all kinds of settings and scenarios, but certainly not a room with the stale atmosphere of an abandoned store room.

"May I invite you to wait here for a short moment, sir?" the butler enquired politely.

"It seems that I have no option," Pierre couldn't help replying, but the door was closing, and the butler had already left the room.

"How right you are!" replied a familiar voice.

Pierre turned around, thunderstruck, to find himself looking into the gleaming barrel of a loaded flintlock pistol. His worst nightmare had come true.

This Is What Friends Are For

François de Toucy had sought refuge in the private dining room of the auberge, a large glass of strong liquor in his hand. Unwilling and unable to accept the inevitable he had been sitting there the whole night, praying to all the saints that came to mind, close to despair. By midnight the landlady had sent a stable boy to fetch the priest. The holy man had arrived early in the morning, and now, they were almost approaching lunch time. The priest sat tired and silent like a mourning black crow in the same room, waiting to be called upstairs to perform the last rites.

But François couldn't accept fate, he simply couldn't accept the idea that Marie was to die – the same Marie who had fought and ridden like a man, never tiring, never complaining. And yet, the landlady had told him with tears in her eyes that Marie's life was coming to an end. Like the flame of a dying candle, she was becoming weaker and more translucent by the hour.

François looked around; nobody was watching him. The priest had closed his eyes, and only the clicking of the beads of his rosary told François that he was praying, not sleeping. Quickly, and ashamed to be seen crying, he wiped his eyes. François was accustomed to death; the sinister figure with the scythe was a frequent visitor in every family, no matter whether rich or poor. Births, marriages, baptisms and funerals were the normal rhythm of life, the Good Lord would call his people whenever He deemed that their time had come. François had fought many battles, he had seen good friends and companions die, sometimes quickly, sometimes a nasty and painful death – but rarely had he suffered like tonight. Why should Marie's life be extinguished, it had barely started! Why should Marie not even get the chance to see Pierre again? Despair spread in his soul like a disease. He found no consolation in his prayers. How could he ever face Pierre again? He had failed!

Wrapped in his sorrow, it took some time before François realized that new guests must be arriving. He discerned the sound of the whinnying of nervous horses, then loud voices shouting imperious orders. Strange, that they should be arriving at this time of the day. They must have been riding during the early morning, maybe the whole night, a great risk even though the weather had improved. Anyhow, why should he care? François took a deep gulp from his glass when the voice drew closer, deep and impatient.

"Is this a post station worthy of its name or have you gone to sleep in your boots? Move your arse, idiot, take care of the horses, we must be gone after lunch!"

François almost choked on his drink. This deep voice with its strange accent – he had heard it before! He wracked his brains, then suddenly he remembered, it had been in Paris, together with Pierre! In a flash he rushed to

209

the door where he collided with a gigantic person who had chosen that very moment to enter the room. A strange pair of eyes, one brown, one blue, looked down on him, then a glimmer of recognition stole into those eyes and the voice bellowed, "François de Toucy! Praise the Lord, you're the very person I've been looking for!" He turned and shouted into the hallway, "Céline, praise the Lord, we've found them!"

He entered the room and François found himself buried in a cordial embrace by this friendly giant. Although his view was obscured by his new-found friend, he noticed that a tall woman had entered the room now. Her riding attire might be stained and dusty, but there could be not the slightest doubt that she was every inch a lady. Self-assured, she strode into the room and greeted François as if they were meeting casually in an elegant salon in Paris, beaming at him. "Here you are! You have no idea how happy I am to meet you finally! We've been rushing all over France in order to catch up with you! My horrid husband wouldn't even let me take a break tonight!"

The horrid husband laughed and protested. "*You* wouldn't hear of a break, you said you'd got a hunch that we were close!"

Céline winked at her husband and turned back to François. "Tell me, how's Marie, have you taken good care of her?" She noticed the sudden change in his expression. Alarmed, Céline exclaimed sharply, "What's the matter, François? Has anything happened?"

François couldn't help it. His eyes filled with tears as he stuttered, "I'm sorry… but something dreadful has happened! Marie's in her room upstairs, but I'm afraid she's ill, seriously ill…" He cleared his throat and fought to regain his composure. "The truth is, we have to prepare for the worst. She caught a serious cold two days ago, but wouldn't allow us to take a rest. When we arrived here at the post station, Marie was already coughing badly, the cold had spread to her chest. I really should have insisted on sending her back to Reims, I feel terrible, I know that it's all my fault!"

Céline knew Marie well enough to have a clear idea how cunningly and ruthlessly she must have coaxed her unsuspecting cousin into letting her join him – and that Marie would never have relented once this unique chance had been given to her to reach Pierre as fast as possible.

"Oh, I don't think for a minute that it's your fault! I've known Marie since she was a baby, she can be as stubborn as a mule!" Céline exclaimed "But tell me exactly where she is, I have to look after the poor child immediately!"

"Not immediately! You haven't even had a bite to eat!" protested her husband. "It won't help Marie if you become sick as well. I insist that you have a bite and drink a glass of wine before you look after her!"

Charles gave quick orders to the gawking servants. His natural authority spurred them into action and in a matter of minutes a plate with cold chicken, bread and a glass of wine appeared. Céline obediently took a hasty bite, swallowed a large glass of wine mixed with water and then – ignoring the noisy protest of her husband – addressed the maid: "Show me to the room of the sick guest!"

François whispered to Céline, "You should know that Marie was riding disguised as a man, but of course the landlady found the truth out. Marie's maid invented a story that they were persecuted and had to flee, so don't be astonished if this should be mentioned!"

Céline shook her head in mock despair. "This sounds typical for Marie, riding disguised as a man. I don't doubt for a minute that *she* came up with such a shocking idea!"

A second later Céline was gone, and the room lay strangely silent while François was still trying to make sense of this strange encounter. He returned to the table where Charles was attacking a plate of roasted chicken. "It takes more than disaster to keep you from eating!" François commented, rather spitefully. Why were the British always so phlegmatic!

Charles looked at him as an indulgent father would look at his cheeky son. "I'm not the nervous type, you know, and you have to admit, there's a lot of me to maintain! Tell me, why would it be better to starve? If anybody can do something for Marie, believe me, it's my wife. From this minute on, Marie's in the best hands one can possibly imagine, so you might as well have some chicken, it's really tender. Stop looking as if the date for a funeral has been set already! Never met any woman before as capable as my Céline!"

François felt strangely comforted by the calm attitude of the friendly giant and realized all of a sudden how hungry he was, as he hadn't eaten since yesterday. Silently he grabbed a plate – the quiet optimism of this giant was contagious. Hope, a feeling almost dead and forgotten, started to stir again.

In the meantime Céline followed a very nervous maid upstairs and braced herself for the difficult situation that must be waiting for her. Never given to hysterics, she managed to stay calm, but as she mounted the stairs her nerves were taut as rarely before. What if Marie's situation was hopeless? They arrived at Marie's room and as the maid knocked at the door, Céline breathed deeply, like a gladiator preparing for his decisive battle, then entered Marie's room. By the light of two candles and a cosy fire, she could see three women, two of them sitting on chairs close to Marie's bed; the third, Marie's maid, was kneeling, holding Marie's hand, crying quietly.

The eldest lady in the room, a stout matron dressed in an impeccably white apron, looked up and glanced sharply at the tall lady who had entered the room. The second one, much younger, didn't look up as she was busily

211

dabbing Marie's forehead with a cloth while the pleasant smell of herbs filled the room. She was frowning and was looking very worried.

Céline looked at Marie who lay in the bed, still and pale as a corpse, her face glistening with perspiration. It appeared to Céline as if Marie's body had shrunk, she looked so small and fragile. All of a sudden Marie started to cough, and her frail body came alive and she started to convulse in pain. Céline needed all of her resolve to keep back her tears. It didn't need a doctor to tell her that François had told the truth, Marie was dying.

She stepped forward and embraced the two surprised women. "I'm Marie's cousin from Reims, how can I ever thank you for all that you're doing for Marie!" she exclaimed in her warm voice.

The stout landlady cleared her throat and answered roughly, "No need to thank us, we're just doing our Christian duty. But I must inform you that we fear the worst, I think it's time now to call the priest for the last rites, she's becoming weaker and weaker!"

Céline swallowed hard, then she looked at the younger woman, hoping that she'd be able to explain more. This woman – despite her young age – must be the wise woman of the village; the maid had mentioned that she had been called to help. The young woman flashed a quick smile of welcome before adding in her soft voice, "We still have a small chance to save her, but the girl must drink something and help us to fight for her life! She refuses to swallow as she complains that her throat is hurting her, but as she's sweating heavily she must drink. It's urgent. If not, I must tell you that we'll lose her today, the fever is too high, it's burning her!"

Céline nodded; she had seen such cases before and knew that the woman was right. Gently she sat down on Marie's bedside before she took the cup of water mixed with herbal medicine that the woman had been pointing at, and ignoring Marie's feeble protest as she lifted the girl's head, she said in a brisk voice, "Marie, my love, this is Céline. Pierre has sent me to fetch you!"

Marie's cloudy eyes suddenly tried to focus and she whispered, "Céline? Pierre?"

"Yes, my darling, Pierre is waiting for you, Pierre loves you! He needs you! But first you have to be a good girl and drink something!" Using Marie's surprise to her advantage she made Marie swallow the first large gulp. Immediately Marie protested violently as the liquid entered her mouth but Céline wouldn't relent. This procedure went on, becoming a battle of wills. Citing Pierre's name again and again she coaxed Marie into emptying the cup, and only then laid her gently down onto the pillow. As she looked up to ask to refill the cup, she noticed that the others were watching her with respect and

212

admiration. Under the spell of the moment, Marie's maid leaned forward and kissed her hand.

The wise woman smiled at her warmly. "You've performed nothing less than a miracle! We've been trying for the past hours in vain to make her swallow something. But you're right, we mustn't stop now, we have to continue. She needs to drink. Let her rest now for a while, but I'll prepare the next cup, the herbs I'm adding will help to bring down her fever."

The next hours tested Céline's strength and resilience to her limits. As could have been expected, Marie passed through a serious crisis and it took Céline all of her force and her willpower to make Marie fight for her life, to coax her into drinking and taking the fresh medicine the wise woman had prepared. Céline felt shattered; a sleepless night spent in the saddle had not helped. She was thankful that none of the other women would waver, and together they were united in the fight for Marie's life. Céline had lost track of time – it came as a shock when Marie suddenly didn't reply any more.

Alarmed by the sudden silence and seeing Marie lying motionless Céline looked up, panic in her eyes. "Is she dying? Have I failed?" Céline whispered. All of her energy suddenly seemed to have left her, and she couldn't help it, she started to cry.

"Signora, she is asleep! It's a miracle! She needs some sleep now. I must say, I've never seen someone fight so hard as this girl today. What did you say to her that gave her this strength?"

"I told her that Pierre, her fiancé, needs her... and I think it's true, and somehow she seems to know it," Céline whispered, drying her tears. She felt tired and spent.

"You were right," the landlady suddenly could be heard as she caressed Marie's forehead. "Only the power of love is strong enough to fight against the demon of death!"

Céline regained her composure. "A true statement, indeed. I must go down now, I need to tell my husband and Monsieur de Toucy that she's improving. They must be scared to death – and I need sleep!"

"I understand that you must do this, and I'll have a nice bed prepared for you. Please try to sleep for two or three hours, my lady, later we'll need your help again, the battle is not over yet, a relapse could happen at any moment!"

Céline recognized the good sense of the landlady's advice, even if the last words had had a chilling effect. She kissed Marie and rose to leave the room, to find that her knees had turned to jelly. She left the room – staggering more than walking – before she gained the staircase and went downstairs.

Later she realized how terrifying she must have looked with her tear-stained face as the two men and the priest jumped up immediately as she entered the dining room and Charles cried out, "Is she dead?"

Céline had a lump in her throat. She couldn't talk, she was afraid of bursting into tears again, but she shook her head and after two attempts to clear her throat she managed to utter, "I think we saved her, thank the Lord!"

François embraced Céline and in a voice thick with tears he exclaimed, "How shall I ever be able to thank you?"

Charles smiled smugly but a treacherous tear was glistening in his eye. "I told you, if anybody can save Marie, it will be my wife!"

Céline protested, "Believe me, without the help of the landlady and the wise woman, I would have given up, their help and their medicine worked wonders. They were simply fantastic! We'll have to thank and pay them handsomely!"

"I'll look after that, but you go to bed now!" her husband commanded sternly. "I know you French like your emotional scenes, but you look ghastly, my dear, and Marie will need you soon again, better have a nap now!"

Céline turned in mock despair to François who grinned broadly at this exchange. "This is what you get when you marry an Englishman, no compliments, no devotion, just sound advice and boring common sense. I'm ready to bet in a minute he'll advise me to go to bed with a hot brick!"

"I was just about to mention this, my dear!" Charles added with a wink. "It's a good sign that you thought about it yourself, maybe there's hope after all of making an English gentlewoman of you!"

Over the next few days Marie's health improved fast. Even if she was still as feeble as a kitten, her coughing improved, and after some days the deadly pallor of her skin was replaced by a more robust colour. But it proved difficult to confine Marie to her bed, as she was a difficult patient and almost drove Céline to madness. Charles, seeing that his wife was becoming desperate, intervened, as he was not willing to dance to Marie's tune.

He looked at her from his impressive height. "Marie, I have spared you a lecture but I'm not going to tolerate any further nonsense! Either you do exactly as you're told by Céline and you're a good girl or I'll have you bundled into the next coach to Reims, and take you back to your parents who, by the way, look ten years older because you have worried them to death with this stupid escapade!"

Marie's eyes flashed and she shot bolt upright. "You wouldn't dare!" she hissed.

Charles was not impressed. "Not only would I dare, this is exactly what I'm going to do if you don't lie down, and if I need to pay a battalion of musketeers and lock you in a cage to get you to Reims, I don't mind, it'll be my pleasure to spend the money to get rid of an ungrateful brat like you!"

Marie might have had a ferocious temper but she wasn't stupid and she knew when it was time to relent. Obediently she reclined in her bed, and assuming the airs of a docile and fragile girl, said, "You must do as your conscience dictates! I'm in your hands!"

Charles grinned at her. "Yes, you are, my dear, and you'd better not forget it! Now stop playing the martyr, the sooner you gather some strength, the sooner you can see your Pierre – but stop driving us all crazy!"

He walked out of Marie's room, but his friends would have remarked immediately that he looked troubled – an unusual state of mind for him. Charles hesitated a moment and decided to look for François to discuss his plans with him further. Earlier on, François had already revealed to him the reason for his hasty departure and immediately Charles had understood the significance of the letter. Cardinal Richelieu must – once again – have changed his position in this odious game of politics. He didn't lose any time speculating as to the reason; changing allegiances in politics was just part of rules. There was no doubt, Pierre was in immediate danger.

He found François sitting with a tankard of ale in the taproom, playing dice with his groom, Michel. François looked bored; apparently the game held no fascination for him. As he looked up, he noticed that Charles was approaching and detected an unusual frown on the face of the person who had become a close friend in a matter of only a few days. "Want to join us? I warn you though, Michel is winning all the time, I'm sure he's loaded the dice!"

Michel only grinned complacently and looked lovingly at the small pile of coins that he had extracted from his hapless master.

Charles laughed. "Looking for a new victim? No thanks! But I need to talk with you." Never a person to beat around the bush, he said, "François, I've been thinking about Venice. I'm worried that we're running out of time!" They looked at each other, both of them calculating in their minds how long a messenger from Paris would take to reach Venice. Coming to the same conclusion they exchanged a worried glance.

"Yes, there's no doubt, we're running out of time!" François agreed with a sigh. "Marie's sickness has destroyed all of our lead, now there's a risk we'll be too late to warn Pierre and Armand! The Cardinal's messenger may reach Venice any day now."

"Let's hope that the Venetian bureaucrats will take their time, but we can't leave before Marie's entirely recovered. Céline told me that this will take at least another week. The worst is, we'll be slowed down further as we'll need to travel by coach, it's impossible to put Marie back on a horse."

François nodded in agreement. Suddenly he slapped his forehead. "Why don't Michel and I ride on our own? You can look after Marie and join me a fortnight later in Venice!"

Charles looked at him. "Marie will hate this, but you're right! You should leave immediately. I'll look after the ladies and tell Marie once you've left us!" He paused and grinned. "I think you've got the easier task…"

Michel grimaced and pocketed the coins. He had understood enough from this conversation, there would be no more card games, it was time to saddle the horses again!

Adventure In Venice

Armand was happy. No wonder he was whistling a popular tune as a servant helped him into his velvet waistcoat. Today the sky was a spotless blue but he didn't trust the winter sun, and a chilly wind kept blowing from in the shore. As Jean had taken the afternoon off, Armand had called a servant from the hotel to help him dress. The Albergo Leon Bianco might be abominably expensive but its service was above reproach, as was its delicious food. Never given to worries about trivial matters such as money or the pettiness of discussing the prices of lodgings, Armand cherished every minute in this wonderful hotel, just as he was loving every minute he stayed in the city.

Today he was in the best of moods. Not only had Pierre been his old sunny and witty self, the tempting vision of a hot bath and a nice chat with Edo were an enticing alternative to a boring afternoon spent in the albergo. Maybe there was even hope that – finally – Pierre would accept his friend's advice and would forget this childish infatuation with the infamous Contessa. "How can Pierre be so blind and so stupid? It's so obvious the kind of game she's playing with him," he muttered to himself before he descended the staircase in the hope of finding Edo.

Not only was his friend already waiting for him, in his impulsive manner Edo rushed forward to embrace him warmly. "Armando!" he shouted in his Italian accent, "You look fabulous, *bravissimo!*" he exclaimed and looked admiringly at his friend.

Armand looked very pleased. He loved receiving compliments. Without much success he tried to maintain a modest expression as he replied, "It's nothing, just some old clothes I asked a servant from the hotel to grab for me as Jean is out today! And you, you do look great, really!"

Now Edoardo looked very pleased, indeed he had dressed with special care and as he remembered why, a shadow crossed his face.

"Anything amiss?" Armand inquired, seeing the change of expression.

"Yes and no!" Edo replied. "I won't be able to accompany you to the Turkish baths as I have *finally* been able to get an appointment with the official of the Republic who's supposed to be in charge of the administration of the mining rights. I say 'supposed' as things seem to be very complicated here in Venice, everybody seems to possess a pompous title but you never know what it really signifies. Honestly, I wonder if they do themselves. But a good friend told me that the man I'm going to meet has the right connections in the highest government circles, and this is exactly what I need in order to obtain support for the Count of Salo!"

217

Armand looked crestfallen. "This means that we have to cancel the Turkish bath?"

"No, not at all!" Edo cried out. "First, I'll accompany you to the place and introduce you. If my meeting goes smoothly, I'll have ample time to join you later. Just start without me, anyhow when one of the big Turkish guys is massaging you, we won't really be able to talk. I mean, it's fun of course, but sometimes, you're afraid that the masseur might break your back, they've got arms like this !" and he indicated something three times the size of a normal bicep.

Armand looked sceptical. "Strange kind of fun! Not my idea of a great afternoon, actually." He paused before adding with a mischievous grin, "In truth, I'm still waiting for the invention of a Turkish bath run by female attendants…"

Edo grinned, he liked that idea as well.

"I confess, I'm really longing to have a decent bath, you can't imagine what kind of commotion I create in this establishment whenever I simply ask them to bring in what must be the only bathtub in the whole hotel – they must think that I'm completely mad!"

Edo laughed. "I can just imagine, but taking a bath is simply not the fashion! Most people here rarely take a bath, they think it's unhealthy. They just put on some more musk, a new layer of powder or carry a perfumed pomander!" Armand made a disgusted face but Venice wasn't any different from France in this respect.

It didn't take very long before a brightly painted boat came along, willing to take them for a modest fee to the more popular parts of the sprawling lagoon. Here the city looked less orderly and much more crowded. The proudly painted and marble decorated facades of the palazzos of the rich and the noble had disappeared, and only numerous and richly decorated churches, monasteries and chapels remained as undeniable proof that Venice was a very wealthy city. Many houses and shops appeared to be in dire need of fresh paint and plaster, as a succession of winter floods had left their ugly marks.

Children playing and their busy mothers were crowding the net of narrow paved streets visible from the small canals. Here, in the popular heart of Venice nobody seemed to be idle. Clothes and linen were being washed, workmen were pursuing their crafts, linen bags, cargo and piles of colourful vegetables arriving from the mainland were being unloaded. In general the level of noise was deafening, church bells were chiming, hammers were clanging, peddlers praising their goods while everybody else seemed to be crying, laughing, shouting or talking all at the same time.

Edo and Armand loved this friendly chaos; it reminded Armand of Paris, a city that never slept. As they meandered their way through canals that became less crowded and more narrow, they entered the older and poorer part of the city until they finally reached their destination, a jetty close to a paved lane that led towards an unobtrusive but well-kept two-storeyed brick building crowned by low domes in the ancient Byzantine style. They disembarked and Armand found himself shoved into a neat but unassuming entrance hall that smelled of a promising mix of hot water and perfumed soap. Edo negotiated a price with the fat owner of the establishment, an immigrant from the Ottoman Empire. He sported a proud moustache and his bulging arms left no doubt that he must have been an excellent wrestler in his younger days. The transaction was sealed by a hand-shake that made Edo wince with pain and money changed hands to the satisfaction of both sides, then Edo gave Armand some quick hints as to bath etiquette before disappearing back in the direction of the waiting boat.

Armand followed the owner and entered the baths section, to be agreeably surprised to discover how big the building was inside. The baths were decorated with beautiful mosaics and polished marble of different colours. The use of generations had stained and marked the stone, and the baths looked to Armand like a relic of Byzantine times. Maybe this impression was strengthened by the sudden appearance of a group of older men who had draped their white towels like Roman togas around their bodies as they sat down at their leisure in the warm halls, chatting and preparing to play chess with their friends. There were younger men present as well, proudly displaying their fit bodies, only wearing a loincloth to adhere to the rules of propriety. The baths were lit by sunlight streaming inside from the top of the vaulted ceiling from where windows with coloured glass distributed a soothingly mellow light, reflected by the ripples of the water where the bathers were soaking their bodies in the warm water.

As Armand succumbed to the pleasures of the different baths he lost track of time. What a heavenly feeling it was to be floating in the water – this felt like a haven of peace, an earthly paradise. His dreams were suddenly disturbed as someone called him; apparently it was already time for his massage. A young man gave him a friendly smile and although Armand still vividly regretted that no female staff was admitted into this male sanctum he was relieved all the same – the friendly young man didn't look like someone who'd amuse himself by torturing his limbs or his back. Edo had exaggerated, as usual.

The young man proved however to be a master of his art and Armand spent a blissful time, soaked in oil, as he felt capable hands hammering, stretching and kneading him until his muscles reached a degree of relaxation he had never experienced before. But the blissful experience ended – far too soon for his taste! The young man covered his head with a towel and made signs that Armand was supposed to stay for short nap – and suddenly Armand discovered that this prospect held a charm of its own, as he felt strangely tired.

Wrapped in a warm towel he fell into a peaceful slumber; how long for, he had no idea. Armand only realized that the young man must have come back as hands were touching him again, but roughly this time, hurting him. He protested violently, but the towel covering his head muffled his voice and blindfolded him. The man must have heard him but there was no excuse; on the contrary, Armand could hear the echo of scornful laughter.

Armand was still trying to get rid of the towel that impeded his view when several hands gripped him. His arms were grabbed, bent painfully backwards before he could react, let alone think of any defence. Now, the towel was ripped away. Still drowsy, Armand's unbelieving eyes saw before him a group of four soldiers clad in colourful uniforms. A fifth man, their captain, strode pompously forward, unfolded a paper and read the text aloud. Armand could only understand parts of the text that was cited in rapid Italian, but those accusations that he could grasp sent a chill of fear down his spine: "The Imposters ... declaring themselves to be Armand de Saint Paul, Pierre de Beauvoir ... having been identified as spies and enemies of the Republic ... are to be arrested in the name of His Grace, the Doge of the Republic of Venice, the Serenissima ... and remitted to the care of the Institutions of our Holy Church... "

As the captain came closer, Armand noticed that his uniform showed large wet stains and that he was sweating profusely. The heat and steam of the Turkish bath had left their traces. Armand wondered why he was paying attention to such trivial matters, although it was clear to him that his life was in danger. He had been trapped – but who was behind this arrest? Had he seduced a girl of a family with connections and this was their revenge? But Pierre's name was mentioned as well... The infamous Contessa? These thoughts flashed through his brain as he grabbed the pile of clothes that one of the soldiers had thrown like a bundle of rags at his feet. Armand started to dress, an awkward task as he was sweating heavily, both from the heat and, he hated to admit, from fear. It proved almost impossible to put on his stockings and breeches under the scornful stare of the soldiers. All other persons with the exception of the owner of the Turkish bath had disappeared; nobody wanted to be seen close to an enemy of the Republic!

The voice addressed him again: "Do you admit the charges brought forward?"

With all the dignity he could muster under these strange circumstances Armand stood up and replied haughtily, "I *am* Armand de Saint Paul, Earl of Worthing, the youngest son of the Marquis de Saint Paul – there is nothing to admit, this ring shows the coat of arms of my family! I can promise you that my father will intervene personally with the King of France if you don't set me free immediately!"

The official was not impressed. In his loud voice he addressed the empty baths: "The imposter has repeated his claim and therefore will be arrested in the name of the Republic of Venice!"

He turned towards the owner of the bath who suddenly looked much less imposing, his moustache drooping – Armand wondered if it could be possible that even his impressive biceps had shrunk.

"Where's the second suspect?" the captain bellowed. "Better tell me the truth immediately or you can join us at the prison! We saw that two persons entered the baths and my warrant of arrest covers a second suspect, calling himself the Marquis de Beauvoir." He sneered the last words to show his contempt.

The owner of the bath bowed reverently. "Signore, *effendi*! Of course I am telling you the truth, I have nothing to do with enemies of the Republic! But his friend left, he never even entered my baths, he told me that he had an appointment!"

The officer looked disappointed but he recovered quickly, and addressing his men he shouted, "Who was in charge of supervising the entrance?"

There was a long leaden silence before one of the men took his courage in both hands and answered, "Nobody, sir, you only gave us orders to check the back doors and windows! We only followed your orders, sir!"

"Did the Lord give you a head to think or for decoration only?" their superior roared while Armand felt a wave of relief: if they didn't know that there were three of them, there was still hope that Edo or Pierre could get him released from custody.

The officer now turned back to Armand and roared, "Tell me immediately where your friend is hiding or you'll regret it!"

"My friend is not hiding, he's right now meeting an official of the Government in the mining department, but I have no idea of his name!"

"We'll find out – and you'll regret it if you've lied to us! Nobody can hide in Venice! We know how to find and eradicate enemies of the Republic!"

The soldiers took this rightfully as a command to move forward and Armand had no choice but to follow them as chains were closing around his wrists now. As the soldiers started to march, his chains were pulled hard and the steel bit into his flesh. Then he was pushed into a waiting boat where he was blindfolded. Armand wondered why and he didn't like the possible answers. Would they dispose of him in the lagoon?

He smelled the waters of the lagoon, heard the voices of the people that must be looking at him as he could hear their jeering and insults, usually reserved for criminals on their way to the gallows. He listened to the oars of the boat touching the water and felt the rhythm of their progress. He had no idea where they were heading, in any case not near the bath house as it took them quite a long time before the boat halted. The rag that had been used to cover his eyes by now sat slightly askew and allowed Armand to glimpse his surroundings. He realized that they had arrived at Saint Mark's Square, disembarking just in front of the Doge's palace and Saint Mark's Church. At least they weren't going to dump him in the sea!

Armand was only briefly wondering why they were heading towards the Doge's palace (had he offended a relative of the Doge?) when he was already pushed forward along the front of the imposing cream-coloured building that faced the waterfront. It was then that he realized with trepidation that his destination was not to be the Doge's palace, but the infamous prisons that were located behind this sprawling complex. His heart sank; their Venetian friends had told many stories about those terrifying dungeons, especially about the chambers underneath the lead roofs. The stories had seemed entertaining – but now Armand remembered the terrifying details, a prison that was scorching hot in summer and freezing cold in winter. His Venetian friends had joked that this institution was not only an excellent deterrent against crime, often enough it would spare Venice the expense of an executioner. Then, lowering his voice in confidence, another friend had added, "Everybody talks about those lead-roofed chambers, but I've heard from my father that the worst prison cells are those close to the wells, it's so dark and damp down there that you can't tell apart what's left of the prisoners and what's vermin in there!"

"Easy to tell," another friend had interjected. "If it's still crawling – it must be the vermin!"

They had all laughed; it had all sounded like a capital joke then.

Armand inhaled deeply for the last time the fresh air with its peculiar smell of the lagoon as they entered the building and the heavy oak doors with their wrought-iron hinges closed behind him, almost noiselessly; the massive hinges must have been well greased. The rag that was supposed to cover Armand's eyes had fallen down in the meantime but his guards didn't seem to care any longer. They were only too eager to get rid of their charge as fast as possible.

They dragged Armand down a long corridor. It was dark in here and the first notes of the unpleasant smell of a prison, the sour and nauseating smell of unwashed bodies, excrement, damp, mould and rotting straw were already filling the building. Armand started to perspire. Don't show your fear, he admonished himself, be a worthy member of the de Saint Paul family!

They entered a small office and stood to attention in front of a supercilious prison officer whose silken clothes heralded his superior rank. He took his time before condescending to have a closer look at the new prisoner who was presented to him and at the documents that the officer of the guards who had arrested Armand had placed on his desk. While the latter stood to attention, the prison officer read them slowly and thoroughly, once, then once again before he looked up and sneered, "Officer, this warrant states clearly that the suspect is to be brought into the care of His Eminence, the archbishop; the episcopal prisons are not located here! You should have been on duty long enough to know this. Anyhow, I have no space available right now, the weather is too clement, we've had no natural departures during the past week." His voice held a note of disapproval that his prisoners had not shown the decency to succumb in a timely manner and make space for the never ending supply of new inmates. He paused, and now looked straight into the eyes of the officer. "Furthermore, the warrant states that you're supposed to deliver two suspects, where's the second one? Lost him, eh?" he chuckled. "Your men seem to be an immensely capable troop, I'm sure you'll be recommended at the highest level!" And with these last scathing words, it was clear that they had been dismissed.

The face of the officer turned scarlet and quickly he lowered his head to check the phrase on the document that the official of the state prison had referred to. Apparently he had overlooked instructions to deliver his charge to the Patriarch of Venice, and still looking flustered he gave orders to his men to march on to the palace of the archbishop. Armand decided rightly to take this as a lucky sign from heaven – the choice between lead-roofed chambers or cells close to the prison wells hadn't seemed very enticing.

Their small group marched on for some time until they reached the palace of His Eminence, the Patriarch of Venice, who resided in another imposing building, luckily located not too far away from the Doge's palace. The episcopal palace was decorated with marble statues of countless saints, the proud coat of arms of the archbishop and – of course – the golden lion, representing the Evangelist holding the Holy Scripture. Not surprisingly they skipped the official entrance, the officer leading them straight to the back of the building where a small, inconspicuous door was hidden. Only those souls unfortunate enough to come into close contact with the Inquisition ever got to see the episcopal dungeons, but the officer knew his way around.

The procedure already known to Armand was repeated, only this time they faced an ascetic-looking monk who seemed to be long since detached from the woes of mankind. This didn't hinder him from scolding the officer severely for bringing only one prisoner.

"His Eminence will not be pleased! His secretary gave orders to inform him immediately when the two imposters were in my safe keeping. Now I'll be forced to tell him that one of them has escaped..." He shook his head slowly and looked accusingly at the soldiers. The officer swallowed and protested feebly, "The second suspect has not escaped, Brother, he never entered the baths! How could we have arrested him? Please let His Eminence know this important fact. We'll arrest the second suspect as soon as you've taken charge of this one!" and while he was still pleading with the suspicious-looking monk, he pushed Armand forward, kicking him hard as if he needed to alleviate his frustration. Armand suppressed an exclamation of pain. He didn't want to show any sign of weakness in front of these commoners who had dared to treat him like a criminal.

"You had better hurry then!" answered the monk. Only a slight raising of his eyebrows betrayed his disbelief in the truth of the officer's statement. "His Eminence is not known to be very lenient in matters of discipline…"

He gave a sign, and immediately two soldiers wearing the coat of arms of the archbishop stepped forward and took charge of Armand. The others took their leave, their officer looking decidedly troubled.

Armand was led through the marble paved courtyard to the remote part of the palace that housed the prison, an unobtrusive part of the building, where only heavy iron grilles and doors would tell the casual observer that guests housed in this part of the palace must enjoy a very special form of care and attention from His Eminence.

The soldiers pushed Armand inside a small prison cell, but compared to Armand's nightmares of ending up in the lead chambers, this cell looked like pure luxury, neither freezing cold, nor damp and – at least for now – no rats or other vermin in sight. Yet he felt far from comfortable as he was chained to the wall. All Armand could do was to squat and wait, uncomfortably aware of the iron handcuffs that were biting into his wrists. But his mind was dwelling on more important issues: Would they find and arrest Pierre, could Edo help them to get out of this mess? Who was the mastermind behind all of this? If the Patriarch of Venice was involved, could it be that Richelieu was playing dirty? He was still pondering all of these options when the door of his prison opened, squeaking loudly, betraying the fact that this prison was in less frequent use than the municipal one.

A prison guard entered the room, a sad-looking, haggard man with a bald head which shone like a mirror. Strands of black hair were stuck to his temples, and a thick drooping moustache underlined the sadness of dark melancholic eyes, half hidden under heavy eyelids. He approached Armand and stated in a low voice, as if he were to share his condolences, "You're the new inmate, the imposter then, you'll soon regret your wrongdoings, the Inquisition has the means to purge the souls of even the worst sinners!"

Armand rose as if he had been stung with a needle and forgetting that he was chained to the wall and in Italy, he shouted in French, "I *am* Armand de Saint Paul and I will not tolerate being called an imposter by a stupid simpleton like you!"

The prison guard opened his sad eyes in surprised admiration and shouted, "Oh, Monsieur, you are truly from France, I can hear this! Monsieur also has a noble accent! I cannot tell you how delighted I am. This reminds me of the time when I was the personal valet of our ambassador in Paris, years ago… ah, those were the times… the ladies of Paris…" He seemed to be dwelling on pleasant memories, and even his moustache appeared to be looking more lively.

"Tell me, why in God's name am I here?" asked Armand bluntly, rightfully interpreting the comments of the guard as an invitation to share confidences.

"I pride myself on judging a person immediately," the guard answered with a slight bow. "I will therefore address your lordship with your correct title." He paused and closed the door to make sure that nobody could listen in. "If your lordship is not an imposter at all, your lordship must have greatly displeased an influential person in this city. But let me tell you in confidence, your lordship wouldn't be the first!"

"So, what can I do?" asked Armand bluntly.

"I sincerely hope that you have some money, my lord. As long as you can pay me, I can make your stay here comfortable. I pride myself on being an excellent valet and I know exactly that persons of your standing have needs…"

"I didn't want to discuss my comfort." Armand tried to steer him back to the subject.

The guard nodded and continued. "In essence there are three options: either your lordship's relatives intervene and pay handsomely to make His Eminence change his mind, or – after some period of time – you'll be handed over to the Inquisition, or…"

"Or?"

"Or your lordship will simply be forgotten. It happens quite often actually. In this case, you'll stay here until your lordship runs out of money and I won't be able to supply with you food anymore, a very sad option, indeed. I would really regret this very much, your lordship is such a healthy and handsome person."

"You're not telling me that the Inquisition would be any better?" Armand replied, but his irony was lost on the guard.

"Oh, no! This would surely be the worst imaginable scenario, my lord. Their chambers for painful interrogations are just on the other side, but luckily the walls are thick enough to shield your lordship from the

225

inconvenience of having to listen to the cries of the poor souls that are being purified!" and he quickly crossed himself.

What a damned hypocrite! thought Armand.

"Bring me some food and wine! I'll pay you, don't worry!" he ordered curtly. "I'm sure my relatives will soon have me set free. If you've lived in France, you should know that our family has access to all circles of government, my father is the godfather of King Louis!"

The prison guard nodded and bowed reverently, no valet could have been more punctilious in his attentions. "I shall immediately make sure that your lordship's request is attended to. I shall also suggest – if by any chance your lordship should have one more silver coin to spare – that this unworthy chain should be replaced by some lighter ankle chains. If you have a gold coin, I might be able to forget to chain you altogether and bring you a table and a chair?"

"A good suggestion, I'm starting to feel like a horse chained up in its stable."

Apparently the guard found this remark very funny as he started to chuckle and was still chuckling as he left the prison cell.

"Your fate could have been worse, Armand de Saint Paul," Armand said to himself. "And now let's pray that Pierre does not fall into the hands of the constabulary."

A Family Reunion

Pierre stared at the barrel of the loaded pistol. Was he dreaming? But reality quickly caught up with him, strong hands grabbed him from behind, and pushed him backwards into a heavy armchair. In no time at all he was bound and gagged, watching helplessly as the man he knew so well walked to the windows and opened the curtains to let in the daylight.

Now, as the light flooded into the room, he could see his cousin in full splendour, dressed with his usual easy elegance. Brushed curls of golden hair were shining in the light, and a large diamond ring was gleaming malevolently on his finger. Slowly Henri de Beauvoir turned around and looked arrogantly at his younger cousin as he stowed the pistol back in its place.

"I always find it wasteful to use a precious bullet and powder on commoners, let alone bastards!" Amused and relaxed he watched his cousin wriggle in his chair, trying to shout back an insult – but Pierre was helpless. His cousin's servants had done a thorough job. All of a sudden Henri's face changed. It lost its slightly amused and condescending expression, and the mask of the civil gentleman dropped. Hatred oozed from every pore of his body.

Pierre looked at his raging cousin; he had no illusions, this encounter was the prelude to his end. But all he could think was, *If I'm going to die, I've merited it. My own vanity and stupidity will kill me! I betrayed love and friendship, blindly I walked into this trap ignoring all good advice. Dear Lord, only grant me one favour, let my end be quick!*

While Pierre's thoughts wandered to Marie – whose love and faith he had betrayed so shamelessly – he felt his cousin's hand closing around his neck, strong and cold, cold as death. As those hands closed around his neck and pressed harder, Pierre didn't fight. Hadn't he merited this punishment? The Good Lord dispensed justice, the Church had always taught, and today it was certainly true!

"Henri, stop it!" a dark voice drawled from the back. "I fully understand that you want to kill this cockroach – and doesn't this feel good? But we need him alive for a few more days as bait! Remember his dear friend Armand is still running free and the best way to make him come to us will be to use your cousin. His beloved Armand will come running in due course, although he seems to be a bit more intelligent than this stupid bastard; he guessed from the beginning that my adorable Eleanora is not a true gentlewoman." He chuckled. "A great woman she is – and very skilled indeed – but how anybody could mistake a whore like her for a Contessa really beats me!"

As he came closer, Pierre saw an attractive man with dark curls approaching him. With a flash his memory came back: this had been the man who had entered the *chambre separée* in Paris together with his cousin Henri when Armand and he had been trapped in the gaming parlour. The man loosed Henri's hands; his way of touching Henri was surprisingly gentle, almost intimate. "Look at me!" he commanded Pierre and involuntarily Pierre followed this order. He watched the strange man open his shirt. If he hadn't been gagged he'd probably have gasped: a large section of the right shoulder must have been severely burned, white and red scars marred the perfection of his olive-coloured skin. Now the man removed his wig and Pierre could see the same terrible scars covering part of his neck and the right side of his razed skull.

"Nice, isn't it?" the man drawled. "This is the result of the fire you and your friend set when I had the pleasure of meeting both of you last time – I won't even bother mentioning the insignificant detail that you burned down my entire house as well! But this time I'll make sure that *we* shall win this game – and before we send both of you to Hades, I want you and your friend to suffer as I had to suffer!" He broke off and looked at Henri. "Let's store your cousin in a nice damp and freezing place to keep him fresh. We'll heat him up later. I suggest that he watch us as we make love to his 'Contessa', he'll see how skilled she is and it will add a bit of spice! I'm sure your cousin will love watching us!"

Both men left the room roaring with laughter while a devastated Pierre saw himself trussed up like a lamb destined for slaughter. He was dumped in a small room, damp and airless as predicted. Lying there helplessly with aching bones in solitude and total silence he had the opportunity to grasp the full extent of his misery. But Pierre was too proud to let his tears run. He closed his eyes and started to pray, but this time not the quick superficial phrases of the daily routine of morning and evening prayers. Here in this dark room his soul was desperately crying out for help and praying that his best friend might be spared the same ordeal.

Meanwhile Henri and Nicolas walked to the spacious drawing room. Henri dropped into a chair opposite Nicolas, who had already settled comfortably in an upholstered armchair, his legs sprawled apart. A liveried footman served glasses filled almost to the brim with a ruby-coloured wine. They grinned at each other and Henri saw Nicolas empty his glass in one go, radiating a glee and satisfaction so different from his normally guarded self.

Watching Nicolas savouring the excellent wine, Henri's thoughts went back to the dark afternoon in February when his servant Mustafa had finally succeeded in finding a boat willing to ferry them over to Venice. He still remembered vividly how he had fallen asleep on the boat and how he had been brutally woken up, fighting – as he had thought – for his life as the hands of a stranger wrapped around his neck.

But once he had come to his senses, he had recognized the mischievous face of Nicolas, the uncrowned king of the Parisian underworld. Nicolas had disappeared without trace after his carefully concealed home base and gaming salons had been burned down by Henri's cousin and his precious friend Armand.

"Nicolas! What the hell are you doing here?"

"You never change!" Nicolas had exclaimed, laughing. "Still closer to citing hell than heaven! I knew of course that sooner or later you'd come here, I know you too well, you'd never give up the hunt for your cousin! I placed my spies in the port to keep an eye out for you. Who's that black servant travelling with you, my men told me that he was inquiring for a boat in the port for both of you, he seems to be a clever fellow!"

"Too clever! He had the impunity to insult me and will pay for it as soon as we reach Venice!"

"Still a proud unforgiving devil, aren't you? I guess that's inevitable when you've been born and raised to become a Marquis!"

Of course Nicolas had been curious to learn of Henri's journey; he had expected him to arrive in Venice much earlier. While Henri gave an embellished version of his prolonged stay in Verona, Nicolas had almost exploded with laughter. "The proud devil as a lover boy for a low-born countess, no wonder she had to pay with her life for this offence!"

Henri had made a face. "Now, tell me about your fate!"

Nicolas gave a brief summary of the weeks after the fire which he had spent in terrible pain close to death until the burns had started to heal.

"I knew all the time that I had to leave Paris. Cardinal Richelieu had turned a blind eye to my establishment as long as I could keep it silent and did not annoy him, but once the truth had leaked out, he'd never tolerate my return. But I was lucky. About three years earlier an elderly Italian count had come for a visit to Paris. I had sent him one of my best girls for 'entertainment', but my Eleonora was a clever one, and quickly made him believe that I was the villain in this story and was keeping her against her will. You can imagine the story: the imprisoned orphan girl originally from an impoverished noble family, trying to survive. It took her only three weeks to have him wrapped around her tiny fingers! The count fell in love, like a young boy having his first love affair, desperate, deaf and blind to any sound advice. She married him and I made sure that her husband met an early end. Then she left for Italy – to take up her inheritance and set up an establishment with the help of some of my men and my mother, acting as her chaperone. No need to tell you that Eleonora was extremely successful; behind the respectable façade of the dowager countess Montefiori she and my mother established a nice little enterprise with gaming tables, entertainment..."

"... and extortion," Henri threw in.

"You're always so crude, Henri! Let's call it fair trading of security against information and money!"

Forgetting all time and place, they had chatted until the boat hit the jetty of the obscure fisherman's lodge.

"Now let's grab your belongings – where the hell is your servant? He should be ready with all of your stuff. Some punishment might truly do him good!" remarked Nicolas casually as they started to search the boat. But no Mustafa could be found and once they had finished rummaging around the boat, not only had Mustafa disappeared, but the same had happened to Henri's possessions with the exception of the money and jewellery Henri had been wise enough to carry on his person. He was seething with rage but Nicolas had laughed. "A clever little devil, I told you so! Who cares about this trash jewellery from Verona, you'll see, there is enough around in Venice, until then, be my guest!"

Nicolas hadn't been lying or exaggerating – the gaming tables and salons showed the same exclusive taste as previously in Paris, and no expense had been spared. Nicolas had created a new kingdom of elegance and distinction – at night his salons were crowded with the cream of Venetian aristocracy, that is, the male half, of course.

"The difference compared to Paris is simple," Nicolas explained. "In Paris we could work as long our existence was ignored by the authorities. In Venice it's impossible to keep a secret, the spies of the Council of Ten know everything; I guess they know my income better than I do. But here we're tolerated as long as we share our profits with the right people, that is, pay them handsomely. Some of the members of the Council may look like long-dead mummies, but their brains still work like clockwork when it comes to money!"

"Who are those men? I've never heard of the Council of Ten?"

"The secret government, officially a body that was created to make sure that no doge would ever become powerful enough to declare himself king, and now they run Venice in truth!"

Nicolas and Henri spent exciting nights with Eleonora, making love together. Soon Henri realized that Eleonora craved every kind of drug. "It's the best way I can control her," Nicolas had explained. "She needs the drugs, and I give them to her whenever she's been a good girl..." he laughed. "And the good girl has your cousin dangling from her fingers already, a few more days and he'll do whatever she asks."

Carefully hidden from society, Henri watched his cousin entangle himself more and more in his blind passion; the day of his revenge and final triumph came closer and closer! But Nicolas warned him to be patient. "We don't want a scandal in Venice, the bastard has to disappear by his own doing, and believe me, Henri, he's ripe. In a matter of days, he'll be ours!"

Today Nicolas had proved that his strategy had been right, today was the day of their triumph and Henri was prepared to cherish every second.

"Santé!" he toasted back, flashing a smile at Nicolas; had Henri ever tasted a better wine?

*****

The horses' hooves pounded on the road, its surface hard as rock. The mud covering the road had dried in the cold but sunny weather, and smallish clouds of dust were forming behind the two lonely horsemen who were riding eastwards along the deserted plains of the River Po. François de Toucy reckoned that they'd need to ride at least two more hours until they'd be able to find a station to make a rest and – hopefully – change horses for the next day. Rarely had he been seated on such a lame duck – a total insult to his superior riding skills. What luck that his friends couldn't see him; he could easily imagine their scathing comments!

He had learned the hard way that only a few post stations in Italy still offered the luxury of keeping horses for exchange – let alone horses of acceptable breeding. Now as they had finally entered the hemisphere of the Republic of Venice, there might be hope after all. He squinted at the sky in order to estimate the time. It must be early afternoon already but as the days were still short, they'd be obliged to stay at the next station overnight.

After a night spent in a rather dubious tavern they continued their journey, still on horses that were a disgrace to their breed. And yet François was not totally dissatisfied. Their journey had been smooth – no villains or racketeering soldiers looking for a bit of fun with foreigners or for booty had stopped them, nor had they encountered any highwaymen who could have hampered their progress. With the tacit understanding of his groom they rode from the early morning on as long as daylight permitted, only interrupting their journey to give regular respite to their horses. François knew that they were fairly close, and by tonight at the latest they should reach the gateway to Venice.

"What day is it today?" François interrogated his groom. "I guess it must be Friday, if I haven't mixed up the days. Since we left Marie and her maid in the care of Charles every day seems to be the same, we get up early, we ride,

231

we drop into our bed, well, from time to time we eat and drink, but even the food seems to be same everywhere, mostly cabbage soup with millet... it's time we had a decent meal!"

"Aye, sir," Michel answered. He had rightly interpreted his master's lengthy outpouring as a monologue.

"This means that we should be able to catch a boat and already be in Venice by tomorrow. I wonder where we can find Pierre? Maybe we should check the best guest houses and start our search there, I have no real clue where to look otherwise. But I wouldn't think that he's rented a house or even a palace, it was meant to be rather a short stay..."

"Aye, sir," answered his groom, long since accustomed to his master's habit of talking to himself.

"That's settled then," replied his master in a cheerful voice. "I always find our discussions most helpful!"

"Aye, sir!"

They arrived in Mestre at noon, much earlier than François had expected. It was not difficult to find an inn in the busy town, but it proved much more difficult to find an inn that would be able to accommodate them for the night. To François's anger they could only find a room in the most expensive establishment in town and soon he was to find out why.

"We need to cross over to Venice tomorrow, can you recommend me a reliable boatman who won't rip us off?" he asked the proud owner of the establishment who had approached him, eager to open a conversation.

The innkeeper was all smiles as he replied, "It will be my pleasure to arrange all of this for you! I assume, Signore, you have the necessary papers, a passport and letter of recommendation? In this case we could approach the authorities Tuesday and if there are no objections, you might be ready to leave by next Friday!"

François had the feeling of being punched right in the stomach and he exclaimed, "That's out of the question! I must be in Venice tomorrow!"

"There is a more speedy procedure, of course, if Signore would be willing to pay..."

The innkeeper named the amount, which roughly translated to two French gold livres. François became upset, he hated being ripped off.

"It's a lot, I know, Signore, but we'll need to bribe some very high-level officials of the Republic and they know their value! In this case, you might save three days, and maybe we can arrange everything for Tuesday!" he added, trying to bring a cheerful note into the conversation.

"Why not tomorrow?" François asked incredulously.

"Because tomorrow is the day of our local patron, there will be a special mass in our church and a fair. Maybe you have noticed that the town is full with visitors from the neighbouring villages. The next day is Sunday and of course nobody would dare to work and offend our Lord. This brings us to Monday and I know that the officer in charge of delivering the documents is rarely seen in his office before lunchtime..."

François was still trying to cope with this disappointing blow; they might lose even more precious time, as although he did possess a passport, it was valid for the Spanish Netherlands (and now in the hands of his hopefully successful friend). He had not dared to apply for a second passport – this would have made Cardinal Richelieu highly suspicious. So far they had been able to navigate around all official border posts without too much difficulty; a bit of money and sometimes a sentimental story had done the trick.

The innkeeper cleared his throat and continued in a gossipy tone, "Signore is French, by any chance?"

"Indeed, I'm French!"

"I could see immediately that Signore is of noble birth, of that there can be no doubt!" He paused, unsure how to proceed further. "It only seems strange to me..."

"What seems strange?" François asked politely, not really interested in going into details.

"Normally Frenchmen are always dark, sometimes difficult to tell them apart from us Italians. In a period of only two months I had two other French gentlemen staying here, as strikingly blonde and handsome as you are, Signore, if you permit me this compliment!"

He cleared his throat. "Signore cannot imagine the effect on my female staff, gawking at my visitors as if my establishment weren't used to men of standing, I really had to tell them to pay attention. When the second gentleman came to stay with us, I was flabbergasted – he looked so much like the first one that they could have been twins. But he was very arrogant, if I may say so, he wouldn't really talk to people of lesser birth like me, so I never raised the question! But would you happen to know them, are they of your family by any chance?"

François felt as if the anonymous boxer had skilfully repeated his first blow, once again in the stomach. There could be only one conclusion: besides Pierre, Henri de Beauvoir must have been here! Trying to hide his inner turmoil, he answered coolly, "No, I'm sorry, I have no real clue who they could be, I've spent a lot of time outside France lately. When did they stay here? Maybe I can try to meet them in Venice!"

"The first signore was here in early January, the second passed through about three weeks ago? I'm not sure, please excuse me, Signore, I have so many guests staying and it tends to confuse me. I could be a month ago or only fourteen days ago. He suddenly disappeared, but he paid his dues first, a true gentleman!"

François looked up and noticed that his groom was standing close to them, making signs. Michel approached François with the reverent attitude he always assumed when he deemed it necessary to make his master look important in public.

"May I show you a problem with the horses' hooves, my lord?"

"Who cares about the horses, we'll be selling them anyhow!" François replied, still ill at ease.

"No, my lord, I would *really* like to show you the horses!" Michel insisted.

François sighed and got up from his chair. The innkeeper understood that their conversation would be paused for a moment. He shuffled back to his table where paper and a quill were waiting for him, a silent witness that the innkeeper was one of the rare people who could read and write, but then turned round and added, "Please let me know if I should approach the official, and I'm sorry to insist, Signore, but I will need to have the money first!"

"Why are you dragging me into the stables?" hissed François once they had left the taproom. "Didn't you hear, Henri de Beauvoir is already in Venice, any minute we lose may be a disaster! And that stupid idiot inside wants to extort two gold livres for getting us there – maybe – by the middle of next week at the earliest!"

Michel was unperturbed by the moods of his master. "There is no problem with the horses, I wanted to talk to you privately, sir, this innkeeper is as nosy as a magpie!"

"May I know then what's so important?"

"I happened to pass along the fish stalls this afternoon, very busy of course, after all it's Friday!"

François looked at his groom disbelievingly. "Don't tell me that you dragged me here to talk about fish stalls?"

Michel flashed him one of his rare smiles. "Of course not, my lord. One of the fish stalls looked less well attended and I started to chat with the fishmonger. It appears that they only moved here a year ago and are having a hard time because the locals don't like strangers. But they had to leave Venice because they couldn't afford to pay their rent there any more when their seventh child was born..."

"Do you want me to become the godfather for child number eight? My God, will people never stop making children? Michel, be reasonable, I have no interest in fishmongers or their offspring!"

"No my lord, but because they're so poor, her husband would be happy to take on extra jobs, even on a Sunday... Such as taking us to Venice..." Michel added, unable to hide a small note of triumph in his statement.

François looked at his groom, not knowing if should hug him or whip him. "You like to keep up a bit of suspense, don't you? Maybe I should whip you for your impertinence, but you know of course that I won't! To do you justice, you just saved us from sitting here paralysed for days or weeks, being milked by the innkeeper or some inflated Venetian bureaucrat."

Michel only grinned gleefully; he knew his worth.

"Tomorrow morning at sunrise, he'll set sail, my lord. I've met him already and he's confident that all will go smoothly. His boat is well known, there will no awkward questions if he is just visiting his relatives on a Sunday in Venice."

François inhaled deeply. Heaven had suddenly shown mercy. "Thank you!" he simply said and with a broad grin he added, "You're aware that a bit of a whipping would have done you good?"

Michel grinned back. "May I propose to leave this to my future wife, my lord? I promised Antoinette to marry her once we're back in France!"

"That's no real surprise... you haven't already anticipated the pleasures of this marriage, by any chance...?"

Michel didn't answer, but his skin turned a shade of pink. Well, François concluded, it was a kind of answer!

The fisherman proved true to his word and as soon as the massive red ball of the sun was rising tentatively on the horizon, they set sail in a ramshackle fishing boat towards Venice. Fascinated, François watched the majestic rising sun and the golden trail of light that glistened on the silvery water as the boat glided almost noiselessly across the sea. Slowly the spires and buildings of Venice emerged from the morning haze. He had already heard much of the beauty of this city, but only this morning did he understand the uniqueness of Venice, a beauty beyond comparison.

"Would you know of a place where we could stay for the night?" he asked the fisherman as they approached the city.

"I can recommend you to stay with a friend of the family, he's a tailor, Signore. The family is poor, but they're honest and hard-working people, his wife is my sister-in-law. If you don't mind staying in simple lodgings, Signore, they could certainly vacate a room for you and your groom tonight and would only charge a modest fee."

François looked critically at his own clothes and exclaimed, "A tailor is exactly what I need, there's no doubt of that." He looked critically at his breeches and his coat and exclaimed, "I cannot possibly roam around Venice in these rags. That's an excellent idea and don't worry about the lodgings, as a soldier, I've not been spoilt in this respect." *And I'll stink like a fishmonger after this journey; one more reason to get some hot water and acquire new clothes as fast as possible!*

The tailor's humble lodgings were located in one of the narrow cobbled streets, far away from the luxurious waterfront of the Canal Grande with its palaces belonging to noble families or the imposing and gold-studded elegance of St. Mark's Square. The fisherman gladly accepted his pay after he had introduced François and his groom to the tailor, his wife and his growing family of six children, soon to be joined by a new member as witnessed by the heavy belly of the tailor's wife.

"Thank you for helping us to continue our travels!" François shook his calloused hands to say good-bye.

"When you have as many mouths to feed as I have, Signore, remaining idle on a Sunday is impossible. If you need my services again, let me know!" the fisherman answered simply and strode back to his boat after kissing his sister-in-law and taking leave of his relatives.

As was customary, the tailor and his wife shared their bedroom with their youngest children. The family would move to the kitchen to make room for the guests and the tailor would sleep in his workroom. A room in the attic was occupied by an ailing grandmother, more lively children and an apprentice, a young boy aspiring to learn the art of tailoring but who also acted as general factotum as the family was too poor to afford a true servant.

"I urgently need some decent clothes!" François stated and as his glance met his groom, he added "and my groom as well, as far as I can see. Can you take care of this?"

"Of course, Signore, with pleasure!" The tailor rubbed his hands with glee. "Just clothes for travelling, or is Signore planning to attend some social events? I understand that Signore is of noble birth, I imagine that you'll need at least a velvet or silken waistcoat?"

236

François suddenly realized that he might have to mingle with the more elegant side of Venetian society and he exclaimed, "You're right, I'll need some formal clothing and livery for my groom as well."

Quickly the tailor noted the essentials, from breeches and stockings to shirts and nightgowns. When François saw the completed list, he realized that he would have to part with the majority of his golden livres; this adventure was proving to be expensive.

Anxiously he waited for the tailor to name a price. Finally, after checking his notes and having taken François's and Michel's measurements the tailor reluctantly named his price and François couldn't help exclaiming, "Are you sure about that?"

The tailor turned scarlet and defended himself immediately. "I apologize if I have upset you, Signore, maybe I can reduce the price by a few lira, but I'll have to work at night together with my cousin and my apprentice and it's impossible to work with tallow lights, the smoke would spoil the precious fabrics and we'll need good light to do the stitching. My wife will have to buy several dozen genuine beeswax candles and they're outrageously expensive here in Venice, we would never dare to buy those for our household."

François made an effort to keep his expression under control – his tongue had slipped because the price had been far too low! Never would he have been able to buy such a vast number of shirts and oufits in Paris for such a ridiculous amount. To keep up appearances he pretended to ponder the tailor's proposal. After lengthy consideration that left the poor tailor looking at him transfixed like a rabbit at a snake, he replied, "I accept your price. In fact time is of the essence, if I can have some clothes for Monday morning, you'll have merited your price!"

The tailor beamed with joy. "Signore is a true gentleman, I'll start working tonight, Signore will be very happy with his choice!"

He paused a moment and added in a small voice, "May I ask Signore for some money in advance, as my wife will need to buy candles and buttons made from genuine mother of pearl, we wouldn't normally have those in our house…"

François opened his purse, chose a golden coin and passed it into the trembling hands of the tailor. Apparently he rarely – if ever – had touched a heavy coin of genuine gold. François could imagine that many of his customers would pay in kind but not in money. The tailor's wife however had less scruples, and seconds later the precious coin had disappeared into the cleft of her bosom, and used to taking command, she shouted, "Why are you still standing here, Mario? Hurry, go to the workshop, don't keep our noble guest waiting! I'll fetch the candles and the buttons, anything else you need? I imagine the gentleman will also want a nice dinner, but we're still in the fasting season. I can cook the fresh fish my cousin brought this morning, but what about a nice cabbage soup to begin with?"

François and Michel looked at each other and shouted simultaneously, "No cabbage soup, please, anything else will be fine!"

Later a breathless younger member of the family brought a bowl of hot water from the kitchen. He stared at François and Michel open-mouthed as if he'd never seen a foreigner before in his life. While Michel changed roles, and assumed the tasks of a valet and sponged down his master who had taken off his shirt and breeches, François started to discuss their plan of action, mostly in the form of a monologue, as usual.

"We'll need to find Pierre and Armand as fast as possible. I propose that we try to find out which guest houses have the best reputation here in Venice or are popular with foreigners. I don't think that they'll be staying in the French embassy, their mission is too delicate to be official and Richelieu wouldn't dare to meddle with an official guest of the ambassador, the ambassador has got too many ties with the de Saint Paul family, I might even know him from court..."

He glanced at his groom who interpreted the look rightly as an invitation to comment on his master's train of thought.

"Aye, sir!"

"So that settles it. I'll start putting a list together and then both of us will stroll around tomorrow and check out the guest houses, I don't want to lose any more time. Do you agree?"

"Aye, sir!"

"Excellent!" but just as he was about to continue, François heard a light tapping at the door and before he could grab his shirt or breeches, one of the tailor's daughters had walked into the room, a young beauty of probably thirteen or fourteen years, the usual age when marriage was to be seriously contemplated. Blushing to the roots of her dark hair she stuttered, "My father has quickly altered a shirt he had already made for one of his customers, he thought you, I mean Signore, I mean your lordship...." She was lost for words and François suddenly had to laugh, which didn't help as it made him look even more attractive. The girl dumped the shirt into the hands of the broadly grinning Michel and fled in total confusion out of their room.

Evening dinner was shared with the family and the tailor's wife, who – when given the means – proved to be an excellent cook. The dark-haired girl sat opposite François, still a bit flustered. She looked exceedingly beautiful with her curly dark hair tumbling like a waterfall onto her delicate shoulders.

What a beauty, if I only had some more time – and she didn't have her parents breathing down my neck... I'll need to keep Michel away from her, she's far too attractive, we don't need any more trouble... And turning his eyes resolutely away from the young beauty, François tried to start a conversation. This proved to be difficult as François only spoke broken Italian and his hosts no French at all. "Can you tell me, which 'albergos' in Venice can be recommended for foreigners?" he asked politely.

But his hosts misunderstood his question. Convinced that their noble guest must be unhappy with his room, they were alarmed, as secretly they had hoped to rent out the room for at least a fortnight.

"Signore is not happy with his room?" the mistress of the house pleaded, close to tears. "But it's the best room we can offer! Would you like more blankets, a carpet?"

"No, you misunderstand!" François tried to explain again. "I'm searching for a close friend, *mio amico,* and I think that he must be staying in an albergo, *si capisce?*"

He could see the relief in the eyes of his hostess but she couldn't help him. They knew some inns frequented by the locals close to their house – but surely those would not be the kind of albergo where a foreigner, especially a gentleman of noble birth, would stay. Suddenly the young beauty intervened, speaking some rapid words in Italian. François could only discern the words 'uncle' and 'Giovanni', but wasn't half of Italy called 'Giovanni'?

While he was still trying to figure out how 'Uncle Giovanni' came into this equation, he noticed that the tailor's solemn face suddenly glowed, first with stupefaction, then with pride. "*Bravissima!* She's right!" the tailor exclaimed, "Uncle Giovanni will know!" and turning to François he explained in slow words, " My wife's brother Giovanni was working as a valet for a noble family until last year. He knows the ways of the nobility!"

A younger son was immediately dispatched in order to fetch his uncle. Most probably driven as much by curiosity as by the noble motivation of wanting to help, only half an hour later Uncle Giovanni appeared. He not only proved to be helpful as he knew – of course – which guest houses were likely to house foreign gentlemen, but he also spoke a surprisingly fluent and elegant French.

"Signore, the best establishment in town is undoubtedly the Albergo Leon Bianco, excellent, I can only say, a class of its own, the choice of the most discerning guests!" and he closed his eyes in rapt adoration of this establishment. "There are others, of course, yet I would recommend looking there first, if Signore's relative can afford to stay in such a house, as regrettably it's as expensive as it is exclusive!"

He named the price for renting a room for a week but the mistress of the house scolded him immediately, eyes flashing indignantly. "Stop telling fairy tales to our guest, Giovanni! A man must be insane to spend such kind of money for a simple room!"

François and Uncle Giovanni exchanged glances in tacit companionship, aware that the mentioned rate was by no means a fairy tale. There was never a limit to the amount of money people were ready to spend if it came to a question of their comfort and luxury. François quickly jotted down the names of the other establishments that Uncle Giovanni named on the sheet of paper that had been reluctantly provided by the tailor's wife together with a quill, ink and a knife. She had not been able to hide her reluctance to part with something as expensive and rare as a sheet of paper.

"Would you know where the Patriarch of Venice resides?" François asked innocently – after all, he had been trained in the refined art of hypocrisy during his duties for the Cardinal de Richelieu – effecting a change of subject. "I've heard that he's one of the most important bishops of our Church!"

Instantly Giovanni's chest seemed to swell with pride. "Indeed, Signore, our venerated patriarch is almost as important as the Holy Father in Rome, no wonder Signore has heard about him! Tomorrow I can show you the magnificent palace of His Eminence but before – if Signore wishes – I could be your guide to the Albergo Leon Bianco, if I may humbly propose my services. Signore might find it very useful to have a local guide, as Venice is full of hidden traps for foreigners – I daren't even mention the plague of pickpockets!"

I know very well how to deal with pickpockets from my past duties in Paris; Cardinal Richelieu was a good master, he must have been the biggest of them all, I guess, François mused, but accepted the proposal with gratitude all the same; having a guide at his side was bound to save a lot of time. *Time!* a voice in his head suddenly seemed to cry. *You don't have any time to lose!*

The next morning Uncle Giovanni was already waiting for him, high-spirited, and punctual as a Nuremburg clock. As François stepped out of his room he saw him leaning comfortably across the kitchen table, gossiping animatedly with his sister, all ready and set to serve as François's personal guide and saviour from the perils of Venice.

The mistress of the house had risen to the special occasion and fetched some freshly baked sweet pastries for her illustrious guest. Still warm, their delicious smell filled the room. A thick sweet glaze dripped lazily onto the wooden plate, as enticing smells of honey and nuts mingled with the powerful scent of freshly baked dough. Did he even detect a note of cinnamon?

Unable to resist, François stretched his hand out, looking forward to tasting such a delicacy, and what an irresistible temptation – a wonderful

240

change after so many mornings he had had to start with porridge – or even worse, cabbage soup! As he looked up to thank the mistress of the house for this special treat, he couldn't help but notice the children of the house (had they multiplied?) who were eyeing these rare delicacies with awe, waiting like a flock of hungry sparrows for some precious morsels to be distributed after their guests had finished their breakfast.

He swallowed deeply – he loved sweet pastries. But pretending not to be hungry after yesterday's copious dinner, he started to distribute the delicious pastries among the children, just leaving a piece for his hungry groom who didn't look particularly happy at this show of charity. No wonder that François, from this minute on, became the children's undisputed hero!

François was still sipping from the cup of warm milk that had been meant to accompany the pastries when the door to the workroom suddenly opened and the tailor, his eldest son of maybe eight years and the apprentice entered the room. At first, François was taken aback – the small group looked like ghosts having escaped from the underworld. The tailor's face, hollow-cheeked like a corpse, was covered by the black stubble of a beard that cried for the urgent attention of a barber. Their eyes were bloodshot as they must have been toiling through the wee hours of the night, stitching and cutting by the poor light of the candles. And yet they were beaming with satisfaction and pride as they presented the result of the night's hard work.

François couldn't believe his eyes: with the flourish of a conjurer the tailor presented an elegant formal velvet waistcoat, a shirt made of the finest linen imported from the German empire, new breeches, even a new pair of silken stockings were presented to him. The tailor had even found the time to make a new shirt for Michel, certainly a lesser and rougher quality of linen – and yet François could see how pleased his groom was to receive his shirt – and that the tailor had taken the pains to work for him overnight.

François thanked him profusely and went back into his room together with Michel where they changed into their new clothes. The tailor knew his business, for sure, as everything fitted to perfection.

"I almost feel human again." François sighed with pleasure as he viewed himself in the polished metal mirror that the tailor had provided. "You can't imagine how much I resented looking like a peasant, I was sure that the smell of manure was following me, how upsetting! Now I can dare to set foot in the most elegant guest house in Venice without risking being thrown out by the landlord – or worse – by his servants!"

Michel grunted some kind of affirmation and being apparently in a talkative mood today he added, "Don't think though that anybody could throw you out, if you didn't want them to, sir!"

François nodded and added cheerfully, "I think you have a point there, I'd probably teach him a lesson he'd never forget!"

On their way to the albergo they passed by the palace of the Patriarch of Venice, but – not really to François's surprise – nothing unusual could be seen from the outside. He was not really interested in Uncle Giovanni's praise of the architecture and the gilded decorations and statues; his soldier-trained eyes only registered that it would be quite a challenge to penetrate the fortified entrance or to climb the steep walls. The Patriarchs of Venice might count on the hand of the Almighty to protect them, but they had obviously chosen to leave nothing to chance if ever the Almighty might be busy dealing with priorities that might not match theirs.

They continued by boat to the Albergo Leon Bianco while François grew more and more impatient. What would he find? Would Pierre and Armand be there, happy and oblivious to any danger or machinations by the Cardinal to bring about their undoing? Had they chosen some other place to stay? Had they already fallen into the hands of the enemy?

François – having been employed by Cardinal Richelieu in the past for the most delicate of missions – of course didn't show his concerns; only a slight frown was a give-away sign, telling his groom that his master was worried, an unusual state mind for him.

A grinding noise and heavy swaying heralded that they had landed at the jetty of the palazzo that housed the prestigious albergo. With the self-assured voice of an officer accustomed to commanding his men, François demanded curtly to be shown upstairs and to meet the guests from France that must be staying in the guesthouse. Not knowing if Armand and Pierre were using their true names, he preferred to avoid this touchy subject. Uncle Giovanni noticed the servant's hesitation and intervened rapidly. With a suave voice trained by long experience in a noble household, he explained in rapid Italian that his illustrious French guest wanted to surprise his friends.

But the doorman only murmured a quick excuse and left, almost fled, from the entrance hall. Minutes later a diminutive but rather pompous major-domo appeared.

"You've requested to meet some guests from France?" he addressed them in Italian. "I'd be very obliged if you would be so kind as to offer me some further explanation?" This last statement was uttered with only a thinly veiled note of hostility.

Uncle Giovanni ignored the frigid reception and politely explained their request once again with the greatest politeness while François remained silent and scrutinized the short, hostile man who had entered the scene. He sported a well-groomed moustache dyed the blackest of black and a beard as prescribed by the latest fashion. Impeccably dressed, he kept himself erect on his high-heeled shoes, but it was fairly obvious that the man was ill at ease; François had developed a sixth sense during his years as an officer, and it didn't need any further words to convince him that his friends must have been here – and that they were in deep trouble.

"I do regret, Signori, that we won't be able to help you!" The major-domo cut Uncle Giovanni's lengthy explanations short with an abrupt hand gesture. "We have no such guests staying here as you've described and – let me add – I find it very strange that you don't even seem to know their names. May I ask the gentleman to leave my house now?"

"What's that I hear? You have no French guests staying here?" a voice from the entrance could be heard. François saw a young man with a sympathetic face striding towards them, an enterprising sparkle in his eyes betraying the fact that he'd probably be open to any kind of mischief. "You know very well that Pierre de Beaulieu and his friend Armand are staying here!" he added good-humouredly, "so don't tell fairytales!"

He bowed to François and added, "May I present myself, I'm Edoardo Piccolin, a good friend of Pierre's!"

François bowed back and answered, "I'm honoured to meet a good friend of Pierre's, I'm a cousin of Armand's, in fact, my name is François de Toucy!"

They exchanged a quick glance, sizing each other up, and liking what they saw. Edo now turned back to the major-domo: "Where are my friends? Yesterday they were here as your revered guests, and no wonder, the prices that you've been charging them!"

The major-domo's face changed from haughty to sulky before he broke into a rapid stream of bitter complaints. "Your friends are scoundrels! We've been interrogated by the authorities, they treated me like a criminal, my wonderful house has been searched, it's a disgrace! Never has this happened to us, there is no finer guest house in the world, princes of noble blood have stayed with us! All of this because of your 'friends'!" and he almost spat out the last word.

Edo looked puzzled and slightly alarmed. "Tell me immediately who came and what they wanted!" he demanded.

The major-domo – a picture of insulted indignation – continued to recount his woes. "The constabulary was here, your 'friends' are being searched for by order of His Eminence, the Patriarch of Venice, as in truth they're just imposters, bandits." He dabbed his forehead. "Bandits in my house! Can you imagine? It seems that they got hold of the individual going by the name of Signore Armand, but the signore who calls himself Pierre is still missing!" The major-domo dropped onto a chair, he was exhausted.

"Let's go to their apartments," Edo answered with a bewildered look on his face, "and send the servants up who served on them regularly, I want to speak with them!"

"Absolutely not!" The major-domo suddenly jumped out of this chair. "We have already packed their belongings. This chapter is over and I don't want to hear from them ever again!"

"I assume they left you with a large unpaid bill?" Edo asked casually.

"Huge!" The cloth reappeared and the major-domo dabbed his forehead again. His moustache was drooping, and he looked more like a frightened dwarf than the imposing manager of the establishment. "Just the bill for the flowers will cost a fortune, I'd never have recommended that flower supplier if I had known that he'd never pay... I'm ruined!"

Got a nice bribe for it though, I'll guess, François thought. He knew the type, and a quick glance at Edo showed that he shared his thoughts.

"Well, I could help you by settling the bill, but only under the condition that we can keep the rooms for several days – and that I can talk with your servants, alone, without your presence!"

The major-domo was fighting with his conscience. He knew that he might get into trouble for letting these strangers enter the apartments but the idea of getting paid and not having to answer to his choleric master was simply too tempting. "How can I be sure that I'll be paid?" he asked slyly.

"Give me the bill and I'll ask someone to fetch part of the outstanding money straightaway."

Thus Uncle Giovanni was sent on an urgent errand to the Bank Piccolin and Edo and François were led upstairs to the deserted rooms that had been Pierre's and Armand's apartments until only recently.

"How are the prisons of the Patriarch?" whispered François to Edo. "As bad as the infamous lead chambers?"

Edo grinned. "Not as nice as this palazzo, but frankly speaking I was almost relieved to hear that the archbishop is behind this arrest. I think we should look for Pierre first, his disappearance worries me greatly!"

François nodded his consent. "I agree, let's first search for Pierre. A night in a prison won't kill my cousin and as I suspect that their worst enemy might be in Venice as well, Armand might be safer in prison than outside!"

"Henri de Beauvoir?" Edo whispered back. "You might be right, we're almost sure he followed us to Milan, but how would you know?"

"An experienced soldier simply knows… I guess!"

Coughing and puffing as if mounting the steps would cause his premature end, an asthmatic servant led them upstairs. Thin as a skeleton, he looked like a mummy, his skin dry and shrivelled, a perfect match for his skull-like head.

He looks like a ghost, as if the Grim Reaper himself were leading us. Edo had to suppress a shiver. He crossed his fingers behind his back.

After regaining his breath the servant announced in a husky voice fit for the mortuary, "Signori, these are the rooms of the gentlemen that have disappeared."

This one likes a bit of drama, François thought, amused, less inclined to be impressed than Edo. *I expect we'll be the gossip of the day downstairs in the kitchen if he ever succeeds in getting back down there without dropping dead first.*

They entered the silent and abandoned suite of rooms – well, not so silent after all, as they could hear some noise of stifled protest emanating from one of the rooms that was located at the back.

"What's going on in there?" Edo's sharp voice echoed through the room

"We caught and bound the servant of the two missing signori," the servant answered proudly. "A true devil, dark as a heathen and he fought like a Turk until we succeeded in gagging him. He kept swearing at us, I've never heard such filthy words before!" His voice was still flat but he couldn't hide his glee; this experience must have helped to enrich his vocabulary.

François and Edo looked at each other and exclaimed almost simultaneously, "That must be Jean!"

They rushed to the source of the voice before the mummified servant could stop them and opened the door of the room where they saw Jean tied to a heavy armchair that was rocking backwards and forwards in his fury. A frightened young servant sat there keeping vigil, a pistol in his shaking hand.

"Drop that bloody pistol immediately!" François roared in the tone of command he employed on the battlefield and instinctively the servant followed the order. He dropped the pistol and it went off with a loud bang, blowing a gaping hole in a Gobelins tapestry that was covering the wall behind Jean.

"Idiot!" Edo shouted, rushing towards Jean to loosen his bonds.

"Oh, Mr Edoardo, how good to see you! Please tell me what's going on, I've been out of my mind, my master hasn't returned, nor did I see Monsieur Armand. These idiots here wouldn't tell me a word. It's all my fault, I should never have taken my afternoon off, I should I have known that my lord was up to mischief!"

Suddenly he realized that François de Toucy was standing close to Edo and he exclaimed. "Monsieur de Toucy, I can't believe my eyes! How wonderful that you've come to Venice! I cannot say how happy I am to see you here! You must help us to find my master and Monsieur Armand, we can't wait, any minute might be too late!"

"Slowly Jean, first you must tell us all you know. We've a very good idea where Monsieur Armand is at the moment, but you're right, we must do all we can to find your master, we're afraid his cousin Henri is in Venice as well. Do you have any idea where your master could be?"

"The damned Contessa!" Jean moaned. "There can be no other explanation!"

"The Contessa?" François replied, bewildered.

Edo slapped his forehead. "I'm afraid that Jean is right, that's the most likely explanation."

François looked at him disbelievingly and a very embarrassed Edo cleared his throat before he answered. "Well, I think it's about time we sat down and discussed everything in detail. I must tell you, Pierre has been behaving very foolishly lately. Armand and I have tried everything possible to get him away from a lady of dubious reputation – the infamous Contessa Montefiori. But I wonder how she fits into this now? She's known to ruin men, but first she usually empties their pockets. Somehow it doesn't seem to make sense."

François was about to reply when they heard the sound of clacking heels arriving in a hurry. It didn't take long before the furious major-domo stormed into the room, accompanied by an army of servants from the kitchen armed with butcher's knives and pans, ready to pick a fight.

"Will you surrender!" the little major-domo cried, his voice almost cracking under the strain. "I warn you, stop shooting in my hotel!" His voice by now was becoming quite hysterical.

"We didn't shoot, you idiot!" answered Edo calmly. "Your brainless servant dropped his pistol, look, he even ruined the precious Gobelins, and one thing's for sure, I'm not going to pay for it!"

The major-domo rushed to the precious tapestry and with tears in his eyes he wailed. "It's ruined! A work of art, brought at great cost from far away, ruined! Confess, it was you who did it!"

"Stop talking nonsense or I'll test these butcher's knives on you first!" François growled. "Don't think for a minute that your ridiculous army of kitchen servants will stop me! The only person to have a pistol here was your stupid servant. Now let's be clear: I am François de Toucy, nephew of the Marquis de Saint Paul, peer of France, godfather of the King of France. You've dared to insult his youngest son by calling him an imposter. I've been sent here by His Majesty, the King of France to make sure that the son of this most noble peer of France will be treated with all the respect that is due to his rank as rumours have reached France that secret Spanish agents are intending to create a diplomatic incident. You know Monsieur Edoardo from the famous Bank Piccolin. He is well known to you and his identity and integrity are beyond any doubt, so I can only give one piece of good advice: shut up, try to be helpful and send your servants back to the kitchen, their smell is assaulting my nostrils!"

The major-domo looked at the elegant blonde stranger, opening and closing his mouth like a fish out of water, completely at a loss as to what to answer. There could be no doubt that François de Toucy was every inch a gentleman and it dawned on the major-domo that the story of imposters might have been fabricated – clearly this was no commoner nor had the two other guests ever appeared to him as anything else but noblemen – and generally he could smell fraudsters or imposters from miles away. The major-domo started to understand that he might do well to change sides. He started to speak but only a gurgle came out of his throat.

François appraised him with a lethal glance that had reduced more robust men to mere ash. The major-domo – by no means a goliath – shrank further under this scrutiny, as François's grey eyes had turned to icy steel. Realizing that he had met his match, the major-domo bowed so low that he almost touched the floor while he lisped, "I must apologize, your lordship, there must be a misunderstanding, a misunderstanding the most *terribile!* By no means did I intend to offend your lordship or your lordship's friends, I swear by all the holy saints! I'll have some refreshments sent up immediately – on the house, of course – and please feel free to use the apartments in the meantime. I'll take care of the Gobelins later and will of course not fail to punish my careless servant. Please accept my apologies for any inconvenience, as your lordship mentioned, it is probably some foreign agents who have misled the authorities."

The troop of servants from the kitchen followed this sudden change of attitude with silent disapproval; they had been looking forward very much to a brawl with some foreigners, an exciting change to their daily routine.

As soon as the door had closed behind the last grumbling servant, François turned to the others. "Where to start? I propose to trace Pierre's actions from yesterday. I understand you took an afternoon off and didn't see your master after you left the albergo in the morning?"

"That's true, my lord!" Jean looked guilt-stricken. "And I should have known that he was up to mischief, I know him so well. His lordship had been

247

unusually moody during the past weeks, if I may say so, because the Contessa had kept him waiting and hoping in vain. Yesterday morning his mood suddenly changed, he was even joking with Monsieur Armand and me." Jean looked puzzled and suddenly exclaimed: "The letters! Of course..."

"The letters?"

"Yes, that morning his lordship was going through some notes that had been delivered and I'm sure that one of those must have been a note from the Contessa as my master's mood changed completely. Oh, I was so stupid and so blind! I was convinced that he was going out together with Monsieur Armand, but I'm sure now that he deceived his friend as well, as Monsieur Armand kept telling him straight that the Contessa was worthless, she was just playing with him."

"Can someone explain to me more about this Contessa?" François insisted. "Who is she and where does she live?"

Now Edo suddenly joined in. "She's a young widow, as beautiful as she's devious, I must give this to her, her beauty is stunning, outstanding. No wonder Pierre fell for her! I love Pierre like a brother, but I can't help feeling that a monastery school is poor preparation for the pitfalls of life – especially when it comes to women. The Contessa met him at a ball and swept him off his feet. He had never met a woman like her. Here in Venice her record of breaking hearts is impressive – and every time her wealth grows, she drives men mad, then she plunders them. I'm sure she played with Pierre, but he was such a fat goose to be plucked – and she hadn't yet started..." Edo was frowning. "It somehow doesn't seem to make sense!"

"Maybe the goose is so fat, that she's planning blackmail or kidnapping. This might yield more than her usual tactics?" François suggested with a grim face.

"Or someone is behind her?" Jean intervened. "I took the liberty of visiting her palazzo as his lordship insisted that I should find out where she lives. I chose a disguise and presented myself as a servant of a proud Spanish duke, but an impoverished one. This house is run like a business, and only rich suitors are admitted; I was not even allowed to see her and present the letter I had prepared. A duke's title is nothing to her if it isn't backed up by a fortune. Inside, her palazzo is decorated in the latest fashion, regardless of expense and I found out from her butler that all the buildings around belong to her as well. I simply cannot imagine that all of this wealth is possible simply because from time to time a gentleman is infatuated by her beauty!"

"Brilliant, Jean, I think we're getting closer to the truth," Edo exclaimed. "*Bravissimo!*"

"I think that Jean is on the right track, but I must say, it leaves me totally confused!" François commented. "I happen to know that the Cardinal has changed sides again, he's certainly behind Armand's arrest. We all agree that most probably Henri de Beauvoir is in Venice chasing his cousin – have we discovered a third dangerous enemy now? This is becoming really messy!"

"The Cardinal has changed sides?" Edo exclaimed. "How do you know this, are you sure? He granted them a letter of protection, didn't he?"

"I happened by chance to see the Cardinal's request to the Patriarch of Venice to detain our friends and make them 'disappear' under the pretext that they're imposters. I can only guess that he's afraid that the King might become too fond of Pierre or Armand once they're back at court. The Cardinal never likes independently minded people to get close to the King, especially as Armand is a member of the de Saint Paul clan. He'll never stomach a member of this influential family coming too close to His Majesty," François explained grimly.

"This might explain why the major-domo told us that Armand has been detained as an imposter!" Edo whistled. "He might be a complete ass, but I doubt that he's been lying to us. Maybe Pierre has been arrested as well in the meantime, he wouldn't know! The Contessa might not even have her fingers in this pie," added François and sighed. "The whole situation still seems a complete riddle to me, I must confess!"

He paused and looked at Edo and Jean. "Did Armand have any other contacts that might come in useful?"

"I introduced both of them to a group of young gentlemen, good families, there might be one or two connected to the Patriarch's family, I'd need to check!" Edo replied, going over in his mind the potential candidates.

François now looked at Jean, who answered immediately. "I know that Monsieur Armand recently visited Mademoiselle Julia Contarini. As she lost her father and stepmother, she now lives with her aunt." He cleared his throat. "It seems that Monsieur Armand was *quite* well acquainted with her in London... her father was on a diplomatic mission there."

"I understand then that she must be rather special!" François grinned. He knew his cousin's tastes only too well.

Edo suddenly jumped up. "This is exactly what we need. Julia Contarini's aunt is also a close relative of the Patriarch and she's so influential in Venice that even the Doge wouldn't dare to ignore her wishes. Hers is one of the biggest fortunes in the city – of course we should know, my brother has been trying to win her as a customer." He grinned and added, "She told him straight that she was capable of managing her fortune better than any banker ever could – and she certainly gives a very capable impression of it. She could

249

help us in dealing with the Patriarch, we could offer him money through this aunt to have them set them free if Pierre has been detained by the Inquisition!"

"Not if I can help it, there must be another way than squandering Pierre's fortune. I propose splitting our forces now. Jean will discreetly – or with a bit of force – interrogate the servants here to check where Pierre has gone to. Someone must have noticed him leaving, how he was dressed, where the boat was heading. I leave it to both of you how you obtain the information, but I expect results!"

Jean nodded and replied curtly, "You'll get results from us, don't worry, sir. I'm ready to kill if I can help my master!"

"That may be going a bit too far at this stage," François flashed him a quick smile, "but we might need you later. If Henri is involved..."

"...things are bound to become nasty." Edo finished his sentence grimly.

"That is settled then. Edo and I will leave immediately to meet Julia's aunt; even if she's a clever dragon, there must be a way to appeal to her for help. We'll meet in about five hours' time at the house where I'm staying here in Venice. My groom Michel will guide you there. It's the house of a poor tailor, so don't expect anything magnificent, but at least he won't betray us or listen in to every word as I'm sure the charming major-domo will."

"Let's go, I think the plan is clear now!" Edo's face showed a grim determination. "I must compliment you on your ability to handle a command!"

"If I didn't I'd be rotting in a damp grave on some forlorn battlefield by now!" François commented drily.

Edo smiled. "I propose to keep one of my servants stationed here in the albergo, he'll inform us if Pierre should return; let's hope that he turns up unscathed."

Uncle Giovanni thus saw himself dispatched to fetch Michel, who was to work under Jean's orders. Meanwhile Jean set himself with resolve to the task of interviewing the servants of the albergo, a task not helped by the fact that they still regarded him as being on the side of the enemy. Whatever these foreign gentlemen might say or explain, word had spread that the agents of the Inquisition had been searching for Pierre and Armand. Maybe they were not imposters after all – but if the Inquisition was involved, they must be regarded as heretics in disguise and it would be the duty of every Christian soul to keep his distance from such people who were damned to burn in hell forever.

Jean descended to the kitchen where he was received in a frosty, hostile atmosphere. No glass of wine was offered in exchange for a bit of gossip like the last time. The fat chef goggled at him with suspicion and clutched his ladle as if he'd love to swing his weapon against Jean's head. Jean's questions were met with the blankest of stares, as if his interlocutors had lost their capacity of speech overnight. He realized soon that talking to the servants as a group would yield no results, so he changed his strategy and questioned the remaining servants individually, but once again, the results were scant. Jean was close to giving up on his mission and simply couldn't suppress a frustrated moan while questioning one of the young laundry maids. A nice-looking girl of sixteen, she suddenly whispered, "I can see that you've taken your master's absence badly. I can give you some clues, but never tell the others that I talked to you, they'll all be listening in behind the door!"

Jean winked at her to show that he had understood and shouted, "So you won't say anything, you obstinate girl! I have time... I can wait!"

She giggled silently. Apparently she was enjoying acting out a drama and wailed loudly, "I won't say nothing! I've got time too!"

Then she lowered her voice and whispered, "Yes, I saw your master. I was bringing up some laundry yesterday noon and saw him going downstairs to the jetty. I always liked to see him, he's such a dashing young man and yesterday he was dressed in his finest!" She gave Jean a long glance which he rightfully interpreted as her being open to flirting with him as well.

"I'm still waiting!" he roared aloud. "And then?" he whispered.

"I asked the servant who was in your master's rooms if he knew where he was going, dressed up like that at noon, it's a bit unusual!"

"And did he know?"

"He looked arrogantly at me: 'this is of no concern to you', so I teased him and told him that he was just playing arrogant as *he* wouldn't know. He then told me triumphantly that he *did* know, as this very morning he had personally delivered a message from a certain person to him, but that I'd be too stupid and low-born to understand those things!" She was grinding her pretty white teeth; apparently the servant's remarks had angered her greatly.

"Let me tell me, you're not!" Jean whispered back. "You're a very smart and beautiful girl." He took her hands in his and to his greatest pleasure didn't encounter any resistance. She smiled: "You'll have to scold me aloud, they'll be wondering what we're doing here!"

Jean reluctantly got up and kicked the chair loudly, then he stamped with his boots up and down. "Tell me what you know or I'll report your disobedience to the major-domo!"

251

"Hah!" she shouted back. "I couldn't care less, I don't know anything, that's the truth and now let me leave, you're a brute to keep a helpless woman here!"

"So who was the 'certain person', do you know?" Jean whispered. He had moved behind her and his fingers were caressing the stands of curly dark hair that had escaped from her modest cap.

"I think everybody knows that your master is madly in love with the Contessa Montefiori, we've been talking about it often enough in the servants' quarters. The message must have come from her, I'm sure."

"Thank you!" he whispered and planted a quick kiss on her cheek. She blushed with pleasure and answered, "Don't forget me when you've found your master, I'd like to… I mean I could show you a bit of Venice."

Jean drew her close. "I'd love to see more… of Venice," he whispered back.

Then he stepped back and shouted aloud in the direction of the door, "Get out of this room, you obstinate girl! I'll have words with your major-domo!"

She winked a last time and left the room, looking demurely to the floor as was to be expected from a simple, yet not too frightened, laundry maid.

Jean finished the last interviews quickly; most of them were conducted in the face of a stubborn silence from the other side, but he didn't care anymore, his mind was working at full speed. The laundry maid had confirmed his worst fears; there could be no doubt that his master had been going out to meet the infamous Contessa. This was no real surprise, as he had of course noticed that one of the most expensive embroidered waistcoats was missing, so his master had evidently dressed up before he had left the albergo. But was the Contessa acting on her own, what did she really want? Money? A title, marriage, or worse – some kind of sinister revenge? Or was the shadow of Henri de Beauvoir looming in the background?"

As soon as Uncle Giovanni arrived, dragging François de Toucy's groom behind him, Jean was ready to leave the albergo. He wanted to take a boat to the Ca' Montefiori as quickly as possible. Making sure that they could not be overheard he rapidly repeated the maid's account and why they needed to leave immediately for the Ca' Montefiori.

"Do you really think we'll find something?" Uncle Giovanni now felt so much a part of the adventure that he couldn't help getting involved.

"Frankly speaking, I don't know. But we must look at the building in every detail. Meanwhile I have a mission for you, Giovanni: I want you to present yourself as the faithful servant of a young Venetian admirer and find out if the lady is in her palace or not!"

252

"I don't know I could do this!" Giovanni protested. "I have no idea who might have sent me, what should I say?"

"You have to!" Jean insisted grimly. "You should know all the noble families of the city, think of some of those who have younger sons with no hope of any title or fortune, they'll kick you out anyhow. But at least you might find out if the Contessa is here or not!"

Giovanni gave it a thought and smiled suddenly. "Yes, there are plenty of those, I'll pretend to be a servant – and my master has fallen desperately in love..." He mimicked a heartbroken lover and rolled his eyes.

"Exactly, they won't be surprised if a new suitor appears, the Contessa seems to break hearts by the dozen. So that's settled, let's go!"

Giovanni waved and shouted to a small boat that was passing along the canal in search of passengers. He insisted that they depart in the opposite direction to begin with. "I could swear that all these nosy fools are standing behind the windows to watch our departure!" he explained to Jean.

Only once the albergo could no longer be seen did he change the instructions to the boatman. The gondolier who'd been rowing at full speed started to argue angrily but as soon as he realized that not only would he be paid for this strange detour but that the foreign guests also wanted to hire his boat for several hours, he swallowed the curses that he had been about to let fly and turned immediately to the agreeable task of negotiating a hefty increase in the price. Unluckily he was to discover that Uncle Giovanni was wise to his tricks and knew the rates. Giovanni made it clear that even if two of the guests were foreigners, the gondolier was dealing with a local. The gondolier tried to object but now Jean joined the discussion and showed his excellent command of Italian argot. Recognizing a brother in spirit, the boatman grinned and the deal was sealed. About twenty minutes later their small boat moored close to the Ca' Montefiori and Giovanni was dispatched to investigate if the Contessa was at home.

All Jean and Michel could do was to wait for his return. As they were looking around to kill time, they spotted a narrow lane close to their mooring. "Let's have a look down this lane!" Jean suggested, always curious by nature.

Michel didn't mind a bit of a diversion and they climbed out of the boat. They found imposing brick walls enclosing a vast garden that must belong to the Contessa's sprawling estate. The short lane ended in a paved cul-de-sac but a careful examination left them disappointed. Not only were the brick walls many feet high and crowned with spiteful-looking iron spikes, they were also impeccably maintained and plastered. *It'll be a tough job to mount these walls*, mused Jean, *even for an ex-pirate*. His thoughts were interrupted by the echo of sharp commands and the noise of barking dogs, a sure sign that the garden was heavily guarded. In a subdued mood they climbed back into the waiting boat, looking at each other with thoughtful glances; they didn't need any words to communicate. Jean was still pondering how to broach the walls when Uncle Giovanni reappeared, bursting with news and his own importance.

"You look like the cat that's got the cream!" Jean greeted him, "Or should I say perhaps, you look like an inflated windbag?"

Giovanni ignored the remark, cleared his throat and declared, "You sent the right person, I have *very* interesting news!"

"Tell us! Is the Contessa in Venice?"

"Not only that!" Giovanni exclaimed darkly.

"I arrived and announced myself as the servant of a certain Roberto... when the butler cut me off mid-sentence! 'We had another servant calling for your Roberto here yesterday!' he shouted at me, 'Tell your master once and for all, her ladyship is not interested in meeting your master! Please stop harassing us, or her ladyship will need to let it be known among his friends that she feels intimidated! We also told the servant that she's out of town, so there's really no use calling on her again!'" Giovanni was a born comedian, skilfully imitating the arrogant voice and attitude of the butler. "I answered – of course," and Giovanni now changed role and played the love-sick young gentleman's servant, "that 'my master can't sleep, he won't eat and although he intends in no way to be a nuisance to the lady he worships, we'd appreciate just a small sign from her ladyship, merely that she acknowledges his existence...' The butler only laughed and sneered at me: 'Understand once and for all, your master is not the only one, they all arrive here making the same brainless platitudes!'"

Giovanni rolled his eyes in comic despair and continued his acting. "I told him that my master is different, he'd just be happy to know her ladyship is close, to breathe the same air! Now the butler looked at me as if I'd gone completely mad but he replied: 'The same air, never heard such stupidity! Your master's out of luck, tell the boy that he must travel to Bologna if he wants to breathe the same air, her ladyship is visiting her relatives over there!'"

Giovanni paused for a moment, savouring the fact that Michel and Jean were hanging on his every word.

"Now, just as the butler was showing me to the door, I could hear a female voice upstairs, calling in *French*..." Giovanni was by now clearly relishing his role: "*Nicolas, Henri, mes chéris, où êtes-vous? Je vous attends!*"

Giovanni looked with satisfaction at the effect of his little speech and couldn't have asked for more: Michel whistled and Jean looked as if someone had punched him right in the stomach.

"I pretended of course not to understand the significance but couldn't fail to remark how fast I was ushered out of the house. That creep of a butler almost slammed the door in my face! I am guessing this information is important...?"

"It is!" groaned Jean. "You have no idea how important! There's only one conclusion: my master's cousin Henri is in league with her, what a nightmare!"

"Nice cousin!" Giovanni couldn't help commenting. "But let's face it, every family seems to have a black sheep, noble or not, I could tell you stories... But what should we do now?"

"Go back and inform my master, François de Toucy!" interjected the taciturn Michel with quiet determination. "I've been in many tight situations in my life, but my master has always found a way out, he's really clever, we need him now!"

Jean looked suspiciously at Michel. "You seem to have a lot of confidence in your master, shouldn't we better try to find a way to get into this building and help my master?"

"And be killed by the dogs or the guards?" Michel commented and spat into the water. "If I have learned anything with François de Toucy, one of his golden rules is: A good plan is more important than any army; acting without a plan will only bring failure!"

Jean was itching to grab his rapier and storm inside the building, but – he hated to admit it – Michel was right, and a cool head was what they needed. His master, Pierre, was in the hands of a man as dangerous as he was cruel and ruthless, and the building looked like a well-guarded fortress. They'd need a plan – and a very good one indeed! He sent a long glance to the Ca' Montefiori, looking so peaceful and innocent in the sun of the late afternoon, and yet his heart almost broke as he thought of Pierre who must be rotting there in some part of the building.

Love, This Strange Feeling...

Edo and François were en route to the Ca' de Muro, the stately home of Lady Alessandra. Edo had pleaded in vain to stop at his lodgings first, as he couldn't imagine paying a social call on one of the most prominent and noble members of Venetian society in his simple morning suit. A crushing stare from François, combined with some scathing words, reminded him that they had no time to waste on social niceties. A contrite Edo therefore ordered a boatman to row them directly to an address apparently known to everyone in Venice.

The grandiose façade facing the Canal Grande was only the prelude to an awe-inspiring entrance hall. The hall was vaulted like a cathedral, and gigantic murals depicted the sea battles and glorious victories of the Serenissima. Arrogant, cold-eyed marble statues stared disdainfully at those visitors who dared to enter this place. The palazzo breathed wealth, a silent testimonial to the importance of the family that had resided here for generations.

Nervously Edo requested the honour of being received by the Lady Julia as soon as an old butler condescended to inquire after their requests. Only a slight raise of his eyebrows betrayed the butler's emotions as he critically appraised the two strangers who dared to enter his sanctum without an invitation. Politely but firmly he started to explain that he doubted that the Lady Julia would be receiving any visitors at all today.

"Spare your breath!" François intervened curtly, "and announce us immediately. I'm François de Toucy, cousin of Armand de Saint Paul, a close friend of her ladyship and I have important news for her. I demand to see the Lady Julia immediately!"

The butler recognized the voice of authority and the name of Armand de Saint Paul. The household had been gossiping with delight about the visit of the handsome Frenchman with the curly black hair. Miss Julia had looked extremely animated after meeting him. It therefore seemed wise to follow the orders of this self-assured visitor who spoke with the ease of good breeding.

The butler bowed with a little more reverence than he had shown initially and asked the guests to be so kind and take a seat in the green room while he'd inquire if their ladyships were disposed to receive guests today. There could be no question of Lady Julia receiving two young gentlemen without being chaperoned by her aunt.

"Pompous ass!" Edo commented as the butler withdrew without showing any undue signs of precipitation. "That's why he's a butler," François replied with a grin. "At least he didn't keep us waiting too long! Now let's hope that

Julia will receive us – and that she can convince her aunt to help us set Armand free!"

"She might even have an idea as to where Pierre may be found!" Edo added, always the optimist.

The butler came back all smiles and invited the gentlemen to follow him. They ascended a sweeping staircase and then walked along a seemingly endless gallery, their footsteps echoing on the typical Venetian floors made from colourful polished broken marble. The gallery seemed to be overflowing with statues and gilt-framed paintings, although it was impossible to determine any style or century, as portraits of saints were mixed at random with paintings of ancestors or vanquished heathens. The palazzo looked like a museum, but a museum without any sense or order to its exhibits.

They entered a salon, fittingly called the red salon, as the heavy curtains were made from a dark red, almost purple, velvet. Two ladies were sitting close to a gilded table, the older one covered in jewels but having long forgotten any pretensions of beauty. Her dark eyes were sharp and she radiated the force of a personality to be reckoned with. Edo and François bowed politely and started their introductions. But the Contessa Alessandra didn't seem to have any interest in social niceties today; she interrupted Edo's flowery introduction, and directing a piercing look at François, she addressed him in immaculate French. "So... you *claim* to be a cousin of Armand de Saint Paul? Let me tell you, you don't look like him at all!"

She had meant to be provocative but her shot failed. François remained serene, and just flashed a quick understanding smile at her while he answered, "I do regret, my lady, unluckily not everybody in our family is endowed with the same good looks. I take after my father's side of the family. We're from the north of France, we're all fair – my mother is a de Saint Paul!"

You know that you're every inch as handsome as your cousin, you conceited devil, Contessa Alessandra thought in amusement, *but you prefer to play it coy, you're not stupid! This meeting promises to become most entertaining...*

She took an immediate liking to the tall elegant stranger and was satisfied to hear that his French was of the purest breeding, a reminder of the wonderful time before her marriage. As a young girl she had spent several months in Paris, a time when her father had served as counsellor to the young Medici queen who had recently arrived from Italy. She sighed; it had been a good time but seemed so long ago now... She nodded majestically and addressed the two visitors in her concise voice. "You're welcome, may I introduce to you to my niece, the Lady Julia Contarini!"

Edo bowed politely, then stepped back to allow François to take his place and greet Julia in the correct manner.

François turned to face Julia, and executed a formal bow to greet the young lady. His eyes caught hers and he held his breath, as sparkling eyes held his in a spell, eyes set like dark jewels in a face of rare beauty, a beauty that was so much more compelling as it seemed to hide a tragic secret. Time stood still. François de Toucy had never been a believer in the concept of love at first sight. His plans had always been simple and clear: the day he retired from the service of the crown, he'd choose a suitable and docile bride from a good family, a bride who'd assure him a comfortable life (and a nice dowry would be helpful). They'd settle peacefully on the family estate under those boundless grey skies of northern France he had learned to love so much. But in this minute, all of this seemed meaningless. Overwhelmed, François had only one desire: to protect Julia, take her in his arms and never let her go! He looked into those dark eyes, lost for words, spellbound. Whenever he had heard his friends professing (usually after too much wine) that true love was like a bolt of lightning, he had sneered, but it had only taken this moment to make him realize that he had found the love of his life! How could he know this so clearly? He couldn't, but of one thing he was certain, this very moment, his life had changed.

A coughing sound from behind woke him from his daydreams, and turning scarlet as a schoolboy François stammered his apologies.

"It would be helpful if you mentioned your name...?" Edo suggested, ever ready to be of service.

Julia forgot her own confusion and laughed; her big eyes were laughing now in delight – the fleeting shadow of sadness had completely disappeared. "Please don't bother, it doesn't matter, the butler had announced you already!" she chuckled. "I'm Julia, and I must confess – I'm most curious to know why both of you came at this unusual time with an urgent message. I hope that Armand is all right?" She had spoken lightly but her beautiful eyes were still fixed on François, who couldn't take his eyes from her either.

"We've come to appeal to you for help!" Edo's sobering voice could be heard. "Our friend Armand de Saint Paul has been arrested and we hope that you might find a way or use your influence to help him!"

The amusement in Julia's eyes died. Agitated she threw her hands up and stifled a cry. "Armand arrested – but why?"

"It's a long story." François had regained his senses – and his voice. Quickly he explained how he had come to see the copy of the instructions of the Cardinal Richelieu to his Brother, the Patriarch of Venice.

"That's not all!" inserted Edo. "His best friend, Pierre de Beauvoir, is missing too and we have no clue if he's been arrested as well or if something else has happened to him, but we're extremely worried!"

258

The calm voice of the Contessa Alessandra interrupted Edo's passionate plea. "No wonder that this Pierre should be in trouble, although I heard a different name when he arrived in Venice, Pierre de Beaulieu..." and she rolled her eyes. "He could have been a bit more imaginative if he wanted to stay incognito. Let me tell you, nothing stays secret in this city, and don't forget it!" The Contessa Alessandra brutally interrupted Edo's explanations.

"Anyhow, your friend has been asking for trouble by hanging around this little slut, the so-called Contessa di Montefiori!"

"Darling aunt, how can you speak like that!" Julia exclaimed, scandalized.

"Pffft, don't play the shy lady with me, my generation is used to speaking the truth. If this Montefiori slut is a genuine countess, I'm a fishmonger. All of Venice has been speaking of nothing else since your love-blinded Pierre was foolish enough to send her a boat loaded with flowers – imagine, flowers in winter! No idea where he got them from, but it must have cost him a fortune!"

"He's not exactly what you could call a poor man..." Edo couldn't help defending his friend.

"What rubbish, squandering money is a sign of either stupidity or senility – or of the newly rich, not of our class. You should know better as his banker than to encourage him in such follies!"

Edo swallowed hard; Lady Alessandra didn't mince her words.

Unperturbed she continued her little speech. "The problem of Armand can be dealt with easily. The Patriarch of Venice is one of my countless nephews – and he owes me a lot of money. Let me tell you, he's always been a simpleton. How could he have swallowed the bait the Cardinal must have given him? I'd bet that Richelieu promised him either a fortune or the French votes when the next papal elections come up. He should know better than to trust a parvenu French Cardinal! I'll send my nephew a message, you can consider your friend a free man already!"

François had to laugh. He was starting to like the old lady. "May I ask you, Lady Alessandra, to wait one more day with your intervention... unless of course the Patriarch's prisons are really terrible. Armand may be safer inside the prison than outside. We suspect that Pierre is not only in danger from the infamous Contessa di Montefiori. Pierre has a charming cousin who's sworn revenge and wants to murder both Pierre and Armand. We're almost sure that he's in Venice at this very moment as well!"

"Sounds like a delightful cousin, anyhow, it's never good having too many foreigners in a city..." the lady added darkly.

259

"But aunt, your own mother was a foreigner, wasn't she French as well?" Julia protested, blushing.

"Not at all!" Lady Alessandra replied indignantly. "My mother came from Spain, of the purest Castilian blood, the best! But that's different, that's not *really* foreign. Better for us to discuss now what we can do for both of your friends!"

"We need to find a safe place for Armand and I'll need some reliable men, I think I'll need to pay a visit to the palace Montefiori; our reception there may be a little cool…"

Julia looked up at François, the admiration in her eyes making his heart beat faster. "Promise me to pay attention to your own safety as well!" she whispered.

François had never felt better. "I will, I promise," he whispered back, and was rewarded with a smile.

"Armand can stay with us, he'll be safe in my house. And I have some good men for you, don't worry. What's your plan now?" the Contessa replied.

"Thank you very much, with your help I'm sure that we'll succeed. We'll still have to work out a clear plan of action. I think we'd better leave now. I dispatched Pierre's and my own valet on a mission to find out more about the last known whereabouts of Pierre. I need to talk to them first before I can give you a clear plan. But it's a great comfort to know that we may count on your support, I'm afraid we'll need it!"

Before François left, he looked once more into those dark eyes – did they hold a promise? Julia allowed him to kiss her hand and didn't seem to mind that he held her hand rather longer than would normally have been allowed for a formal good-bye.

After the two gentlemen had left the red salon it suddenly seemed deserted. The ladies looked at each other in silence; it had been an eventful meeting. Both ladies seemed lost in their thoughts until Julia's aunt broke the silence. "I think you liked the blonde Frenchman, *cara*, I must admit, if I were younger… he has something about him."

"He's the one, I'm going to marry him!" Julia replied simply.

Her aunt swallowed. "Now you've taken me by surprise! You don't even know him!" exclaimed her aunt. "I've never heard anything like that from you before, don't forget that you're a Contarini! Don't be silly, half a year of imprisonment must have confused you. Don't throw yourself at the first handsome man you set eyes on!"

"Dearest aunt, he's the right one, I simply know it." Julia jumped up and embraced her aunt before she added guiltily, "I confess, I may look fickle. It's true, I was a bit in love with Armand, he's so handsome and charming. But I never felt like this before... and you saw François. Oh, I could embrace the whole world!"

"François was swept off his feet, I could see that much!" added her aunt drily, "just as he swept you off yours! Well, if he's a relative of the Marquis de Saint Paul, his family should be good enough to contemplate a marriage; but I warn you, he won't have a lot of money and he's merely of the lower aristocracy. I would wager he's a serving officer, he has that air about him!"

"I have enough money for both of us, I couldn't care less!" Julia snapped back. "If I want him, I'll have him, nothing will hold me back. I've inherited plenty of titles, now that papa is dead!" and she swallowed hard, as the memories flooded back.

"Poor François de Toucy." Suddenly her aunt smiled and the tension broke. "His fate would seem to be sealed... he doesn't know it, but he seems to be in so much greater danger than his cousin and his friend!"

*****

Armand had been in worse situations before this. Sitting sloppily in a comfortable chair, his satisfied glance roamed around his prison room. His prison-guard-turned-valet had performed a miracle, the bare prison cell with its cold chiselled sandstone walls had been transformed in a matter of hours into a comfortable salon.

Armand spoke softly. "The power of gold! There's nothing like it."

A bed with inviting pillows and blankets had been installed in a corner – no dirty straw would be assailing his nose and hampering his slumbers. No longer hindered by rusty handcuffs, Armand sat at his leisure in front of a table that showed the remains of an appetizing dinner. The tray had been brought in as night was falling, and expensive beeswax candles were now lighting the room, spreading their scent together with their warm light.

He held a cup of wine in his right hand; there was ample time now to analyse his situation. Never given to bouts of hysteria or panic, he had decided to ignore the guard's veiled allusions concerning the dangers of the nearby chambers of the Inquisition. Optimistically he had concluded that either Edo or his father would find a way to get him out of this prison, of that there could be no doubt. And yet his forehead wore a slight frown, but it was not his own situation that concerned Armand. For the past hours he had been listening hard to detect the approaching steps of the guards bringing the next prisoner – but the hallway had remained silent. *Where the hell is Pierre?* It seemed rather unlikely that in a city like Venice with its densely woven web

261

of agents and spies, the authorities should have failed to arrest his friend. Armand closed his eyes and tried to visualize once again their meeting that morning during breakfast. Rarely had his friend been in such a good, almost exuberant mood lately... They had joked like in the good old times. Pierre had even been willing to accompany him to the Turkish baths, if it hadn't been for his appointment for a fitting...

Suddenly Armand slapped his forehead and cursed. "Damnation and salvation! Pierre was having me on! There was no fitting!" He now remembered that only the day before Pierre had been showering curses upon the head of the same tailor because Jean had told him that nothing could be ready before next week.

"I'm a total idiot," Armand moaned aloud. "Pierre, you sly little fox, you've fooled me! I could bet that the message Pierre read this morning came from the Contessa!" Frustrated and angry he banged the empty cup on the table. Minutes later the door opened and his guard-turned-valet appeared. Bowing reverently he enquired, "Did Signore require my services?"

Armand looked at the guard in disbelief but then remembered that he had banged the cup on the table. The cup was empty, so he decided to at least make use of the guard's services. "Bring me some more wine, it's quite good actually. Tell me, where did you pinch it from, I can't imagine the Patriarch of Venice offering such good wine to his prisoners!"

The guard looked visibly offended. "Signore! Never would I touch the wine of His Eminence. I bought it for your lordship of course! For prisoners of rank, only the best is served, that's my principle! Value for money, no scrimping!"

Armand looked at him suspiciously but the guard's sad eyes didn't blink; either he was telling the truth or he was an excellent liar. Armand decided to change the subject. "Have you heard anything about my friend, Pierre de Beauvoir? You remember, his name was mentioned with mine on the same warrant!"

Warily the guard looked around as if he expected spies to be hovering in every corner of the prison cell. Slowly – almost tip-toeing – he approached Armand. "I shouldn't be telling you," he whispered conspiratorially, "but I can see clearly that Signore is a man of honour. Your friend hasn't been spotted yet and the officer in charge will soon find himself in the biggest trouble imaginable as the Patriarch's right hand is convinced that he let your friend escape at the Turkish baths. It's impossible that someone should vanish without trace in Venice, it has rarely happened before!" Armand parted with yet another of his precious coins to thank him for the information, but the guard had done nothing to alleviate his fears – on the contrary!

As soon as the door closed and he heard the heavy iron bolts being drawn shut, Armand's frown deepened. If Pierre was not in the hands of the authorities, there was only one place he could be... The thought chilled him. *The best scenario is that she'll pluck him like a golden goose.* He tried hard to stop his imagination running wild; he didn't even want to think about the worst scenario...

*****

The King looked tired. Nonetheless he had granted Cardinal Richelieu a private audience; never would he deny such a favour to his prime minister – he owed him too much.

Richelieu had arrived, ascetic as ever, but with a smug look on his face. He was accompanied by a handsome young gentleman of good build, dressed in the latest fashion, his hair dark and curly, his demure eyes half concealed by long lashes. The King wasn't surprised to find that the young man proved to be a remote relative of the Cardinal's. The young courtier kneeled reverently and the Cardinal smoothly explained that his relative dreamed of being granted one great favour, to be invited to one of the King's famous hunting parties.

Richelieu, you can be more subtle than this! thought the King, disillusioned. To be sure, the young man was handsome and maybe some years ago King Louis would have desperately longed to make him one of his few select, intimate friends. But times had changed, though Richelieu never seemed to have understood this. Strange, how such an intelligent man could have become so blind.

The King closed his eyes for a second and the face of his long-dead favourite Cinq Mars appeared. *Why was I so attracted to Cinq Mars or later to the Marquis de Beauvoir and his friend Armand de Saint Paul? – not because they were exceptionally handsome! These men shared the same spirit of freedom, they were independent, daring and wild.*

Talking to them, Louis had – if only for a wonderful moment – cherished the dream of true companionship, of finding the holy grail of genuine friendship. He longed for friends who would like *him*, the human being called Louis, not the King of France, who had become a symbol and sometimes even a stranger to himself.

This young gentleman looked like a lamb not only ready, but actually eager for slaughter. He'd do whatever Richelieu would ask him to do, report every word and every movement of the King back to the Cardinal. The King opened his eyes, smiled graciously and promised an invitation to his inner circle. The young man rose, cheeks flushed and glowing, happy to have pleased the King – and his uncle.

"Now leave us alone!" the King commanded firmly but with a gentle voice. "We want to talk to our prime minister in confidence!"

The young man bowed, almost touching the floor, and content as a young puppy he retired from the small room the king had chosen for the private audience.

"Put some more logs on the fire before you leave us, our prime minister likes it warm!" the King ordered the footman who was standing to attention. He obliged immediately and heaved some more heavy oak logs onto the fire that was burning brightly. Richelieu was flattered and agreeably surprised. Rightly he understood that the King intended to please him tonight.

"Your Majesty!" he protested, "There is no need to take care of me, it's Your Majesty's comfort that's my only concern... and reward!"

"No need to play the courtier with me!" the King replied, suddenly dropping the majestic 'we'. "Richelieu, did you ever think about your or my end?"

The Cardinal looked taken aback. He was shocked. The King had broken a taboo, never had he expected this kind of question. Was it a trap? All the Cardinal's instincts warned him to be on his guard. "Your Majesty, as a man of the Church, of course I have, but as the holy scripture teaches us, death is not the end for the faithful, paradise will be waiting for us!"

"I may be a faithful son of the Church, but I'm not so sure about paradise, dear Richelieu! Of course, I'll have an army of monks praying for my poor soul and to save me from purgatory – and for yours as well – but can we really be sure? And what will happen to my kingdom? If I passed away tomorrow, I don't even dare imagine the consequences. The Queen is a foreigner in her own country, with no experience of ruling, and the dauphin is only just learning to speak! Richelieu, I must confess, I have nights where I can't sleep, I lie awake and I'm in agony!"

"With all probability, as Your Majesty is at the peak of your life, I shall be the first to leave this earth!" Richelieu answered, suddenly dropping the pretence of lightness; the King seemed truly worried.

"But if ever the Good Lord should decide to call both of us, I must confess, there is reason to worry. The old noble families would try to ascend to power once again, France will be tormented by civil war, the heretic Huguenots will try to regain their hold and all I have been fighting for – spending many years in the service of Your Majesty – will vanish! I know only one man who's capable of assisting Your Majesty's heir or the queen in holding this country together until the dauphin is old enough to take the reins into his own hands: Cardinal Mazarin!"

264

The King looked respectfully at Richelieu. "This is why you tolerate him at court? I've always wondered, because it's obvious that you don't like him!"

"Your Majesty's observation is as sharp as always! Yes, here in front of my sovereign I can confess, I detest Mazarin, but I can see a situation where the kingdom will need him one day!"

"You're a great man, Richelieu!" The King suddenly took the Cardinal's hand and clutched it with surprising force; the Cardinal winced with pain, but the King didn't notice.

"Only a very few men would have put their personal feelings aside in favour of the greater and noble interest of our kingdom!" The King paused for a moment, still not fully comforted. "Are you sure that paradise will be waiting for us? Don't tell me the usual stories. I mean doesn't the bible command us 'Thou shalt not kill!' – and how often have people been arrested in our name, executed on our orders?"

"Earthly justice has to be dispensed, Your Majesty!" Richelieu protested vehemently, "this is also part of the holy scripture – as long as there is evil, it has to be fought!"

"As you're so sure, my dearest Cardinal, I'll believe then that paradise will be truly waiting for us!" the King answered, relieved from the torture of his conscience.

The Cardinal felt relieved as well; there was nothing worse than having to pacify a guilt-stricken king when it came to the worldly task of running a kingdom. But why did Richelieu then suddenly have to think about two young men in Venice who were about to be sent prematurely to paradise? Maybe the doors of heavenly paradise might remain closed to him; he'd better confess tonight and donate some gold to a new convent, just to make sure...

A Sacrifice

Pierre watched the last of the daylight disappear. He sat tied to a heavy armchair, bound and gagged. Sharp cords were cutting into his wrists; never had he imagined that the mere fact of being bound could be so painful. Now, as he sat in total darkness, left in solitude, he listened to the strange noises seeping into the deserted room. He heard the sound of gurgling and splashing water, cats yowling and fighting, wooden beams creaking. Scraps of conversation and laughter, and the clattering of dishes were telling him that life must be going on outside, busy and unperturbed – but he was no longer part of it.

And yet Pierre was not alone. His conscience, long ignored and almost forgotten had risen like a wrathful ghost from those depths where it must have lain dormant, emaciated and almost dead. Released from its spiritual prison it tormented him relentlessly: "*You* wanted to be a worthy Marquis de Beauvoir? *You* pretended to be a genuine duke? You're nothing but a weakling, a traitor... whatever fate is waiting for you, you have merited it! You betrayed Marie's love and confidence, the trust of your best friend, the memory of your parents – and all of this for a worthless bitch! How stupid, how brainless, how humiliating!"

Every single word, every reproach was so true, every word hit him like the thrust of a dagger. Now, sitting in the darkness, suffering the unbearable pain of heart and body, Pierre could no longer understand how he could ever have fallen under the spell of the Contessa. She was beautiful, but so were others – had she bewitched him? During his childhood in Reims, from time to time witches had been brought to justice and burned – although this was a rare occurrence. There could be no doubt that witches existed, just as it was certain that the devil existed. And yet, in the depths of his heart, Pierre didn't really believe in this cheap excuse. When the day of judgement came, he'd need to answer for his sins – would he be condemned to stay in purgatory forever?

Sitting there in the darkness, Pierre was slowly growing aware that something else was starting to torment him. At first, easy to be ignored, it was a mere feeling of discomfort, but the sentiment was growing, slowly and steadily until it started to overshadow all other concerns. This was the sort of problem that never happened to true heroes, it was degrading and embarrassing. Soon his mind was totally obsessed by this thought, by the panic that he might be found here by his cousin, having wet his breeches! This would indeed be the ultimate humiliation, something that simply must not happen. Pierre clenched his teeth and held on.

As soon as he picked up the noise of approaching steps, he almost welcomed the unknown visitors, whatever fate they might have in store for him. Pierre was ready to face torture or death – if only he'd be allowed to relieve himself first! Suddenly he heard dark, good-humoured voices; whatever their mission, they seemed to be looking forward to it. The door opened and two footmen entered, bulging muscles hidden under tight livery. The older one had a large nose positioned decidedly askew in his pockmarked face, his bald head shimmering in the light of the stinking tallow lamps they had brought along. The younger one had a scarred face, where a fight with daggers had left its marks.

Pierre swallowed hard. They were wearing the livery and colours of the de Beauvoir family, his livery. *As if I were dead already*, he couldn't help thinking. Not ready to wait, his cousin was already claiming his heritage.

The footmen came closer and without wasting precious time on explanations, they loosened his bonds, callous hands clumsily untying the cords that were biting into his flesh. Seconds later Pierre felt the blood flowing back into his throbbing hands, a strange, unpleasant feeling. Desperately he made a sign to take his gag away. The two footmen looked at each other; apparently this had not been part of their orders. The older one with the strange nose seemed to be the leader. He looked into Pierre's eyes and replied, "I think our little birdie wants to sing for us! But take care, if you sing a song we don't like or sing too loud, we might break birdie's little beak!"

His mate laughed; he thought that this was a good joke.

The older one took the gag off, and Pierre breathed deeply and croaked, "Get me a commode, quickly!"

The servant broke into laughter. "Our hero needs to piss!" he bawled across the room, but Pierre was too desperate to care.

"There is no commode here, you spoilt little brat," and he spat on the floor. "You can piss in the courtyard like we do, just make sure that you don't let it out before you get there!"

They went downstairs, every single step a torture. Pierre's legs seemed to have acquired a life of their own after he had been bound, as he could scarcely control his steps – furthermore, every movement seemed to threaten to make his bladder explode! Pierre was convinced that he had never descended so many stairs in his life; it seemed an eternity until he set eyes on the courtyard. Pierre was close to despair.

As soon as he had made use of the corner the grinning footman had indicated to him, Pierre came back to his senses – and to reality. His most pressing need might be answered now, but the sober truth was that these two men were meant to guide him... but guide him to where? To his end? Quickly he let his eyes roam around the courtyard – but it was built like a fortress, entirely closed either by the surrounding buildings or high walls, with no chance for a quick escape.

The older footman must have followed his glance. He grinned complacently while he gripped Pierre hard and he spoke in his broad accent, "No chance of escaping, birdie, don't even think about it! We'll bring you now to our master, he'll decide what to do with you – and he's got a lot of imagination, I can tell you that much!"

"Yeah, handles the whip like a real devil!" the younger footman suddenly intervened. He seemed to be able to talk after all. Pierre pretended to ignore this remark; his pride wouldn't allow him to show any weakness in front of these low-born louts. But he knew there would be no mercy for him, his cousin was indeed the devil incarnate.

He was marched up the stairs again as Pierre braced himself for the inevitable. The small cavalcade crossed several galleries and antechambers lit by an ample supply of candles. No expense was spared in the Contessa's household. Never had Pierre expected the Ca' Montefiori to be so vast and sprawling. Like its owner, its façade was a *trompe l'oeil*.

They halted in front of a door where another servant on duty was waiting. No questions were asked, and the footman disappeared to announce his arrival.

Pierre was dragged inside an elegantly appointed bedroom of vast proportions, lit by dozens of candelabra and warmed by two luxurious fireplaces. The servants forced him to sit down on an armchair where he was bound and gagged again, a routine he was starting to dread. As the two footmen finished their job and left the room, Pierre was able to study his surroundings.

Two men were standing close to a table loaded with food, watching him with a conceited smirk on their faces. Nicolas and Henri were at their ease, having a good time. Although the two men were looking at him, they pretended to ignore his presence. In the best of moods they were joking and exchanging scathing remarks about stupid green boys chasing girls – not difficult to grasp that they were speaking about him.

What is he up to? Pierre's thoughts were racing. *I'm still alive, what kind of devious scheme does he have in mind?*

Pierre saw the delicious food on the table, could smell the wonderful aroma of roasted meat and suddenly realized how hungry and thirsty he was. He had been kept without water and food since he had left the albergo. A very different Pierre this had been: joyful, young, naïve, stupid.

Henri left the table and strode closer to Pierre's chair, holding a cup of wine and a piece of meat in his hands. Pretending to be surprised to find his cousin, he exclaimed, *"Mais voyons,* Nicolas, we have a guest! I don't actually remember inviting him... usually I only invite guests of good pedigree, not bastards with shady ancestry. Shouldn't we invite him all the same to share some wine or a piece of this delicious suckling pig?" He stepped closer; Pierre could smell his breath, reeking of wine.

Henri spat at him, then emptied his cup of wine slowly over Pierre's head. Pierre struggled against his bonds, but was utterly helpless. Henri laughed, then slapped Pierre's face hard with the meat he held in his hand. Then he dropped the greasy piece of meat onto Pierre's lap and cleaned his hands using Pierre's fine waistcoat as his napkin.

"How clumsy of me!" he drawled. "Nicolas, look, the wine is gone, and see, our guest won't even touch his meat, I guess I shall have to call the dogs to take care of it... they'll clean it up, they love fresh meat."

Nicolas grinned, filled a new cup and handed it to Henri. "Take a fresh cup, Henri, this wine is simply too good to be wasted! Let's wait a bit until we call the dogs; this late at night they'll be really hungry, I gave orders to starve them. It'll be fun to watch how they fight for a piece of meat. I'm just afraid, though, the dogs might get a bit confused..."

"Why confused? Roast pig or a live pig, they won't care. You're right, that will be fun to watch. But we have ample time for this entertainment!" Henri conceded and walked back to the table.

Pierre was mad with rage, but what could he do? Bound to this heavy chair, he helplessly listened to their terrifying threats and had to endure this humiliation – and if that wasn't enough, he heard the voice of his conscience, oozing with smug reproach. It wouldn't stop reminding him: *It's all your own fault, you betrayed your friends, you're paying now for your stupidity!*

"I think our guest has merited some entertainment before he ends up as dog food!" Pierre could hear the drawling voice of the man called Nicolas.

"Any good ideas?" Henri enquired. "You're right, he looks bored, I'm not sure if he likes our company!"

"Well, I'm sure your bastard cousin will appreciate my little idea very much. Henri, don't forget, we're his hosts, your little cousin merits something special, something he'll never forget, even if his life won't last very long afterwards!"

Pierre went rigid, bracing himself for the next humiliation – or pain. There surely wouldn't be any mercy, he was in the hands of the devil himself.

"Let me see then what kind of surprise you have in mind!"

Nicolas clapped his hands and a door opened. But no blood-thirsty dogs with dripping spittle or black-hooded torturers appeared. Music could be heard and then, out of the dark shadows, the slender silhouette of a veiled woman entered. Accompanied by a flute player, she danced into the room, hips swaying, a man's dream come true. Pierre could see that her tunic was almost as transparent as were the veils she wore to cover herself. In the light of the candles every detail of her slender body became visible, the veils doing nothing to hide her body. Dancing to the rhythm of the flute she dropped veil after veil, then her tunic came off until she stood in the room in naked perfection. Night after night Pierre had dreamed of the Contessa di Montefiori, imagining her naked body, yearning to make love to her. Now here she stood, so close to him he could see the glow of her skin, the perfume he knew so well filling his nostrils.

But no feelings of love, let alone desperate longing filled his heart. If ever any doubt might have lingered in his mind, tonight – right before his eyes – was the undeniable, painful proof that the woman on whom he had spent a fortune, sacrificed love, friendship and all of his principles, was nothing but a cheap courtesan, ready to go with the highest bidder.

"Show our guest what he has missed." Pierre could hear the amused voice of his cousin.

The Contessa smiled and bowed forward until her hair tickled his skin. Like a playful cat she licked some of the remaining drops of wine from Pierre's skin. Then she walked to the large bed and invited the two men to join her. Henri followed first; Pierre saw her loosening the belt of his cousin's breeches, while Henri caressed her black hair that glowed in the candlelight. He closed his eyes in disgust but seconds later he opened them again. Nicolas had approached him silently and had dug his strong hands into his crotch. The pain was almost unbearable.

"Open your eyes and watch us!" he heard his excited voice. "Tomorrow you'll be taking her part! If we don't feed you to the dogs before, that is…"

The sudden pain almost made him vomit, the gag making his breathing difficult. He faced Nicolas with all the dignity he could muster, but in his heart Pierre just wanted to die, quickly, now.

Nicolas joined Henri and the Contessa. Knowing that Pierre would be compelled to watch and listen to their noisy antics and to their insults, they did everything to make him suffer.

Most of the candles had burned down when Henri, Nicolas and later the Contessa had fallen asleep on the huge bed. Tired from their sexual exertions, drunken and drugged they succumbed to a deep slumber. This must have been the sign for the two footmen to appear. Silently they took Pierre back to his prison cell. Here a jug with water was waiting for him and never in his life had Pierre welcomed a simple cup of water so much. Maybe the water had been drugged or poisoned, but he was beyond caring. The door closed, and finally he was alone in the darkness, yet still not really alone – the maddening voice in his head had started its remonstrations once again. *I think I'm going mad*, Pierre thought, before he fell asleep, worn out, every bone aching, desperate as never before.

He must have been sleeping deeply as he didn't hear them coming. When the dagger cut into his flesh, he wanted to cry, but nobody would ever hear his cry as the gag had muted him. The blade cut deeply and all he could think was: *Die with dignity, Pierre de Beauvoir! You've lost everything else, now at least keep your dignity!*

Armand – Appearances Can Be Deceptive

Céline was brutally woken from her sleep; a cry, desperate, shrill and alarming ripped through the silence of the night, followed by violent sobbing. They had only found a small room in the ragged inn that was their home for the night, therefore she had slept close to Marie, and the men had been expelled to the stables for the night.

"Marie, what's happening?" Céline cried out, still drowsy from slumber. Then she understood: Marie, still asleep, was in the grip of a terrible nightmare. As Céline gently touched her, Marie kicked her violently, speaking to the enemy in her dreams, but Celine couldn't make any sense of the mumbled words escaping from her mouth.

"I'm afraid more drastic measures are needed," Céline said to herself, and skilfully avoiding further kicks from Marie, she pinched her arm hard. The drastic measure proved successful and Marie woke up, but it took her several minutes to come back to her senses and to comprehend where she was. As soon as she started to realize that it was not the ghoul of her nightmare but Céline who was sitting on her bed, she looked at her friend and whispered, "Céline, I had a terrible dream! It was horrible, I was so terrified!" and tears welled up in her eyes and rolled down her cheeks.

Céline took her in her arms, and rocking her gently like a frightened child she whispered, "Come, on tell your aunt Céline, what's so terrible!"

"It's Pierre!" Marie sobbed. "Something terrible has happened to him!"

"Calm down, my love, Armand is with him and you know that François will be there as well, most probably they're having a wonderful time already, while we have to sit in this terrible coach drawn by horses that are not even worth the name! I'm sure they sold us donkeys in disguise!"

Marie had to smile under her tears. Confidence restored, she looked at Céline. "Are you sure? I mean we know that Cardinal Richelieu is trying to get hold of Pierre and Armand, what if his messengers were faster than François?"

"The Cardinal is far away and I've rarely seen a more capable man than François, he can deal with any given number of messengers, I'm sure!"

Marie giggled. "I hope Charles never hears this, he'll be jealous as hell!"

"A bit of jealousy keeps a husband interested," Céline smiled back. "Maybe I should drop or word or two about François's skills into the conversation, Charles has become a bit complacent lately."

Marie snuggled into Céline's arms and drifting back into sleep she murmured, "I'm so happy that you came. I think it wasn't just my illness you saved me from. I know something is amiss with Pierre, I simply know it – but you keep me from going mad with worry. How many days until we reach Venice?"

"Charles told me about three to four, so close your eyes now and stop worrying, soon you'll be wrapping your arms around Pierre – well, if we allow it..."

But her last remark was uttered in vain. Marie was fast asleep already. Céline closed her eyes – but it was now Céline who couldn't sleep. What if Pierre truly was in danger?

*****

"Are you sure that you heard the Contessa speaking... and that she was really speaking French? Don't be making up any fancy stories!" François de Toucy was using his sharp voice, usually reserved for those unlucky specimens of mankind that had merited his special – albeit mostly unwanted – attention.

But Uncle Giovanni didn't budge. He nodded enthusiastically, pressing his right hand to his heart, and exclaimed, "Yes, Signore, as sure as there is a pope in the Vatican! It must have been her, she did speak French and she called two men, Nicolas and Henri!"

François exchanged a telling glance with Jean. The conclusion seemed clear enough.

"Let's go to the Contessa's palazzo tonight and free my master!" Jean pleaded, his voice cracking under the strain, as wild pictures of Pierre suffering at the hands of Henri de Beauvoir flashed through his brain.

"Excellent idea, Jean!" François answered scathingly. "In that case you might as well order your master's coffin right away! Didn't you say yourself that this building is guarded like fortress? By the time we find Pierre he'll be dead and we'll find ourselves in a gigantic trap to be butchered like pigs. I know how much you love your master, but we must keep a cool head and devise a sensible plan to save him! Henri de Beauvoir is a dangerous enemy to be reckoned with! He hates Armand as well, and I'm sure that he'll want to have both of them in his grasp. This is the only element that might give us some time." *And some hope*, he added to himself.

Jean hated to hear those words calling for patience, but even if every fibre in his body was urging him to act immediately and not to wait, he understood that François was right; a rushed decision or untimely action would spell disaster. He swallowed hard and replied meekly, "I apologize, my lord, you're right! But what can we do? We don't know the building, we have no idea who lives inside this palazzo, how many guards there are, all of these details that we'll need to develop a plan. "

"I think I can help!" Giovanni interrupted his lamentations. Astonished glances met his triumphant one.

"Well, that's a real surprise, tell us how and why – and don't waste our time on unrealistic suggestions, it's too serious!" François commanded.

"It's simple, Signore, some years ago the palazzo still belonged to its previous owner, actually, the family owned several palazzi in the city. At this time I used to work as a footman for them. I know the building in and out. I can tell you even how many rats live on the lower floors…"

François whistled. "Giovanni, my apologies, I underestimated you!"

Giovanni smiled and replied. "Apologies accepted, Signore!"

"Now, could you draw the layout of the palazzo? Give me all the details! Where do you think they'd keep such an important prisoner?"

All sorts of questions were raining down on Giovanni and Jean was ordered immediately to look for the tailor's wife and wrest another piece of precious paper from her thrifty bosom together with a quill in order to draw the layout of the Contessa's palazzo.

Jean had not even reached the door, when they heard a heavy hand hammering impatiently on the door of the tailor's house. Automatically François and Edo gripped their rapiers; this could only herald an unwanted visitor.

"Who's there? Announce yourself!" They could hear the piercing voice of the tailor's wife.

"I'm the servant of Signore Edoardo Piccolin, signorina, he told me to come to this house – it's urgent, please open the door!"

They heard the shuffling feet of the tailor's wife as she walked to the door. Having recognized the voice of the servant he had placed on watch at the Albergo Leon Bianco, Edo had to fight a rising sense of panic. This could only mean that something unusual must have happened to Pierre! With frightened eyes he looked at François, but the latter kept a straight face. It would take more than a messenger to unsettle François de Toucy!

The servant was led into the small room where Edo, Jean, Michel, François and Giovanni had gone into a huddle. Intimidated by so many people looking at him expectantly he started to stutter: "S-signore Ed-Edoardo, I have a v-very important m-message for you!"

With clumsy fingers he fumbled nervously at his waistcoat. Jean was tempted to lunge forward and rip his waistcoat apart. Having lost precious time, finally the servant managed to wrestle the document from the folds and hand it over to Edo who took the message, unfolded it and went as white as a sheet. Unable to utter a single word he handed the sheet of paper to François. François read the short message. In fact the content was a simple command, addressed to Armand:

If you want to find your friend alive, come to the Ca' Montefiori tomorrow evening without fail, or he's a dead man.

Underneath the message only two words had been added, written in a brownish kind of ink:

Help! Pierre.

François looked at the message and his expression froze, while Jean, unable to wait for explanations, had moved closer. Silently François showed him the message.

Jean's face became pale, and he swallowed hard. Looking straight into the eyes of François he said curtly, "Henri de Beauvoir will pay for this, I don't yet know how, but I vow by the Holy Virgin, I'll not relent until I have paid back everything, an eye for an eye!"

Edo interjected with a feeble voice: "The brown ink?"

"...is blood, most probably his own!" François finished the sentence for him.

"Bastards, barbarians!" Giovanni spat on the floor. "Are you ready to spend some money to get into this building?" he asked.

"If I have to buy a battleship and shoot the palazzo to its foundations, I'll do it," growled François.

"Signore, you're in Italy, those crude methods may be suitable for France or England, here in Venice, we fight more elegantly!"

"Just get on with it!" Edo intervened. "Tell us how we can get into this building, we must free Pierre urgently!"

And this was exactly what Giovanni did.

*****

Henri stood close to the open window that offered an excellent view onto the Canal Grande. The Serenissima was looking her best today as the grey veil of wintery clouds had disappeared and a perky sun was showing its face.

Temperatures had risen, and spring was in the air. Sunlight was playfully reflected by the waves that rippled the surface of the Canal Grande as there was a lot of traffic on the Canal. A flotilla of boats made up of all imaginable sizes, including fishing boats, colourful gondolas and simple rowing boats, was bustling along below the window of the palazzo, creating a colourful and ever changing kaleidoscope.

There were the usual faint echoes of shouting voices, cursing and yelling, but it seemed that the benign appearance of the sun made the voices sound more conciliatory than before, as from time to time even snatches of laughter reached the first floor of the Ca' Montefiori.

Greedily Henri inhaled the fresh air; he had a headache. As he turned his head he could see that Nicolas was looking pale as well. He had replaced his wig with a knotted scarf and was looking ever more like a corsair.

"We added too much of the Spanish fly to the wine yesterday!" Henri groaned, "sometimes I think it's pure poison!"

"I guess it is, expensive poison," Nicolas agreed, "but we had a great night! I thought you'd never grow tired…"

"Oh yes!" Henri flashed him one of his rare smiles. "And my dear little cousin went mad with rage… any nice surprise you have in store for him tonight?"

"Tonight, dear Henri, will be the *big* night of our revenge. My name's not Nicolas if Armand doesn't arrive here in a blaze of glory as soon as he receives the desperate message from his helpless friend, and then our trap will snap shut." He made a telling gesture. "Two mice to play with, we'll have a lot of fun!"

"Don't you think that Armand will come with some friends, I mean, he may only be a kid, but he's not stupid…"

Henri looked sceptically at Nicolas.

Nicolas waved his hand deprecatingly. "I know the gang of young gentlemen he's been hanging around with, most are actually customers of our little establishment running up high debts with our pretty Contessa. All have big mouths, but as soon as they see that trouble is brewing they'll bolt like frightened rabbits, don't worry!"

"What about this banker, they seem to be friends with him?"

"You name it, he's a banker. He won't meddle too much – what's in it for him? In any case Armand will be met by our men, he'll be disarmed and his friends, if there are any, will be packed back into their boats. What can

276

Armand do? I guess he'll offer you money, a title, land… his father still has a lot of connections!"

"A title! I *am* the true Marquis de Beauvoir, that's the only title that counts! *We* were the true power behind the Valois kings before these Bourbon upstarts came from their stinking stables to usurp the sacred throne of France, heretic peasants who married merchant daughters for their money, that's what our kings have become!"

"I know, Henri, calm down, I too want to see Armand suffer before he dies at my hand, you know what he did to me!"

"I know!"

The door opened and the Contessa entered. Dressed in her favourite red she looked like a ripe cherry to be picked. Her lustrous black hair flowed freely onto her shoulders as she had not yet finished her morning toilette. "Why are both of you looking so gloomy? Didn't you like last night, I must say, I rather liked it…" She smiled mischievously as her melodious voice filled the room.

"Not gloomy, just imagining how we shall deal tonight with our French guests. But you look lovely, as always!"

The Contessa blew him a kiss. "I think I'll order a coffee for us, I think that's what we need now!" She rang the bell and gave a quick order to the black page who appeared from behind a hidden door.

"What are the plans for tonight?"

"We play cat and mouse," Henri answered sardonically.

"Sounds enticing, can I play the cat?" said the Contessa. "I think I would be a very good cat!" and playfully she formed claws in the air.

"I'm convinced that you'll be a wonderful cat, digging your sharp little fingernails and teeth into our little blonde mouse…. And tonight you'll even have a second toy to play with!"

"Little Armand, I guess," she laughed. "The ever so faithful friend can't be far away when his best friend is in trouble. Well this sounds entertaining enough. When must I be ready?"

"Our little game will start in the evening, it would be nice little touch if you'd wear the ruby the bastard offered you – the colour of his blood."

*****

"Can you help me? I need your aunt to use her influence right now! Things are moving quickly, we must free Armand today, it's the only way to save Pierre!" François still held Julia's hand; somehow it seemed difficult to let her go. He noticed though – with pleasure – that she didn't object to holding his hand longer than the rules of usual politeness permitted.

"I know that she has spoken with His Eminence already," Julia replied and added with a whisper, "I can tell you, she was truly upset after you left us yesterday! The whole afternoon she kept complaining about her nephew and his foolishness at being manipulated by Richelieu. By the early evening she had worked herself into such a fury that she ordered her private gondola and visited the episcopal palazzo."

"And do you know if she was successful? I guess the Patriarch of Venice might have different priorities than meeting one of his numerous aunts!" François was curious, although somehow he couldn't image that anybody could resist the force that was Julia's aunt. She was worth an army.

"Of course she was! She simply walked into one of his audience rooms and ordered his visitors to leave them alone." Julia giggled. "She said that her nephew was trembling in his boots as soon as she mentioned the name de Saint Paul. He apparently offered all kinds of excuses and lies, but this doesn't work with my aunt. He didn't stand a chance, she made him sign the papers before her very eyes: Armand is a free man!"

François planted a quick kiss on Julia's hands before he exclaimed, "Excellent, that's wonderful news!"

With satisfaction he noted that his kiss had not displeased Julia, but before he could make further advances, the Contessa Alessandra swept into the room.

"What kind of new rules are those that allow an unmarried lady to be alone with a gentleman?" she chided Julia, but her tone was not unfriendly. Evidently, François de Toucy was in her favour.

"No new rules, dearest aunt!" Julia protested. "I let you know immediately that I'd receive Monsieur de Toucy and if you take ages to arrive, it's not my fault!"

"You're a naughty little kitten, I had to finish a letter first!" She turned towards François and addressed him now. "To what do we owe the pleasure of your visit this time? I didn't expect to see you back so quickly! Is anything amiss with Pierre de Beauvoir?"

François could only admire her sharp perception. He bowed and answered, "You're absolutely right, Contessa, we need to act fast, and I'll need the help of Armand. I understand that you have been able to arrange his release already?"

"I did, I'm not the kind of person to dally when work has to be done. Your cousin is free to go, I've brought the document for his release with me."

"Please let me thank you from the bottom of my heart, you've done us a great service."

But the Contessa was not to be impressed by his smooth words. "Don't talk nonsense, it was my duty. It allowed me to save my foolish nephew from a potentially disastrous situation, Armand's family would have caused a scandal – and rightfully so!" She paused and her sharp eyes examined François. "You might need more help! If Pierre de Beauvoir really is in the claws of this so-called Contessa, I can imagine that you'll need some good men. I've heard her palazzo has been turned not only into a brothel but also into a veritable fortress."

François could – once again – only admire her perception. The lady seemed to know everything that was going on in Venice. "I greatly appreciate your offer, I could use some good men. Actually we do have a plan for how to enter the Ca' Montefiori tonight," François answered with grim determination.

"I can imagine! I don't see you walking into a trap unprepared," the Contessa replied placidly, "and I wish you luck. This vermin must be smoked out!"

Julia looked at him with huge eyes. If he was not mistaken, he could even detect tears shimmering in her eyes. "Take care!" she pleaded, then not knowing what else to say she added lamely, "Good luck!"

"I'll take care – and your aunt is right, it's about time we liquidated the infamous Contessa and her friends, they're of the purest evil!"

"My major-domo will be instructed to select five of my best men, they'll be ready in about two hours. I suggest that you go and find Armand now, you have no time to lose," the Contessa Alessandra replied in her calm voice. Turning to Julia she said, "Don't shed any tears my little goose, François de Toucy will handle this, he seems to have a good head on his shoulders – I'm sure it's not just for decoration!"

François understood this rightly as a compliment, and smiled and bowed to the ladies before he took his leave.

"What a pity that I'm an old frump now," Julia could hear her aunt sigh. "He's really devilishly attractive!"

Uncle Giovanni was waiting already, ready to guide François to the palace of the Patriarch of Venice. As usual, most of their trip was made by boat. After they arrived at the jetty, they needed to cross a large square paved with coloured marble and walk further down one of the narrow streets that were so typical for the city. The guards at the entrance of the episcopal palace looked snootily at the unknown visitors but quickly changed their attitude as soon as Giovanni presented the document signed and sealed by the Patriarch – accompanied by some scathing remarks in the local dialect.

Immediately they were led to the ascetic secretary who supervised the activities of the Inquisition and the episcopal prisons. He seemed well informed as he greeted François de Toucy with the greatest respect. "I have been informed, Signore, that there has been a small misunderstanding – one of our officers has shown an… ahem… excess of diligence. He will be taken care of. In the meantime I would like to present my apologies for any inconvenience that might have been caused, also of course in the name of His Eminence; the Patriarch was shocked to hear about this error!"

Slimy creature, thought François, accepting the false apologies with a straight face before replying, "I will recommend that my cousin forget this little – shall we call it 'unfortunate' – incident. I hope that he didn't suffer too much this past night though, otherwise we might find him a little irritable."

"Oh, I really don't think so, you'll understand as soon as you're reunited."

François was slightly surprised by this statement, but the busy secretary had already given orders to guide François to the small prison building and left them without offering any further explanation.

A sad-looking prison guard stepped forward to guide them to the episcopal dungeons. François looked at him critically – and could only wonder. Having worked for Cardinal Richelieu (frequently assigned to extremely delicate missions) he had seen many kinds of prisons in his life – far too many for his taste. Usually prison guards were a filthy and highly unsavoury species, as were the institutions they represented. But the guard in the episcopal prison was not only dressed in a clean livery, he spoke and acted more like a servant than a prison guard.

As soon as the heavy iron bolts of Armand's prison door had been drawn back and the door opened to allow a view onto the cell, the truth dawned upon François: this was no ordinary prison cell: from the Gobelins that covered the wall to a luxurious bedstead, and a table covered with tin plates and cups, Armand's prison cell looked like the well-appointed apartment of a gentleman. Any compassion would have been wasted; there had obviously been no suffering on Armand's part.

His cousin jumped up from the bed. He had been reading a book that he dropped carelessly to the floor. "François, what the hell are you doing in

Venice! I think this is the second time in my life that you have rescued me! Can't tell you how delighted I am to see you here! I was bored to tears, they gave me a prayer book, can you imagine?"

"Armand! It seems to have become one of my favourite pastimes, saving my little cousin from calamity! You're the reason, by the way, why I came to Venice," drawled François but his laughing eyes belied the haughtiness of his statement. "But tell me, how did you manage to turn a prison into such a luxurious dwelling, I've never seen anything like it! I imagined finding you miserable, chained to the wall, squatting on some dirty straw, rats nibbling at your bones..."

"It's my charisma, cousin!" Armand smiled, full of mischief. "And maybe the golden coins that I always carry in case of an emergency!"

"I agree, those were wisely invested, this was indeed a true emergency!"

Armand suddenly became serious. "You needn't have worried about me! I was born under a lucky star. But where the hell is Pierre? I know that these crazy Venetian constables wanted to arrest him as well, but did they get him after all? I've been worrying about him the whole night! By the way, do you have any clue as to why I've been arrested?"

"Too many questions at once! Have mercy! First: you were arrested because Cardinal Richelieu is playing his dirty little games once again – I guess the King liked you too much for his taste. But regarding Pierre, why were you worried, do you have any suspicion that something might be wrong with him?"

Armand sighed deeply. "François, it's useless beating around the bush, my dear friend Pierre is in deep trouble, I'm almost sure of it. He fell in love with a lady, well not a true lady in my eyes, you know he's as inexperienced as a new-born baby. She calls herself a Contessa, but I know her type – great flirt, but highly dangerous. Pierre fell for her, he wouldn't listen to any advice! I'm worried to death that he's been trapped by her, she'll milk every last drop out of him. It's not love, I'm sure, but he was overwhelmed by her, she made him mad with desire. One day he'll wake up and hate himself... I did what I could, but he wouldn't listen to any of us!"

"Giovanni, can you please make sure that we won't be overheard, I need to talk privately with Armand!" François commanded.

As soon as the door had closed and they were alone, François looked into the anxious eyes of Armand and replied, "You're damned right to worry, Armand, it's far worse than you think. The Contessa was a juicy piece of bait laid out by Henri de Beauvoir. I know for sure that Pierre is in his hands now!"

Armand didn't comment; he only swallowed deeply, then he grasped a cup of wine which he emptied in one go. "I'm not really surprised, everything about her seemed false. If she had just intended to milk Pierre, well, she certainly had ample opportunity to do that before now. She played a very clever game though. Now I understand what she was after, she wanted him mad with desire beyond reasoning. François, we can't wait, we have to help him, what can we do?"

"I have a plan, but it can only work if you are willing to take a great risk. Are you ready to risk your life for Pierre? I don't see any other way!"

Armand shrugged his shoulders. "I know for sure that Pierre would never hesitate for a second to risk his life for me, so what kind of friend would I be to hesitate? Tell me what I'm supposed to do!"

François opened his waistcoat and showed the message that he had received the day before. As soon as Armand recognized the dried blood with Pierre's signature he threw the cup against the wall and shouted, "These swine, these bastards, I'll kill them, I'll cut off Henri's balls and boil them in hot oil!"

"It's difficult to stay calm, but try to listen. I'll explain my plan now, and if we do it right, you may cut off and boil any part of Henri that you fancy, with pleasure!" answered François and started to outline his plan.

*****

Night had fallen. He could hear the gurgling sound of oars touching black water, he could see other gondolas gliding along, lanterns swinging like delirious fireflies. Black shadows against black water – what better camouflage could there be than the veil of darkness? Whether it be first innocent love, adultery or crime, the night would keep any secret.

Soon, almost too soon, Armand recognized the façade of the Ca' Montefiori, lit by torches at night like most of the noble palaces along the Canal Grande, competing proudly to display their owners' wealth and magnificence. He disembarked and was greeted almost immediately at the jetty. He had been expected.

"*Buonasera*, Signore! You've come alone? We appreciate your discretion. Her ladyship is already waiting for you!"

Armand answered with the mere indication of a polite nod and followed the liveried servant inside, then up the marble staircase to the first floor. Here he was led into an elegant room of ample proportions. The glaring brightness almost blinded him; there were burning candles everywhere, from crystal chandeliers to candelabra spreading their light and the pleasant scent of beeswax.

Standing decorously next to an array of red roses was the most beautiful woman in Venice, the Contessa di Montefiori. She wore a velvet evening dress of scarlet red with a scandalously low neckline. The dress enhanced the effect of her pale skin, and a single ruby the colour of blood glistened diabolically on her bosom. Her white teeth gleamed in the light, but her smile was not a kind one. Armand was alarmed.

"Good evening, *mon cher Armand!*" she greeted him in her melodious voice. Her eyes remained cold however, her smile never reaching her eyes.

"Good evening, Contessa, may I come closer? I've come to propose a deal, my family is ready to pay a substantial ransom if you will help to set my friend free," Armand replied stiffly.

"I'd love to, but in fact I have different plans!" she answered, and snapped her fingers.

Two servants with bulging muscles lunged forward and before Armand could react, he was trapped, while arms of steel started to strip him from his waistcoat to his shirt and then to his boots. His breeches were thoroughly searched but he was spared losing those. A satisfied grunt signalled that the servants were happy with the result of their search. A rapier, a gun and two daggers were proudly displayed and presented like a valuable gift to the Contessa.

"What a naughty boy!" she exclaimed, mocking him. "To visit a lady of rank with a dagger hidden in his boots, I don't think that I can leave this unpunished!"

"You're right, I wouldn't need this for a true lady!" Armand couldn't help answering.

"Armand de Saint Paul. You'll never change and you'll never know when it would be better to keep your pert mouth shut."

Armand turned round as if stung by a wasp to identify the man who now spoke to him.

"You didn't expect to find me here, did you?" the amused voice asked, an obviously rhetorical question.

"Not really, Henri de Beauvoir! I can't say that it's a pleasure to meet you here though!"

"I'm not really interested in knowing whether it provides you with any form of pleasure or not," Henri replied in a bored voice. "By the way, there's someone else who's delighted to meet you here tonight," the voice went on.

283

A shadow detached itself from the dark corner of the room. Armand recognized the same man who had joined Henri in chasing them in the *chambre séparée* in Paris, the man who had been in animated discussion with Henri over how best to murder Pierre and himself. Fate had decided otherwise, then, and hopefully he'd be lucky once again. He remembered that the man had worn his hair long and curly – like an aristocrat – but tonight he wore a scarf, and looked like a pirate.

"Now, my dear Armand, soon you'll understand why we went to all those pains to lure Pierre and you into our little trap. Frankly speaking, I had expected rather more of a challenge, it was not very difficult after all to catch your stupid little friend. Pierre was an ever so consenting victim, but not a very clever one – it's actually an insult to be confronted with such debility in one's own family. But I mustn't complain, that's the result if the blood is not kept pure."

Armand felt his anger rising but he commanded himself to stay cool. *That's just what he wants to do, provoke me, but I'll pay him back!*

Henri's appraising glance ran over Armand's naked chest. "Almost a pity that such a nice body will not survive this evening, I could have taught you some nice little tricks... What do you think, Nicolas?"

"We might have time enough to make use of this nice body tonight...." Nicolas suggested and approached Armand as if he wanted to caress him. Instinctively Armand tried to shy away but the arms of steel held him tight. Nicolas uttered a short laugh before he spat in Armand's face.

Before Armand could pay him back, hands of steel had already closed his mouth.

"You thought you'd come here, offer me some of your filthy money and get away with it? We don't need your lousy gold, I probably have more than your conceited father has ever seen in his life! I want revenge... for this!" With a dramatic gesture he tore his scarf away. Armand swallowed. The man's skull was covered with some remaining strands of hair but most of his head was covered with a disgusting layer of scarred pale skin, glistening in the light of the candles. The man had been very attractive, but without his scarf, he looked like a monster.

I can only hope that it gave you a lot of pain, Armand thought defiantly as Nicolas approached him. Close to his ear, Nicolas hissed, "Tonight, you'll suffer as I have suffered! You'll become mad with pain as I was crying with pain! You'll plead for mercy in vain, you'll regret ever having been born."

Armand's thoughts ran away with him: *You may have to risk your life, François said to me. I know I agreed to help Pierre, but I had no idea what was waiting for me here. I can only pray that the Lord will save me! These people are not only evil, they're utterly insane!*

"Let's start with our little entertainment then!" Henri cried, now in the best of moods.

"Bring him in!"

The door opened and Pierre was dragged into the room. Armand had until this moment felt as if it was all somehow not real, as if this conversation had been more of a staged drama than real life. But now his heart almost stopped beating, and tears sprang to his eyes. His friend could barely hold his head up; he must have been tortured, as instinctively he looked for protection. Never had Armand felt such compassion for his friend, and so much hate for those people who stood there, smirking, radiating smug satisfaction.

Pierre suddenly noticed Armand and protested, "No, Armand, no! You should never have come, it's all my fault, I should never have dragged you into this!" and tears started to roll down his face.

"How endearing! A reunion between faithful friends! Nicolas, I feel so enriched by this experience!" Henri's mocking voice filled the room. "Look, my dearest Contessa, your proud Marquis is here!"

"Maybe he's thirsty!" the Contessa suggested and sipped from a cup of wine in a mock toast to Pierre. "I'm afraid we simply forgot to give him some water since.... Ah yes, it was yesterday, indeed... my people are so appallingly negligent. Therefore let me drink to your health!"

Armand noticed how dry the lips of his friend were. He hated every second of this distasteful comedy, he felt sick with disgust. Alarmed, he saw that his friend must be suffering with a high fever as his face was flushed, and he had problems focusing, as he clung unsteadily to the footmen who held him.

"Yes, let's give them some wine!" Henri took his cup and threw it in Pierre's face. Armand was ready to commit murder, there must come a moment when the guards would let him loose, just a second's inattention would do! But the guards must have sensed his fury, as their grip only tightened.

"Now let's start our little game, if we shall call it that!"

"Yes, let's call it the game of revenge!"

Nicolas clapped his hands and the doors opened again. Two liveried men in the colours of the de Beauvoir family appeared. Each of them carried a long knife, and one of them had thumbscrews and evil-looking tongs dangling from his belt. Armand's heart started to beat wildly, his stomach contracted.

He had to summon up all his courage, all his pride. A noble mission, intended to rescue a friend, was turning into a nightmare.

Henri walked to the window where a low table with glasses and a carafe of wine were standing. He poured himself a glass, ready to celebrate.

"Show me those beautiful little instruments!" Nicolas commanded and invited the Contessa to come closer. "Have a look my dear, doesn't this look nice? I think we'll have a lot of entertainment tonight, I have plenty of ideas for how to use them, skilfully, slowly. I do so hate artless butchery!"

"You know that the sight of blood excites me, Nicolas." Her perfect teeth were shimmering in the light, excitement and lust glowing in her charcoal eyes, too big to be natural.

"She's drugged," thought Armand. "I should have realized this much earlier, those bright eyes…"

The servant with the crooked nose grinned idiotically. "Yes, master, those are little beauties, all nice and sharp, as you ordered them."

All of a sudden his tone became cunning. "Would my lord like to try them first, make sure that they've been sharpened to your liking?" His strong arm moved forward and the sharp butcher's knife went straight into Nicolas's belly, as smoothly as if it were cutting through butter. Mercilessly he turned it while Nicolas's cries of agony and dying spasms echoed through the room, filling it with his anguish.

The second servant hadn't remained idle. Swinging his knife like a skilled butcher, he cut a gaping hole in the Contessa's throat. Blood gurgled like a waterfall, spreading onto her bosom and her velvet dress, sticking to her expensive pearls and the ruby. She staggered, moaned, then dropped down, to die close to Nicolas, her eyes and mouth still opened in absurd surprise.

All of this happened in seconds only, taking all of the bystanders by total surprise. Armand's guards, flabbergasted, loosened their grip. Grasping his chance, Armand lunged forward and grabbed his abandoned pistol. Quickly he turned and shot at Henri. The crashing sound of glass could be heard as Henri tumbled out of the window right into the Canal Grande. Did they hear a cry – or just a splash? Or was it just their imagination? Armand hurried to the broken window and looked outside, but all he could see was the black night with random gondolas and their lanterns. There was only an eerie silence.

The silence was broken as the doors of the room crashed open. Accompanied by several armed men François de Toucy entered the room. Taking immediate command he disarmed the remaining guards and servants while Armand hastened to embrace his friend. He wasn't sure if Pierre had really understood what had been going on. But Pierre opened his eyes and whispered, "Thank you, I was so blind, forgive me, my best friend of all!" and then fainted in his arms.

Satisfied, François looked around; everything had worked exactly according to his plans. How lucky that Uncle Giovanni had known how much the Contessa was hated by her own staff and which servants were willing to open doors and change sides, provided that enough gold was flowing. It was money that had been wisely invested. Still relishing his victory, he detected Armand struggling with the body of his unconscious friend.

"I think you need some assistance, the burden of friendship can be heavy!" he joked as he helped to place Pierre on a low sofa. "Armand, you did a brilliant job, you were very brave tonight!" he added.

Armand was flattered. "I must confess that there were one or two moments when I was not really at ease, nobody could really guarantee that those men with the knives would change sides, you took a great risk!"

"There was no risk, the two servants were our own men, recommended by Julia's aunt. We killed the others once we knew what had been planned tonight. I was betting on the fact that Henri and Nicolas would be so absorbed by their own hate that they'd barely notice the faces of mere servants – and with the liveries and hairstyles they looked almost identical.

"You could have told me this part of your plan!" Armand protested.

"It proved far better not to have told you, you were a far more convincing victim showing genuine fear! Nicolas and Henri were convinced they had you in their pocket, conceited devils that they were!"

Armand didn't know if he should admire or hate his cousin.

Love And Faith

He woke up, or was he in heaven? Marie was sitting at his side, smiling her lovely smile at him – satisfied, he concluded that he must have landed in heaven! In real life, Marie was far away, staying in Reims with her parents. Heaven was a good place to be then, he decided. He smiled, sighed and fell asleep.

"He's coming back to life!" Céline stated with satisfaction. "Don't cry, my little lamb, he'll be all right!"

"I'm not really crying!" Marie protested. "But not everybody can be as unfeeling as you!"

Céline looked at her with an understanding smile. "I admit, I'm most shockingly even-tempered, I guess it's my deplorable lack of imagination! I can only defend myself by saying that I must have inherited this trait from my grandmother. I remember how she knocked out a burglar who had dared to enter her bedroom. Her only complaint was that his blood had stained her best carpet!"

Before they could discuss the subject any further, Jean announced the arrival of François and Armand. Back in the Albergo Leon Bianco, word had spread that the two foreigners were not only titled and of the highest nobility, they were known to enjoy the protection of the influential Contessa Alessandra de Muro, the de facto queen of Venice. Even Jean was now treated like royalty whenever he condescended to enter the servants' quarters.

"How's Pierre doing today?" François asked, as he took his hand and touched his forehead.

"Much better. Did you really open and clean his wound?" Marie shuddered; it must have been very painful for poor Pierre.

"Oh yes, he did!" Armand intervened, "like a barber-surgeon. I can still see him cleaning his big knife before he cut into his arm, you'd think he'd done nothing else all his life!"

François laughed. "Well I have done it often enough. I can even amputate an arm if need be, I learned the hard way out in the field. And I had to clean the knife thoroughly – just imagine mixing Pierre's blood with the blood of that frightful Nicolas – what an insult!"

"I suppose you saved his life, but why did you do it there?" Marie asked, still shocked by the picture Armand had conjured.

288

"He had fainted – so that was the best moment as he wouldn't feel the pain and I could see that his arm had started to fester, that's highly dangerous. I know this from war, if you don't cut it out fast, a man won't survive!"

"But what happened to Pierre, how did he ever happen to come into the hands of these villains?" asked Marie. "Are they all dead?"

"I'll tell you every detail as soon as Pierre is awake and can listen!" François answered, avoiding a straight answer, but wouldn't be cajoled into saying anything more.

Once news had spread that Pierre was on the mend, his bedroom was almost bursting with people. In the morning Armand had sneaked alone into his room. At first an embarrassing silence had reigned; Pierre hadn't known how to start. Finally he stuttered, his face flushed with mortification, "Armand, I don't really recall every detail, but I know I owe you my life, I also remember that I behaved like a complete idiot..."

"Quite so, my dearest Pierre, like a total ass!" Armand answered cheerfully. "But I'm sure you'd have come to my rescue without hesitation, that's what friends are for. Let's close this discussion, but next time your best friend Armand tells you to keep your hands off a bad girl, you'd better listen!"

Pierre sighed. "You're right, I was a total ass. I hate to admit it though. Should I come clean with Marie? It almost kills me to see her, to see the love in her eyes – and to know that I almost betrayed her with this bitch..."

"If you dare to breathe a single word to Marie, you might as well never call me your friend again!" Armand answered forcefully. "Trust me for once, your friend knows best! No confessions or self-pity allowed, is that clear? This chapter is closed, forever!"

"Clear!" Pierre had answered meekly. "I learned a lesson, Armand always knows best! At least when it comes to dealing with women..."

"Finally, a sign of intelligence! I'd almost given up!" Armand laughed and hugged his friend – carefully though, so as not to hurt his bandaged arm.

In the afternoon all of his friends gathered around Pierre who held court, lying on a sofa in the middle of the sunlit room. Jean had begged his master to stay in bed, but Pierre wouldn't hear of it. His arm was still hurting but he felt much better. Now he was reclining comfortably, cherishing the attention of his friends. Marie's presence had mended the wounds of his heart – and of his mind. Had this really been him, the same Pierre who had been pining at the feet of the Contessa and had gone to the madness of sending a boat full of flowers? He must really have been bewitched!

"Now, François, please tell us how you saved Pierre? Who were his enemies? I knew that something terrible was going to happen, I told you already in Reims! I'm bursting with curiosity and I'm still worried, tell me the whole truth!" Marie pleaded.

Pierre's elation suddenly abated. Nervously he looked at François who appreciated that the attention of the room was suddenly focused on him. Never a victim to modesty and well aware that his tailor had surpassed his expectations, François was very pleased with himself.

"Marie, you really have a sixth sense! As I told you before, Pierre and Armand were being chased by an agent of Cardinal Richelieu. The Cardinal must have decided that their return to the French court was not desirable. When I arrived in Venice, Armand had just been taken into custody and the constabulary was searching for Pierre as well!"

"I spent a night in the prison of the Inquisition!" Armand interjected, not wanting to leave all of the limelight to his cousin.

"The Inquisition!" Céline exclaimed. "But that's terrible! You must have spent a terrifying night!"

"I could hear the cries at night..." Armand added, ready to go into more details, but François found it about time to revert to his storyline. "I found out that Julia Contarini's aunt is very influential, and she helped me to set Armand free – but indeed he had to spend a night in the clutches of the Inquisition!"

"How brave you were, Armand... and how clever of you, François!" Céline was impressed.

"But what about Pierre? Armand always finds a way to survive, I wouldn't actually worry too much about him!" Marie insisted.

Before Armand could protest, François took up the tale again. "Pierre was missing. It took a lot of effort to find out when and where he had disappeared! I myself had been hiding in the house of a tailor since I had arrived in Venice, it was important that nobody should know of my arrival. Thanks to Jean we finally found a clue. Soon we realized that Pierre had been abducted by his cousin Henri and taken to a sinister palace that belonged to a Contessa with the most shocking reputation. I don't want to go into details as there are ladies present here, but I can say that the Contessa and Henri were not just friends. But we were unbelievably lucky – Giovanni, the brother-in-law of the tailor where I was staying had served in this palace as a valet some years ago when the palace still belonged to a noble family of good reputation. He still had many friends among the servants there and together with Armand we devised a plan to enter the palace and find Pierre!"

"*We* devised a plan...!" Armand commented. "That's a joke! He used me as bait. He knew that Henri wanted both of us!"

"That's true!" François smiled, full of mischief. "I needed Armand to incite Henri to lead us to Pierre, and thanks to Armand, we succeeded. Armand took a great risk. With the help of Giovanni we were able to convince some of the servants to help us and turn against Henri and his infamous allies!"

"I guess that a bit of gold helped to convince them?" Charles interjected.

"That's the way this kind of business is usually conducted. And not only a bit, I'm afraid that I spent a considerable amount of Pierre's money."

"Who cares!" Marie cut in. "You did well, better a Pierre who's alive and poor than a dead one, just imagine, Henri de Beauvoir!" And her eyes were full of tears as she added, "I really do thank both of you, François, and also Armand, for saving my Pierre. Both of you acted like true heroes, I'll never forget this!"

"Has Henri's body been found?" asked Céline.

"Not yet. But people tell me that the current is so strong that it's rather unlikely that he'll be washed ashore in Venice."

Suddenly the room fell silent. Everybody would have preferred to see Henri's body firmly shut in a coffin. A big cloud had chosen this very moment to obscure the sun, and the room suddenly lay under a shadow, the shadow of Henri de Beauvoir.

"He might still be alive then?" Céline whispered. "I don't like that thought at all!"

"Let's raise a toast to Pierre, Armand and François!" Charles interrupted the sombre mood. "They've merited our full admiration! To our heroes, long may they live!"

"Look, Pierre's face is flushed!" cried Marie full of concern. "I think reliving those memories is not good for his health, let's change the subject!"

The next days passed quickly, and as all of his friends had moved into the Albergo Leon Bianco Pierre had no more time or opportunity to mope about the past. Back to his cheerful self, Pierre couldn't even understand how he could ever have become so blind. Even François had moved by now to the albergo, accompanied by Giovanni who had ascended to the position of private valet for Armand and François. He made his presence felt immediately, and never before had the servants of the albergo been under such a strict regime.

It was Jean who noticed one afternoon a grandiose gondola approaching the albergo. Painted in bright colours with gilded lanterns and carved woodwork it was a vessel fit for a king. He could only marvel at the precision of the oarsmen who handled their oars with impressive efficiency. "Who would that be, my lord?" he asked Armand, who happened to be close by. "In France I'd say a member of the royal family was approaching, but Venice is a Republic."

"A Republic by name only, Jean!" Armand stretched his neck to get a better view. "It is royalty," he grinned. "Almost! It's the coat of arms of the Contessa Alessandra, her family is linked to almost every reigning doge of the city and she once mentioned that she has still to find a king or prince in Europe who's not in some way or other related to her. You'll see – she's an impressive personality!"

It took almost half an hour though until Giovanni (having informed the major-domo haughtily that he was far too insignificant to deal with such important visitors) announced the arrival of the Contessa de Muro and her niece, the Lady Julia Contarini. Jean was curious to meet such an important person – what a disappointment to see a rather small and portly lady enter the room. And yet, it only took a minute and she seemed to dominate the room.

She had brought fruit from her famous glasshouses. "I understand you survived quite an ordeal!" she addressed Pierre. "You can be happy that François de Toucy arrived at the right time. I understand that it was a very close-run thing; the lady – not that I should even call her a lady – in question was not known to take prisoners."

Pierre nodded and swallowed hard. Her ladyship seemed to be well informed, too well informed for his liking.

Their conversation was interrupted as Céline and Marie entered the room and the usual round of introductions took place. The Contessa gave a sharp glance towards Pierre and commented, "I understand that this young lady is your fiancée... a very nice girl."

Pierre blushed and stuttered, "Yes, indeed, ma'am!"

"Better keep a good eye on your handsome future husband! He seems to have an awkward tendency to end up in trouble."

Marie smiled and laughed. She liked the outspoken lady. "I promise, Contessa, as soon as we're be married, he'll be kept safe and under the closest supervision!"

While all attention had been focused on the Contessa de Muro, Armand had time to discover something else. His cousin François had fallen head over heels in love with Julia, and what's more, this was a feeling that was clearly shared by Julia! Both had detached themselves to a corner close to the French windows that opened onto the balconies. For a second he was taken aback, his male ego greatly damaged. But as he had never seriously contemplated matrimony, he quickly came to terms with this new situation and decided to tease his cousin mercilessly as soon as the Contessa left.

"Now, I must confess, I'm still curious about one thing!" the voice of the Contessa could be heard. "If I may ask so bluntly, why did you come to Venice and why were you trying to stay incognito?"

Her question was met with a long silence. Finally Pierre cleared his throat. "It's a secret, but I can disclose this much: Armand and I had promised to reunite three ancient rings. The first is the ruby ring that I'm wearing, the second one is a diamond ring that has been in my family for centuries. Jean, please show the Contessa the second ring!" While Jean hurried into the adjacent bedroom to fetch the precious ring, Pierre continued his story. "The third ring is a sapphire ring, it has been designed in such a way that it will fit together with the other rings – and once the three rings are reunited an ancient script will become visible. We had committed to reunite the three rings and we know that the third one is here in Venice, so we came to Venice in order to find out where..."

"Why the secrecy? You wanted to steal it from the owner, tell me the truth!" the Contessa stated, eyebrows raised.

Pierre looked taken aback. "We intend to offer a high price to the owner! But you're right, we were prepared to look into unusual methods if need be, the problem is that I gave my word of honour to find it. In fact we don't need the ring as such, we just need to be able to read the inscription once the rings are reunited! I only need to hold it in my hand for a short moment."

Jean came back with the diamond ring and handed it to Julia's aunt. Critically she examined both rings before she continued to speak. "I think I know where the third ring is, but it cannot be sold!" the Contessa said firmly.

"Maybe you could talk to the owner? I'm sure he'd listen to you."

"I could, but *she* won't listen..." the Contessa smiled. "The ring has been in our family for generations and I'll bestow it on Julia as her wedding gift... somehow I have the feeling that this date may not be so far away." Her piercing eyes glanced at her niece who turned a flaming red.

"I understand – congratulations!" Pierre laughed. "But could we come to the Ca' de Muro tomorrow and reunite the rings to read the inscription?"

"Why is this so important to you?" The Contessa was openly curious now.

Pierre hesitated and looked for help to Charles, who had followed the conversation so far without interfering.

"Allow me to explain, Contessa!" Charles took over. "It seems that the inscriptions on the ring will indicate the place of a treasure to be found, with a value far greater than the value of the rings themselves; the Marquis de Beauvoir has committed to locate this treasure in exchange for help he received in claiming his inheritance in England!"

"This sounds very secretive, and I understand that you prefer to be rather obscure. If I remember, my late husband dropped a remark once that the ring was a heritage, straight from the ancient times of the Knights Templar..."

Pierre was dumbstruck; this lady seemed to know everything!

The next day he arrived at the Ca' de Muro, but he was not alone. Armand, Charles and François had insisted on coming too, and were burning with curiosity. By chance Edo had turned up as well. As soon as word had spread that they wanted to visit the Contessa to see the famous ring, Marie and Céline had insisted on joining the party as well.

"Charles, you cannot even think of keeping us here waiting, these rings were the origin of this whole adventure and the reason why we're all here! There can be no question of Marie and I sitting demurely in the albergo and letting you have all the excitement. We're coming! And then, my dear Charles, it's time to go home, I am missing our child and Marie's parents must be mad with worry!"

There was not a lot Charles could say, and finally he gave in. If the Contessa was surprised to find that the number of her guests had multiplied, she didn't show it. Refreshments were served until the big moment arrived and a servant brought in a tray with a small velvet-covered box.

"This looks like quite a family reunion!" the Contessa couldn't help commenting, as she opened the box and took the ring out of its confinement. The sapphire came alive in her hands; as soon as the sunlight touched it, the ring glowed a wonderful deep blue colour. Pierre presented the two other rings and as the three locked together, an inscription could be read.

"What does it say?" asked Armand, holding his breath. "Does it mention a treasure?"

"I can't read it!" Pierre looked at the inscription in disbelief. "I've never seen anything similar before, it's a short text, but looks like a mix of Latin, Hebrew and Arabic script – I've never seen anything like this."

"The languages of the three religions that were reunited in Jerusalem at the time of the Templars," the Contessa remarked.

"According to legend this ring was a gift from the famous sultan Saladin," Pierre added, "but who could help us to decipher the words?"

"I had a foreboding that a question like that might be forthcoming." The Contessa smiled and whispered something to her servant.

The servant bowed and disappeared, then only minutes later he reappeared accompanied by an old man dressed in a simple suit made from black silk who wore the cap of the Jewish faith.

Pierre almost forgot to breathe; he hoped that the earth would open up and swallow him then and there! This old man was the very jeweller who had sold him the ruby and pearl necklace he gave to the infamous Contessa di Montefiori. Would he recognize him and mention his foolish purchase?

The old man greeted them politely and listened to the introductions. As the Contessa presented him to Pierre, the jeweller greeted him formally as if he had never seen him before. A weight fell from Pierre's mind and he vowed to buy a suitable gift for Marie before they left Venice – but no rubies, never would he touch rubies again.

The old man took the three rings and studied them with a polished crystal that magnified the inscriptions. After five minutes he laid them down carefully; it was evident that he held the rings in the greatest esteem. He smiled at his audience who were holding their breath – what kind of treasure was hidden behind this inscription?

Then he started to speak, changing to fluent French to the surprise of everybody. "These rings hold a secret indeed, a treasure of the greatest value imaginable. The inscription is a citation: 'Faith, hope, and charity – and the greatest of these is charity.'" He cleared his throat. "The greatest treasure is charity, or love – this is what the great Saladin wanted to remind his Christian adversaries when he presented this precious gift, as these words come directly from the New Testament!"

"A polite hint, as it were, to restrain their greed?" Charles could be heard. "I admit that our forefathers created quite a mess in the Holy Land!"

"I can't believe this! I travelled all over Europe, nearly got myself killed, not once but several times, met crazy people beyond all possible imaginings – and all of that for a treasure that doesn't even exist?" Armand was upset. "You mean all of this was for nothing?"

"I don't agree, Armand!" Pierre could suddenly be heard. "I found love and friendship that is worth much more to me than stupid treasure."

"I'm not sure our friends in London would quite agree, I think they were hoping for real treasure," Charles interjected.

The Contessa raised her glass. "I tend to agree with the Marquis de Beauvoir, let's drink to love, faith and that hope may never leave you – and let's pray that his murderous cousin has disappeared forever!"

Her last remark had a sobering effect, but everybody followed her example, although Armand could nevertheless be heard muttering, "Even a little treasure would have been a good thing after all that, wouldn't it? I mean after so much pain and so much effort, to then be fobbed off with some unctuous words… "

"Oh, Armand!" Pierre sighed. "Best friend of all, you'll never change!"

Suddenly Charles tugged discreetly at his sleeve and made a sign for Armand to come closer.

"What is it?" asked Pierre curiously.

"Ever thought about the possibility that this might be some sort of code? I somehow don't see my fellow Templars sending us to Venice simply to find a quote from the New Testament…"

"Oh, no!" groaned Pierre. "For me this mission is finished, no more adventures!"

He seized his glass and raising a toast to Marie, he cried, "I hereby invite everybody to our marriage in Paris, a toast to the future Marquise de Beauvoir!"

A cheer went the through the crowd and congratulations were showered on the young couple. Jean looked sceptically at Armand. "Do you truly believe this? No more adventures, my lord?"

Armand grinned. "Do you believe in fairy tales? I don't! But let him marry Marie first, it'll probably be his biggest adventure of all – taming a tiger would be far easier!"

Made in the USA
Coppell, TX
26 September 2020